Wakefield P

T0358144

Long Afternoon *of the* World

Graeme Kinross-Smith is a writer of long standing in the Australian literary scene, perhaps best known for his collections of epigrammatic lyric poetry. In addition, his recent prize-winning fiction has appeared in *The Best Australian Stories* of 2004 and 2005. His several other books reflect a variety of life interests, including photography and, in *The Sweet Spot*, the story of Australian tennis – both of which underpin events in *Long Afternoon of the World*.

His best-selling *Australia's Writers* and his texts on the craft of writing reflect his role as a pioneer in the teaching of creative writing in Australia. An Honorary Fellow in Arts at Deakin University, he has given many readings of his work to audiences across Australia and overseas. He lives, writes, teaches and takes art photographs in Melbourne, Geelong and Port Campbell.

By the same author

Mankind's Spies: How Writers Work, 1972
The Book of the Murray (with G.V. Lawrence), 1975
Turn Left at Any Time With Care (with Jamie Grant), 1975
Australia's Writers: An Illustrated Guide to Their Lives and Their Work, 1980
The Sweet Spot: One Hundred Years of Life and Tennis in Geelong, 1982
Window to Australia (with Joyce Evans), 1987
The Oxford Literary Guide to Australia (Associate Editor), 1987
Writer: A Working Guide for New Writers, 1992
The Oxford Book of Australian Sporting Anecdotes (Associate Editor), 1993
If I Abscond: New Poems and Short Fictions, 1997

Long
Afternoon
of the World

Graeme Kinross-Smith

Wakefield
Press

Wakefield Press
1 The Parade West
Kent Town
South Australia 5067
www.wakefieldpress.com.au

First published 2007

Designed by Liz Nicholson, designBITE
Typeset by Clinton Ellicott, Wakefield Press
Printed and bound by Hyde Park Press

National Library of Australia
Cataloguing-in-publication entry

Kinross-Smith, Graeme, 1936–   .
Long afternoon of the world.

ISBN 978 1 86254 737 7.

I. Title.

A823.4

This is a work of fiction. All characters and events in it are inventions.
Graeme Kinross-Smith asserts the moral right to be identified as the author of this work.

 **Government of South Australia**
Arts SA

 fox creek

 Publication of this book was assisted by the
Commonwealth Government through the
Australia Council, its arts funding and advisory body.

In memory of my brother Ian
26 February 1940 – 5 December 2001
who might well have known all of Tim's close people

—

The fact of the *very shadow of the person* lying there fixed forever!

Elizabeth Barrett in a letter about photography to Mary Russell Mitford in 1843

I have been burdened always with too much affection for people, places and things. Passionate love of relatives, of friends, of the ranges, the streams, the trees, horses, cats, of the beauty in the dawns and sunsets and starry nights – a multitude of experiences that other people take more mildly . . .

Miles Franklin, *Childhood at Brindabella*

Examine for a moment an ordinary mind on an ordinary day. The mind receives a myriad impressions – trivial, fantastic, evanescent, or engraved with the sharpness of steel. From all sides they come, an incessant shower of innumerable atoms; and as they fall, as they shape themselves into the life of Monday or Tuesday, the accent falls differently from of old; the moment of importance came not here but there . . .

Virginia Woolf, *The Common Reader*

It must be this rhapsody or none.
The rhapsody of things as they are . . .

Wallace Stevens, 'The Man With the Blue Guitar'

Contents

I sit in the older chair with the rubbed corduroy cushion. I think. My thoughts loop down and settle on a page waiting white and empty, a space white with intriguing doubt. One thought after another – they hand each other back. I value them. I hug them to me. They come to me constantly, everywhere, any time. There is no rest from thought. And these musings are mine: only I have proprietorship over them. My name is Tim Menzies – and these are my inimitable wonderings. If my thoughts prove to be erroneous I can think them through again, revise them.

Someone has told me about a man who comes into another man's office. He is carrying an old linen shopping bag with jute handles. It's a deep bag. The grimy linen has carried many loads and has slid sideways out of shape. But now the bag is full of paper.

The first man dumps the bag and its load on the unoccupied end of the other man's desk. That's a novel in there, he says. The other man, who knows him, looks up, surprised. He is an editor. He reaches over, draws the bag to him, feels inside for the first few pages. He looks up. Are these in order? he asks. Are these numbered?

Did someone tell me about this or am I dreaming? Has this happened? I'm not sure. I must be thinking about what a novel is and what it would be like to write one. It might be satisfying to write down all my provisional wisdom one day as the man with the linen bag has done. It would make a statement. It would be saying: this is what my experience has told me to say. And yet there are pages I must not know. I must not know too much. One day I might set down all my puzzlement and just let it stand there on the page.

Yes – it could be that one day I will write a novel.

—

Grandpa John's Cadenza in
the Face of the Sea

I can often feel the sadness in things.

Darkness in the Box Hill Town Hall with my grandmother Pearlie. We are eating boiled lollies, waiting for *Casablanca* to come up on the screen. It is the War. I do remember this. Grandma is wearing a Scotch Pebble. She is dressed in black. She is big and broad, and in the dimness I can't see her eyes for the shine on her glasses. She breathes heavily, like the heavy Wimmera-Mallee lady she is. She has left Grandpa John at home – he's not keen on the pictures.

Ingrid Bergman is sad. I see her pinched face – this woman, remembering, her nose nearly crying for the past. I hear Sam's broad, dry voice, and the piano behind. He sings about a kiss. He sings about sighs. Ingrid Bergman is sad, but he looks at her as he sings, because he wants her to remember. He's not smiling.

I think about kissing. Does it mean Ingrid Bergman is in love? I'm not sure. I don't really know what that sort of kiss is like, or why people sigh and think it is important. (What's 'fundamental'?) Joyce, my aunt with the blonde hair and the diamond ring from David, kisses like that. I've seen her with David in the kitchen at Mont Albert. I see their big bodies. I see their shoulders straining, David's fingers spreading and pressing Joyce's back so hard through the cotton. It is a different kiss from Grandma's saying goodbye, or Aunty Ellie's buttery kiss at Gerogery, saying she is pleased that we brothers are there with her boys after such a long time. I am her brother's son – the eldest. I don't like being the eldest. Sometimes I don't like being my father's son. 'This is my son, Tim.' I don't like that. It makes my stomach curl.

—

I watch the cursor blinking at the end of the story I'm writing. It waits there after the last full stop. It waits for the story to go further.

I can make it go further. I can conjure it up from what I know. Often I feel the stories under my hands, like baby birds pulsing in their protective down. What stretches about me is a continuous present. I can tell stories about myself as a kid in Melbourne in 1942 if I want to, and I can smell the lilly pilly tree in front of our house at Cicero Street and see the concrete of the street in the setting sun like expanses of pink sugar. I can write about my uncle Candles, or my mother Louise and her tomato dress, or my father Will, who sucks in his cheeks as he applies a match and draws on his pipe. He might be sitting under the blood plum tree having a rest before he starts on the garden again.

When I'm writing it's as if I'm a child. Even as an adult I'm still a child, and so are all the people around me, although they pretend to be adults. I divide people into those I can see as children, and those I can't. I distrust those I can't, because they have become so practised and intent in covering their childhood. There are some people, I think, who wear their childhoods around with them like gentle scarves. It shows in their smile, their way of walking, their need to play and read and touch balls and enter water. Even though they can be stubborn, greedy, self-centred, I can see where these people are going, can allow for them. I trust them.

Sometimes I sit in the old church I bought near Port Chalice, in Victoria, in Australia, watching myself put the stories on the screen. If I go outside and walk to the little gate under the wattles, I can hear the sea thundering in, pestering the cliffs at Campfire Bay six kilometres away. Other times I write in the front room at Hawthorn in Melbourne.

I write about my uncertain life. I tell stories that could be about myself – that acned teenager who likes to use an axe, who wonders how gentle a kiss is, who watches a girl's eyes coming round again and again in the square dance, who later listens to the sounds of his own footfall walking home past dark street hedges. Sometimes I catch closer snatches of myself in the story – who is this man called Tim Menzies; this father, brother, failed husband? I ponder my travels out of the state of Victoria to the long sweeps of country without hills in New South Wales, to the secret dark density of Tasmania, to the hot, clear breath of Western Australia, to green, pendulous Queensland. As I write I unearth myself. I can begin to see what has made me.

I discover that I can write and draw myself into another way of happening.

Some of what I write tries to be what actually happens in time's continuous present. But it changes as I tap the words in and look up to see them on the screen. I can see that some of it is what I wish would happen, and some is what I know has happened, or will happen.

So I am a man telling a story that flows around me. Sometimes I see the path of what might happen – it comes right to my feet. Sometimes it's like feeling in the dark for a light switch – and if I'm lucky I find my fingers going straight to it. But how many people have I been? I hear other voices, some of which must be mine. And what is remembering? I write – and it's as if things that have happened brush against me in the dark. I can feel the breath of their passing on my cheek. I don't know when they will come to me. I suppose the half light in which I sit is imagination. As I write the past comes and goes as it has to in time's long present. I look up in my mind's tramping and I am here – or is it there? Is that remembering? Is that how memory insists on its own peculiar order, mounts its little explosions in me as I think? Who am I? How is it that I find myself coming back to touch my close people again and again?

Some people are real when I first think about them and put them in my story. But then they change. I have to take them into my mind as a sculptor takes a clay manikin into his hands. I work them, feel their gaze, listen to their voices, follow them where they walk. I find out things about them that no one has ever told me, that my life has never shown me. I find out surprising things about myself. I find that I am capable of loving many people, when all along I have thought myself deficient in reaching out. I have despaired of finding the love that I see in my dreams, that I smell on those days when everything seems possible. Yet now I think I see it here before me. I hear the warm orange of a woman's voice and I know it is Rosa. Although I have not yet met her, I can sense her deep voice's purity high in my throat where taste and smell and intuition meet.

So I find myself in the story. I seem always to be present, hovering, watching. But soon I can't remember exactly how things happened, whether I or someone else did something, or whether I imagined it, or whether this person or that broke the news or took the photograph. Then I know I'm getting near the truth.

—

When my mother Louise dies, I have the feeling that she has also lain here long ago, in just this place, at just this point on time's circle. They have called me at the College. I have quit the first seminar of the afternoon. I have driven straight over.

She grasps my hand and draws me down. I know I have felt her breath, seen that bed-head and its starched wings of pillows before. It is as if I will know the words she's about to whisper. 'Tim, Tim. Goodbye, my darling,' she says. 'You'll watch over Will and Alex, won't you?' She knows that during the night she'll slip the traces of the deep-windowed hospital in this street of pin oaks.

I nod, my heart draining. I am seeing a long aisle of pale, trodden earth through trees, leaves drifting and falling across it. I come back to the descant of her breath. Her eyes roll away with the morphine and then close over the pain.

Will, my father, has left only minutes ago, a reed bent by fatigue and worry and yet still drawing out the required words for the nurses. He'll probably be home by now, the Toyota parked just short of the peeling garage door in case he gets another call to the hospital. 'Watch over Will and Alex,' my mother has said. Alex Cumming. I look at my Louise's terrible, suppurating face, listen to her breathing. Why Alex, from so far back, from among so many? I can't ask her.

—

It's hard to know when I first hear the drumbeat, when I first feel the chill that stops my heart. I know it has been lying in wait for me since I was a child. When I think of it I still see the back door at Cicero Street and my scooter abandoned on the grass. I hear the bells of lily-of-the-valley shivering in the wind near my father's shed. I see my brothers' blonde heads lost in concentration. I hear my uncle David's thudding words. I feel again that first desperation to speak to my mother.

—

'. . . From what I'm *told* . . .' I hear someone saying, and at first in the thickness of anger in the man's voice I don't recognise who is speaking. 'From what I'm bloody TOLD!' And then I know it is my uncle David. Then I can hear someone panting. I can hear a whimpering.

At first I don't know where they are. I hear his last spitting word. Then I hear a heavy thud against weatherboard and I know they are near the old store-room. I'm in the long chook shed in the midst of collecting the eggs. Auntie Jean asked me to. I'm looking out through the chook wire. Then I realise I can see my Auntie Joyce there. Her shoulder is backed up against the wall. She is on the ground, one knee bent back under her poplin dress. She is crying. David is standing over her. His thumbs are stuck in his belt.

I can hear their voices even now when I think about it. I can hear their voices and the whimper of pain. It was all that time ago. Can the trail have started so early? So early!

I'm there. They are not far from me, but the loquat tree is in between. It's Mont Albert. Something tells me to be quiet at all costs, and not to move. I crouch there, half-standing, with the billy hanging from my right-hand fingers. I'm aware of the tight little mounds of chook-poo here and there around my feet and the long perches dangling away into the darkness along the far wall. And now I know it's David's voice I'm hearing. I don't like David. I'm frightened of David.

'Get up! C'mon, GET UP!' he's saying. 'Get up or by God I'll get you up!'

Auntie Joyce starts to raise herself with her arms, but she winces and slumps back. She's crying. She refuses to look up at David. She looks along the ground towards the house as though it's a long way away. A sob shakes her. She gives a sad neigh.

Then I can hear her words. 'David. Stop this. Please!' Her voice is a half whisper, a wavering murmur.

'Stop it? You slut! All right, stay there if you like. You witch! You're telling *me* to stop it! God!' He draws his foot back as though he's going to kick her. He's hissing. 'What I need to know is when did you start on with him, you bitch?' David is bending down, leering into Joyce's face. He grabs her jaw, turns her head so she has to look at him. 'When?' He gives her jaw a parting twist and lets go. He stands over her. His face is set, thrusting towards her. 'When, eh? WHEN?'

Auntie Joyce chokes a moment. She sobs. But she looks up into David's eyes. 'I've told you,' I hear her say. 'I've told you before. I've told you all the time. I haven't "started on" with anyone. I haven't started on with Rourke.' She sobs, raises a hand to wipe her eyes. David looks over towards where I am. He seems to be glancing angrily towards the chook-shed, but he doesn't see me. He looks as though he's going to spit on her. I don't even breathe.

'You're a lying bitch! I go away for a few minutes and when I come back to the bloody Members' you're gone – and so is Rourke! Yeah, it runs in the family, doesn't it. You and your sister both, eh! From what I've been told. You and Louise, eh? What little secrets has she been hiding? Eh! EH! Dear little teacher Louise, eh? Butter wouldn't melt, would it! How about poor bloody Tim, eh, who can't even get out of his own way? What about all that? From what I've been told there's a lot more to find out about that.'

I see Auntie Joyce's eyes flare. 'Leave Louise out of this. You don't know what you're talking about.' She tries to lever herself up, but falls back. 'You've hurt my arm,' she says. 'You've hurt me!' It's as though she's just discovered it. David shoves his thumbs in his belt again and just laughs. 'You had it coming,' he says, his voice sing-song, rising. 'You've had it coming for a while.'

There are streaks of dirt on Auntie Joyce's forehead and down one cheek. The back of her hand hovers near a bruise. I can see it now, blue on her temple. But she isn't crying now. She is brave. She looks straight up at David now. 'When you went off to the betting ring Ian Rourke offered me a drink. We went into the other bar and sat down – and – we – had – a – drink.' It is my aunt I'm watching. She measures her words out. She is brave, looking up at David, her other hand absently trying to put one fold of her dress over the other again. 'We had a drink. That's all.' She looks down at her dress and sobs. She catches herself again. She continues, but she's crying now, and it twists her voice. 'And you missed us. You went off on a wild goose chase. And then you start all this!'

'Good story!' David says and he snorts. 'I know that bastard Rourke. I wouldn't trust either of you.' He paces three or four steps down the path towards the house, then paces back until his shoes almost touch her sandalled feet in the dirt at the path's edge. 'Now bloody get up and get inside. And make damned sure you go through to the back room. You don't want any of the others seeing you until you've fixed yourself up.'

David paces away, fuming. Then he comes back to her quickly, as though he's just decided something. I think he's come back to hit her. But he swears and reaches down, grabs my Auntie Joyce by the arm and yanks her up. She cries out like a hurt dog. She stands for a second or two, swaying, wavering against the shed wall. Then David gets his weight behind her. He shoves her, propels her down the path before him with sharp nudges in the middle of her back. I can't see them now. I can hear Joyce crying in a low whimper.

I'm staring at the loquat tree. I'm looking at the dark perches. I'm looking at the wall of the storeroom. Then I'm back with the three eggs in the billy – two brown, one white. I'm wondering how I will get inside with them, but I'm still hearing my mother's name, Louise. I'm hearing my mother's name on David's lips – and my name too.

—

Louise and Jean smoke together. This is my mother and her sister, I remind myself. I've seen them do it from when I am small and I want the packet. I watch them too when I'm bigger. They sit in the old chairs outside the back door at Mont Albert and smoke and talk. Joyce sometimes smokes too – with David. David spins out his gold cigarette case from his pocket and shows it in the light. Then he opens it and slips a cigarette out and puts it in his mouth. Then he slips out another one for Joyce. Then he snaps the case shut. He likes everyone to watch him. He looks at us all. I don't like him. Now that he and Auntie Joyce are married, he's my uncle. But I don't like calling him Uncle David. He sneers at me. He says nasty things. Soon Joyce will be having a baby. But I still don't like David.

—

Three weeks after Louise's death, Mr Stephen Tremearne, solicitor, rings me. He tells me that accompanying her will there is a signed statement addressed to me alone. I see my mother's face as he speaks. The statement, he tells me, is to be delivered to me one year after the date of her death, unless my father Will determines that it should be surrendered to me earlier.

As I put down the phone, I see them. It's unnerving. Just for a moment there are two identical wooden, flat-top tennis racquets lying beside a towel on a wine-coloured velvet chair. They are both Cressy Perfects like Louise used to play with. They have the familiar little flourish of feathers above the insignia. They are new, the transfers on them fresh and bright.

—

I know there is a State. It is very big. It is called Victoria and I think sometimes about the 't' sound in it. There are fences going across it everywhere because a lot of people have bits of it. I ask my father Will if we've got a bit of it. He laughs and points down the back yard at the chook house and says that's our bit of it.

I don't think about the State much. But sometimes I do, when we're going to drive up to Gerogery, because Uncle Roy and Auntie Ellie live in another State called New South Wales that I can't think about so much because I don't live in it. In New South Wales they have different trains with bigger engines, even bigger than the *Spirit of Progress*. I can't really think about New South Wales because it's just too big. It's much bigger than Victoria. You can see it on the map. I know that people from

New South Wales are different and sunburnt, with freckles on their arms. That's where Will's family are – his brother and his two sisters. They live in Sydney.

But then there's Alex. His name is Alex Cumming. Mum says that he played tennis in New South Wales sometimes. He nearly played in the Davis Cup but that was when he was playing in Melbourne. He had to go to Canada and New York and California but he didn't like it. Alex was born near Waitchie on a farm, and then he lived in Sea Lake because he came from the Mallee. He played tennis in Sydney once. He played in Tarcutta, too, in New South Wales, and at a place called Dubbo. Cattamundra, Tarcutta, Dubbo – I know some places in the other State, but they're different from places in Victoria. People are different and there aren't so many fences.

Sometimes people call Alex 'Uncle' – but he isn't a real uncle. It's because he played football and cricket with my real uncles. He played with Candles and Flute in the Mallee. Candles and Flute are Mum's brothers. And then there's Des – he's her blind brother. Alex used to be one of the best tennis players in Victoria. He was famous. I like Alex. One day he takes me for a walk when it is the War. Will is in the War too. He's away. Uncle Alex comes to the beach at Parkdale before he has to go back to the Islands. Mum is in her apricot dress that you wear with bathers. I can remember that. Alex says that the Islands are hot with palm trees. He says he has to go back there to fight the Japs.

I can remember there's a boat at Parkdale out where it's deep and its sail comes down on the people.

—

To me the mystery is inescapable, precious.

There is my mother, in the photograph, her head cocked queru-lously, a curl shadowing her left eye, standing in the dust along the tennis court fence beside two of her baggy-pants brothers and her sister Jean. It is the Mallee of the thirties. And now, in another shot, here are Louise and her mother before her, both sitting forward attentively like echoes for the camera on a rustic bench at somebody's wedding in

Melbourne. It is the 1950s. Here are my mother and her father John huddled over the old stone sharpening-wheel near the fruit trees in the Mont Albert yard late in his life. Here are Louise's brothers and her two sisters. I know each of them so well – their eyes looking into mine, or their hands spreading on their knees; eyes looking up, when they can't work things out. I know each voice. I know the stories they've told me. I see Joyce's eyes half closed, her turn of head, as if she's listening. That's how she considers. I listen to the stories my mother tells me about them. Sometimes I look up to catch her weeping as she speaks about them, then laughing at me through her tears.

Here am I, writing about them as I look back on my own marriage breakdown. Even so far from its end it still springs back on me from time to time. I'm looking down on us – Patricia and me – standing near to each other, but now we're strangers again. Or were we always strangers? And yet we are a generation, even as we part. Something I've never dreamed. Parting. And even as we part our children are the next generation.

I think about others who married, other generations. There before me, time and again, I see my mother, and behind her, her mother and father, Pearlie and John. My grandparents. I can't see clearly who in turn stands behind them. Pearlie's sister Mollie stands beside them, an innocent face, trembling with enquiry. But behind Pearlie and John, I know, the Sutton and Barnes families are joined in the hazy sunlight of colonial afternoons. I can sense it.

What does it mean when people marry? Is it too much to expect a man and a woman to step forward out of their families, to meet each other, to hope, to love, and then to stay together for the rest of their lives?

I think about it and I can see John's parents ushering him forward through time towards a young woman called Pearlie who they will never know. It simply comes to pass in Adelaide, in the colony of South Australia, in the year 1880, that a Welshman, Isaac Barnes, and his Cornish lady, who was Esna Seton, beget a boy-child who they give the name of John and that he will become my grandfather.

Pearlie's father, though, comes to me in a soft-lit image backed by the dour stench of a sea-weed beach. I know it. He has left farm labouring in East Anglia. He comes from the Vale of Dedham. His name is William Sutton. It is 1879. He walks down the gang-plank to a reeling pier at Sandridge in the colony of Victoria, from the ship *Ben Nevis*. He expects to find himself within sight of the streets of Melbourne, but sees only salt flats and the glint of water. He is carrying his cricket bat and a canvas bag with metal clasps. In this place where he knows no faces but where sometimes, like a sudden clearing in a forest, he hears a voice that comes from the Suffolk valleys. He finds work tending the horses and carts in a brewer's yard in Richmond. Three years later, he marries the pale sapling limbs, the dark candour in the eyes, of Jeanie, who was Jeanie Pettman. He makes love to his new Scots wife during a stupefying Melbourne heatwave and they conceive a baby girl. In the tiny church in Hawthorn she is christened Pearlie. She will become my grandmother. She will sit beside me in the dark of the Box Hill Town Hall watching Humphrey Bogart's hanging face for signs of fear and finding only sadness, listening to his globular, tough words from across the world. Behind the imaginings of both of us we will detect the khaki drill, dispassionate smell of the War in the darkness.

From John and Pearlie come the tumble of people with the ineffable, good-willed Barnes' dawn and sunset in their eyes – Archie the eldest, then my mother Louise, then Candles, then Flute and husky-voiced Jean, then later Des, and finally young Joyce whose body begins to mean things to me when I am still a boy, a pillar of woman on whom I hang disturbing dreams. These are my close people. These are at least some of the things that I know.

Have I always known these things? Do I sit in the midst of a story that is a slow un-packing of my own secrets? Is that how it should be?

—

Is Melbourne where Myers is, where the tram stops near the river, where all the people walk? Melbourne. Melbourne. Melbourne – where I live. I try to see it. I can feel it, smell it, hear it, even in Camberwell. I live at 8 Cicero Street, Camberwell. But is Camberwell Melbourne?

Sometimes down in the park, or even just sitting on the gutter in the street with the football, I can hear Melbourne over the hill, if there is no wind and it's still. It's like a low rumble that never stops except at night. Melbourne.

My father Will works in Melbourne. When Flute comes down from the country he asks Will about what it's like to teach. A cigarette that's gone out is stuck to his lip. Flute's farm just waits up there in the Mallee while he is away in Melbourne. He sleeps in the back sleep-out when he stays with us in Cicero Street. He talks to Mum while she irons. He grunts. He says he should have brought down a lamb for me and Alistair to have in the back yard.

From Melbourne you can go to Fernertreegully. From Melbourne you can go to the beach if it's hot. From Melbourne you can go to the You Yangs. I remember a wedgetail eagle there, circling in the blue. The rock is warm in the sun. From Melbourne you can go to Gembrook. You have to go past Fernertreegully to get there, and there are creeks. Fernertreegully? says our father. Fernertreegully?? Yes, says Alistair, Fernertreegully! You know! You can go anywhere from Melbourne in the Chrysler. You can go to New South Wales where the trains are different, where Aunty Ellie and her buttery kisses are, and Uncle Douglas goes out after lunch with his horses. You can smell the horses in the stable. You can smell their sweat, because they never have a bath.

But the creek's in Camberwell. There's a car in it, with the water going round it. It has been there all the time. No one wants it any more. That's where the McLellans play and I sometimes go with them, just to the first part of the creek, if Tom or Ralph look after me. One day I see Patrick McLellan climb down in the grass to where the big tunnel is with the iron rungs up its sides. The creek comes out of it from Camberwell, and it gets darker and darker. Patrick climbs up the concrete on the iron rungs and into the tunnel, and then he stands and calls out like Tarzan. We can all see him. We can hear his voice go way up the tunnel. Then he walks into the tunnel beside the water and soon you can't see him, but you can hear him calling like Tarzan. Mr McLellan says never go in there, but Patrick does. Mr McLellan doesn't know.

16

So the happenings push themselves at me. I write about them in the old church that no one wanted. I stumbled upon it and bought it one winter ten years ago. It's weatherboard and pinnacled. Its floor slopes. Hills flock down on me, roads ribbed with tree shadow run away from me towards a horizon of gums. It is Victoria, surrounding me in the notes on paper and the map brushed by the cheek of my hand. I look up to see half of a sheep shear from the Berriwillock farm, hanging from a nail near the door of the church. A boot scraper now, and way out of its true country. There was a spent tank in the yard of John and Pearlie's old house when I was up there, and the bees coming and going from the corner of the veranda roof, and some corrugated iron wrapped round a tree like a piece of limp seersucker. Ah, the place where my mother had part of her growing up with Flute and Candles and Joyce and Des and Jean; the place that Archie was too old to get to know much; the farm that Flute ran after John and Pearlie had moved to Melbourne just after the War had begun and the others had spread to the four winds. A boat in the shed, too. Did Uncle Flute use it on the dam? Did they cart it to the Murray? The old wood is trying to blossom through several coats of paint. The rowlock has gone from one side, leaving a grey gap in the timbers.

For a moment I see Flute there, standing just under the machinery shed's shade, turning something over with his boot, then walking a few paces in the dust, stopping, scratching his head.

As I write I'm aware of time's circle far out there, a bright bracelet. It surrounds me. I can sense happenings, afternoons, dire weeks with no words, nights of breathing and skin's touch, days of illness waiting for the body to signal all right again. They are all strung along the brightness. I smell an opening into light and sound.

I am seeing a man's hands. They are young, the hairs on them still dark and sharp against the sun-browned skin. The hands are carrying sheaves of oats to the chaff cutter. I see only the hands, the rolled-up sleeves of a striped shirt, creases outlined in work grime, the ears of oats.

I hear the steady stutter of the engine, rollicking on its stand, the bucketing of the belting running, running. There is a welter of stalks crowding the smoothed steel mouth of the cutter. The hands bring two more sheaves. The sweet-smelling crush of stalks is sitting there, held back by the matt of stalks further in, not descending, not bending to be drawn in to the blades. The hands dump the two new sheaves on the ruck of stalks, push them down and in. I can feel the young man's shoulder muscles tensing against the crush, pushing. Once, twice, and then a change of position. Three times. Then suddenly I feel a voiding, a release, the hands and straining fingers plunging down with the fragrant grain stalks. There is a blinding hurt, a scrabbling in the maw of the cutter, a scream, a yell. The belting rips on, bucketing, running. Then other hands grab, miss, grab again and pull a lever with desperate strength, and the belting stops. I can hear a crying, suddenly cut off. There is breathing, a low voice swearing and whimpering. Then there are words that lose their resonance as soon as they are uttered against the straw of the piles of stooks, the pile of chaff, the closeness of the earthen floored shed, the hewn rafters grey with dust. Suddenly, as though they have been thrust at my face, I see the bloody stumps of fingers, some of them points of incredible white against the red pulp. It is Flute. I hear Flute's whimpering, swearing. They are Flute's hands. It is what is called the past.

I get up from the chair, my gall rising, and walk to the church window. Half an hour ago, hail was bounding all over the truck's cab outside in the yard, but now the sun's golden rays are reaching into the boobiallas, dappling, weaving, catching and shining the wet trunks and branches. I am fretting, breathing hard, my heart racing. It is what is called the past, and another place, that has grasped me and released me.

I leave the computer seething to itself on the desk, push against the heavy door, tread down the steps and out onto the wet grass.

—

I listen to her words. 'I haven't asked him,' she says. It is Patricia. Her flat, curt words echo there, all those years back now. Our marriage is broken.

Her lips purse shut. I snatch a look at my wife's eyes and her face as they turn to the sink. I look for the closure, the humping of the shoulders. My question hangs in the air. I watch Patricia's steps to the stove with the saucepan. It's as though I feel her steps tread my oesophagus. Then just the faintest pause in her coming to the refrigerator, because it's closer to where I hang in the doorway. I am standing, questioning. She is busy. Each step is a knell. Then her relieved stepping away from me again to the table. No touch of reconciliation in any of it. I have merely asked a question about Jesse's books for History. Even as my anger swells at the repetition of the same grey domestic rondeau, I look at her and grieve. This is my wife. I have done this to her – the grey, sealed face. We have done this to each other in seventeen years and in the company of children. This is my wife to whom I promised things. I cry in the pit of my stomach.

It is another morning. I am in the shower. I transfer weight to my right foot, feel the water fall now past the other side of my head, curl now down the left side of my neck, shoulder, trunk. How long have I been thinking; thinking here, my marriage plunging past me, meeting the false marble of the shower base, splintering wetly, fragmenting, gathering itself in an inexorable, impatient pool and edging to the plughole, dribbling down, dribbling down? It's gone, our time together. The admission comes to me like a hand smartly slapping my forehead. Finished – whatever that means.

I think if the sun would declare itself first thing through the windows rather than waiting until mid-morning to expel the cloud wrack, I could cope better.

I think people act and say themselves into a corner of bitterness and then cannot change, cannot emerge again open-faced into rooms of choice and forgiveness. I think it's worst at night and in the morning. The still, steady sunlight in the afternoon seems to suggest that morning's leaden re-awakening to the desolation of knowing, and night's wide-eyed tension, are both mistaken dreams. Everything will come right again.

But it won't. It's a long time thinking under the shower. A long time to come to the same conclusion every morning. I've run out of mornings now.

—

You get ready for tennis.

I know that. Tennis is different shoes. It is a different dress. It is a white hat with only a front on it, and green under it. I watch my mother. The sun is reaching in the bay window at Cicero Street and putting a square of light and warmth on the edge of the carpet. I can feel it with my fingers.

There's a racquet in the back of Mum's wardrobe. It's heavy when I get it out, because it's in a thing with screws. Mum says: Tim, you can take the racquet out of its press. She shows me. She leans close. I can smell her cup of tea and I can smell powder. I unscrew the screws she has loosened. The press falls off. Mum says: take off the cover; we don't need the cover. I know how to do it with my fingers. I pull at the little things. I pull the cover off. I can hold the tennis racquet in both hands.

I know how to hit. Where are the balls? I don't know where they are. I ask Mum. She says never you mind. She closes the front door. It's heavy. It rumbles. We walk past the roses and I don't know where the balls are. We pull the front gate closed. It rings. We walk down the street and round the corner and past the Kennedys' house and the McLeishs' house and into Milton Road. I don't know where the balls are. We walk up towards the shops. Mum is carrying her straw bag with a cardigan in it. Sometimes I carry the racquet. You can hit the grass with it. Then Mum takes the racquet.

We don't go to the shops where Miss Bell has ice cream. We turn down a path. It is in someone's garden. We walk past a window with curtains. I can see a table inside with a vase of flowers on it. We walk down the side of the house where it is cold. Then we come out into the sun and there are the tennis courts. They are waiting like a pool. I look at the white lines. They just wait and wait there all the time, even when I'm asleep.

No one is playing tennis.

—

Our marriage is broken and gone.

There are days, weeks, months that are a sad indistinctiveness in my memory. When did it start? When did our heavy silences begin to follow the cutting words? When was our posturing drawn back like a false curtain to reveal that the climb back to warmth was now impossible; even though we could still practise habitual tenderness because there once had been tenderness, even though we could still come out of the shadows with an offering of consideration because there once had been consideration.

Patricia and Timothy. We are merely two people. It's as if I look down upon us as distant, tiny beings, nothing beyond the ordinary.

In the mid 1970s our marriage still stumbles on. The stolid indifference between Patricia and me is kept at bay by the trusting, needful eyes of Jesse and Susan, by my work under the searching lights at the college and Patricia's at the ad agency. The East Malvern house appears grey to me. I dread nights lying beside Patricia. The reading light goes on and she reads beside me in her nightie, rubbing left thumb against forefinger obsessively. She seems to be able to concentrate on what she reads. I can't. I face away from the light, lying on my side. The tense minutes, half hours pass, punctuated only by sighs and shifting of legs or the curt words necessary to keep a household going.

And now Patricia's eyes are often puffed and half closed with bitterness and weariness. I can't look at her. She is no longer the one I know. I know that what she is saying has been festering slowly in her for weeks. She who says little. I pity her, even as she attacks me. I can feel the slapping blows she would like to give me, feel the stinging skin on my cheek and neck, and know that now I would take them, hear the thud of them near my ear, feel the hot assault of them, and not move, because it is too late.

'You bleed us dry, don't you.' Her words belabour me. 'Where do you think money comes from? What about Jesse's expenses? And Susie coming up to university too? It all goes on your research, all your gallivanting around. You haven't got a financial instinct in your body. I think I'm putting in – at the moment I seem to be working for nothing else but the children's education! And you can be off at the drop of a hat! Your precious courses, your books, conferences, your precious articles – they take everything!'

I have never been, can never be, what Patricia hopes for.

—

I am reading my book in the little canvas chair at Cicero Street. I'm seven years old. I glance up from the page and look across the back-yard. It's all sunny. But a chill comes to clamp my heart whenever I think of it. I know what will happen, what I'm going to see. I know how the coldness will creep on me. It has happened before, the chill just waiting there, ready to return, waiting to remind me of where it all starts.

Will is making a wooden wheel-barrow for Greg to play with around the sand-pit. Greg is waiting. He doesn't know what the wheel-barrow will look like. While he waits he sings to himself. He croons. My little brother waits, and plays with his Christmas fire engine in the sun at the shed door.

In the shed I can hear the lever fall back as the vice goes home around the wood where Alistair is working at the bench. Will, my father, is helping him. It's half dark in there. It is father and son. I hear Alistair start to pare at his piece of wood with the sand-paper as he has seen Will do. I can see their faces, Will's and Alistair's, looming like moons in the darkness where the light from the shaft of sun at the shed door floats up to them. From where I sit I can see their heads nodding over the vice. I can see the bristling stack of bits of wood under the bench and the worn-out tyre a dark circle further over and the O's of the tins Will saves stacked up towards the roof.

Then Will comes to the door to see better. He's prying in the wood with the awl to widen a screw hole. Then Alistair slips his wood out of the vice and comes out into the sun to look at its smoothness. Greg gazes up at them and croons, and then bends over his fire engine to run it with his hand on the old bricks near the door. The three fair heads bob there together like birds over seed. That's where the fear begins. I feel the chill. They are not me. I am not them. They are fair, like Will's family in Sydney. I am dark. I'm sitting here near them, but I'm alone and different. Where is my mother? Where is she?

I look at the secret, dim mouth of the shed door. It doesn't want me. It has what it wants. I look at the three heads. They don't want me. They have forgotten I'm there in the chair. They are complete. They are with each other. But I am not with them. Where is my mother? I look up at the veranda window and my book slips from my knees. I know she's not there. I need to hear her words, see her face. But she's not there. She's far up the hill towards Camberwell visiting the McLellans' Auntie Jess. Who am I? I can feel my heart beating out across the sun-filled grass, with a fear that I've felt dimly many times before. Where is my mother? I must speak to her, hear her words. I want to ask her things and watch her face. Will people say hello to me if I'm different? For a moment it's as though the world disappears. Can I believe that the street – our street with the lilly pilly – is still there just up the drive? Am I somewhere else? Where is the place for me?

—

Joyce is going up to the back shed at Mont Albert to take Bing some chops scraps and some bones from the soup. She's my aunt, but she's only eight years older than I am.

Bing is a kelpie. Flute uses him sometimes with the sheep, if Joyce is staying up at Berriwillock long enough. But he's a city dog now, Flute says, and he's soft and he doesn't know what to do. Poor bugger. Flute squats down and rubs Bing's face and pushes him about and rolls him over. Bing likes it. Joyce does it too. Now, with the soup bones, Bing comes right out to the end of his chain. He's jumping and whining. He's excited to see Joyce, because no one has been to talk to him the whole afternoon. His chain rasps on the little tank when he moves, and Joyce says 'Bing, will you sing? Bing, will you sing?' and he loves her and he licks her face.

We haven't got a dog since Taffie got killed.

—

I'm writing about my close people.

I'm watching Grandpa John as a young man. He has a shock of fair hair, a sunburnt face, his cheeks peeling close to his ears. No one knows that this is the day he will meet Pearlie. He has come over to the sheds at Ibis Plain with old Rodgers, his employer, to help crutch the hundred Sutton sheep cowering in the corner of the home paddock. It is two years into the new century. I see John's shoulders and hands working through the morning under the sugar gums. I hear the rasp of a whetstone, see the glint of shears. I see John, legs and boots splayed, eating lunch with another man and a tawny dog against the wall of the shearing shed. The Grampians are drawn faintly across the horizon to the south.

At afternoon lunch a billow of white leaves the house – Mrs Sutton and Pearlie bringing a basket with scones, some milk and hot tea. Ah yes, says old Rodgers as they stand round in the bark detritus near the sheds, John is a cricketer and a tennis player. Pearlie steals a look at his awkward new face as he sips the dark tea, at the certainty in his tanned hands and forearms.

This cameo comes again, bringing other days. I find these two people alone in the crowd, the white and red-rusted roofs of the town swarming behind them in the hot Wimmera weather. I have seen Pearlie switching her gown with one hand as she talks to John at the change of innings on the red earth fringe of the ground near the scoring box. I see them again, hear their voices damped by the trees, hear the pluck of racquet meeting ball, see Pearlie's white skirt brushing the gravel as she bends to a forehand on the old Sutton tennis court. Her father is striking out with his round-arm swing at the other end, her mother watching, shimmying, shifting her feet in expectation of John's next shot. Pluck, and the ball leaps away. Self-deprecating words of laughter filter through the trees, through the leaf shadows.

I see a stepladder standing in the dimness of a hall. I see light pressing against frosted glass windows. I see feminine hands that come, trailing streamers. I see male hands hanging the streamers, reaching

24

up, pinning them under the ceiling's swarming darkness, then work-boots descending the ladder. I see a storeroom where Pearlie is arranging cups and saucers. I watch John come from the hall in his work-faded blue shirt and enfold her from behind, take her in his arms, her bountifulness, her breath expelled and drawn in again in the dim, dry room.

—

Sometimes I will find myself writing about a State called Victoria. I will be a man writing about other men called Flute and Alex and I will enter that country. Flute and Alex know I am describing them, making them move, and they don't know what to do about it.

I am also a man writing to the future. I find myself making words towards a woman who I think is called Rosa. She seems to hover near me, although I have never met her. I tell her about herself and myself and about what it is like to write. I tell her that we will meet and that I will love her. She will be my beautiful woman. I write that, and I am sure. I see her colour – a warm charcoal orange. I know she has a contralto voice when she is speaking passionately and intently.

—

There are questions.

Just how good a tennis player is Alex Cumming? How far does he run every night from the silos and out along the Mildura Road? Is a Cressy Perfect the best racquet? Alex has two of them. Who can Alex hit with? He gets up a sweat hitting against the wall of the Sea Lake bakery just off the main street, but that isn't enough. He has a strong farmer's wrist and big shoulders. He wears a white floppy hat with green under the brim. When he beats Willard at Kooyong in 1926, what is the temperature? What is the score? When the man from Kooyong in formal coat and tie takes him for a walk out into the street from the Royal South Yarra Tennis Club so that they can talk and says something about Davis Cup out of the side of his mouth, is that when Alex's secret ambition starts? The bees are prospecting photinia hedges and lavender in the gardens as the man and Alex saunter back to the clubhouse. Alex doesn't know how to saunter. He doesn't know what to say. He doesn't know this immaculate suburb. He has never before walked along a concrete footpath. He only knows how to farm for wheat and sheep and how to play tennis, how to launch himself sideways to get volleys that other players miss, how to measure with his eye before he serves, how to climb up for the smash, so that he is seeing the ball like a moon against the background of the grass banking and the people, swimming down, swimming down, waiting to be hit. He plays tennis after his early morning rounds of the big paddock behind the horses on autumn Saturdays and when he goes to Mildura and Swan Hill for tournaments in the summer, if he's not harvesting.

One year, I know, he goes to Geelong for a tournament at Easter and he wins the singles with the wind blowing off the sea. He beats O'Hara Wood, and no one speaks to him during the rest of the afternoon until the president beckons him up to the dais to get his trophy. As he stands waiting he looks at the strange buildings on the street opposite the courts. The pavements and parked motor cars between are hidden by high palings. But doorways and white arches above street level catch the low sun as the president speaks, and a loneliness closes in on Alex like a piece of cold steel clasping his chest. For a moment it is as if he doesn't know where he is or what he has been doing there. He is far from home. All he wants is to pack his clothes and his racquets on the bounding bed in the hotel and start for Sea Lake and Waitchie. He can see in his mind's eye the pepper trees trailing their tresses over the gutters in Sea Lake's main street. He yearns for them and the stillness of the Mallee evenings away from the seething coastal wind.

—

Jean is my oldest aunt. Jean sings. She's got a husky voice. Jean looks at American magazines. She sometimes smokes American cigarettes. They're called camels, but they're cigarettes. They've got a camel on them. Cec brings them home. He gets them from the Yankee soldiers near the Trocadero. The American soldiers are lonely. So are the sailors with white gob caps. They always look clean, because they wear white uniforms, but the soldiers don't. The sailors and soldiers write letters to their mothers and their sisters and brothers and to their fathers and to their wives and their girlfriends. But in Melbourne they're lonely, especially when it gets dark. I can remember all this.

Sometimes Jean sings to them. She sings to them, and Cec tells them funny stories at the Army camps when he's in Melbourne, but Louise says sometimes they don't understand his jokes. Sometimes Des plays jazz for them and they clap and then they smoke another cigarette, but Des can't see it. But I can remember their lonely eyes.

What does Jean think of Candles? He's her blustery brother. What does she think of Archie? She doesn't see them very often. What does she think of Flute, who still has to run the farm up in the Mallee even though he's lost three of his fingers? I know what she thinks of Louise, my mother, because I see them together and watch them and listen to them talking to each other. I see Jean with Joyce too. 'Li'l sister,' she sometimes says to Joyce, 'What are you thinking?' Joyce thinks a lot and doesn't say much. She's like Flute.

I think about them all, and my grandmother Pearlie and my grand-father John. I wonder how big our family is, when I think about it. Pretty big. I've got ten cousins – and Joyce is going to have another baby soon and that will make eleven. I can write them down. And I've got another five cousins in Sydney where Will's family lives.

I have to look after my cousins sometimes when we're at Mont Albert. We play outside while Louise and Jean and Joyce talk inside. But Joyce's little daughter Gwenda runs into a branch when we're playing hidey and it sticks into her eye. When the doctor comes he says she's lucky she can still see with it. Even the weekend after Gwenda's eye is still puffed up and you can only just see the white in it. When we're waiting for the doctor Joyce says these things are sent to try us – and she's nearly crying. David says what the hell was Timmy doing, that's what I'd like to know. Timmy was supposed to be minding them, wasn't he? I can hear David even when I'm in Des's side bedroom. Bloody useless, I hear David say. Came down with the last shower, if you ask me, he says. Hell! Then I catch the sound of the first words of my mother saying something very low, but I don't know what she says. Will is not here. He's in Albury.

I don't like David. Neither does Jean. I don't think my mother does either. But Joyce does and Annie does, because he brings them things when he's had a win.

It will be like before. I will watch my mother reading. I will watch her and wonder where she goes when she opens the book, when her breathing settles and her toes at the far distant other end of the bed stop rubbing each other. She says she is reading a novel. I can tell that it is not a time to speak.

She has brought a glass of water from the kitchen. She pads in barefoot and stands it on the dresser, just within reach in the corner. She grabs both pillows, Will's as well as hers, then picks up the book from the dresser and rolls onto the bed. She stuffs the pillows under her shoulder and neck so that she lies partly on her right side, her left hand tinkering with the next page of the book, waiting for the words to finish, then turning the page. This is how you read. She is breathing. She is soon still. She is gone into another place.

I look at my tennis racquet that Auntie Jean gave me where I've left it in the corner near the wicker chair with the blouse and dress over it. I think about it. I listen and I can hear the sparrows outside in the guttering.

It is like before. It's like before, but now I know what the words on the pages might be saying. Because now I can look at the words that I think at first are running across the page like rabbits. Now I can see the squads of words and the white spaces – and I'm starting to learn what they say.

—

David is going up the back at Mont Albert to get the tricycle for Little Gwenda. I'm walking up the drive behind him. I like the back shed. There are spider webs on its windows that haven't been touched for years, and the big old vice on the bench. No one has used it since Grandpa John died. This is where Grandpa John used to make cricket balls out of golf ball cores and twine.

Bing hears us before he sees us. We know because we hear his chain running out on the edge of the bit of tank where he sleeps. He's waiting for us. He gives a couple of yips and rears up at the end of where the chain will take him. He wants to see me. I'll cuddle his head and he'll squirm and he'll lick me. He's running back to the tank and then out to the end of the chain waiting for us. I go to him, but the chain catches his water bowl and it tips it over. David turns round. You bloody dog, he says. I see Bing's ears go down and he flattens to the ground. His eyes look up at David as though he might be hit. He tries to slink back to the bit of tank, but his chain catches David's shoe. You pest, David says. You bloody mongrel! He kicks Bing as he slinks back. He kicks him again. I hear his shoe sink into Bing's chest like a soft football. Bing crouches and hobbles, with little yelps. He's winded. He crawls into the bit of tank. He's crying in little mews like a cat. Bloody mongrel dog, David says. Useless bloody Mallee mongrel! Get out of it! David goes and pulls back the door of the shed so hard that the shed shudders.

Bing, will you sing? Bing, will you sing? It's Joyce's voice I hear. But it's not real. She's not here. She's back in the house. She doesn't know. Bing won't sing. David is in the shed, pulling the other things away from the trike. I don't like David. What does he mean when he hisses at Joyce about my mother, about me, out near the store shed? Why does he hurt her? I've got to get back inside before he comes out with the tricycle. I run back down the drive, past the privet and round to the path and along the concrete to the back door. I grab it open, get inside. My heart is racing. My mind is bursting. I slip through to Des's workroom and close the door and sit on his chair to think. What does David mean about my mother's little secrets? What does he mean butter wouldn't melt?

—

'Can you recite it, eh, "The Man from Ironbark"?' our uncle Des is asking in exaggerated disgust. He purses his mouth, smartly rubs his hands together at arms' length towards us. 'You can't, can you! You can't. After all my teaching!' He hisses, rubs his hands at us again like a condemnatory final statement. We're watching his mouth for his grin, but he withholds it.

I look away from the computer's soft shirring and the white of its keys, and there we are. I can remember. It's just Alistair and me. It's before Greg is born. We are boy brothers lolling on our uncle's bed in the back sleep-out at Mont Albert. We're in Sunday-tidy-but-worn visiting clothes.

Des sits on the simple wooden chair, his back to the lowboy and the bedside shelf with his hair brush and some white soap in a dish on a shelf, handkerchiefs where he can put a hand on them. His abraded black leather tool bag, closed like a big purse, is lying just visible on the top of the lowboy. Des is in old suit pants and white shirt. He has rolled the sleeves up above his wrists.

I laugh. Alistair looks up and smirks. We've been flipping through the *Saturday Evening Post*s we've found in the kitchen. There are either *Life*s or *Saturday Evening Post*s – and we like them. They are American magazines, better than Australian ones. Aunty Jean gets them from Cec. Cec is in New Guinea, where the Australian soldiers are fighting the Japs. I can remember when the War started and Cec went away for the first time. It was two summers ago. Summer. I love summer, because it means hot days and swims at the baths. Summer is the time I measure things by.

'Can you do any of it?' Des is saying. 'What about "The Bush Christening"? No, you can't, can you. I'm blowed if I know. After all the times I've told them to you.' But he has turned away from us towards the window to hide his face, and the grin is coming to his mouth. He knows what we want. 'Oh, yes, you do it better, Des! That's what you say, isn't it! You do it better. Please, Des, please recite it. Cripes, you little ninnies. You can't give me one word!' Now it's starting. Now it's happening. The laughter comes up in our throats like bubbles from our bellies.

'All right. All right!' Uncle Des snorts. 'But you're going to pay for this!' He turns his face to my shifting of position on the bed. That's how he places things. I slew slowly, lower my feet to the floor, try to move silently from bed foot to bed head. 'And don't bother moving about.

30

I can hear you.' He looks directly at me, and his eyes seem to burn sorrowfully. I feel a mingling of great love and great sadness for him. 'Come here, you little ninny.'

I take a daring step towards Des and in one movement he grasps me firmly by the shoulders and upper arms. He draws my face to his. 'You're going to pay for this! Not one word can you give me!' His strong hands cup my head about the ears. He brings my smooth cheek against his all-day growth of stubble. He rubs his sandpaper chin abrasively down my left cheek, then my right. I writhe. The laughter is frothing in my mouth. I'm caught and Alistair is jealous. I'm caught, I writhe, I laugh in bubbles – and then explode with joy and fart a single, staccato fart.

'Aha, the first word at last,' Des chortles. He laughs. I can see he laughs at himself, at vitality, laughs at these two stainless souls who are with him. I feel his love fan me. Then he swallows. His face changes. 'All right. You've got to tell me how to start. OK? OK! "The Man from Ironbark".'

'It was the Man from Ironbark that hit the Sydney town . . .' I say, the words bliss in my mouth. And we're away into the story of the bushman, the Sydney streets, the barber's shop. And I'm reciting with my uncle.

''Ere, shave me beard and whiskers orf. I'll be a man of mark. I'll go and play the Sydney toff up there in Ironbark . . .'

I'm watching Des though, his eyes facing away again towards the window, his face fallen to that of a man now. I notice the change as he recites. I feel my breath catch. What if something happened to Uncle Des? My uncle who is blind. My uncle who sang a spiritual in a church when they asked for him. My uncle who plays the piano in the jazz band. My uncle who wears long suit pants and is old – twenty-nine years old, Louise says. Des's eyes, with their blue pinpoints, look far away into loneliness sometimes. I watch him. I have forgotten Alistair. I watch Des, I hear the words. I scan Des's face and mouth. A pang that has a distant day in it crosses my heart.

Uncle Des for a moment is waiting, listening, seemingly unaware of me. Then he stirs, picks up the line, transforms his face and voice to a snake-like cunning, and continues:

'The barber man was small and flash, as barbers mostly are. He wore a strike-me-fancy sash and smoked a huge cigar . . .'

He's away again. We wait for each scene we know in the poem to unfold for the fiftieth time in this suburban bedroom in Mont Albert, Melbourne, Victoria, Australia, the World, the Universe. I can see the barber man and his plan. I see his dark, puffy jowls. I've always felt his fatal pause with the razor in his hand. Many times I've seen the bushman's craggy face, his waiting, scraggy beard. I've felt that red hot slash across his Adam's apple, the stinging line of it. I know how the bushman towers over everyone in the shop in his baggy pants and his rough white shirt, enraged and stung.

'And all the while his throat he held,

To save that vital spark. And "Murder, bloody murder"

Yelled the Man from Ironbark . . .'

'Murder, bloody murder,' Alistair is mumbling to himself. He seems to be saying it to the quince tree and its yellow globes beyond the wavery window glass. But we are waiting, waiting for the barber's whining and the bushman's spitting outrage and scorn:

'And then at last the barber spoke.

"'Twas all in fun. 'Twas just a harmless little joke a trifle overdone. A joke!" he cried. "By George, that's fine! A lively sort of lark! I'd like to catch that murdering swine some night in Ironbark."'

The poem washes over us. I picture the flowing beards. I see the shearing floor like the one at Berriwillock, where Flute comes from, when the shearers stretch their legs across the greasy floor and slurp on tin mugs of tea and yawn and mumble and laugh.

Des has finished. Where I lean against the wall at the lowboy end of the bed his fingers find my shoulder. His hand squeezes it, then pats it for confirmation. 'Aha! Eh? Considerably more than one word you gave me in the end. Eh?'

'Can we do "The Bush Christening" if we . . .?' Alistair starts, but Des is shaking his head. What's Des doing? He's groping forward, running his hands along the wood of the shelf beside his bed. His fingers feel the edges so deftly, creep onto the shelf, touch Brylcreem jar, scissors, the soap in the dish. Then they retreat.

'Damn! I had that bit of paper with the address on it,' Uncle Des says. 'I had it, didn't I? You know I had it, don't you. Where is the damn thing?' He stops, face turned to the door, listening. Then he starts to call in an urgent, carrying voice:

'Jean! Jean!'

We can hear Auntie Jean bite off a sentence in the murmur of the kitchen, her voice rising on the last words to a 'Yes, what is it?'

'Did you give me that slip of paper from the phone with this afternoon's address on it? I can't find the damn thing.' Uncle Des stands taut, his head on one side, face fronting the wall near the door as if intently searching it.

'You've got a copy somewhere, and I've got a copy, Des,' comes Jean's voice. 'Have another look around. Not in your suit-coat pocket? I'll be there in a minute.'

This afternoon Des will put on his tie and dark-blue suit, take his white stick and his bag of tools from the lowboy and set off down the street, tap-tapping, sometimes stumbling a few steps when a tree root throws him out of stride. He'll go to the tram, armed with his address note and its time of appointment. People will help him. He will ask questions in his clear sing-songy voice. He will find his way from Mont Albert to Prahran to tune a piano – among all the voices, footsteps, tram bells, purring and receding car exhausts. Tonight, if they've got a booking, Charlie might come to pick him up to go to the club in Kew to play jazz. Des's piano, Charlie's sax.

I think about Des and his blind tracks across Melbourne and how, while he's away piano tuning, he leaves behind him, at the closed gate of the Mont Albert house, a sign, inexpertly hand-lettered but clear. I think Jean did it for him. Its cream and black board worms its way deeper every spring into the encroaching privet of the hedge:

'Desmond Barnes – Piano Tuner – Apply Within – Telephone WX4362'

—

I know now with a new certainty that I'm going to write about Alex Cumming. And yet I can't tell myself why. Under my eyelids I am wondering about him. I feel him thinking towards me. I'm thinking him into my forehead and keeping him there.

First, it seems that this is happening not far from me around time's circle. Alex will be waiting in the soft, even light under the Kooyong stands where it is cool. Suddenly the rush of the crowd's clapping comes down the stairs from the stadium above. But the sound is invisible. The concrete stairs just loom there, completely empty and still, letting the light down. The sound circles in the dust and the cluster of ice cream papers and fades away. Alex Cumming walks to the foot of the stairs and looks up them towards the light. His hat is in his hand. His hair is grey. He glances down at his watch.

Now, in a smooth elision, it becomes another happening, another place. These are Alex's shoulders in an Army shirt under the pure white boles of the trees at Fern Tree Gully. It must be further back on time's circle. I smell the beer on Alex's breath. Sometimes I smell beer on my father's breath, a tired smell that brings me pictures of the lines of crows' feet crouching at the corner of people's eyes. It's like sweat, the smell. I see beer and open shirts together. When my father drinks beer his voice changes and comes deep and thick from the back of his throat. My mother says Will is in Sydney, doing War work. Mr McLellan across the street does War work. He has an important uniform. He sometimes goes to Sydney on the train, too, but not on the same train as my father. Will and Mr McLellan have to get special tickets to go on the train. I have listened to them talking about them at the front gate.

But now I can hear that Alex will call from the sodden log bridge over the creek at Ferntree Gully. He will call and I will watch my mother leave the fire and its black billy blushing to itself as the flames take it and retreat. I will see Louise walk over to Alex across the leaf detritus and bark and damp earth. Alex will have his uniform on with the V's on the arms of the shirt and the tight webbing belt and faded trousers and orange-brown boots and khaki gaiters. His hat will be resting on its chin strap on the thick grey wood of the picnic table that has to stay out in the rain all the time in the bush. I hear myself thinking. I hear the trees dripping on it. I hear myself saying it is the War in 1942. I remember the day and how the air even now feels cold. I smell the real chewing gum that Alex has brought. He can get it, he says. PK chewing gum. Alistair wants a piece, but he's too small. He might swallow it. Greg is in the basket, asleep in his shawl.

The gentle circle of happenings slides away again, dims. I see that, yes, Alex Cumming is still waiting under the Kooyong stands, in his pale-blue summer shirt and his wide hat from the Mallee with its thin leather band. But I can feel the picture fading. I don't know enough. I haven't stood there with him. There is a lot about Alex Cumming I don't know. I watch him pace slowly back into the light towards the clubhouse. People pass him, working their shoulders round him. People overtake him. There is his hat still moving, then it is gone. He is lost. I can hear a red train gurgling out from the city above the green ranks of courts.

—

My father Will still lives. But he might soon die. I puzzle over him. He is one of my close people. I have seen so many things happen to him. It seems I have always been with him. I have seen him reel at Louise's death. I have watched his face at my wedding, suavely presented but uncertain. I have heard his voice for so long. Little Dig, he used to call me. Now he calls me Dig when it's just the two of us and no one else to account to. I have for so long heard words, heard ideas issue from him. It's as though he seldom tries to teach me anything – he simply thinks aloud, discloses himself, draws things out to lay before me. When I am at university it's the slow, wise voice of Whitman I hear from him, sitting at the tea table at the back of the house in Cicero Street, Camberwell, the light infiltrating, inflating the terracotta roofs attended by dark islands of trees across the suburb:

'I do not doubt but the majesty and beauty of the world are latent in any iota of the world . . . I do not doubt there is far more in trivialities, insects, vulgar persons, slaves, dwarfs, weeds, rejected refuse, than I have supposed . . .'

Will lets his knife down to rest against his plate and looks at us, his eyes glazing. 'Vulgar persons, slaves, dwarfs, weeds, rejected refuse,' he intones, and shakes his head. He takes up his knife again.

How many times have I watched him as he works at the bench in the shed? He just accepts his skill with tools, his methodical work at the bench, his hands that make things fit. You've got good hands, he says to Alistair. Alistair always wants to make things with wood. I don't. But I like to watch them using the tools. Now Will my father stands there planing, knees flexing with each stroke, then hits the vice with the heel of his hand and takes the wood from its grip, raises it, sights with his eye along its blond length. He loves the smell of wood, of linseed oil, of paints. He wears old ARP black overalls. It's wartime. He's chewing a match, his pipe lying unfilled on the ledge near the door. I am watching him from the step. He is in a talking mood, prepared to ask me to get things. 'Stick your arm in under there, will you, Dig, and pull out two of those rods? See this? I'm going to string one down each side of it. A bit of metal support should strengthen it, stop it twisting. What do you think? It'll look like a steam pipe running down the side of the engine, don't you think?'

Will is proud of his car. It sits behind him in the gloom of the garage as he works, its headlights catching the light balefully. He is proud of his well-judged driving. He keeps a car log of where he goes, where he gets petrol, what it costs, mileages he drives. He snaps the little notebook shut on these details and strings a rubber band round it and its stubby pencil and pokes them back under the dash.

But I am younger then. I look at my father's head bowed over the developing bolt of the locomotive and I don't know that he's thinking; perhaps about Chaucer or Thomas Hardy or Milton, or Emily Dickinson or Melville. I don't know about the American history he teaches at the college. I don't know that he thinks about Paul Robeson, Joseph Furphy, Henry Lawson's stories. All I see is his shed with its clocks under repair and the old radio he's making work again, and the collections of tins that are stacked up the walls into the gloom.

Sometimes I write to Rosa. I sense her there. It is a sort of speaking. I tell her about myself. I tell her where I am and what I've been thinking and doing. Sometimes I tell her stories about the people I know. I tell her these things so that I can hear the stories again myself, so that I can see whether they have changed.

So I write to Rosa, but I'm not yet certain when I will meet her. Why she comes to me I'm not sure. I sense her there at my elbow, knowing things I don't know.

—

I am searching the past for my grandmother Pearlie. I am searching for Grandpa John beside her, as I put the words down. On bad days they elude me. Those are the days when the false leads present themselves. I have to retrace my steps, shed whole pages.

John and Pearlie take their honeymoon at Lorne. I can picture it, Pearlie's long dress dragging in the sand near the stolid piles of the pier, the water barely hushing at her feet. It has to be in the slack time of the year: April and warm and calm. I know it. The December harvest at Ibis Plain has been very hard and hot, but a good one. There's never the time in the full summer for a marriage or honeymoon. Now, three months after the harvest, I can feel Pearlie's happiness and ethereal unease sweeping over her in turn in this strange bright morning, in this strange place smelling of the blood of the sea and the secret cool wine of gum leaves. When she wakes here there are no plains crossing her mind. She misses them. She misses her mother. When the day ends here the sun slips like an eye behind forest and she searches again in dismay for the sweep of the Wimmera horizon. But John is warm and gentle.

He sits now on a rock, watching her fossick for shells. He thinks of the plains, too, and of the simple wooden cottage among the box trees near the yards on their new block back home at Lallat East. He watches the moody swell turn up a shining fin of kelp thirty yards from shore and let it go again. He doesn't understand the sea, doesn't trust its blue stare. He tries to comprehend the depths with their misty light, their eyes and fronds and the willowy fish he has seen from the pier.

My grandparents are young. I watch them. They are unsuspecting. Pearlie in her perfect, firm body knows nothing of the children who will tear it, of her future dreams of blood. John has thought hazily of sons, but sees only the paddocks, furrows running towards the veil of sugar gums. How to tell either of them about a son who will lose the fingers of his right hand, swearing against God? How to tell them of two daughters who will come four miles from the school walking their pony, stumbling hand over hand from fence post to fence post in the darkness of the dust storm? How to tell them of a son who will go blind as a boy, born just sixteen years into the new century, with the beat of the recruiting drum sounding against the corrugated iron walls of the smithy in the town? I reach for the two of them as I write, but for a time I encounter only air, hear only the strutting of the small clock in the shadows of the bookshelves on the other side of the room.

They start to move before my eyes now. I can hear their voices. The day has become pink evening. They walk the pier, Pearlie's hand seeking John's wrist, her hips sidling beautifully against his. Is he a man of the world, he wonders, in these strangely bright shoes, his open silk shirt and maroon blazer? A fishing-smack rides the grey-green water that rises moodily against the piles of the wharf, then falls away again. A man with a pocked face looking up from under a faded Trilby hat sets his knees against the gunwale and heaves fish up to the pier's decking. They fly, land, slither to find a place among the other fins and eyes.

'Oh, a shark!' John hears a woman say, and looks to where she points. Her beau mutters and pulls her arm again through his, dragging her off, her face craning back. On a rough wooden trolley resting on its shaft on the decking, John and Pearlie see a nine-foot monster of bronze perfection and inert power, one of its pectoral fins riding up over the trolley's side. A fisherman lolls not far from the big fish at the railing, his leather apron wet and blood-tinged from fish cleaning. He watches bemusedly the departing waist and bustle of the woman and the approach of John and Pearlie. John side-steps, Pearlie's hand still in his, so that he can come round to the shark's head. The fisherman shifts his pipe in his mouth.

'Give it plenty of distance!' His voice is peremptory and deep. He doesn't move.

John starts. Pearlie murmurs in compliance, starts to move away from the unbelievable, perfectly sculpted snout, the unblinking round eyes. But pride and curiosity are working in John. He avoids the monitoring eyes of the fisherman, leans down closer to the head and the cruel gape of the jaws. The fish is still. With his free right hand John reaches away to touch the barrel of the body. He encounters sandpaper and damp and the muscular rise of the dorsal fin.

'Keep away! He's just out of the water. He can still take ya hands off.'

John starts, draws his fingers away, looks up at the fisherman, his face prickling with anger and abashment.

'I heard you!' he says, taking a fresh grip on Pearlie's glove, making to move around a winch's tethered bulk to the pier's edge on the other side. But before his words are clear of his throat the shark, not four feet from him, suddenly leaps in a paroxysm and snaps at the sides of the trolley, its weight trembling the planks, its head following its pectoral fin over the trolley's side, then sinking back, eye staring, in grey, expressionless chagrin. The shark is still again, its outline drawn in, reeling down again towards death and final stillness. But the trolley threatens to topple. John has stood his ground, while Pearlie's quick scream still echoes in his ears. She strains at John's left hand and tries to break away. The eyes of two near couples and a group of boys mooching along the pier swing in their direction. The fisherman waits to be sure the trolley will stay upright, shifts an elbow against the rail, allows a puff of his pipe in the still evening. Behind him the sunset paints the shifting fields of water with charcoal.

'Oh!' Pearlie cries. 'Oh, John! Come away. We'll go back now.'

They turn. A dim light or two pricks the dark shore. John drops Pearlie's hand, and determinedly runs his own over the uncompromising blade of the shark's tail as he goes.

'John!' Pearlie remonstrates.

It all comes together in light, in sound. It's like Grandpa John's cadenza in the face of the sea.

John shrugs, falls into a measured tread beside her, thinking of their airless, warm room in the guest house, of the bed, of his night shirt, of Pearlie's ivory backed brushes and her golden hair coming down. He wants to kiss her perfect belly. It is as if I can feel his mouth drying. It is as if I too measure off, as he measures off with his eye, the distance to the shore and the track that will take them through the trees. In that distance he must rearrange himself, regain composure and a certain swagger on this coast with its whispers, where he has no keys to knowledge.

—

With Victoria the Great Divide is the thing, my father Will says. North of the Divide. South of the Divide. It makes all the difference. My father, a New South Welshman, talks compulsively, longingly about the Divide, as though beyond that bright line sleeps everything good. Once we're north of the Divide we'll see the sun, my father Will says, driving north, driving north in the Chrysler. Even then I can see the Divide in my mind's eye. It's like looking along the pitch of a tent: that's how sharp it is. I look at the map of Victoria in the atlas in the dim tiers of the fire-smoky schoolroom in Camberwell and I can see the Divide running down from New South Wales in yellow and pinches of brown, rising above the green fringes of forested hills that separate the mountains from the sea through Gippsland. I can see the tailing away of the yellow ranges into the plains of the north-east near Wangaratta and Benalla and Euroa. But it's a long way across the Divide. I think of Will's Chrysler driving through all the country where the yellow and the brown are, its engine protesting, grinding, becoming hysterical, overheating. Blasted overheating, Will says. We'll have to give her a rest.

We drive over the map when we go to Sydney – over the blue lines of the rivers, over the little thin lines of the creeks, along the red roads and the black roads. We know what's coming if we look at the map. Dandenong, Berwick, Nar Nar Goon. But there are so many names, so many places with their stores and their hotels and their railway stations. It's hard to think about it. Warragul, Trafalgar, Sale. We drive all day. When we start it's so early the streets are quiet and there's only one bike and a paper truck on Riversdale Road. We drive and I sometimes feel sick and Alistair complains too. Will just keeps on driving. Alistair goes to sleep beside me. When he wakes up at Trafalgar his eyes are narrow and he's cross. I tell him we've been through Warragul and there was a steam train. Alistair says who cares and turns towards the other window. I can sit up and see the trees washing the Chrysler's bonnet. I like watching the strong water cap far up front on the radiator with its silver wings. It forges ahead, ahead through the country.

We drive until it's late and cars are putting their headlights on. When it's getting dark and the trees are reaching down to the Chrysler's lights we come out of the bush and there's Bairnsdale. We stay the night in Bairnsdale, because we're in East Gippsland and it's all bush and it's all dark. Will wants to cross the Drummer in the morning, taking it steady. She might boil on the Drummer, he says. Will we all have to get out of the car? The Drummer is a big mountain. The Princes Highway goes right over it.

We stay in a hotel. It's very smart and modern, with cream walls and polished wooden stair rails. In the bathroom there's a hot water tap. Will gives Mum a quick kiss while they're standing looking round our bedroom. Then he unsnaps the suitcase on the bed. Tomorrow, he sings, we'll be in good old New South. Mum looks at him across the strange bedroom with its wood varnish smell and makes a face.

I go to sleep with a headache when I've had tea.

In the morning I wake up and for a while I can't see and I don't know where I am. Then I remember. The bedroom is dark. I look at Alistair. This is my brother. His arm is down the side of the bed against the wall. His mouth is open and he's neighing quietly as he breathes. I know it's morning. I want to see where the daylight is. I get out of bed, go to the door. I can open it quietly by pulling down a bit on the knob. I'm quiet going along the hall in my bare feet. There's light. There's a room with a window. I can hear a horse clip-clop outside. It goes past. I want to see down to the street. I find a way across the room. There are sheets on the floor, and a towel and some clothes and a hair brush. I pull back the window curtain to look out. I can see the street down below and some verandahs and roofs. I can still hear the horse's shoes, sharp on the street somewhere, but I can't see it.

'Hey,' a voice says and it frightens me. I look round. I can see better in the room now. There's a man in bed.

'Hey, what do ya think you're doing?' says the man. He's getting up. He hasn't got pyjamas. He's red furry. There's a lady in the bed too.

'Where did you spring from?' says the man. His hair is messed. He picks up his pyjama pants from the floor. He's putting his leg into them. He's grunting. I want to go back to Mum and Dad. The lady in the bed gets up on an elbow. She's yawning. She says: 'Room 23, I think.'

The lady hasn't got a nightie. She's tired. She yawns. She's the lady who owns the hotel. I remember her now. She showed Dad where our room was, but her hair was shorter. Now she's sitting up, swinging her legs round and out of the bed. I can see her back and her long hair and her bottom. She reaches down and when I look again she's got a nightie on.

The man puts a hand on my shoulder. I don't like him. 'C'mon, back to your Mum,' he says. 'You know where to go? Just near the stairs. See ya.' He pushes me into the hall.

That's Bairnsdale. The sound of the horse's hooves in the morning before anyone's up, and the red furry man and the lady with no nightie. That's Bairnsdale, always, no matter how many times I go there.

—

Forget that you're dark, my voice says to me. Forget your dark hair. Just let the months go on, let things go on happening around you. There'll still be movement and voices, the days will stream on in the sun without any reminders. That's what my voice says.

—

I am on tenterhooks whenever I talk to him. That's how it seems.

I look into the eyes of Patricia's father. He sits, one knee crossed over the other in the lounge at 42 Cremorne Street, the nest of rosewood occasional tables beside him where his wrist lies along the arm of the chair. His eyes, I think, are looking at me with the burning of that ultimate interest he must practise in the surgery. And yet they are cold when I look a second time.

'And how are your parents?' he is asking me.

'Mum's enjoying her teaching,' I say. 'She's glad to be back with a sixth grade this year. More of a challenge. Minds opening up to all sorts of things.'

'Yes, indeed,' Patricia's father says. 'All sorts of things. And I see the teachers are after more money again. Is she involved in that?' He looks away towards the mantelpiece as though he's just thought of something he should have done. Then his eyes swing back to me. But they burn again with only a dutiful attentiveness. His fingers drum for a moment softly on the armchair, then stop.

'No, she's not. She can only just keep up with the work. Large grades, a lot to bring home. So no unionism for Mum at the moment. If she were younger, maybe.'

'And is your father still at the school – or is it "college"?'

'Yes,' I say, wondering how to put it. 'Yes, he'll always love the teaching. But he's found one of his students is on drugs at the moment. She's been acting strangely. Vague, slow speech, no answers to questions. But the Head of Department doesn't seem to want to act on it. So Dad's at least going to have a talk to her parents off his own bat.'

'And to what end will that be?' Patricia's father asks, unfolding his legs as he speaks. I'm at a loss to answer him. To what end? Before I can form words he groans and then rises. He smiles a wide, enquiring smile, looking down on me. 'Now, what can I get you to drink?' he says.

It's a far echo of chill days, days on tenterhooks, days when I am still too inexperienced to know, days that are part of a dead marriage.

—

So here I am writing to myself again so that I can see the story and not mistake it. I write about a woman called Marie, one of my Mallee relatives, my uncle Flute's wife, and about all my mother's brothers and sisters. I write about the Wimmera, another neighbouring part of the State of Victoria, where my grandmother Pearlie and grandfather John were children, where they grew up to know cropping and sheep, to play cricket, to cook in the big kitchen at 'Ibis Plain' after Pearlie had been to school in Adelaide and then to get married and start their own farm at Lallat East, carrying their things into the pine-scented rooms of their new house.

What I write at first is almost all on my mother's side of the family. My squat, slightly portly, blond-grey, handsome father and his family are absent much of the time and when they appear they come only as wordless dim figures stepping around the actors who are my mother's family sitting in the light and speaking their lives. That's how it works out, it seems.

I discover as I write that people leave a tincture of themselves in the places where they live and love and hate. I can find people's spirit in these places, even though they have been dead for a long time. I have felt it in Suffolk, in the Vale of Dedham, among the Sutton graves under the green moss thicket. I have felt it in the dry farm yard at Berriwillock. I have felt it as I dive in Loch Ard Gorge. I have heard voices surging down with me, all strangers, where the white rock appears among the weed like bones, the crayfish under the ledges backing away from me, reminding me that I have only breath. But standing alone at the foot of the cedar staircase in Pinninarra House, home of the forebears of my father Will, where his two maiden aunts taunted each other year after year and died within two years of each other among those closed rooms with their draped furniture I hear no voices. I just yearn for Will to tell me more. But that is another story: Pinninarra House sits among its trees in another State that is warmer and moist, where the red coral trees light the pudendas of rainforest in the hill clefts running up to the Illawarra Range.

—

44

It's the Mallee. Grandpa John is standing at the wood heap. Considering his age, he is satisfied with how his wind is lasting. He can still keep chopping and splitting. He is seventy. His head sometimes reels as he straightens up. But his eyes are still good. No glasses, except for reading by the lamp at the kitchen table at night. He's a good shot still, but guns are a burden now. Even so, he shot that last fox from this very woodheap two nights ago. No more pullets gone for a few weeks, eh! And Grandpa John loves his Pearlie, who he still sees as a girl. She knows him. He knows her skin and hair in its rough bun. But she sees his neck getting more and more like crepe above the flannelette singlet when he comes in. She sees his knees bend slowly to set the small wood blocks down near the stove. Flute should take over this place, she thinks. We should go down to Melbourne to be near Louise and Jean.

—

With the suddenness of light I'm there – and it is when I'm very young – it must be the late 1940s – and it is Artarmon. I can feel again the excitement of Sydney's direct sun, the thought of the Harbour, the movement of waters, the musty smell around the glossy fern branches near the sleep-out. The sun is flooding in through the shutters in the sleep-out and there is the sound of a train weeviling down the valley towards the Sydney Harbour Bridge through the pittosporums, along the red-rusted ballast of the line, through the red-brick walls of cuttings and factories. It is the slam, slam of the brown and black Sydney trains thrown back by brick and rock. It is Sydney. It's warm and I can smell porridge and toast and there's the broad-leafed rasping of a banana tree near the fence in the back garden. Bananas! They won't grow in Melbourne. It's going to be a new day with Auntie Con and Uncle Douglas. It might even be hot. My father Will is still asleep in the other bed. He's driven a long way from Victoria. He's tired. It's only me and Will. My mother and Alistair and Greg are at home in Victoria. It is just us. We have come up in the Chrysler with the trees and the paddocks and sheep. We stayed in the hotel at Gunning. It was cold. The hotel had a big fire. In the morning there was a frost, all white. But in Sydney it's warm. Afterwards Uncle

Jack might come over. He lives at Vaucluse. His house can see the Harbour at the bottom of the street. We might go on the ferry to Manly. We might go for a swim, it feels so warm. And yet my heart feels a chill.

I sit at the table in the Artarmon house. I'm eight. I'm having porridge and then I'll have some toast. Uncle Douglas looks at me. Auntie Con is standing behind his chair. She is Will's sister. She is pretending to be a Scot. 'Will you have brown sugar or treacle, my bonnie lad?' she's asking me. I look at her red hair. I look at her blue eyes. I look at my father and his blue eyes and the sandy hair falling down near his ear and his gold and copper whiskers. He hasn't shaved. Maurice comes in. He's got shorts on. He hits the back of my chair with his hand as he sits down to tell me he's here. Maurice is my cousin. He reaches for the bowl of porridge Auntie Con has spooned out with a wooden spoon for him. She says, 'Steady, Maurie, my bonny boy. Say hello to your cousin and your uncle.' Maurice smirks at me. We played cricket down the side of the house yesterday. I look at his very white skin and his freckles and his soft red hair. I look back at my father. I'm glad he's with me, because I'm dark and I can't look out the window to get over it like I can at home. There's a curtain and I'm not sure what the house next door is like. I look back and I can see myself reflected in the sugar bowl. It's silver and it makes me look as though my face is round. A dark-eyed face like a ball. I look at the others. They are my relatives, my mother has told me before we start driving from Melbourne. 'You'll see all the relatives you've forgotten,' she says. They are all red-haired or sandy and pale. They are not like me. They are my fair aunt and uncle and cousin. And soon Uncle Jack might come over to see us with his blue eyes and the gold hairs on his arms. He sometimes takes his boat out through the Heads from Vaucluse to fish all day when it's calm and all he puts in the boat in an old bag are a couple of bottles of beer and three bananas and a big hat. I look at my father and I can almost see Uncle Jack there in his face, because they are brothers.

I'm happy with my aunts and uncles and cousins. I'm happy to be in Sydney where the sun is warmer in the banana leaves. But the dim

46

unease is there. I'm glad my father Will is with me, because I haven't got gold eyelashes or sandy hair.

—

What about my close people and their mysteries?

I see Candles, dragging on a football boot, reaching for the tongue, pulling and spreading it, then locking fingers in the laces and drawing them tight. Candles is really Uncle Murray. Uncle Murray and 'Uncle Alex', my mother tells me, won the doubles at the 1933 Swan Hill tournament. I have to remind myself that Candles' real name is Murray. The adults call him Candles, just as they call his brother Jeremy 'Flute'. When far back round time's circle I am a schoolboy nephew I can call him both.

Later, when he comes down from the Mallee, Candles plays football for Collingwood during the War – just a few games with the firsts. Then he plays with the seconds. Then later he is captain and coach of Camberwell. I see his big shoulders and bald head away down beyond the curve of the ground where legs running look like fast sticks, where sometimes from the fence you can't see legs at all. Then Candles plays with Glen Iris on the smaller grounds, with cars at their boundaries and old gumtrees beside the cricket scoring boxes.

Sometimes I find myself wandering among mysteries about these people I cannot fathom. I seem to be in a house where things will happen to them. Sometimes, inexplicably, my hand is stayed just as I am about to push open a door. Sometimes there is a touch on my forearm telling me to wait for what will be vouchsafed to me. All the while I watch my close people move against the overcast mornings or across sun-fretted ground under trees. I love them. I fear for them. I still wonder how it is that I have been chosen, how it is that they were meant for me – the living and the dead.

—

The most interesting photographs have shadows in them. Lying there on the floor at Cicero Street I'm sure of that.

I'm thinking of the cameras in the house. I know that Will, my father, keeps his camera in the lowboy near the double bed, wrapped in a bit of old sheet. But my Brownie Box, the one I took Alistair with, is in the top of the cupboard in the back bedroom, with the stamp album. The cameras could be taking pictures, but they just sit there with their film inside them and wait.

The best photographs I've taken have shadows that recede in them. I took a picture of Alistair in that straw cowboy hat when we walked through the bush down to the shops at Emerald. There's Alistair with the shadows and sun crossing the track behind him and into the distance. I had a feeling about it and so I took it. It was my first photograph. And then I took the McLellans in the creek at Upwey. I had to step in closer over the fallen branches in the bracken to get the picture. You can see Barry's face shivering with the cold water, but he's trying to smile. I waited for that, so that Barry's face came into the patch of sun on the water. Tom's face and shoulders are in the shadow, and there's a branch near him and the rest is darkness. I took that. You look to see what the camera has got and if it is all right you press the lever. That's all. And you try not to let the camera shake.

I've come home from school and I've found them in the cardboard folder in the little cabinet in the lounge. My photographs from the Brownie Box are bigger than these ones Will has taken with his folding camera. I'd forgotten about them. 'Ilford Film' says the folder. Beside the words is a picture of a camera like my father's. I've pulled out the pile of photographs and settled on the floor to look through them, turning them over, reading what's on the back. I can remember some of them, but they still come to me like discoveries. I see new things in them.

There are some photos of babies. There are some of me as a baby in the wicker pram. There are some of Alistair in the pusher, and you can see the eczema on his face. It's painted pale pink with calamine. There are even three or four of Louise on the day she married Will. Who took them? There's one of the house in Gardiner where I was a baby – the house I can't remember, the rented house, the house before Cicero

Street. And yet I seem to feel its dark side wall and its hydrangeas. I can see the back of Dad's car down the drive in the photo.

It's as though I might be turning the photographs over now. I watch my fingers reject two photographs and pick up another, turning it over. My eyes rove its detail. The backyard of 8 Cicero Street, Camberwell. It's the same backyard that is at this moment just through the hall, through the kitchen and down the back veranda steps. I could go out there now and look at it. It would take me about thirty steps to do it. There in the picture is the Jonathan apple tree, the shed door, the stepping stones to the clothes line. But it's another time, because Sandra from across the street is there and Taffie is alive: he's under the lemon tree with a bone. It's before the car got him in Riversdale Road.

I sit unblinking for a moment. It is all there, familiar, as though I could touch it. But it is another time. The sun is afternoon, lighting the side of the manure drum behind the shed. As I look at the picture I can smell the grass, hear the mean little wind rattling the white bells of the Lily of the Valley under the sleep-out window. What would happen if I went out there now? Would I be in this other time? Would Sandra and Taffie be there? Would the sun come through the cloud and shine on the manure drum?

I decide that I'll try it. I think about the steps I'll take through the hall and kitchen and veranda. I go to get up from the floor where I lie sideways, legs curled up behind me, leaning on one wrist, the prints fanned out in front of me on the carpet. But something heavy with instinct prevents me getting to my feet. My eyes are drawn only to the photograph. I have to keep looking at it, pondering its sky, the shadows of the apple tree falling on Sandra's shoulders as she reads, the corner of the eaves of the Fraillon's house, the sun prying though the lattice work near the back gate. I'm frightened that there might be nothing outside in the backyard if I go to look. I don't move. The photograph's folds of grey tone edge in to surround me. I'm reeling. I'm searching. I'm floating above the yard painted there in light.

—

There's a thing called bracketing when you are taking photographs, my father Will says. And there are things to think about when you're burning off on a bush block before the bad fires come in the summer. You don't learn how to do these things overnight, my father tells me.

—

Flute is called Flute because he has been playing the flute for eleven years when his fingers are caught in the chaff cutter. Sometimes, before his accident, in the still harvest nights after tea at Berriwillock, even when he's only nine years old, he plays 'Drink to Me Only with Thine Eyes', sitting out in the cool on the chopping block away from the house. He plays 'Danny Boy' too, and sometimes, at Pearlie's request, 'Abide With Me'. It is his father's dark wood flute he plays, which was John's father's before him. Its silver dampers catch the sunset as he breathes the notes.

Candles is called Candles because of the fire in the hayshed. He was the one who had the idea of the candle to light the crackers.

Yes, I know all this. But I feel the chill beside my heart. Yes, I know it all, but what does David mean when he says how about poor bloody Tim? I don't know. He's talking about me. There he is near the old store-room, with his fingers in his belt. I don't like David. What does he mean? He talks about my mother. Why does he say dear little teacher Louise? I know what he's saying is nasty. What does he mean when he says butter wouldn't melt? What does he mean that my mother has been hiding little secrets? He's my uncle but I don't like him. I don't know what it's about. He hurts Joyce. I don't like him even if he is my uncle. I don't like him and I don't know what he means.

—

Flute's Story

It is so sad to me even when I first hear my father Will sing it at the piano in Cicero Street. The pipes, the pipes are callin'. And no one comes, I say to myself. I see the valley hushed and white with snow. This time it's Auntie Grace, Will's other sister, at the piano. She plays and hums, letting her eyes sweep up to mine. Her face is sad, her eyes falling further away as she leans down to the notes, but she is listening to my father and matching him, waiting for him. She is his sister from Sydney. She lives in the house at Narrabeen now, but she used to play the piano in the house at Vaucluse with the sea close. I can see her fingers finding their way over the white keys and outside the sea is glinting in the Sydney heat, in the sharper light at the foot of the street. In the music I can see the summer in the meadow. I can hear insects murmuring. I don't know whether I am hearing it then or now, as the music flows.

One day further round the circle of time my uncle Des will play it for me in a dark hall. It will be a sort of blues then.

—

Greg seems only little. He is drawing Flute's tractor working in the crop.

His arm reaches around the top of the butcher's paper. He's got the thick pencil, but he's making light lines. Later he'll paint the picture. I can see the insides of all his fingers as he draws because his hand is turned over as he makes the lines. His mouth is pursed with concentration. It is the past. This is my little brother. We are on the back veranda at Cicero Street. Outside the sun beats at the towels on the clothes-line and the side of Will's shed and the lid of the manure drum. Even the bricks of the veranda wall are hot. Greg's in his shorts. I'm in my swimming togs. I've just come home from the baths.

My brother Greg is left-handed. He draws and paints all the time. He's eight years younger than I am. I like watching him make his pictures. I want to keep them afterwards, but he doesn't. He just loses them.

Now he reaches a brush into the jar of water and softly dabs the red paint in the paint set until he's got enough colour. But there's too much water. He squeezes the brush drier and then dips into the red again. He paints the side of the tractor. The bonnet is like a lozenge above the engine. He paints it in one slow stroke and the red fits with the lines. His mouth purses and then draws away as he puts the last little bit of red in. Then he sits back and he looks at me for a moment, but he doesn't really see me. He's thinking, but he doesn't mind me watching. Then he wets the brush again in water and just strokes the little dish of yellow paint, screws the brush in it a bit. He leans over the paper and turns his head on the side and just touches the tractor's side along its top with the yellow. Now the tractor is not new-bright red. Now it's Flute's tractor, red and baked in the sun and tinged with rust.

How does Greg do it? His brush knows where to go. Now he leaves the first brush in the water and picks a finer one, wets it and takes a dab of yellow and a dab of white and puts in the dry oat heads that are hiding the tractor wheels where it's slowly moving down the paddock. He looks at it, then wets the brush and squeezes the yellow out and washes it again. Then he dips into the black, coming back to it with more water so that it's not too thick and sticky. He touches in the steering wheel and the tyres and then he makes the engine with small touches of black and then other little dips of white here and there.

I want Flute to see his tractor, but he won't. He's up on the farm. The painting will lie around for a few days and we'll all pick it up and look at it. Then it'll disappear and we probably won't see it again. Greg will be drawing or painting something else then.

—

How can Des play jazz piano? How can he know all the chords? How does he know all the songs? He knows the names. He tells me the names and he sings little bits of them. You know, he says, da, da, da, dah – di-di-di-di-diii. Remember that one? He says, 'After You've Gone.' You'll remember that all right. It's about someone in love.

If he's near the piano in the lounge at Mont Albert, Des will feel his way across the room, hand over hand, his body bent in a sort of slow rush to round the back of the armchair in the corner to get to the keys. The keys wait white for him to find them, reflected there in the shining dark wood of the piano cover which is always up, never closed. Then his long fingers reach out to touch them. Then it's beautiful. This is what I wait for. Sometimes he slides onto the stool. Sometimes he feels the shoulders of the piano with his hands, then reaches forward with his foot for the pedal. He starts to play just standing there. How does he do it?

—

Is it scenes from a marriage?

Do all fracturing marriages go on echoing long after they have finished, even go on persisting as some sort of practised shell of indifference when in reality they are dead? I suppose Patricia and I each hear our brief whispers of doubt as much as six years before Louise dies. The separation comes two years later and the divorce three months after that. Is that how marriages sadly carry their echoes into the future? And then there are our children, I say to myself. Our children, our living echoes.

Scenes from a marriage attempting survival? Sometimes I try to imagine Patricia, my former wife, as though she is someone else's – but pain blurs the picture. Yes, Patricia is my wife, daughter of a doctor I find difficult to talk to, mother of my children Jesse and Susan, principal legal officer and secretary to two advertising agencies in Clifton Hill. Former wife. It sounds strange and sad. I toy with it. I'm imagining her now that the Heathmont years of small children and gum-scented streets and hope are over and she has become mother of teenagers, housewife and hostess, still in the same Heathmont house we all love and that almost seems in its sun-slatted rooms to be trying to sustain the unsustainable.

But Patricia has few enthusiasms. She makes me out to be a malingerer. She thinks I evade work. She resents the way I stalk away into music, like someone walking into the sea and immersing. She is suspicious of my love for the forest and the sea, suspicious of Pat Friar, my friend, who declares his love for tennis, trying to describe it to her. She doesn't approve of those who declare themselves. I watch her close over as she listens to him. He is banished. She is suspicious of my love for words and the time they take to make. 'What you really want,' she says, 'is to stop working altogether and just write, don't you! Don't you!'

Patricia has few enthusiasms. She doesn't understand them. She cannot declare them. So what loves does she have? I ask myself.

Scenes from a marriage broken? Portraits of a former wife? It seems mean to say it, but they flood down on me in my pain. They come unbidden. Patricia knows her power and it hurts. She is incisive. Time and again I've heard her cut through the slow, imprecise wash of conversation with just the one question. Like her father with his diagnoses. Walking intellects, both of them, as though their bodies are present only to ferry conclusions. She almost never weeps. When I do, drawn out by wine on an empty stomach and in sympathy with the welling eyes of a Vietnam veteran on television or watching the camera catch an autistic girl's terror of being touched as she talks to her counsellor, Patricia looks at me levelly for some seconds. Then her eyes slide away as if pained, she fiddles with a serviette or a glass, then heaves herself up from the chair and quits the room. She busies herself in the kitchen. She is proud of her intellectual toughness, proud that emotion seldom sways her. She will be asked her advice often on money and legal matters and office politics and she will have good reasons for what she says. She will be asked her advice about me and she will just give a hollow laugh and look away.

Scenes from a marriage finished? One day early on I buy a print of Chagall's 'L'Anniversaire'. I buy it in the first place because I see hope there. I see myself and Patricia in it, feel marriage in it, feel man and woman in it, and shyness and love and personal secrecy and reticence and limitations in it. It's just a small colour reproduction. I would have to travel to the Guggenheim in New York to see the original, it tells me. The print seems to follow me in my life-changes, room-changes, house-changes. I never get it framed. It becomes grimy at the edges and slowly yellows. But it stays with me. Marriages echo. Images echo and return. I can see it there, pinned to the wall in a corner near the phone, or later propped on dust against books in my Hawthorn house that I never take down. It is a red-based picture of two ghosts that were perhaps us, two human swimmers in whom love is young. The young man's body curls and arches round to bring his lips to her cheek. It's shy love. His love floats. Her surprise lifts her towards the ceiling. She's caught even before she feels the warmth of his touch. It could have been us, so far back, Patricia and me. But no longer. We have wasted each other through the years. It's years since we floated across the room to each other, if we ever floated.

—

Sometimes I lie alone and beside the water in the lee of the cliffs during the heat waves, waiting to have another drink from the thermos, waiting until the day calls me to dive in the green glass of the water again. I think then that perhaps all of time comes to me. Everything is elemental. Salt on my lips, sea-washed pebbles under my fingers, the sky deep blue, the rock of the small cliff running yellow-brown against it. I hear the water running fingers in among the rocks, then a pause, then the start of a tiny chattering again, mounting to a chuckle as the wave ambles in. Stippled cloud far up, baked against the blue dome. It is frozen lace, although in half an hour it has moved imperceptibly from north west to south east. I am somewhere in the long afternoon of the world.

That's when I see the sister we never had standing beside my mother and I catch the grip of their joyous tears in my throat. That's when I see my brothers bending with my father over what he is making in the shed, and Alex Cumming putting down two sparkling tennis racquets and taking up a white towel. That's when my close people leave their messages, their marks in air. That's when I fold Rosa in my arms, sinking into her eyes even before I know her true name . . .

—

I drive north. I drive north to the country of my mother, who is dead, to my mother's people who are my people, to my mother's past in the Mallee and the Wimmera. I suppose I drive towards the places where the Barnes family's warmth and mousy-haired understatement and quiet determination counted, where they had their own spirit of finding out, which is different from my father Will's fair-haired and freckled finding out and his quotation of the Americans and their poetry. I drive to find out, even though I tell myself it is a teaching trip, a work trip. I am driving to find out.

I bore away from the city in the Nissan, away from the sea, over the northern edges of the Western District, across the corner of Central Victoria and then to the west and north through the Wimmera, with the Grampians scalloping the skyline further to the west. I am driving across some parts of my own life, across memories, crossing particular days that stud the thread of all my years. I'm getting towards fifty. I love this country. I drive north. I cross mornings; wheat crops riding on red dust; red dust climbing through fences, spilling to the road's edge; fences running to distant palisades of gums that are dark messages against the sky; delicate dark flurries of gums running towards silos; silos waiting far down the plain like modernist temples that draw me to them paddock by paddock.

I'm not sure what I search for. I know I am seeking my close people. I know I am seeking something to tell me about my mother Louise. I know I am going to the Murray, the river that in one way and another has flowed brownly in and out of my life since I started teaching and writing, although I have never lived within sight of it. I see Flute's farm at Berriwillock ahead of me, just the touches of shade on walls under the Mallee spars. He knows I have been thinking about him, writing about him, although he has been dead now for seventeen years. I might meet him there. There will be others stirring around me. When I get to Mildura I will try to find out about Alex Cumming, farmer and tennis player, friend of my mother Louise and her brothers, who is now who knows where. Probably his sister Elsie knows.

Somewhere ahead it's all laid out like an invitation. There's the

Murray–Darling junction and the reed beds and red gums. Already I smell the north's direct sun among the timber. My mind simmers. I drive towards lives. Somewhere here is my mother and her brothers and sisters. I will search for them.

I sense Pearlie and Grandpa John more dimly in the background. I want to bring them up close. I want to see Pearlie's vast elbows working over an earthen mixing bowl, see her sweep her hair from her forehead with the back of a floury hand. There is Grandpa John in the paddock, stumping in the stubble in grey drill trousers, white shirt. He is hatless, testing the red soil with the toe of his boot, squatting to dig his fingers into it, raise it, smell it, let it run between his palms to the ground.

I think of Grandpa John's sons – these brothers, my uncles. They are proud of each other. My mother Louise is proud of them. They tuck into each other's thoughts. Flute and Candles look up to their older brother Archie.

But when I think about Archie I don't see him against the country. I have never seen him at the home places with the Wimmera and the Mallee around him. Archie is always down from the country in the holidays, but he's teaching in country towns – Edenhope, Charlton, Elmore, Violet Town. He leaves his kids to play with us in the sunlit back yard in Camberwell while he pays people visits. He's busy. He thinks of tomorrow. He organises. He's serious. He holds serious conversations with my mother, Louise, in the kitchen, near the kitchen cabinet. He runs his hands along the shelves above the stove. He is Louise's brother, I have to tell myself. This is a brother and a sister talking. Archie calls my mother Louie. Louie, I say to myself. Louie. I've never heard that before.

Flute and Candles don't think of tomorrow. Flute plays his football, drives his tractor, talks to his horses in the red earth stable, stands with his hands on his hips. Candles rides his bike across Melbourne every morning to work at making hot water services in Footscray when he loses his job with the bakery in Auburn. He rides with his lunch in an Army haversack slung over his shoulders and a bike pump sticking out at the corner. He rides home again at night, holding onto the backs of trucks when he can, careful of the tram tracks, sweating, concentrating.

He plays cricket on hot Saturdays. He plays football on the grey winter Saturday afternoons when the mist and fire smoke settles early over the houses.

Then there's Des. All the brothers and sisters love Des, even though he nags them, pesters them with questions and words. Des is the youngest brother. Des is simply Des, probably because he's blind. Desmond James Barnes. Young Des, my father calls him. Sometimes my father is a sort of father to Des, a mate to him in his quiet way. And sister Jean is simply Jean. And younger Joyce is Joyce with the wide laugh and dancing eyes.

It's forty years ago, I think as I drive. I am writing in my head. Forty years ago since I see Joyce and David kiss in the kitchen at Mont Albert, hear Joyce's breathing, then a warm hmm of satisfaction and then a gasp for breath and a sigh through her hair. And yet it was yesterday. They don't know I'm near the telephone table, fingering the Braille on the telephone's numbers. Later, as I think it into words on paper I feel dust in my mouth. It was only yesterday.

—

I find the house. It's just out the Swan Hill road, on a dirt side track that hives off to the left as the bitumen veers right, three miles from Berri. I stand here. This is where Flute lived and died, and his son Frank died not long after him under the tractor in the paddock. And this is the house paddock. This is the wood heap where John and Pearlie stood. This is where Des went blind. This is where my mother Louise took the morning lunch out through the crackling yard to the men when the harvesting was on. This is where Alex Cumming came to play tennis in the red evenings, sweating.

I don't remember some of the things I'm seeing. I don't remember the house as being so close to the town. I can see a transport stuttering down the highway's shadows, its engine's baying coming to me, its cabin and blunt nose reaching the town's walls and roofs and then barging through them and away again into the scrub to the south. Do I recall the mallee growing in the yard? It frets the side of the house with shadows.

I don't know whether I want to stay and explore it or not. There's guilt here, knowing my years of forgetfulness, even indifference towards this branch of the family, while I was chasing my professional tail in Melbourne. Then suddenly here is my mother's face simply looking at me, not accusing me, but awaiting what I will do now that I realise these things. Her eyes are questioning me.

But behind it all the silence is complete, except for a repeated rasping, like the screech of a white cockatoo, as the wind opens and shuts a corrugated-iron door on one of the far sheds.

—

I write. I think. I find I can create scenes that are like paintings. Each one is different, speaks in a different tone. Some are funny, some are twisted, ironic and slow. Some are filled with a finality like death. Some are discoveries. Some just open themselves and lie there, like a sun-bather who is not aware of being watched. They hold what I've heard and smelt and sensed through my skin and the back of my head where realisation comes like a flush of blood.

I find connections, as if ultimately everything runs a thread, not at first apparent, to everything else. Even people who have never met each other connect, I can see, through third parties or through having touched the same thing, or having heard the silence of the same place. All the time there are people who walk winningly near me, enter my life briefly and for just so long, and then depart.

—

I am still waiting for the house to admit me. I have climbed through the fence, leaving the truck at the gate. The sun splinters into the mallee between me and the white statements of the house roof and the sheds at the back. There must be something. There must be a sign.

Dry ground, dry leaves under my boots as I walk in the gently seething wind. The house has a fly-wired sleep-out down its near side and a rolled corrugated-iron veranda at the front. My mother lived here. Her sisters and brothers lived here.

Flute died here in the 1960s, his heart boiling over. Little Frank, his spitting-image son, died here under the wheels of the tractor only six years later. Marie, Frank's mother, let death cradle her here in the same year. Oh, a sign, just a slim sign.

I see them. Pearlie and John, Grandma and Grandpa, red with dust. I hear the crackling of bark at noon among the spears of mallee, the mice in the walls at night. Twenty years earlier at their first farm the deep blue range of the Grampians lies along their horizon. 'Hope Farm' they call that place, looking across the dam to the gums. But as soon as they move north, drought and dust and the taut red Mallee horizon beat them. Sucked dry, they come to Melbourne to die. Flute takes over the farm with no name.

The house is inert. It does not glower. It is saying it is up to me. A sign? There's the house yard, inside the house paddock and its sheds. The house yard fence is gone. I tread around a clump of dark-green cactus near the gate-post, a concrete path running to the front veranda. I don't remember. Broken glass, dark brown. The veranda is hooded. A dark balloon of bees pulses from the sprung weatherboards at its far corner. The wind moves the door of the shed up the back. It screeches.

I can't go into the house yet. I'm not permitted by the past. The past must open to me.

I walk towards the back, following the shreds of chicken wire of the house-yard fence. Then I see the squat position of the old car shed twenty yards from the back of the building. I can feel it like a grey, familiar glove. Dull and undemonstrative corrugated iron, melting into the red earth, laced by thin shade. Closer to it, I see the white path of concrete to the back door, red earth ebbing against it. Ah! I see yellow chickens on red dust. Ah! I feel the sun. It beats on me, melts my eyes. I am carried from bed. Ah! I hear Uncle Flute's voice: 'Won't do him any harm. Won't do him any harm'. I am high. I can't touch the ground. Flute is carrying me. I look down from his arms at the chickens. Two yellow balls put their heads down and run to the hen. She is white. Ah! I see nail holes in darkness. I smell a dog. It is close. Its name is Bull. It licks me on the cheek. I am in the old Dodge with its side curtains. I am driving. I am four. Bull pants beside me on the front seat, tongue lolling, then collapses to a sprawl to scratch. Bull knows. Bull approves. He comes with me. He stops when I stop. I say stop. He stops.

I drive in the car shed. I dribble. It is dark, and the nail holes spring at me from the walls.

—

Dim in my mind is my brother Alistair beside me. It must be the early 1940s. We are thin wartime kids in handed-down clothes. Greg is our brother too, but he's smaller. He seems not to come into the picture so readily. I see my mother, I see Alistair and Greg. I see my father Will. We all seem to be waiting for the sister that we'll never have. I feel air that is fraught, raw. I hear my parents' voices tolling on the other side of the house. They are arguing again. I can imagine Will's face, his eyes gone cold and blue. I feel suddenly all alone. I can hear my mother muttering her responses in a low voice, almost like a man's, in her wounding, her misery. I feel desolate. The thin drum-beats.

I see myself. I'm happy in an anguished way. Around me the world of Camberwell and Melbourne is a large landscape of creek, spare paddock, shop and vacant block, rare beach, street games, lumbering planes in the sky that sound like the War, chook runs, bonfires, Cub and Scout camps in the ranges beyond the Dandenongs and summers when in my bed I think of the blue lozenge of the baths under the sky and how I will soon swim there again.

I am predestined to feel happenings in my gut. It seems that nothing of human drama, subterfuge, tensions escapes me. I lie at night seeing my mother's breadth and receptivity as a circle of light set against my father's oblong-shaped quiet, his retreat into his own knowing and prescience, his cussedness, his anger. And yet we all feel his love come through his anger like a forgiving, wet-warm face washer to smooth our doubting brows.

—

I am watching Flute in Melbourne, but he doesn't know. He lolls there in the theatre's dark.

It's strange. I seem to be present with myself, hovering on my haunches over butcher's paper with a crayon in the back sleep-out at 8 Cicero Street, but at the same time I can sense Uncle Flute sitting akimbo in the darkness of an hour-show theatre. He's eight miles away in Bourke Street, Melbourne. It's the bloody Italians on the screen. The bloody Eyties. Flute is watching Mussolini with his fat shoulders, stabbing out the Fascist salute. He watches the old clips of the goose-stepping front rank swinging past. But he knows some Eyties up near Berri. What about the Lanzas, over near Waitchie? Good people. Tony Lanza, with his eyes like dark currants, can play a solid game of football – small and fast. He works hard. As if on a screen behind his eyes Flute can see Tony standing there beside his load of wheat in the dusty yard of the silos, one hand reaching up to the mirror support on the door of his truck. His pale armpit shines out in the shade. As usual, Tony is talking, talking, his free hand waving and describing. Flute's conjectures fade into the darkness, that swarming, grainy grey of the theatre.

Why isn't Flute married? He doesn't think about it too much at home, but down here there are girls everywhere. Faces he sees during the day seem to follow him back to the hotel at night and creep into his dreams. The news-clips, too, remind him. 'Mademoiselles Help Pack Punches Somewhere in Europe' says the screen. The Belgian and French girls are seen packing parachutes for Allied paratroopers, standing at tables in business-like blouses, shoulders working. And then they are shown in off duty hours at a dance, sweeping in a rondelay past the camera in the arms of men with berets folded under the epaulettes of their battle jackets. Why isn't he married? His arms ache for a woman.

—

I try to think of it. When I'm very small I imagine it as a big cloud with trucks in it. The War. It has been there always, even in Camberwell, although you can't see it from Cicero Street. It is over the hill. Sometimes

I can hear it, though, like a roaring a long way away. It kills people. They lie in mud with their clothes torn.

I'm looking down on myself in full sun. We're playing guns. Barry McLellan makes good gun noises. He pretends to fire the big khaki toy gun under the apricot tree with a 'phut' sound made between his teeth. Then he stands up and walks where the shell is going, making a whistling sound. The shell goes a long way, up past the loganberry stalks against Wilson's fence to where Alistair and I have made a road and a bridge, and the shell comes down on the truck that is just at the bridge. 'Crump', goes Barry's mouth, and the air blows out of it and he dribbles a bit. The shell hits the truck. 'Direct hit! Direct hit!' yells Barry and he sweeps the truck down the slope with his hand and it rolls over and over. 'Now the Germans can't get their trucks and supplies past the bridge,' Barry explains to the air and to me looking up from my crouch, and he walks back to the khaki gun. But Barry looks tiredly at the filigree of roads and secret hangars with dirt over their tops and the trucks and the planes on the dirt airfield. He's getting sick of this. He shuffles his boot in the grass. 'You wanna game of cricket?' he's asking me. 'I've had playing guns. I'll get Ralph and Tom and we can have a game out in the street. You wanna? I'm sick of wars.'

When I stand up the backyard spins. I'm dusting my bare knees. They're grey with dirt, green with grass. 'Yeah,' I say, and I swell with agreement. 'We can play with my Grandpa's ball. The white twine one.' I can say this to Barry, but I can't say it to Ralph or Tom. They're older, more perfectionist, his big brothers. I can feel in imagination their disdain for a ball made from a golf ball core and knotted twine. They want real balls. But I like to use Grandpa John's ball. It doesn't bounce so high. It doesn't hurt so much. And I know that once the others hear the magic sound of the bat on the ball in the street, they'll come anyway. They won't care what they play with once the game's going.

—

Everybody knows that Flute, through all those years when it's the Depression and the War, leaves his car out at Essendon when he drives down through Victoria from the Mallee to Melbourne. He always does that. I can see him, hear him when he comes to stay with us. 'Too many bloody things moving,' he's saying. He's chewing a match, squinting his weather eye. 'I dunno! I can thread the truck between the pages of a bloody newspaper up at Berri,' he's saying. 'Fence posts'll stay still for ya. Trees stay still. But down here . . .' I see him propping in the kitchen at Cicero Street, one arm running to the kitchen cabinet.

So Flute drives towards the city among the other cars until he gets to a man who runs a garage out near Moonee Ponds Creek. And that's where his dark-green Dodge – later it's a frosted-blue Holden – stays under the pepper trees in the oil-stained gravel of the yard for the week or more. Then Flute gets a taxi. It carries him and his strapped suitcase in along Mount Alexander Road towards the grey and white buildings of the city. Sometimes Flute stays with us at Cicero Street, sometimes at the farmer's pub in Spencer Street, sometimes at the Victoria Coffee Palace. I see him looking in the shops. I see him self-consciously letting the material of cardigans and sports coats run through his fingers in the Mutual Store. Now he's walking, cigarette stuck to lip, along the outside of Flinders Street station and its orange-drink counters and paper sellers, to Prince's Bridge, flexing his bad knee down the steps to the river. He asks about tickets, mutters to the man on the gangway of the boat. He takes a river cruise in the sun up to the landing at Studley Park and back.

I wonder about Flute. I can hear him thinking sometimes when I write about him. I'm wondering what Melbourne means to him on these trips by himself. I hear him thinking about the people. They stream around him in the morning. He's like a blown paper sometimes: that's how he feels. And yet at three o'clock in the afternoon he might have all the shadows along Collins Street to himself for nearly a whole block. Where are they? I hear him thinking about the women, smelling perfume as they twitter past him on the pavement. I feel the thought of the Tivoli under his tongue, its taste, its smell, its suggestion. His laugh rumbles when he thinks about it. He smells Bourke Street. He thinks of the Tiv's small doors jammed with people laughing, calling to each other. He can smell the closeness of beer and cigarette breaths in the theatre's dark. Later he laughs inside his cheeks when he talks to Louise and Will about it, when he scoffs with Candles and Jean about it. They smirk and look at each other at the memory. I have always been catching their winks. Ah, the Tiv! Ah, the white beak of Roy Rene.

Flute keeps his hands in his pockets and walks the shops. He just wanders, I see as I write, with his stumping walk and his short legs and his hair brushed back with oil and parted down the middle like a spine. He just wanders and goes into places and orders things when he sees something he needs for the farm. Melbourne means seed merchants. It means farm machinery out on the Footscray road. It means the pubs in town. Flute drops in to Young and Jackson's for a couple of beers, resting his elbow on the bar, squinting round his cigarette, talking about the seasons and the wheat to city blokes who haven't been up to the Mallee in a long time.

But now Flute is off, I see, up Bourke Street, over into Little Bourke, homing in on the Exhibition Gardens. Or is he? He's going into an alley, tripping along, his white shirt a point of light, slapping a folded *Herald* against his thigh. He comes out on the cobbles into light. It's La Trobe Street. He's standing on the edge of the gutter for a time, watching the traffic. He appears cocky, looking up and down the street, standing four square just out of the path of the evening pedestrians. He has been three days in town. I can see the first-day diffidence is gone. He has spoken to so many people. He's moving with the city now. I watch him. I can hear Melbourne's relentless, tired, opportunist rhythm behind him.

He smells perfume first and the words follow quickly, right at his elbow it seems. He feels a gentle touch on his arm. 'Going my way?' The woman is young, dark. He has never seen her before. She wears a soft wool beret. She is still walking slowly towards the sun, looking back at him, smiling, questioning with just a hint of laughter. Her high-heeled shoes meet their shadows as she moves. He's looking nonplussed. He can only smile: her enquiry is so clearly for him. She stops. She's folding her hands and bag in front of her, looking at him. He shrugs. He takes a step, then wheels and drops the *Herald* in a street bin strung on a lamp-post behind him. He's looking at her dimpled face again, her eyelashes, and he's smiling, running his hands round his belt. He pulls his trousers up and walks over to her against the flow of people. He takes her arm. They walk towards Exhibition Street. He looks down at her. She looks straight ahead.

—

That year when it's still the War I see a film at the Maling Theatre. It's called *Squadron of All Nations*. I see it even to this day. I'm watching the grey pictures of the air field, and of the air force men when they arrive in their suits and sports coats. I hear the thundering throb of the planes, the Spitfires, the Hurricanes with their guns sprouting from their wings and their fuselages. Sometimes it is the long roar of the big Lancasters and Halifaxes taking off with their bomb loads for Germany. These are young men who are going to fly the fighters and they haven't been in a plane before. So they train and train in the cockpit, at a table with maps and instruments. They do PT out on the grass in their singlets, and the wind blows their hair. Their task is to fly with the bombers and protect them from enemy fighters. The young airman I like with a sudden love looks like Patrick McLellan across the street, with a steady jaw when he's thinking, with a face that breaks around his nose when he laughs. Patrick has the same tight curls that run down the back of his neck. And Patrick shaves and he has a girlfriend like the airman in *Squadron of All Nations*.

I can feel the sharp edges of the seat behind my knees and the wooden armrests under my elbows in the dark theatre. I'm squirming with worry, watching the screen. Dougie Frawley and Barry Collinson from school are in the same row, and Sandra is beside me. Sandra used to take me to school when I started. She lives just a bit up the street. She has two sisters: no brothers. I have two brothers: no sisters.

I know that the young airmen in the film are going to get killed. Two have come from America, one is a Canadian, another is an Australian. Others are Polish or Dutch pilots who have escaped from Europe and joined the squadron to fight again. I know that although they laugh and drive their cars with no roofs, they are frightened of going up with the bombers to cross the English Channel and fly to Germany. I know all about the Messerschmitts and Stukas that might shoot them down. Patrick and Ralph McLellan know how to make all those planes out of balsa wood. Ralph's bedroom has twenty-three planes hanging from threads pinned to the ceiling. The McLellan boys made all of them and painted them with the three circles of the RAF or the black and white swastika of Hitler. At night I dream about those planes, about power dives, about seaplanes that have to rescue airmen. I think about the enemy. There is always the enemy and it is the Germans. Now the Japanese are the enemy too, but I don't know as much about them.

Then, towards the end of the film, when the big raid is on and the young airmen are flying over the tiny pattern of thousands of fields in Europe, I see the enemy for the first time. Where do the pictures come from? I think they must be stolen films that the Germans have made of their airmen. In the film suddenly I am looking down on a German bomber from above. The picture is dim – grey and indistinct. Through the perspex of the fuselage I can see the pilot up the front and then the navigator and a gunner further back. They are Germans, intent on their task. They are Germans who are on their way to bomb England, where my Auntie Marie lives in the countryside with Hamish and Pamela. The enemy are terrible because they are concentrating – they don't look up through the sky at the camera. But I can see them moving, writing things, speaking through their headphones, and their plane is creeping over the pattern of the fields away below on its way to bomb London. They are doing their job, concentrating, sitting in their jackets with their epaulettes showing. Epaulettes mean they have been trained to kill, they have power, they have hate, they take a lot of trouble.

At the end there is a dog fight way up against the clouds, and the Spitfires are twisting and turning and the Messerschmitts are on their tails, their guns flashing white. I watch the tracer spitting. I would like to fire the Spitfire's guns. I don't notice the seats any more. I don't know that I'm in the theatre. Just when the young airmen seem to be winning, a

German pilot on the tail of the young man like Patrick presses his firing button. I see the young man stiffen suddenly in his cockpit and just loll there. His plane begins to spiral down towards the tiny pattern of fields. The German pilot smiles inside his goggles. I'm watching. The airman like Patrick must be dead: his plane is smoking and it is going to crash. Then I am watching the airman's girlfriend asking someone at the base about him, and they shake their head and look away. She stops under the trees. She is crying. Then she walks on.

We all come out into the Canterbury streets to the gasping rush of a train coming up the valley towards the railway gates. It is very bright in the low sun. The others are walking on, kicking lilly pilly berries like footballs, laughing about the cartoons, pretending they are Gene Autrey as they come round corners on the way home. I'm walking behind. I can't believe the airman like Patrick is dead, when he was alive and smiling. I hate those dim, shirted Germans. I hate the swastikas they wear. I hate the way their shirts hang on them, with their pockets. What would I do if they came for me with their intent eyes and blond hair?

When we get home, I can see the back of Patrick McLellan leaning over his bike up the side of the house. Patrick looks up and gives us all a wave. He's all right. I look at him with a lump in my throat. I stand for moments, hearing the crickets ringing thinly in the grass.

—

Is this a dream?

I have a big hat on. My eyes go to meet the ball. I am ranged behind it, ready to stroke with the racquet, hitting it against the wall. I am bending down to stroke it, to catch it with the tug of the strings before it hits the gravel. My feet know where to move. The ball leaps away, comes back at me with its seams. It's hot and I've got a big hat on. I can feel the sun through my shirt. Sometimes I'm in the shade of the house corner, sometimes I'm in the sun. But it's not me, because I'm standing now and looking out over paddocks. And I hear a voice saying that it's nearly the year's end. It is not me.

I feel the racquet swing smoothly. It goes to meet the ball. The ball

70

comes back to it as though it has been called. It is rhythm. It is firmness, the tug of the strings. It is wrist that gives the ball an extra nudge sometimes, tips it up the wall so that it comes back in a different place. I can feel the hat now. It is a big straw one with a wide brim. But it can't be me. It's not my hat.

The ball spins as it goes, spins as it comes back. It's delicious to control it, make it come back firmly. I feel my knees bending, thigh muscles letting me down to the ball. I can feel my wrist firm. But the person hitting is not me in this dream. It's nearly 1917, the voice is still telling itself quietly. It's nearly 1917. It is nearly the end of the year. Tonight it will be a new year. The ball flies up to the wall, comes back, flies up, comes back. 1917. Up. 1917. Back. The voice speaks with it, lazily. A new year. What happens in the sky, asks the voice, when a year changes? What happens when a year changes?

It seems to be Alex Cumming who is swinging the racquet, his oval passion. And yet I can feel the tug of the ball hitting the strings each time. But it's Alex Cumming doing it. He's dipping into the old hessian bag at his feet, feeling for another ball, trying it to see if it's harder, flattening it against the heel of his hand as he has seen his brothers do, feeling its tight resistance. It springs into the light. From down the hall of the house comes a whisper of cooler air. But the cicadas festoon the creek bed behind the house with streamers of sound in the heat. Beyond the wheat the low hill waits, wavering. Father is in Swan Hill buying harness and some boots. Mother is lost behind white curtains in the side room, shuffling among preserves. Alex's brothers are out with Tally, the rabbiter, in the far paddock. I seem to be here, standing behind Alex, looking out over the paddocks.

It will soon be afternoon lunch and the men will come in. Wicker will strain and tick under the cloths when Alex's mother and sister carry the tarts and tea out to the men. Then he'll have to stop hitting against the chimney wall.

Alex Cumming is steadily eyeing a keening hen that is advancing cross step and eyeing him near the cactus inside the house fence. Then, holding the racquet in one hand, two balls in the other, he steps out from under the veranda. The sun on hot gravel smites his eyes. There is no one he can hit with. Under the pepper trees the tennis court is seething, a hot red oblong.

He walks round the corner of the house past the rancid butter smell of the drain where the kitchen water seeps towards the orange tree. Now he stands four square on the baked earth in front of the boards of the feed shed wall. His wrist firms as he raises the racquet. In an action he doesn't need to think about, he slides the ball out through the air from his strings to the grey wood, tries the day's bounce, watches for the unexpected joins in the timber, bends to meet the ball with his tender net of strings and send it truly to the wall again. He feels the rhythm coming, drenching his wrist, shoulders, knees. He feels the tug of the ball hitting the strings each time. Beautiful!

It is nearly 1917, he's saying to himself as he bends and hits. It is nearly 1917. He bends and hits, bends and hits, bends and delivers – and the ball flies where he wants it to go. It will soon be another year. After the dark it will be 1917! In my dream he bends and delivers, bends and delivers.

—

I remember. It's the top of the street, the privet street tree making a dark green house. I'm hiding there, hot in my old shorts, breathing against the leaves. I've taken off my shirt. It's back there like a limp green rag on the Haywards' fence. I can hear the others scattering, calling around the street light outside our front gate. Then the street, my beloved Cicero Street, falls quiet. With his head against the light pole Ralph is counting to a hundred: 'niney-eight, niney-nine, one hundred, an' I'm comin' ready or not'. He catches little Jane as soon as he swings out into the light. She's hidden near the lilly pilly, but she giggles. And then he catches brother Barry who comes from the lane into the light and makes a rush at the light pole, only to be tigged on the run as he crosses the McLellans' driveway. What I can hear tells me that now Barry is reduced to sauntering and snarling until he comes on the others. Then he'll be pleased. Then they can call someone else 'hee'.

I'm secure. I needn't ever be found, and even if they come this far to find me, I can probably beat Ralph back to the light pole. I breathe against the leaves, feel for one, break it off. I split its softness with my fingers, stick it in my mouth, look out again towards the street light. No one.

Then suddenly there's a footfall in the leaves. A white form looms beside me, crouched to come into the hideaway, breathing, hissing. I start. Before I can see who it is, a white hip and elbow knock me sideways into a branch.

'You here too?'

It's Sandra Hayward. I can smell her hair, can just see her eyes shining. She's breathless.

'Hidey, eh!' she says, and lets herself down on one haunch. She looks at me, breathing. The leaves lean in around us. I look at her, see her elbow softly supporting her. I love her. I've always loved her, but she's older than me. I love her. I love these games. I love summer nights when the street light is on.

But Sandra suddenly half rises. She rushes me. She's in one of those teasing moods. She goes for my bare chest, my armpits. She's hissing around her tongue as she probes with her fingers, half laughing.

'High school next year, eh!'

She digs her fingers into me in time with her words. I'm surprised her fingers and hands are so strong. She worms under my arms. She tickles. She's laughing quietly, still hissing close to my face. She knows it's the one thing I can't stand. She knows she can make me helpless. She delves, stops, her face close to mine. She delves again. I splutter, roll on my side, my face running into dried leaves. I'm trying to contain my electric giggling. I'm convulsing, writhing, to get away from her fingers, aware of the shouts and movement at the foot of the street. I don't want to give myself away. Sandra doesn't care. She delves, her face close to mine.

'Ticklish, eh! High school, eh!'

I can't stand it. I feel her body arching over me, and I'm swept by something I don't understand. A yearning. But there are twigs digging into the bare flesh of my back. I roll into a ball to escape, and feel a straining in my shorts. But I can't help it. I jerk open again like a jack knife when she attacks my chest and ribs again. I'm whimpering, helpless.

'Don't! Don't! ... Stop!' I gurgle, drag in breath. I groan. She'll stop soon, won't she? She'll have to stop. But she doesn't. She is interested in me, in my flesh, my skin, my knees, my shoulders. Hidey is far away and dimly lit. Oh, God. I'm backed into the leaves and branches, helpless.

Still Sandra bores in, delves, her fingers flitting about my shoulders, my neck, my knees, my groin, my armpits. She's too quick. I can't breathe and protest and cry and laugh at once. I feel as if I'll break, as if my bottom will split open. I feel a tightening and aching in my stomach and between my legs. She is over me, fingers working, laughing down at me. I feel a throbbing, my body going rigid. I can feel my willy coming up. I've never known this before. I don't know what's happening. I'm splitting open. I'm swelling, swelling. My willy and balls and bottom are so tight, so big, so warm. I feel so much power and splitting down there, no matter where Sandra's fingers go. I shriek into the dead leaves with the power of it. I spin on my back. I groan in helplessness and a mad joy. I split right open and shudder, shudder, shudder. I have never opened and felt this pounding before.

Sandra doesn't know. She still delves into me, into my stomach, my armpits. But she is flagging, her fingers running around my neck, my shoulders, but not so much delving now as exploring, her fingers playing around my stomach, but not hard. I lie groaning, groaning, thinking widely, so wide that for seconds it's as though I can see everything. Sandra stops, panting above me in her white dress and her white hair ribbon. I moan. I'm glad. I lie back. I smile at Sandra. My limbs loosen, spreading and pushing against the branches in the dark. I feel cleaned out, aching and wet between the legs. I groan. I croon. I can hear myself doing it. I can feel Sandra beside me, white in the dark. I seem to be thinking furiously, randomly. I know Sandra is looking at me. I settle, feel the wetness and warmth in my shorts, and feel a wave of tiredness sweep over me. The power is running away from me like a steady rivulet. I will soon be able to speak again, but I'm tired, open, and I've never been open before. Oh, God! I'm so open.

'They're up the top of the street.' It's Barry McLellan's shout.

We can both hear the running feet coming, clapping across driveways and then thudding into the grass of nature strips. Another voice. 'Well, tell them I want them in now.' It's Mr Hayward. He'll be standing almost invisible at his gate in the darkness. Even now, parting the leaves, I can see his cigarette red in the blackness. 'Time to come in,' he yodels. 'Time to come in.'

The running feet have slowed, but voices are still coming up the street. Sandra rolls, slides her feet out from under the privet, her dress catching for a moment on a branch. Then she's clear, standing, brushing down her sides, fiddling with her hair ribbon.

'We've got to go. Are you coming?'

'Yair,' I say, surprised at the sudden dry sound of my own voice in the darkness.

My body is drained and languid. I'm walking light-headed home. I am open, languid. I will walk open into the close, hot house and go to my sleep-out and no one will know. And yet I want to tell someone. I want to tell Sandra, but not now.

Sandra Hayward walks down the gutter ahead of me. I can feel that she knows something special has happened at the top of Cicero Street. I can tell she's thinking as she walks. I know what her head down means, her hair falling forward, her eyes searching the gutter. I'd like to tell her that I know something I didn't know before – it wavers before me like weed in water, advancing, retreating. It's not clear to me just what it is. Sandra has reached me deeply without meaning to. How can I tell her that somehow she's touched a person, not just a boy. That's how I feel – a tired person, walking. Somehow I feel older and more important, too. I walk on.

—

It's possible that there's a man reading in a garden.

Above him, I think I see a silver birch leaning its tresses down against a blue summer sky.

When he looks up from his book, letting his gaze wander, the man notices the reflection of the tree's leaves move back and forth in the dark glass of his watch.

The man holds his watch still and studies the lit green of the leaves' shapes as they wash back and forth across the silver figures of the hours on the watch face. He wonders idly where he is, where reality lies, where the tram he hears fretting uphill behind the houses fits into his consciousness, into what is predestined for his time on earth, into all the happenings that will present themselves to him before it is his time to die. The tram is the only thing he can hear at this moment that puts him in mind of people. It is probably full of people sitting, or standing hanging on to its straps, or propped in corners near its doors. It is late afternoon on a hot working day. The man can imagine there will be other men in hats and open-necked shirts and with glasses in their hands spilling from the doorways of pubs onto hot footpaths closer in to the city.

He knows there are other people not far from him. They are probably standing looking at their vegetables, stooping down for hoses, hovering over saucepans behind thin curtains in a dozen kitchens, filling a bird bath, oiling a hand-mower, sitting at a dining-room table reading aloud pieces out of the *Herald*. But he cannot see them, hear them, smell their sweat and the smokiness in their clothes from trams and trains. He might be alone on earth with his book. He looks again at the leaves moving in the face of his watch like fish in a pool. Then he opens his book again at the page where his forefinger has kept his place. His eyes glaze with transition, and he starts to read again. But as he begins anew on these pages, these words, he knows he is reading all he has ever read, all the wisdoms he has tasted like fruit in books' pages.

It is Will. It is my father. He can still feel the catch in his throat, still taste the hospital APC, the sting of the lemonade they gave him, the ice cream's cool promise of healing. He is still four days from speaking to his classes, still four days from the chalk and the sweeps of his illustrating hands that impress on people what there is to think about in history and literature. His tonsils have stopped bleeding, his voice is coming back through whispers towards full vowels and consonants. He will soon be complete again.

It's quite possible that all this has happened, that it is 1947, that it is the year I turn twelve in the Camberwell sleep-out, just round the corner of the house from where Will, my father, sits convalescing now.

—

That's Melbourne. Melbourne where I've always lived. Melbourne. Melbourne. You can hear it moving. You can hear it thinking.

—

Pearlie detects it first through the wall. The dull thud, and another thud. I'm watching her sleep-puffed face. The house is hot in the moon-light. Insects shirr-shirr along the gums near the dam. Pearlie turns slowly, heavily against John. He flings an arm, his white singlet bulking as he humps over to his right side. He sighs, rubs furiously under his nose with the back of a hand. Thud. I know she hears it. Thud, thud and then a strangled cry.

Pearlie is up, pulling the broad shoulder strap of her nightie straight, standing on the rug for a moment, arms hanging, getting her bearings. She pads to the door, into the hall. She stops, listens. The centre of the house is deep in darkness. She shuffles back to the robe inside the door, reaches for the matches on its top, fidgets, strikes a match and lights the small lamp and takes it ahead of her into the hall again. She pushes the door of the boys' room ajar. Thud. She hears sheets pulled taut by move-ment. Jeremy lies, just a head and shoulders facing away, into the corner, breathing steadily with a glottal click. He's a motionless sleeper. No, it must be Des. He lies close to the window, the moonlight running along the white of its frame, competing even now with the pale gold light of the lamp. She sees Des's leg pull up, stretching the sheet taut. He moans, flings on his back, face to the ceiling, eyes closed, then turns and rams his forehead against the wall. Thud. And thud. He cries softly 'Aw! Aw!' in a strangely adult tone of desperation. She sees that he's awake, in pain, and yet asleep.

Pearlie lowers herself onto the edge of the bed, reaches for Des's shoulders, pulls him to face her.

'Des, boy, what's wrong?'

He opens his eyes, stares, says nothing. The night quakes silently around them. Des's face is a pale orb in the room's half darkness. Then his legs struggle again under the sheet and 'Aw! Aw!' his face contorts again and he strains to run his head against the wall. Pearlie grasps him firmly by the shoulders, loses her grip as he moves, makes an awkward grab and finds his neck, so that he almost gags. He's awake now.

'Des! Des! What is it?'

Des finds her face, her voice. 'Aw!' His voice complains as if straining his pain through his breath. 'My head. There are spears in my head! It's like before. It's like spears. I can see them. They're white and they go down and down.'

'What else can you see?' she asks, a shiver of premonition in her voice.

'It's black, Mum. It's all just dark.' He looks towards her.

Des's brow is knitting. His eyes move as though he is listening. Pearlie realises in a sudden chill that he can't see her in the rapt frost of moonlight reaching in from the window to touch the sheets, or in the gentle lemon wash of the lamplight from the other side of the room.

'John. John! Come here, will you? John?' A hot weatherboard cracks in the gloom. She stares into the warm darkness of the hall which seems to have swallowed her words. She can feel the house settling again. Where is John?

'John! Come quick! It's Des.'

—

Now I am standing at the drink counter. I have come into town on the train to buy a watch. My father Will comes with me. I am a schoolboy looking at the Melbourne people coming for their trains with Gladstone

bags and briefcases. It's the big world. It's busy. It is the end of the day
and the sun is swarming hot from over the river in the west, making all
the buildings stand up. We are in Flinders Street station. The orange-
juice Will gives me is in a heavy glass with flutes in its sides. It is rich and
cold. The oranges come from Mildura. I am going to buy my first watch
soon with my own money. We will go to a jeweller in a lane off Collins
Street, Will and I. My father will talk to the jeweller about a sweep
second hand, but I haven't got enough for that. So he says I'll put this in
to make the difference – and he reaches for his purse, pulls something
from it, flexes a five pound note in the air and slaps it onto the counter's
glass. I keep looking at the watch's face on my wrist when we are on the
train, when we are at Richmond and Burnley and Hawthorn and Auburn
and Camberwell and when we get off the train at East Camberwell and
walk down under the bridge into the cool air in the dip.

—

When I look back on it now I see the touchstones. I see
Sydney in the sun and I hear my cousins' voices, see their
sun-reddened noses, their freckles. I see how the days have
made me, keep on holding me. And still they do. But now
everything is changed. Now it is as if the light falls
differently. I hear Elsie Cumming's bitten-off reticence about
her brother – 'Water under the bridge now,' she says. 'It's all
water under the bridge.' Then I hear her knocking the kettle
in the kitchen. When I trace it back now I see the
photographs, feel the letters in my hand as I sit covert on
that bed beside the stacked detritus of my father Will. He is
not there. I am surrounded by the quaking silence of a house
he loves but has decided to leave. I think about the
photographs and the first thing that comes to me is their
innocence – their innocence in the face of their telling power.
They can condemn. They can reveal what people don't want
known, or don't want to recall to themselves. They can stop
time. They can unlock time, as they did for me. But all in

such grey-black tonal innocence. Time opens up. Time closes over. Time offers itself again.

And the letters and cards? I suppose they have their innocence too. When Alex wrote them in his meagre South Yarra flat, or when Will quit the card games to write them in the cold of the Mount Buffalo Chalet, they meant just the one pressing and innocent truth — love. I can sense my mother's silent receipt of them, and then her secret rapt reading. Now that I have read them they mean another truth. There are no letters, no cards from my mother. No voice. I realise that all I have heard from her for so long is her breathing silence. It wrenches me. It won't go away.

—

I am thinking of Pearlie. She is sitting in the chair near the Berriwillock fireplace. It is April and getting cold at night. Soon there will be a dusting of frost on the red earth in the mornings. She is thinking about Louise and Archie, their city collars, their books. They are young and like flowers blossoming. But they come home from teacher training in Melbourne and don't walk out in the paddocks any more. They tell her about cable trams and balls and a grand house they have been to above the river in Kew. They speak about people out of work, about children 'on Susso'. They sit down to read and cannot be talked to. They don't seem to see that here another red drought is sapping the country and its secret places. And now another child.

Pearlie despairs. She feels her heart slipping again into its dogged rhythm that has always ridden her through exhaustion. But can she manage this time? She is weary of the weight, of getting up and down, weary of John's complacency, weary of her body's racked frame of bones, weary of the waiting, the pain, the blood.

She sits there. From outside in the yards come the three sharp yaps of a dog at work. But Pearlie is unmoving. She sighs a sigh that turns into a guttural growl, her breasts heaving. She is forty-four years old. For nineteen years she has borne children, cooked, washed, sewn, felt brows, smoothed butter on lumpen heads, fed shearers, fought fires, read stories to vacant eyes that say go on, go on when she stops with weariness. She has heard tables, asked long lists of spelling and then watched her children leave the farm to live in clothes she has not made. Day and night they work, live, eat and talk far away among misty streets in Melbourne that she has never seen.

Pearlie sighs again, looks around her in a long silence. Then I see her wearily brace her elbow to lever herself out of the chair. I know as I watch her go to the door that she has another twenty-one years to live. She is my grandmother. She will die in Melbourne. I will remember it. I can see again the rime of her battle with death collecting around her lips while she lies in the Mont Albert front bedroom, with the Saturday afternoon football commentary buzzing sadly to no one on David's radio at the back of the house.

—

In the church's cold darkness I am taking off the old jeans, the sweaty shirt and scuffed boots. I have cut the boobialla branches and loaded them in the truck for tomorrow morning. Now the night is coming. Here is the mirror. It starts out at me from the dark corner of the church down near the fire. It does not hold the light like the cheval mirror in Hawthorn, but it's always there, registering the bulking of the bed, the dark angle of the desk. I will put on the thick, shapeless grey jumper so that I can sit and write when it is dark. My body glides there in the mirror's semi-dark pool. I feel a suffusion of warmth that for a moment I cannot place. Something stirs, something I've put out of mind. I'm looking at the mirror's outline as if for the first time, looking at the bevelling of its glass. It brings me up short like a tune on the air. There's the bevelling, yes, and the gentle rise to a pinnacle at its top. Both reach for me with a sudden, strangely satisfying shock. This, I tell myself, although I have forgotten, is the oldest mirror in my life, now limpid in a darkening church. I see it anew. It's the dressing-table mirror from Cicero Street. Of course. How can I have looked so often into it and forgotten its origins? It is the mirror that reflects the first room I ever smell for comfort. It reflects a house I have loved. It is the mirror in which I have first watched my mother getting ready for tennis, changing to go shopping, straightening the straps of her bra, pulling on her stockings. The mirror stays with my mother all her life. But Louise, my mother, dies, and the mirror lives on. I remember saving it, sawing away its supports, separating it from the yellow dust of borer in the dressing table after her death. Then it is stored in Will's garage until I rescue it, bring it flat in the tray of the truck to this valley, and put it where it can comment on things, where it can say that my desk, my bed, the stasis of dark leaves against the road make sense, that they all accompany me. I will persist and the mirror will register me. I will survive. If I be not I then who will be? The mirror lives on. It has served. I have forgotten.

Now I have remembered. It is the smell of talcum in a drawer. It is Will's face and Alex's face behind my mother's. It is Louise pursing her mouth as she puts lipstick on and rubs her lips together. It is her body changing for tennis. It is Will tinkering with a bow tie. It is Alex shrugging on a belt and reaching to turn up the collar of a white shirt. I am looking into a mystery in a bow window filled with light. Then, I am standing, wondering. I am looking into my own eyes again now. I am far around time's circle.

—

Suddenly I'm aware of Rosa with me in the dimness. I stand in the future. I seem to be speaking to her, telling her things. And yet it is Melbourne, Melbourne that moves under my eyes. I see it like a city of gold and ice from the Sydney flight as I come in from the conference, the Bay duck-egg blue in the dusk behind it, the You Yangs a dark lift in the rug to the west as we circle, losing the city from our windows, and approach from the south. All that detail of lights slipping into the hills, and, as we descend, the burrowing traffic running like sluices of gold, factory floodlights smudging yards and the last dams in the fringing paddocks taking away their mirrors as the plane sinks to embrace the earth.

It must be some week soon, some time in what we call the future, in another part of the city, that I will fold Rosa in my arms. Can that be right? Can that be right?

—

Des is blind but his eyes look so clear. Blind since he was twelve. It was either a grass seed that got up Des's nose and travelled through his head to his eye, Louise says, or it was a bad fall he had from the haystack against an iron feed bin.

I try to think about it. Blind for the rest of my life! What would it be like? All those summers dark, and yet I'd still smell the hot breath of the wind down the drive in Cicero Street, or the clean wine smell of Bailey's big gum tree, the lantana by the bow window of the front bedroom, the bland cold of the block of ice when I go to the ice chest. I shudder inwardly. Not to see?

Des is blind, so his hearing is much more acute than ours, Louise says. Des is blind, so his hands have to tell him things. Des is blind, so that he has to smell danger, or feel it near him through the hairs on his wrists or round the back of his neck. Des is blind, so that is why music is so important to him, why he sometimes plays the Jew's harp and the violin and the clarinet – and, of course, always the piano in the jazz band. What does he feel when he sits down on that stool and reaches for the first notes?

I think through to Des. At this moment he is shuffling and feeling around for his tuning fork in the storeroom near the sleep-out in the house in Mont Albert. No – now he is standing quiet, stretching an ear to the talk in the kitchen. No one knows he's there. He can hear that there's talk of Betty, but he can't hear the detail. Voices are lowered.

Betty is the lady who wants to marry Des, our mother tells us. She is sad, she says, because she doesn't think that Des will get married. He's too shy. He's worried about someone having to look after him all his life. Des is only thirty.

Betty takes Des out sometimes and then brings him home and stays for a cup of tea. I hear Auntie Jean say quietly to my mother one day that she hopes Betty won't 'lead Des on'. Auntie Jean has to live at Mont Albert while Cec is away at the War. I watch Jean and my mother tuck into each other's thoughts.

I watch Betty to see what she does when she's with Des. It's late Saturday afternoon and Betty and Des have come home again after the concert – a bit of a jazz session, Des says. The mad, scrambling crescendo of the races comes from the back sleep-out, where David is totting up his bets.

I'm left behind. Louise and Will have taken Greg and Alistair and gone to look at some second-hand chairs in Prahran. I see it all again. I moon along the drive and in and out of the front garden's bushes and leaf litter. What are Aunty Jean and Aunty Joyce doing? I don't know. I've brought down the eggs for Joyce from the chooks in their long shed way up at the end of the back yard. I come up the ribbed concrete of the side path and slip in to the space near the phone. I can see Jean putting some scones on a plate at the sink. David's still out the back with his race guide and the wireless. Where is Joyce? Perhaps she's out in the sleep-out with David.

I don't like David, but I see the others put up with him. I hear him swearing from room to room sometimes, as though he wants to own the house. I see his dark head and eyes like currants. I see his mouth that speaks sideways. I see his fancy clothes, the thick coat lapels, the white silk scarf he wears when he takes Joyce out. I'm watching myself far off in time. I can even smell David's hair oil.

David is in the truck during the week, working in Auburn. What does he do? What does he think while he works with his father laying the carpets in other people's houses? Huh, fuck carpet-laying, he says some-times. I won't be in it for long. I'm just helping the old man until he finishes. David wants to work full time for the bookies at Caulfield race-course. He says he knows all the important bookies. He talks about them. He gambles on the races and he takes bets on Jean's phone at Mont Albert. I hear Will say that's risky, that's very risky. At first David is just Joyce's boyfriend, although he's a lot older. Then they get engaged, so he is her fiancé, even though he's thirty and she's eighteen. Then they get married at the weatherboard church in Hartwell, with the confetti falling and eddying and sticking along its hot asphalt paths out the front. I can remember it. Now they are living in the side bedroom at Mont Albert until David can find a house for them. At the end of the year Joyce is going to have a baby. I hear Des and Louise and Jean talking about it.

I'm watching myself down time's long hall and I still don't like David much, with his smell of brilliantine. A lot of the time he more or less pushes us out of the way. He doesn't take much notice of Alistair or Greg or me. We're no use to him. He doesn't talk to us or show us anything, doesn't even ask us questions. He says one day that I'm mad wanting to stay on at school. He laughs about it. 'You'll get over it!' he says. He's always telling me that in a couple of years I could be out in the world making a packet. So on this Melbourne Saturday afternoon, I don't go out the back where I might run into David sucking his pencil and writing down results and talking on the phone quickly and then slamming it down. I just stay near where the sleep-out comes out towards the kitchen, where I can flip through the American magazines. I've got a couple of *Life*s this time, not a *Saturday Evening Post.*

But through the door I can see Des propped with his arm extended to the kitchen cabinet just like Flute stands sometimes. Des is relaxed, he's smiling, his head listed to one side, listening, so that he doesn't miss anything while Betty and Jean are talking on. But there are footsteps on the lino behind me. The sickness, the sad crying in my stomach touches me. I know what will happen. It is David coming from the races to see what is going on.

He pushes past me through the little alcove where the phone is. He's stretching his arms and yawning. I catch the sharp, sweaty smell of the beer on his breath. Jean looks up from her rinsing of the teapot. Betty is nuzzling against Des's forearm, talking across the room to Joyce about someone they met on the tram coming out from the jazz club. I watch David roll into the kitchen. Movement and voices stop. Everyone watches him, waiting. Suddenly the strange, empty realisation that Will and Louise are not here surrounds me, takes my breath.

'Go for it, boy!' David leans close to Des's searching face. 'Go for it!' He winks at Joyce. She laughs quickly.

I see David turn to look at Betty, challenging her gaze cheekily. Betty is looking at him in sharp panic. She tries to smile, then looks down. She has met David only once before. Des is silent. His head is cocked to one side, in a way that he has, trying to sense what people's faces are saying. I see Jean looking levelly at David, her eyes telling him not to butt in. He sweeps his gaze around the faces. Then he shrugs, spreads his hands out in front of him, and looks at his fingernails. He gives a thick laugh. He says he has to go and listen for another race.

'A man's got to keep working,' he flings over his shoulder as he goes. I see his stubby pencil that he puts behind his ear sometimes. I see the betting slips and the pages of the paper near the phone. He's gone.

Jean looks at Joyce, who laughs and looks away. The tea is ready. Everyone goes into the front room. I'm following. There's a cushion in the corner, and another magazine to flip through. Des sits very straight with his cup and saucer. He doesn't say much. His smile is gone. His head is cocked, listening. I see Betty put a hand over and stroke his wrist. She slips her fingers into his and then takes them away again. Auntie Jean watches what Betty does. She sees how Des settles back in his chair, how his brow unknits, how he reaches for Betty's wrist and nuzzles his face against her sleeve.

It's like a painting with people sitting in it. The afternoon sun spills through the small stained-glass window above the fireplace onto the ring of chairs and faces. I look down. The light is touching my hands as I finger the pages. I look at each of the faces in the room. I'm listening to the talk. I can hear Jean saying something in a low tone to the others about oranges and then I hear Joyce say something about the Tiv. I keep turning the pages of the magazine and reading bits. Then I look again around the faces. Jean is sitting where Pearlie used to sit when she was alive, in the dark chair with the armrests. But why aren't Will and Louise and Alistair and little Greg here?

Betty has to go. I see everyone step and side-step politely towards the front door. I see feet on the thin, brown felt carpet in the hall. Betty leads

Des. I look at Jean. I think she likes Betty. They were sniggering together and laughing in the kitchen. Now they hand each other out onto the veranda. Everyone's talking. I watch Betty lead Des down the steps to the dark shadows of the drive. I watch her give him a kiss on the side of his neck. I see him smile and stumble back. I watch Betty get into her little Austin with its leather smell. She backs out. Then she turns with a wave and drives away down the street. Jean takes Des's hand again. Everyone shuffles back inside.

Even now I feel the sickness again, the crying in the stomach. Even now I wish my mother and father were here. Des takes a towel to dry some of the washing up. I come to help. Joyce throws me a towel – 'Make yourself useful, eh!' – and we dry together. I can see that Des is happy. His face is breaking into smiles, and he draws in breath as he does when he's enthusing. He grabs me when I go past and rubs his bristly jaw against my cheek. I find we're laughing, laughing.

There are footsteps coming past the telephone. It's David coming from out the back again. He's got the *Sun* stuck under his arm. He's carrying an empty beer glass. He's chuckling to himself. He opens the refrigerator and reaches in for another bottle. He finds one and looks back at Des as he takes it out.

'Well, Des boy, she's gone. When's the wedding day, eh? '

'Ha! Wedding day?' Des snorts quickly. His voice is suddenly high and nervous. We can hear him breathing quickly. 'Who says I'm getting married?' We see his face is flushing, reddening. His eyes are darting under a furrowed brow. Jean stops, props deliberately above her work at the sink and looks across at Des. Her eyes are heavy, resigned. There's no fun in them any more. She eyeballs David, who is smirking around at the faces. I watch David, then look at Jean. Jean is waiting, watching David too. My gut begins to cry. I know what this means. Jean and Des and David and Joyce. What will happen? Joyce is four feet from me, fidgeting with the tea towel. She doesn't laugh this time. She says: 'No, David. Don't! Leave it. Please.'

David gives her a glance. 'Fusspot!' he says, and snorts.

He turns again to Des, who presents his cheek, listening. 'She's after you, boy,' says David. He pushes through to lean a hand on the kitchen cabinet, making a loud thing of smacking his lips. 'I'll bet she's not only after your cock. She's probably after your money too!'

'Oh, David,' Joyce mutters, but she doesn't seem to be looking at him. Her eyes seem held by a point just beyond his elbow where it rises in the kitchen like a challenge, his hand on his hip. 'David, stop it!' But Joyce's eyes have swung to her sister, her face distracted and fearful. She looks near to sudden tears.

Jean's face is suddenly a fury of eyes and bared lips. She darts from the sink, hands dripping soap and water, wrests the *Sun* from under David's arm, swings it quickly in the kitchen light and brings it down on the side of his dark head just above his ear. It makes a loud, wadded smack.

I see David ride the blow like a dog struck at first, his head heeling over. Then he hisses, rights himself, plants his feet. His eyes come to a slow, bovine stop. Jean is at him, taking two quick steps, bringing her face close to his. 'If you can't control your tongue you can get out of this house. If Candles or Cec were here they'd cure you. Get back to your bloody form guide! In fact, take it and vamoose. Back to Oakleigh. Go on! You've polled on us long enough. Take your mean tongue and get out!'

I see David rouse himself. He steps forward as though he is going to push Jean backwards into the window, but Joyce's hands grab for his wrists. She pulls him towards the door, his face still leaning dark and threatening into the room.

'You're a hoity-toity bitch, aren't you!' he spits. 'I can buy and sell you and your marvellous Cec and your marvellous Candles. I can buy and sell you and your little teacher sister too. And what about her, eh? She doesn't even wait for wedding days, does she! What about her? Dear little butter-wouldn't-melt-teacher Louise? Eh? Don't worry. I'm going. But I'll be back!'

Joyce's hand is at her mouth. Her eyes rake me. Then she looks away. She is moaning to herself and dragging David. I hear the effort in her breath as she steers and urges him past the phone and its pad and out into the back porch.

'I'll be coming back with interest. With interest!'

I'm watching unbelieving as the kitchen window stares unaltered, as the soapy water from Jean's hands drops to the floor. She takes up a tea towel and mutters into it, 'Spare me that man, spare me!' and then gives the dishes away as a bad job and sits down sharp in the chair next to me. She reaches out damp fingers, covers my hand absently with them.

I see Des is forgotten, standing against the stove in the corner. Now his face has collapsed. It's just hanging, eyes looking straight ahead. Jean sits, her eyes boring into the table top. Then she turns wearily to look at Des. He can feel her gaze on him. He's ready. 'Don't worry about me,' he's saying defensively, his voice breaking and then steadying. 'I'm all right. And he'll cool down. David'll cool down. Don't worry about me.'

Jean spins halfway round in the chair and reaches back for Des's hands. But again he senses her entreaty and freezes further into the corner. He puts his hands behind his back. He's staring fixedly into the wall beside the window, brow knotted, breathing quickly like a side-eyed foal that hopes it isn't seen. I'm still looking past them all at the rose light beyond the window, at the dark, pious tops of the cypresses against the sky. I can feel Des's secret weeping in the belly. I think I hear sounds from the future. I hear the unretracting grind of trams rounding the Power Street corner on their hard rails far away in Hawthorn. How can that be? My gut carries a picture of some long, desolate afternoon with no warmth in its sunshine. It's as though there are creeks crying inside me.

—

An Oval Passion

There I am, sitting on the bed's corner, listening to the noises of the house, moving one image over another in the pile of photographs, searching, amazed, wondering ...

It's a winter Sunday when I find the bundles. It's the winter Sunday when Greg and I move Will from the larger Cicero Street house to the smaller one in Overton Lane. That's when I come on these other photographs, photographs I've never seen. I'm clearing the front bedroom at Cicero Street. To the sound of the lantana twigs raking at the side window in the wind, I come on one photograph after another. The questions grow vaster and vaster as they ride above me, like great unreadable dirigibles straining and creasing against the blue, but undeniable, undeniable ...

—

I don't understand.

My Auntie Joyce loves animals and birds. She is always watching the birds in the garden at Mont Albert. She knows what sort they are. She's got a bird book. My mother Louise knows too. Joyce is very gentle. I see her with Bing, her dog from the Mallee. He rips the webbing of his paw at Mont Albert when he's chasing a pigeon. Joyce washes it and talks to him and then she wraps it up with some old sheet. That's what I see Auntie Joyce doing when I think of her. I can see her eyes concentrating, hoping. I can hear her gentle words while she bandages the paw and Bing pulls away with the pain.

Joyce goes to the boxing with David to see the men fight each other. They can hurt each other all right, she tells us. One night when they are at the Stadium a man is knocked out. Joyce and David see it. Joyce says the man falls near the ropes with one leg out of the ring. He lies there and the referee is counting, but he doesn't move. There's blood starting to come from his nose and one of his ears. He doesn't get up, and they take the other boxer away. They hide him with two towels, so that he can't see. The first boxer just lies there, and a doctor in a suit climbs through the ropes and squats down beside him. He's got a little bag,

Joyce says, but he doesn't open it. They turn some of the lights out so that you can't see. The doctor calls out to the boxer, but no one can hear him, and then he lifts up his eyelid and has a look and then he turns the boxer over a bit to look at where the blood is running out. Joyce says he shakes his head. Joyce says people are leaving the Stadium and some people are booing. The doctor feels for the boxer's pulse. But she thinks he's dead. He's dead with the blood there on the canvas beside him. But nobody knows for sure then. He might have a spark left, Joyce says. But when she looks back some men are bringing a stretcher, and they lift him onto it. Joyce says she mightn't ever go to the boxing again. David says come on, he laid himself open and that's what happens. He had it coming. It had his name on it.

I don't understand.

—

It is always her face I see, even in primary school – those plaits, those dark, nervous eyes. Ellen Proban's dark eyes and water-bubbler laugh. I think I love her. And yet she is unattainable, always just departing, just going away round the corner with her school bag trailing, just leaving the baths, marshalled by her big sister, as I arrive. Sometimes our eyes meet – and I see a challenge there. But often she looks past me, as though she's closed for business. And yet she is the girl I prize, where she lives on the other side of Riversdale Road, where she sits two rows away in class, where she runs like a fawn, her plaits flying, in the school athletic sports on the oval ringed by oaks. I monitor her very breath, even the sheen of nervous moisture under her eyes when we play a mock game of chasey with each other round the table at the small party organised by the teachers on our final day in primary school.

She is the girl I love against the evidence, the girl I love in hope. One day we might sit and talk and I can drink her eyes.

—

The photograph finds its way to me in the end. Alex Cumming's shoulders and knees bend down to a volley – it's a picture that comes to me in the screen of my mind again and again. It is an image that always rides with me.

The photograph in the *Geelong Advertiser* shows him leaning down to the ball, wrist firm, his shoulder muscles straining under the shirt. Among the many photographs taken of him, it must be one of the few he keeps. I can see he feels the strength of his shoulders when he serves, when he swings them through from the hips as he slices into a backhand, or when he reaches up behind him for a high backhand smash. Alex has the Cumming family's broad shoulders and strong wrists. He can lump wheat-bags like his father, so when he steps onto the tennis court and takes the oval covers off two racquets, the strength is there. For him in tennis, it's wind that's important. Farming gives strength but not lasting wind. For that he has to go out on the Mildura road, night after night, when he's getting ready for the championships. Out to Old Friend's Lane and back, running, running, pushing, pushing, pushing further against the stars.

I can feel him doing it. I am breathing with him. It is his oval passion, the stroking, the tug of the ball meeting the strings. But how do I know this? Why is the arc of each stroke so sharp in my mind?

—

It is another time. I can look down on myself just arrived home, musing at my bike leaning against the shed wall. The Malvern Star. I glance at it, yes, making a mental note that I must put it away, but knowing that my mind is full with the thought that tonight I will give myself to it again. I've found it can exist beside other things. I've found that its mystery is invisible.

I know what will happen next. I will set to work on the history essay so as to earn what I will do tonight. After the work is finished, I will give myself to it when the night is still. Some days and nights I feel like this. My whole being is brimming, my penis, my perineum electric with need. I want no family, then, no Alistair and Greg, no meals, no voices. I want solitude, secrecy, the soft sheets. I can't wait for the darkness.

Even thinking about it I can feel the secretion of anticipation in my mouth. And yet a huge love, a generosity, goes with it. I seem to have come over a barrier into another field of my life that I had never guessed was coming. I lean back in the chair and open my arms. It is as if I rove the streets and am lost among the people I know, the stories that have happened to me. In its swelling power it makes me part of the world's long question and its working out. Even so, I still have to climb each time over the edge of guilt that surrounds it. It promises another unfathomable person in me. It is such a secret and private thing, governed by smell and sound and touch.

I shoot glances at my father Will at breakfast in the morning to see whether he has noticed. Will is oblivious. He sits munching his cereal in tie and sleeve bands, one hand propping the *Age* in front of him. I glance at Louise. Hunched over the pan on the stove in her nightie and dressing gown, the black pudding sizzling in the pan she's watching, my mother unbelievably notices nothing either.

—

There are things that lie far back on my time's circle, and yet they seem to belong only to yesterday, they seem still to swim beside me. I write about them. I wonder at how they seemed to me when I was younger and how they appear to me now, how they fit into the strangeness of the world. I think sometimes that I have been more than one person as I've lived on in the envelope the world allows me. I think that perhaps somewhere deep down I've decided what I must do with the days until I come to an end. Perhaps that's it.

My two parents stand like totems. I worry about them. They don't often argue, but Will, my father, thinks things one way, and Louise, my mother, thinks things another way. My father wonders and thinks of tomorrow. He is sometimes passionate and stumbles into things that he should be able to see are going to lead to trouble and unhappiness. Louise lives more for the day. She lives in a calm that is wise. I think it is the Barnes capacity for acceptance.

But now I hear their voices rising and I cringe. When Will and Louise argue it's often about money. Waste, Will says – silly waste! We can't afford to waste anything, especially with a war on. Think about it. And he takes out his little stub pencil and a bit of paper from the desk and his eyes narrow, his sandy hair stands up as though he's been startled. We'd better save that, he says. And so he saves things – rubber, aluminium, envelopes, jam tins, jars, magazines, bits of leather, strips of metal, scraps of paper, wood off-cuts, even bent nails.

You of all people should know, Will says. You, from a Mallee farm where there's never any extra! You know about the Depression and the War. You've seen people do it hard. So why do you waste things? We're not made of money! I've got to watch every penny.

I'm not wasteful, Louise says. I watch what I buy. You've given me little enough over the years as it is. What about the kids' clothes? What about school books? Your little bit extra wasn't enough through those years, was it! I've had to be so careful. And yes, I've had dozens of kids on Susso when I was teaching. I've seen their faces. I've often given them my lunch. I know what it means. For Heavens' sake, I've lived in a War Savings Street all these years – I think the sign is still on that telephone pole up the hill. But the Depression's gone: the War's been over for years. We have to be careful, but we don't have to save, save, save. We don't have to pare away all the time any more. Let's live! Let's live!

When their arguments sound through the house at Cicero Street I wish my father was dead or would go away to New South Wales – when he argues with my mother, when his words batter her and her face falls into itself, when she cries afterwards in the front room on the corner of the bed near the mirror.

It's only later that I feel my father's unpredictable love. He flings up from the table when Louise keeps insisting that Greg should have a new set of paints, a new brush. Spare me, he shouts. Most of the brushes are like new, for God's sake. He's still got paints left. Spare me! We can hear him stamping in the next room, stabbing the mantelpiece with his fingers. Spare me! But then we hear things calm down, and he comes back and his eyes soften, and I know he has been thinking about me, and I look over at Greg and then at Louise to be sure that she has waited for my father to come back to her again and that she loves him even through the times when he hurts her. I see then, when I'm a bit older, that she knows things will pass. I see then that Will hardly ever apologises with his words, but that his long-fingered hands on Louise's neck and his eyes searching for reassurance are what apologise for him. I wonder how I can have seen it one way, felt it one way, when I was smaller, and now see it another way and have hope about my mother and father. I suppose it is something to do with being the many different people I seem to have become through my life.

Will, my father, is curious, doubtful. He's always wondering. He reads a lot. He shuts himself away to think. Sometimes he talks to Alistair and me about what he reads. It's as if he's here now saying it. What he tells us doesn't go away. When I'm at high school he says: 'Did you ever think that Thomas Hardy watched a woman being hanged when he was sixteen years old? A year older than you. What did that do to him, I wonder.' And he looks at me. Or one day he's saying, half to himself, half to me: 'From the first time I saw Dorothy Norman's portraits of Alfred Steiglitz, and his portraits of her, I knew they were lovers. They weren't just partners in the dark room. They're probably lovers even while Georgia O'Keeffe is away with her painting in Mexico for all I know.'

And he looks at me. It's as though he's decided I'm old enough to hear him thinking aloud. And I say who is Steiglitz? Who is Dorothy Norman? Who is Georgia O'Keeffe? Then he tells me, and Louise will be listening in and she'll know some of it, but not as much as Will does because he's a photographer himself in a way, and he knows a lot about the Americans. I think about the photographs I've taken with the box brownie. I wonder about Alfred Steiglitz.

They were lovers, Will says. I like the word lovers. My belly creeps with a thrill of the skin at the idea. I imagine the lovers' bodies coming to each other and light eking through curtains. I see a film about love. One Saturday night Ben Lodz and I say we are going to the Rivoli to see Esther Williams, but we go to the Broadway instead because Ben knows the film is on there. It's a French film about a prostitute in Paris. *La Ronde.* I remember the long plunge of the curtains in the prostitute's room, the silky drapes on the bed, the soft light, and the soldier taking off his uniform. Ben and I sit there in the dark, and our mouths are going dry with curiosity. I remember when the woman is making love to the soldier we both hear a man's voice coming from the darkness down in the front of the theatre. The man is saying; 'Yes, yes, yes' and then he calls louder to the young soldier on the screen: 'Now, in! Come on, in, in, in!

Will never knows about *La Ronde*. Neither does my mother.

—

Ah, the echo of marriage. Ah, the woe that is in marriage. And the signs, the signs.

'Who's miserable?' I hear myself asking. I'm hearing it again. It is echo. It is woe. 'What's miserable?'

Susan's eyes look at me so soulfully and directly that I cringe for an instant. 'You're miserable. Mum's miserable. Separation. Sell the house. Move. It's terrible. We're a family, but now we're breaking up. It's too soon. How can we break up? Jesse's miserable in his own way, but you'd have to know him to see it – like we do.' She pauses, and I know there's more. Her eyes look away out into the lilly pilly tree that shadows the drive. When they come back to me, they brim with tears. 'Too soon,' she is saying softly. 'It's not fair. It's too soon.'

I remember I quit the bed after Patricia's words that burn in the darkness, that sear my mind. As I stand there wondering where to go, I can hear my own guttural words hitting the wall near the bed. I can feel our backs hunched against each other. We are desolate. I look down on us from above and know we are alone in our dilemma, there in the midst of Heathmont suburbia. It seems so long ago. Now in my pain I don't even look in on Jesse in his fuggy room. I don't go to Susan's white door on the other side of the hall. I take the air bed and my track suit to the station wagon. I drive through the stilling suburbs and into the wooded hills, and park on a ridge from where I can see the lights around Westernport. I watch them wavering. My thoughts butt against disbelief. Eventually, I settle and sleep there soundly, once the heavy weight of anger and foreboding has lifted from my heart and throat. I remember it.

I wake to the descending scale of music in my head that tells me this cannot last. I drive home through early shopping traffic that glints in the sun. It's Saturday morning. I feel no better. I am a bitter fool as I push open the back door. Patricia is sitting at the table. She makes no comment as I enter. She transfers more jam from plate to toast as if weighing out some deep debt.

—

Most of the time Des needs Charlie if he's going to play in the band. Most of the time. Charlie gets him there in the old Vanguard. It lumbers up to the house in Mont Albert like a green beetle. Charlie's clarinet and sax are in the back with a couple of spidery music stands folded down. Des gets in unencumbered and off they go in the twilight towards the city. Des can carry the music in his head until he gets to the piano. Sometimes he can get to the halls by tram and Charlie brings him home. The tram is easier, safer. People handle the drunks better on the trams than in the lonely carriages of the trains. People talk to Des, tip him off about where they are and when his stop is coming up.

Des plays at the Scout Hall in the dip of Whitehorse Road. It's a dance. The cars pull up in the side-street. People step off the tram heading towards the twitter of voices in the hall. There's the smell of perfume and hair-oil. Girls feel their feet tapping already as they head to the door. Even before the band has set up, the run-on beat of the quick-step is coursing through them. Their eyes are lighting.

The girls love Des. We know about it – Alistair and Greg and I. They wait for his notes to spill out into the hall with the drums and the bass backing them, with the sax looking in here and there. I have to think that this is my uncle they love. This is my uncle who is playing, looking far off to the curtain on the left as his fingers skate on the white and cajole the black on the keyboard. The piano can't live until he touches it and asks its advice. Then it speaks. Then the girls' eyes light and they hum and their feet cannot stay still.

—

I ain't got a dream that's workin'. My inner voice repeats it.

I hear the words of the song. I hear the sure beat and sliding sax chords of Ellington's big band. I hear Jesse hammering away at his new box in the garage. I can hear someone's motor mower ranting around the shrubs in a garden down the street. I hear, if I listen closely, the tick of the black clock in the lounge.

It is Saturday morning. It is a bit over a week after our second session with the marriage counsellor. The morning is predictable, normal. The bees fossick in the flowers of the lavender outside. The sun shines. Can my tension be real? I know Susan is in the back room doing homework at the deep window. I can hear Patricia's voice from the alcove, talking to her mother on the phone. My heart beats faster at the thought. From the window I can see the careless basalt rocks I settled into the earth when we moved here, and I know that if I walked towards the front gate I could see the pale blue lips of the Dandenongs to the east. The words on white pages of student assignments lie under my elbow. The pen is in my fingers, rotating slowly as I think.

I look again at the rocks, at the white fall of alyssum over their faces to the edge of the drive. Countless times, sitting here, I have focused my thoughts on the round and generous rock that takes the foreground. I have sent my concern to its shadows and vents, and found hope in the fall of light on leaves, on moss, on secret declivities where the garden meets the shining plane of the wet drive. But now, there is nothing. Nothing comes back to me. I am scarcely seeing. What I am waiting for, my heart beating fast in spite of me, is sounds. In the tense air I am waiting for Patricia's voice to cease, to hear whether her footsteps follow, or whether she sits beside the silent phone with her own thoughts. I am paralysed in the waiting. So much seems to depend on the next sounds from the alcove. They will tell me what stage we have reached in our grinding misery.

The pen rotates slowly in my fingers. Why all this human detail and care and yet a cold, lonely ending? Why all this establishment and preparation for a future and now the prospect of a desolate landscape ahead, trackless and un-shining, not peopled by the faces I know and love?

Why this waste of years, of the time allowed for life?

Suddenly the door is sliding open. Patricia's face is there. It is pinched, impatient, impassive. She gives me the briefest glance. 'I'm going into town,' she says. 'Susan is coming with me. Jesse says he's going to Dave's to help him with his car. I don't think we'll be home until eight or nine. I'm going to 42 Cremorne to see Mum and Dad while they're free.'

She swings her eyes back to me to see my reaction, then draws her face away, slides the door home.

I ain't got a dream that's workin'. The song's lines throb in me. I know now – how long have I known? – that we cannot stay together. I quiver at the realisation. So with what speed and what pain, my mind keeps asking. With what speed and what pain?

It is a scene from a failed marriage. I have been an actor in it. I will always be able to recall my part.

—

I am nine. I'm still seeing those three blond heads at the shed door, my father sighting along the piece of wood and then getting to work with the awl, my brother Greg stooped crooning over his fire engine on the rough bricks, and my brother Alistair coming from the vice in the inner darkness to blaze in the sunlight. All thinking their own thoughts. All together, their thoughts going from one to the other like a gentle hum in the sun and I can't hear them.

The emptiness has taken over my stomach now for two days. Where should I be? Who should I be? Where do I belong? Why do I suddenly feel cold and alone? I have come to the kitchen door with my feverish words, my choking questions for my mother. They spill from me with my breath, faster than the words themselves.

'No . . . no,' Louise says. 'No, Tim, you're not different. You mustn't think that.' She stops, seems to pale. Why is her stomach sinking? I can see it in her eyes. Then she resumes. 'Tim, you are the eldest. You are the darkest. You are the wisest.' My mother comes to a stop again. She seems to have no breath left. Then she says, almost in a whisper, 'You are my only Tim. Really!'

I don't feel wise. She dries her hands quickly on the kitchen towel and comes to me. She takes my face in her hands. She looks at me then looks away. She still holds me but she leans away in anguish towards the stove as though she is about to ask it a question. I can feel the warm moisture still in her fingers. Then her eyes come back to mine.

'You mustn't think that,' she hums again, but that is not what her eyes are saying. There's a wavering in her. Are her eyes pinpointed with fright? 'The darkness comes from your grandfather's family. Grandpa John's brothers were all quite dark, you know. All quite dark. That's come right through to you.' In the end her voice sounds quite pleased, quite chirrupy, but her eyes don't say it. I see them melt, then come to a pinpoint again.

She folds me against her apron now, gives me a strong squeeze, then slowly pushes me out to the full length of her arms and looks at me. 'Really – I mean it?' she says. 'No more thinking that? Really! Are you better now? Some people are darker than others. Perhaps it's darker for the eldest – I don't know. But you're part of all of us. What would we do without you?' Her lip slackens just a bit, trembles for a second. She's looking away towards the stove again. I see her swallow.

It's no use, a voice inside me says. It's no use. This is my mother Louise, but it's no use. Where is Will, my father? Now I need his steady blue eyes, his sandy shock of hair at his brow. I need to see his watch, the hairs on his wrist. It's no use with my mother. I thought it would be, but it isn't. When will she be warm and sure again?

'Now, you're OK again, aren't you,' my mother says. 'You worry too much, but you won't any more, will you? Will you!' I shake my head no. It's not any use now. I shake my head, seeing the patterns in the lino on the floor.

'Would you like a scoop of ice cream? It's probably set now. Yes?' she asks me. She's searching my eyes.

'Nope!' I say. I say it loud. I step down from kitchen door to veranda, my back pinpricking with the expectation of her touch, but there is none. I open the back door. My back still quakes behind me for what I can't see, what I can't look back to. I don't know what my mother is doing in the dimness. Is she propping against the chair? Is she looking after me as I go out and down the steps? I don't know. The thin drumbeat is treading in my head.

—

I am far back in the years. Beneath the sleep-out window my homework books catch the sun. That's where they always sit after I come from the tram, after I step into the silken air of the house, calling hello. Then in my room I delve into the bag and its lunch smell, pull out the books and pile them near me on the desk to denote intention. Then I sit down and stare at myself inwardly, collect my newly arranged self together.

I slump there in the chair, pullover draped over its back, school tie off. I realise slowly that my mind is offering glimpses of Pam – Pam, the girl at school who dives. She is in the form above mine. She is rounded and lively. I've watched her. She is rounded and smug. I've heard her talking. I don't trust her, even though I don't know her, even though she's not even aware of my existence. But she is neat as she arches above the water in a dive at the baths. She is neat in her breasts and thighs. I see her pert bottom plummet into the water. Where did she come from? Just lately, just since I watch her in the swimming trials, it's this Pam I see rather than Sandra, although Sandra started it, rather than Ellen, although Ellen is the one I yearn for. They are all girls. I can think about each of them. But perhaps Sandra is too precious, too grown up. I still love Sandra in a warm, brotherly way, but she seems to stand aside from my fantasies. She knows me closely, and I her, much more closely than the mysteries that are Ellen or the distant Pam. Now I see a glimpse of shorts and thighs. It is Pam coming up from the dressing sheds, Pam going home from the baths with her towel and her shoulder bag. In my musings she slips away from me until I cannot see her face. I'm alone. I can run the scene again, in puzzled joy. I can let joy mount to ecstasy. The face retreats. I feel my stomach tighten, my cock start to rise and throb.

—

Still Melbourne growls behind the hill. Still I see Will's shed where he wears his old overalls at night, boot-mending. The light-globe has half of a brown-paper Education Department envelope strung round it as a shade, directing the light down to the littered bench where the boot last crouches among tacks and hammer and slabs of sole leather and Kromide. It must be the War. I can even hear the tired chime of the switch as he turns the light off and comes into the dark yard at Cicero Street.

I can fly this city in my mind. I am over Richmond, the railway line gleaming silver below me. I am over Auburn, the small backyards backing away from it to house sleep-outs, back taps and gully-traps, ferns hanging under weather porches. I see an angry man hustling a woman in an apron round the house-end like a flighty chook. I am over Hawthorn, where I live, preparing for the river. I see the river coming from Kew through its dark trees and shining on towards Abbotsford, shining through Hawthorn, shining on towards South Yarra as it has always done.

I hear voices. I see Joyce and David. They have just come home from the Stadium. They stand for a moment in the full light of the lounge at Mont Albert. It was a good fight, David says, and Joyce says yes, it went the distance, and her eyes are bright and she smells of cigarette smoke. A knock-out in the tenth, she says. She starts to take off her short coat and I watch David's hand go to her bottom and she quivers. Then she turns and he kisses her on the mouth as though we are not there.

—

Here is Patricia's face. I can hear myself saying it to her, see her mouth go down quickly with hopelessness, then right itself, see her lips start forward near tears. I am near tears. There is a tenderness in anguish, I realise, when it has come beyond anger. There is a pacific, inexorable calm to our suffering now that I could not have believed in the last few months. It is a calm that grinds out my gut slowly. We are not worth anything to each other any more. We have come to it at last. We have sailed into another ocean.

'I have to tell you,' I say. 'I have to. It's the only way to explain.

What I'm saying is that I don't think I can put my arms round you any more unless you can bring yourself to put yours around me. I think that's what it amounts to.' I can see that it raises no hostility in her eyes. I can see that it brings very little but a glance of resignation, or is it dismissal? For a moment I suspect that she might be on the brink of smiling at the bumbling nature of what I'm saying.

But now the metaphor is the real, the real is the metaphor. We can no longer touch each other.

Sometimes I hear a Chopin Largo running behind what I see. Sometimes I hear Patricia's strangled voice entreating, explaining to Susan and Jesse sitting on the steps running down to the back room. 'I don't hate him. It's not that I hate him.' From where I prop in the hall all I can see is their shoulders and Susan's hand coming up to the side of her head. She's saying, 'Why then?', and banging her head with her hand three times to see if she can knock some sense into it. Then her frustration turns to sobs. Jesse looks at his sister, then stretches his arms before him, his fingers entwined tightly, his eyes sighting along his arms. But he says nothing. My gaze has become riveted for long seconds on the line where the brown-flecked carpet has been neatly tucked away at the edges of the steps by a carpet-layer unknown. Our children are trying to help us.

—

Will I ever be loved by a woman? How does it happen? What about Valmai of the flashing eyes, who plays with me in the tennis team – her deep and rich lipstick, her swirling wildness when she belts a ball in frustration, her hips swinging? Could she love me? What does she think of me? What about Pam who dives? What about Ellen, whose dark, nervous eyes I love, who manages to walk away from me?

Tonight, I will have to study for the exams again in the sleep-out, look again in the mirror at my face with the question marks of acne. I will be caught in the wondering all over again. Sometimes I find that I have been wondering for half a day and am none the wiser. Then I feel dry and desolate.

My father Will tells me about Thomas Hardy and gives me one of the novels. I see into Hardy's stories. They seem to have lonely, resigned and desperate figures walking country roads. I worry about Henchard each time I come back to the book on the bed in the sleep-out. Sometimes I hear Henchard's voice, see his eyes lose their fire with sadness and despair. I think what it must be like to be a hay trusser. I see Henchard's wife waiting in the shade of the trees with the baby. It makes me think of the tragedy of people who miss each other, or make decisions they regret, or lovers who might enrapture each other but who never meet. It must be that there are people who suffer, who are meant to doom themselves. I look at the people in our street. Is there anyone like that?

Just think, Will says, Hardy and old Joseph Furphy lived at about the same time. They were born within three years of each other, but thousands of miles apart. What different assumptions they must have had. What different lives they were allotted. But what if they had met? They'd both seen a lot of misfortune. I wonder what they would have had to say to each other?

Will, my father, is always wondering, always thinking. No holidays from thinking, he tells me one night at the tea-table. No break from wondering. You can't have holidays from trying to find out. I start wondering, too.

In Melbourne there are roads that mean.

Whitehorse Road means weekends and the thermos and sandwiches in a basket and cake in a tin. It runs out to the Blue Dandenongs and Lilydale. It runs out towards the bigger mountains further east and north, where we can see smoke trailing from gullies far off. It means the dark cypresses and the white rock fences of Coomb Cottage where Nellie Melba lived.

Batman Avenue means my Grandfather John when he was old and grey. I go with him on the train from Mont Albert. We go to the city. We walk along the river to the Yarra Bank. My grandfather is in his hat, with a suit coat and an open-necked white shirt. He is going to get worked up. He is going to the Yarra Bank. His train ticket is in the band of his hat. He is going to listen to the speakers on their bluestone mounds under the bare trees. He is not going to say a word to them or against them. He only mutters a few words to the men around him in their hats, and then he moves to another speaker. We might catch a tram back to Flinders Street, we might not. A lot of the speakers are bloody fools, he says in a grumble. He is worked up.

Burke Road means hot nights and pale bodies flashing into the river at the bridge, shouts coming across the water in the still dusk. Warragul Road means hot nights too, our legs sticking to the car seats on the way to the beach at Parkdale. It means sand for the first time near the golf-courses, and then the railway closer to the sea and then the smell of salt in the air and then the silky cool of the beach sand under our feet.

Riversdale Road has always meant the dray-horse down on its knees on the hill, the council man flogging it, swearing at it, coming round to its other side, flogging it again with the whip, the horse trying to rise again and pull the load. But its hooves slip each time on the asphalt. The leather comes down again on its neck and head. It still hasn't got up when our tram has gone.

The Nepean Highway means Rosebud and the honest-to-goodness smell of sun on canvas and the polite thud of the sea beyond the ti-tree and how dry and salt-eaten wood can become, how long the sun takes to set in charcoal.

Smith Street is another one that means. Ah, the grimness. Will and I have been to the boot factory to look at some shoes for school. It's first thing in the morning. Will backs the car into an alley to turn. I look at the tiny houses, at the smudge of grime around the doorknobs. Suddenly I'm seeing a big rat, brown and grey pepper colours in its fur. It scampers to the peak of a pile of rubbish from the bluestone gutter. Then from behind us comes a phlegmy shout and soon at our window there is a woman in a stained dressing-gown. Her hair is long and stringy, white, and hanging over her face on one side. Her nose and cheek fall into a pit. There's a twisted hole like an old tree-stump in her face. 'Watch where ya goin', why don'tcha, ya bastard!' Her face with its cavern is at the window. Will's arm is clamped around the steering wheel. I can feel his dismay but I cannot see it. 'Sorry,' he says. 'I didn't see you. Sorry.' He turns the wheel while he reaches for first gear, pushes in the clutch, smiles to her apologetically. She snarls at us. She hits the car a thud near the back window with the flat of her hand. I can feel her hate like the heat of a fire. 'Short-prick bastards,' she spits. She is looking at us, pulling the gown close around her neck. She throws back her head with disdain. Her eyes are roving, finding words. She hasn't finished. 'Go back to your precious little missus, ya cunts. Don't come nosing in here.'

I look at my father. He is silent. He expels a breath, makes eyes at me. In them I feel shame and sadness. He lets in the clutch. I watch the narrow-fronted houses pass, the two-storey ones with no fence and windows open and bellying grimy curtains. 'Terrible,' says my father, as if to himself. 'God! It's taken half her face away.' I feel the horror of his words, I see the horror of that face. I can't explain what I seem already to know. Smith Street means that.

Melbourne means these things with its wood-yards and quarries and gasometers and tram depots and railway yards and strings of cars and trucks and the long streets of same houses in Brunswick where Aunt Mollie and Erskine live when they are old and Erskine says in his self-centred way as he pushes his empty plate away at the dinner table – 'Thank the Lord I'm blessed with limitations. No, I won't have any seconds, dear Mollie.'

Melbourne means these things, but why am I thinking of them now?

—

Mr Burchill is my piano teacher. He means music to me. His long fingers climb around the notes of the Schumann, his shoulders and head inclining towards the walnut of the piano and drawing away again in time with the phrasing, the walnut making a dim image of his pale, looming face from where I stand behind him holding the Bach in readiness. His throat murmurs with the melody, as his long fingers climb the octaves, teasing the notes out.

Mrs Burchill stands for a moment at the door with the tea cup and biscuit plate, listening, leaning her forehead against the door jamb. She is so young: much younger than Mr Burchill. She is beautiful, I tell myself, stealing a glance at her, as I listen to the Schumann so that if Mr Burchill asks me a question or suggests I try it I'll be ready. She is unattainable, somehow wrapped round in her knowing, although she throws out smiles that hint at memories. Her note is contralto, deep, beyond me as a sixteen-year-old. With another glance I remind myself of Mrs Burchill's beauty, her mystery. She notices and she smiles. Green eyes and long lashes, her neck and shoulders revealed above the V-neck of her sweater, a tendril of auburn hair trailing down to touch her shoulder. She appears with Ellen in my thrumming nights. In my fantasies Mrs Burchill displays before me like a tremulous rufous fantail, sweeping her beauty around in an arabesque and withdrawing it, while Ellen seems to watch from the side, her dark eyes questioning.

Are Ellen and Mrs Burchill my 'women', I sometimes ask myself, when I'm back home again in the sleep-out. 'Women' – the word rises daringly in my mind and stays there.

All that is music to me. So is Will, my father, letting out his tenor like Richard Tauber, singing 'Danny Boy' or 'Drink to Me Only With Thine Eyes' or 'Swanee River' in the front room at Cicero Street while his sister Connie plays the Ronisch and outside the sparrows fuss in and out of the Virginia creeper on Fraillon's wall next door. That is music to me. Des, as he rocks over the snatches of chord, plucking them out of the piano, is music incarnate to me. His whole being, his shoulders and back, his keening head on its side in the front room at Mont Albert, become 'The Sunny Side of the Street' as he plays it, then they become 'Cry Me a River'. And on another distant Sunday, his whole dim being in the white shirt hovers over the keys. I am hearing the plaintive chords of 'Yesterdays' as the light fades. That is how music and words reach into me.

Will, my father, his hand on my shoulder, says many times that he wants me to learn piano, even though he doesn't play himself. He wants me to have the skill of his sisters, to have Des's glorious free musical knowing and invention.

Down the rooms of the past I hear music. Music is dream. Music informs landscapes, the patient streets, the city's lights spreading across the hills, the noons when the ranges to the north of Emerald and Macclesfield are a stupefying blue, steeped in their forests. I hear Uncle Des play the Ronisch sometimes when he comes over. I hear Aunt Connie play it by ear, head turned to catch what our voices are saying. I play it myself when I practise, knowing that soon I will be riding my bike to Mr Burchill's, where I will moon at the veronica hedges running to the front steps of the house, and the pink of the crepe myrtle against the afternoon grass, and from where I will carry home images of Mrs Burchill's womanly, strong shoulders and the eloquence of the Streeton paintings behind her, speaking from the walls beyond the piano of Gippsland fern-gullies, distant mountains, sun-stippled hills, while the notes of the Schumann flow towards the light and the window's wavering glass. They are two Streetons, Mr Burchill tells me, that have never been seen in a gallery.

—

There's an echo. 'You still have a bit of a regard for Patricia, haven't you.' The counsellor, Meg, is making a statement, not asking me a question.

'Yes, I suppose I do,' I say.

It's just an echo now.

—

I've come in my first car – the little Ford Consul. The smell of the uphol-stery like a new nest stays in my thoughts. I've come to take Des home to Cicero Street for tea.

Even as I get out of the car and tread the damp grass towards the church hall I can hear Des's fingers on the keys, tuning, tuning. There's a pause, a listening, then more tuning and repetition of the one note. I've heard him tuning before. The hall's side door is ajar. I slip in. At first all I can sense is the dark ceiling rising above me and far away a west window filled with gold. But there's no other light. As my eyes adjust to the gloom I can make out the stage and Des's white shirt bending over, then rising as he reaches through the piano top to the wires. He doesn't know I'm there. I can hear him humming to himself, can hear his tuning spanner searching for the right knob, hear wires unintentionally strummed.

For the moment I stand. There's a strip of carpet running to the stage down the hall's centre. There are seats on one side, but not the other. I stand. I see the rafters materialise above me, spearing into darkness. There are two pianos on the stage. I can see Des's coat hung over the shoulders of a chair and his little black bag of tools close to him on a piano stool. Now he starts again, finger on the note, other arm reaching over and into the piano frame, the lid lying back. The note, again and again. 'Huh!' I hear him say. Now he tests seconds against sevenths, thirds against fifths. The piano yearns to break into speech, but Des won't let it. He is waiting for perfection. He stands in front of the piano and tests the notes, tests the pedals. He stops, reaches, scrabbling along the music shelf to find the spanner, then turns, hands outstretched, feeling behind him for the stool and his bag. He touches the stool, touches the bag, drops the spanner in. He feels his way back to the piano, tests two notes, goes up an octave, tests the same third and fifth there. I watch. I listen. This is my uncle who I love, bringing a piano to perfection in the dark. He needs no light. The frosted glass of the west window is gold-filled and still. My heart is beating fast with love for him as I watch, but I don't make a sound.

Now Des's white shirt straightens. He turns, searching with extended arms for the stool, finds it, lifts his tool-bag and puts it on the floor. He drags the stool to the piano, feels for the keyboard, pulls the stool in closer and sits down. I see him pull back his cuffs. And then he leaps on the keys. The piano responds. Des is drawing long chords of light out of it, lifting his face to the ceiling, listening to the notes. 'Huh!' I hear him say. Two more chords, and then the same pattern rising through the octaves. Now he sits back, takes a breath. He leans in to the notes now, entreating them. He begins to play an intro. I strain to hear what it is, but he is hiding its identity, giving only the slimmest of clues, a note here, a phrase there. It is beautiful. It is someone thinking. It is someone appealing. I am reading the gaps in the story. I am listening for what is not said. And then I know. It is Des's beautiful, inventive, exploring jazz. It is not what I expected. It is 'Danny Boy'. It is the 'Londonderry Air' in a church hall, sad and beautiful. There's a lump in my throat. Now that I hear Des playing it I know that the 'Londonderry Air' is a blues and a lament. It is as though I hear it again for the first time. I haven't moved. He doesn't know I'm there.

Now Des stops, swings round on the stool. He seems to be looking straight at me down the hall. I know his brow knits, striving to be sure. I can sense it rather than see it. Now he looks clumsily and puzzled towards me. I've known it before. It's as if he searches not only for me but for what my heart might be saying.

'Tim? That's you, isn't it? Tim? Sneaking up on me, eh?'

'Not sneaking up,' I say. There's a lump in my throat that tries to enter my voice. 'Not sneaking up. I was listening. Just listening.'

'Ah, well, this little pianner's a goer again,' he says. 'So I suppose it's home, James, is it? I'll pack up. Now where did I put that bag? Bag – and coat. And I told Louise that Betty's coming over too. Did I? Didn't I?'

I walk the strip of carpet towards my uncle. 'Yes,' I tell him. 'Betty's there already. She's there waiting for us.' My heart has steadied. The love remains.

—

I remember. Jean is saying: 'Yes, he can know. He can know. Why not, for heaven's sake?'

My father Will and mother Louise look at me with a quizzical serious-ness, debating with themselves whether I can know, now that I'm thirteen years old? Can I know, there in the driveway away from the house where Joyce and David are sitting silent in the kitchen. Can I know? I already know quite a bit. I can feel that there's something wrong. David's being has collapsed into a silence, an inertness, a head-down desolation that I have never seen in him before. Even a quick glimpse into the kitchen tells me that this is serious. From the time we pull up in the Mont Albert drive early in the afternoon I am banished with the others. 'Go up the back and keep an eye on Greg and Gwenda – just for twenty minutes or so,' Will says when it all starts, and I see that Cec is watching him tell me, but that his mind is somewhere else.

And I have seen Joyce's tears. I have seen them twice this last half hour when I drift intrigued back to the house from where Glen and Gwenda are playing bounce ball to each other in the far yard, when I slip in the back door and wait on the back veranda near Des's workroom. I see Joyce come out of the kitchen and close the door behind her to burrow her head and hair into the door-jamb, crying quietly and trembling. Then she rouses herself, still sniffing and wiping her eyes with a handkerchief. She squares herself before the door, reaches for the handle, turns it and steps back into the kitchen. Before Joyce can close the door I see Cec in there with his arm along the shelf above the stove. I can see Will sitting astride a chair near the door with his back to me. I can't see Louise or Jean or David. Then the door is closed again and I stand wondering. I can hear the voices resume, the low thunder of Cec's words, then Will's voice cutting in, questioning.

Now David and Joyce have been left in the house silent and looking at the floor. Scarcely a murmur between them. Why? There is a conference in the driveway, Cec's pale shirt backed into the wisteria, Louise and Jean propping against our car and talking quietly, Will listening to Cec and his suggestions. Why is this happening? Why is it happening when Des and Betty are out? I hear Cec say: 'He'll get comeuppance enough as soon as it gets around.' I hear my mother saying: 'What a hide! Four years, and always the eager helper!' I hear her cluck with disgust. 'Slimy customer, isn't he. Always has been, I suppose.' I've never heard Louise say those things before.

And now they see my eyes watching them from down beside the privet at the gate. They see I am held by it all, that my feet don't know where to go. 'He can know,' Jean is saying to Louise. 'He can know. Why not, for heaven's sake?'

I see my mother direct a quizzical, serious look towards me, as though she had forgotten me. And then a blank face but a shake of the head from Will, who has not been hearing exactly what Jean and Louise are saying, but can guess. And it's no.

'We'll tell him the details when we're home,' says Louise. 'But not here. We've got things to decide, haven't we?' She is committed, businesslike.

Will looks at me apologetically now, but he is still concurring. He winks at me. I feel better. They'll tell me soon. But why not now?

—

Sometimes when I'm at high school it seems that there might be only the four of us – Ben Lodz, Eric Lansell, Pat Friar and me. The wash of other faces, other voices in the corridor fades back. And there are the girls, of course. Estella and Ellen – the two E's, we call them when we sit out on the lawns to eat lunch. I look round the faces, hear the voices and I love each of them. I know how they think. I know how we are different. I love Ellen, but she keeps me at bay with her wit and her dancing eyes. I want her to read what I write, but she seldom does.

I sit writing about them and I miss them. The sounds of Eric's octaves romp in the background as he practises for the Liszt concert there in the big room at the end of the school. Eric tries the school's piano, pulling a face, tries it again. Then he settles, thinks about what the orchestra will play, how it will hand itself back into the dimness to let him in on the piano, gives himself a cue that we can only see in his eyes and in his gentle tap of a foot, and starts some of the Liszt. The piano seems to discover its own unsuspected dignity and power as he plays. We have never heard it challenged this way by Miss Anderson in music lessons. It is its full voice we are hearing. It cries, asks for solace, sets out tragedy and wisdom in the airy room.

We are lucky. Eric will play parts of the Liszt for us but for no one else. He doesn't like the crowd that gathers. He is always being asked to play. I hear people call him 'Eric Lansell, the pianist'. I hear Miss Anderson call him Eric and ask whether the stool is right for him when she gets him to play in class time. Eric says little. His eyes are elsewhere. I have to tell myself that I play tennis with Eric Lansell, the pianist, the prodigy. I am probably one of the two or three people in Melbourne who does. We all have seen his name in the paper when the concert in the Melbourne Town Hall is advertised. Sometimes I try to sort out the ways Ben and Eric and Pat Friar and Ellen and Estella and I fit into school and music and love and tennis. My heart swells with the richness of it all.

Why did I start to play tennis? Because my mother did. Because my mate Pat Friar did, like his father before him. Because when I'm too young to play I go with Louise down to the courts hidden behind the houses and play in the dense green buttercups behind the fence while she walks to pick up the ball and sets herself and hits it to the ladies at the other end. Because I can think of Uncle Alex Cumming playing tennis with Candles and my mother at Swan Hill. Because one day at Kooyong I see Trabert and Seixas and Hoad and Rosewall play a doubles match and can't believe the wide, fast arc of Seixas's serve going away, spearing further and further from the forehand line.

Why do I love the music? Because my father Will and his sister Connie and Uncle Des offer their music to me with raised eyebrows and challenging smiles, because I can see there is something liquid and beautiful that I can make when I play the Schumann or the Bach or the Beethoven at home, or for Mr Burchill in the long-windowed front room of his house as his wife leans sometimes like a pale lily in the doorway.

Now, in the music room, we stand at the back of the piano, leaning forearms on it, feeling the strength of the notes coming through the wood as Eric plays. Ben and me. Ellen has been sitting at the side of the room since the last period ended, feet crossed, hands laced on her skirt in front of her, listening. Sometimes she lifts her eyes to the kids drifting past the windows towards the gate. Some of them stop just outside in a cluster of suddenly attentive blazer shoulders and hats.

We need the orchestra, Eric says, and laughs a quiet laugh to himself. And as I listen my mind roams with possibility and beauty. I'm seeing Ellen at the pool, her eyes for me sometimes as promising as fruit, her legs willowy when she walks to the diving board, her shoulders wide and strong and lightly tanned, urging the small wave in front of her when she swims in the breaststroke. The Liszt contains it all as we listen, the octaves insisting on sadness and commitment to the depths, the trills carrying our lives away into doubt, then into sunlight. I look at Ellen. Her face is far away, her eyes dark and tired. I look at Ben near me. He is fiddling with the music book near his hand on the piano top as though pretending he must open it, as though he is embarrassed at our rapt attention. Ben is tone deaf, doesn't feel music. Once, watching him dance, I can see that rhythm disturbs his legs' directives, countermands his shoulders' tilt. He has to stand with us in the rows of singers in the house choir, but the teachers ask him just to mouth the words.

I know Eric's fingers, hands. They have deeper veins on their backs than mine, the skin not so tight. His finger joints can skitter on the notes much more than mine can. His fingers are so ready to play. He sometimes flexes them and pulls on them as if they were gloves before he starts. He practises for four hours a day, sometimes six if there's a concert coming. His fingers can flash out like the legs of can-can dancers in some of the fast, strong-rhythmed passages. I hear some of the Brahms dances, or the Greig, or Chopin Mazurkas and I see his bony, certain fingers. They don't spill wrong notes. All the parts of being alive are in them. They seem to be separate from Eric sometimes when I see him play, but then I see his shoulders and his neck urge them on, support them, tell them that the music is right, will always be right.

Ben has stopped fiddling with the music books. The music has grasped him. I look over to Ellen. I can see her dark eyes are crying, but she doesn't bring her hand or handkerchief to them. The sadness and joy of the Liszt. The whole world is in it.

There are some parts now where I know what the orchestra will be saying. I have listened to Will's record of the Liszt. 'Liszt: Concerto for Piano and Orchestra, No. 2 in A Major' the record says. I am getting to know where the music will take me. Now, when I listen to the thin oboe gradually opening into light at the start of the record, I'm waiting for what Eric will play when the piano drops into the music like a smooth stone starting ripples in a pool. Even when one day I listen to Eric practise it alone at his place I know that in his head he hears everything the orchestra will be saying. And now I can hear the horns come like glissades of light. I can hear the steady murmur of the piano working up, I can hear the orchestra come in like a dark wolf speaking to the piano, opposing it. I like the way the piano won't be silenced, will thrust through towards hope. I wait for the deepest orchestra, for the dire double basses in the second movement and then the piano entering and starting to rise and then the cello suggesting something and the piano thinking to itself and still rising, always rising, and the oboe thinking with it.

And then, as Eric plays, I am thinking how we play tennis. Often it is just Eric and me there in the afternoon on the Drysdales' court. I can listen to the Liszt now and yet see the court, see Eric down the other end, stepping in, rolling over the ball, switching it sharply down my backhand line, so that at full stretch I have to dig it out with a steeled wrist and plenty of hip swing and shoulder and a bit of undercut. I can hear the Liszt, and I can see the ball fly. I see it scorch the line, a burning winner, cleaning the nail heads in the lead lines, flattening into the bottom of the fence. It is music and tennis. It is rich: the declining chords of the afternoon, Eric's eyes glazing as he serves, the smell of water on hot brick, and momentarily in my hand the soft, secure nap of the ball that flashes me back to childhood, to my mother's straw bag, to a vase of chrysanthemums floating in the dark of a window.

—

I wish I'd been in the kitchen at Mont Albert. I remember it, the wishing. I want to see the faces, hear what the voices say. But I'm not there. He can know, I hear Jean saying. He can know, can't he? But I can't know until later.

Now I know, and it seems as though I've always known. Louise and Will have told me, but they haven't told Alistair or Greg.

Uncle David has been stealing money from Des for four years. Sometimes it has been money that Des has left in his workroom after a few tunings. But mainly it's money that David has offered to take to the bank for Des. David takes the money and pretends to go to the bank in Surrey Hills. But he doesn't go. He keeps the money and takes it to the races. Or sometimes he takes Joyce and his mother to Mario's in Melbourne for dinner and then to a show at the Tiv. Great night, he says afterwards to Will and Louise. Lucky I had that win at the races. And Joyce nods and says yes, we had all the trimmings last night. She says it in her quiet way. Her eyes aren't bright at the thought, but they are contented. She's tired. Little Gwenda comes and holds on to Joyce's dress and looks up at Louise and Will. Louise winks at her, bends to her, picks her up. I can see it. Little Gwenda puts her thumb in her mouth and leans her head against my mother's. They tuck into each other. I can see it.

—

The ocean is such a big blue question that it sweeps all other thoughts away. No more the questions about Will and my mother and the knot of wondering in my stomach about Alex. It sweeps away David's words from so far back and the shock of my name and my mother's name on his lips near the old storeroom. The dawns clear my mind too. So, often, do the soft evenings when the golden light seems to have been hoarded by the grass itself long after sunset.

With the sea there's always the getting in and the getting out, with the swells rising to the narrow wave platform, then sending their clear glass spilling generously over it, prying upwards until they spend some of their urging in the pools cupped in the rock. As I look down I see a dead albatross floating, beak down, in a raft of froth in the middle of the gulf, rocking to each pulse of the sea. As I look down I see the sea gardens plunging away from the surface, sheer walls of green and brown and wine-coloured weed waving. I watch the clouds of bubbles that plunge in white-blue veils down the weed-waving walls when the bigger sets thump their weight into the fissures near the cave's entrance – veils that suggest such secret and deep purity in the depths and then swirl and disappear like spirits. All of my body wants to fly slowly down the sea garden's walls away from the sun and air. And then I'm looking down on myself, it seems, an inconsequential figure against the rearing cliff walls, against the surging water. That's how I want it. I want to feel my irrelevance in the sea. I like the feeling of meaning nothing.

Sometime I will tell Rosa about the ritual of wetting of face and sealing of mask, of fins slapping the spongy weed as I step to the edge of the wave platform. That's how I have to tell it. Three hundred yards away, golden light is creaming the foam. I look down into the pure swelling of water at my feet. As it creeps up ankles and knees to my thighs, I am called. I go. The water accepts me. I stretch on it deliciously. I leave the shore. I fly.

That is how I have to tell it. The running thunder of every ocean is in my ears. I take a breath through the snorkel and look down. What is to come and what is past is far down, discernible as a changing, moonlight-pale outline of rock and weed seventy feet below me. I plunge, dive, fly down into the gloom. Sun shafts plummet past me to what may never have been.

—

Des is shaving. He is staying at Cicero Street. I sit over breakfast with Louise. I've set up Des's shave stick and brush and safety razor above the basin where he can sense them, reach for them, soap up. Then I imagine him reefing away the bristles and soap with the razor, leaning to feel for the tap, running the water, washing up. I see him doing it in my mind's eye. I'm listening. My mother is listening. Des doesn't like us to lurk beside him.

Now Des eases into song. Tentative at first, a hum here and there. Then clear and deep. 'Alas, my love, you do me wrong . . .' Then there's a pause, the click of the razor hitting the basin. Then another hum. 'For I have loved you, oh, so long . . .' Then Des's voice comes to us again strangely twisted, as though he's puckering his face for the razor, feeling the skin and beard: '. . . delighting in your company . . .' More humming and stroking with the razor. Then: 'Greensleeves a heart of gold, Greensleeves a heart of joy, And who but My Lady Greensleeves . . .'

Louise is smiling. Now she calls, 'Who is this lady, brother dear? Is this the new jazz version? Who is this lady, pray?' Sounds of razor being parked, and Des's voice after a delay that may be because of surprise or may be due to new soaping. 'Top secret!' he sings. Louise's eyes dance to mine. She's happy.

Now the humming goes on, more subdued. We hear the razor drop into the basin. We hear it retrieved and parked again on the basin shelf. 'And who but My Lady Greensleeves . . .' More humming – and even the sound of a shoe beating time on the floor.

I'm thinking, watching Louise's eyes, listening to the sounds from the bathroom. This is a different Des. This is not the Des I saw shrinking into the stove corner in the kitchen in Mont Albert. This is not Des snorting with embarrassed misery before everyone, saying: 'Don't worry about me. I'm all right. Don't worry about me.'

This is another Des.

—

That's what sometimes happens to friends. They take other paths. They slip from sight. Their voices fall silent. I've always been close to Pat Friar – my close mate in games of street cricket at Cicero Street, in front of the boys' mirrors at high school, talking about Wordsworth and D.H. Lawrence on the steps at the baths, down the other end of the court at tennis coaching, his father sitting on the dipping seat beside the court and smoking his cigarettes and watching us, calling 'good shot' and then coughing.

I feel close to Pat. He's always there. With his steady grey eyes and grin he knows what I'll do next, where I'll go. Then he tells me what's going to happen at the end of the year, but I only half believe him. And then it comes to pass. At the start of form three Pat goes to the grammar school in Kew. There's no time to get together after school and Pat has to play tennis for his house team on Saturdays. We see less and less of each other. We lose touch.

That's what happens to friends. They disappear into another world. But even then I have the feeling that Pat will come back.

It's Jean who discovers what David has been doing.

Now I can see how it happens. It's when Betty brings Des down to Jean and Cec's house at Mentone. He'll be staying there overnight. Des has work to do tuning at Chelsea and then he'll play with Charlie, Don and Mark in Brighton for two nights. He's tired. He stretches out in the chair, Betty beside him. Betty's staying for tea. Des reaches for her hand, pulls her towards him, gives her a quick kiss.

'Des! Des – you remember those tuning jobs you did in Kooyong and Prahran – one in Kooyong, the other two in Prahran?' It's Jean's voice from the back room. 'What happened to the money from those? Seventy pounds or thereabouts? You remember? When you were here last? You took it back to Mont Albert with you.'

'Gone into the bank,' Des calls. 'David took it in.'

Suddenly Jean's voice is close. She's has come to the doorway. 'Not according to this.' She is holding a bank passbook.

Des looks blankly towards Betty. 'Passbook. Your passbook,' Betty says.

'It was in your suitcase,' Jean says. 'I was checking how you're going, but there's no seventy pounds. There's been no deposit for almost a month.'

'Piffle,' Des says. 'David took it in the day after. Have another look.'

Jean opens the passbook, riffles through to the last page, leans into the doorjamb, then thinks better of that, straightens, and comes to sit down on the couch at Des's side. She's silent, running her eyes down the columns. 'Nothing. Nothing since the sixth, and then it was only fifteen pounds.' She pauses, then raises her eyes to Betty's. 'I'm going to check this with the bank. I think something's fishy. There was that lot – and there was a fifty-five pounds two weeks before, and I can't find that in here either.'

'Oh, it's bank records gone astray,' says Des, but his eyes are pointed, darting about.

'I can't get over to Surrey Hills until Thursday,' Jean says. 'But I'll give Mr Peart a ring. He'll check their sheets.' She passes her fingers through her hair, looking at the floor. 'Dear brother. Dear brother! Is it possible you've been diddled?'

—

I am alone in the church in the valley, where people once worshipped and sang. It takes me an hour or more to pack up and get on the road back to Melbourne. Stove to wipe, refrigerator to empty and defrost, muddy carpets to vacuum with the decrepit cleaner from my marriage now three years gone. Computer to pack, printer to disassemble and box and put in a plastic garbage bag against the dust of the road. Water to turn off at the tank, gas at the gas bottle under the wattles behind the kitchen.

Axe and saw, spade and rake to stack in the church's cluttered porch, where the smell of mower and drying grass and petrol mixes with the intimate smell of mice. And then I load the Nissan – food, sports bag full of clothes, a satchel of books. Then I fasten the stays of the tonneau cover, take a final walk around the church, and come in again to saunter and pry through the rooms, pulling leads from power-points, turning off the electricity at the fuse box in the porch.

With no lights burning, the church settles back into its corners and late-day darkness. The pallor from the southern windows creeps in evenly, just a rouging of illumination on the looming bulk of the old wardrobe, the pale plane of the bed, the rough-hewn pillar of the wood-box near the door.

I go to the old bookshelves tacked to the dark-panelled wall near the bed. On the top shelf the little gold travelling clock ticks its strutting advance into time. I take it in my hand, turn it over. It is Alex Cumming's clock. I know it comes to us from somewhere years ago. I seem to have known it all my life, but not looked at it closely, not thought about it. It is always there in our houses. Someone always winds it. I can see it in the corner of the mantelpiece near the bookcase at Cicero Street. Did I inherit it after Louise died? I hadn't thought about it – but I think so. The thin silver plate on its leather case says: 'ALEX CUMMING –

Winner Invitation Singles Championship New South Wales Hardcourt Championships – Dubbo, 1933'.

I prop a boot on the edge of the fireplace, thinking. This clock has been present somewhere in my life for as long as I can remember. I raise it to my ear, listen to the steady foxtrot of its movement. The church wraps its silence and dark around me. I study the clock's square, implacable face, its square numerals. 'Made in USA' it says. Then I wind it, feeling the tug of the spring at each turn. I set it down again on the shelf, its tick strutting in the dimness.

I look to the door, wait listening a few more moments to the clock. I feel a pinpoint of delight, an expectation of my return in a fortnight or so, in thinking of the clock's steady ticking running on in the silent church for tomorrow and the next day in my absence. I will be driving the Melbourne traffic and walking the corridors to my office while the clock's slow nodding runs behind the empty church's spaces of air and light and reaches out towards its trees filtering the sun in the yard.

It's becoming a small duty I perform at every departure from the valley. Sometimes as I perform it I could swear that someone watches me from the shadows.

—

I know it all now. Mr Peart at the bank turns up nothing. Cec says he always knew he wouldn't. Candles and Chris have just moved up to the milk-bar and the coaching job at Nhill, but they know about David. Louise talks to them on the phone. No one has told Flute yet. Mr Peart says it's hard to know how much is missing unless Des has his own record of earnings or a full set of receipts. Then he asks Jean and Cec if they want to make it a police matter. They say no, not at the moment. That's why we all go to Mont Albert to see Joyce while David is out. That's when Alistair and I see Joyce crying, but we don't know why she's crying. We've never seen her cry like this, so abandoned, in front of everyone.

—

I told them no, Jean says. I remember her words, husky and compelling. But she sounds as though she doesn't know what to do. I told Mr Peart no, too, she says. I told them all we don't want to take it further. But they rang. Police station Camberwell here, they said. I told them no. But they still said they wanted to have a talk to him. They came round to collect him about half past six. Hell!

We are all at Mont Albert again. It's just after tea on this hot December night. The cicadas are cutting the air into shreds in the trees along the street. The chooks have been in bed in the dark corners of the pen up the back since six o'clock. Louise asks me to take Little Gwenda and Little Ian up there to have a look. But I know she's waiting for something. I know she wants to be ready to think. Then she decides she'll come too. We peer in at the chooks, white leghorns, wrapped up like tight sheets on the perches. Then we can hear voices, so we head back to the house.

Everyone is at the back door. David is home. He's tried to come in the back way without being seen, but he's met Joyce looking for Little Gwenda and Little Ian. Now Jean and Cec are there. Des is there, just inside the door. Will is beside him, tamping down his pipe. He doesn't say much unless someone asks him. I think he thinks this is not his family, but he's looking at David.

David is quiet. He looks hot and greasy. He looks used. He wants to go inside and lie down, he says. But Joyce is crying again. As he turns we see David's right eye is red and puffed, nearly closed. Joyce puts an arm around him and he starts to cry. Joyce opens the flywire door and pushes David inside. They go into the dark side of the house away from the kitchen. My father Will pulls Des closer to him to let them past. Des's face is pointed with attention, with listening.

'Just a few questions,' Cec says, looking around at Jean and then at Will and Louise. 'And his eye is almost closed up? Just a little talk?' He looks at Jean. 'I don't like this. It's nice of them to deliver him back, isn't it.' He snarls and kicks at the edge of the concrete. Then he seems to shed something. His face changes. 'But what do you reckon? It's all about comeuppance? Most of us get our comeuppance in the end, don't we!'

My mother's voice surprises everyone. She is looking at Jean. It seems a long time ago now. She still holds Little Ian's hand. 'Yes,' she is saying in the sudden quiet that lets the evening's sounds in again. 'Yes, the trouble is that everyone around David gets their comeuppance too. That's the rub.'

—

I'm yawning, after an almost sleepless night with Jesse, but I'm listening, seeing Louise's picture as she speaks. She's tired too, at the end of the school year, but her eyes dance there on the Cicero Street veranda as the afternoon sun probes the weatherboards. She has to touch people. Big Ross – there he is, I can see him as she talks about him – sometimes a laughing stock, barely capable of a written sentence, restive, short concentration span, slow, but fascinated with trains and railways. His eyes go to the ceiling in frustration and failure during class work, Louise says. But into the seat beside him slides Little Ian, the brightest kid in the school, small and bespectacled, non-physical, non-sporting. He nudges Ross over in the desk and curls his head around the blank page to help Big Ross make his sentences. Louise knows to let the process run, sees the relief in Ross's eyes to find that someone has come to him. She knows he comes to Little Ian's aid in the rough and tumble of the schoolyard.

She has to teach, my mother – has to touch people, has to watch them bloom. She tells me about it and for a moment she is close to tears. Then she breaks free of it and goes to make a cup of tea.

—

Yes, I've found Pat Friar again.

One night six years after he goes to the grammar school, I see someone balancing a plate and a cup in the queue at the university caf. God, it's Pat all right. I can't miss the nose and chin and the way his dark hair falls straight past his ears. Older, darker round the eyes, more muscly – but it's Pat. We can feel our grins slide across our faces.

He's doing Engineering. We talk at the caf table, the steam rising

126

behind us from the bain-maries, the babble of voices around us, the lights, the awareness of the cold outside. It's as though we can both still read each other's signs. But there are lectures to get to. He'll ring me soon.

He does ring two days later. So we're mates again. Not long after he comes with me in the little Consul to hear Des play at the jazz club above the river in Kew.

—

There is no future. The world has taken us over, Patricia and me, Susan and Jesse, and grinds on into new grey days without consulting us.

I have been looking for it in my tired, dispirited way. Real estate. House after house, living place after living place. I turn the pages. Real estate, alphabetically by suburb. Another page. Then, starting out from among them all, there it is, as though it is meant to swim up to my eye. 'Heathmont. 8 Roomed Family Home'. It stabs me to see it. I look up to the ceiling, then out the window. Waste and loss. All these years.

Each description stabs me. Spacious and attractive brick veneer property looking to Dandenongs, with additional rear unit. Handy to schools in pleasant residential area. Nicely established garden. It is dismemberment. I know all these corners. I am invested in them. We all are invested in them, where the rear unit – 'the rear unit'? – backs towards the sugar gums, where the leaves gather, where the spoutings fill and I lean from the ladder clearing them and look up to see the grey tiles running to a sky of surprising blue, where Susan and her friend Jeanie skip with their ropes below me on the side lawn, their skirts and pigtails flying, their figures impressed in leaping shadows on the grass by the high summer sun, their breathless chanting losing itself against the fence and the privet – their sharp, girlish voices singing:

> 'Red, white and blue.
> The boys kissed you,
> Took you to the pictures,
> And undressed you . . .'

But the advertisement persists. The main home includes lounge room, modern kitchen, dining room with excellent built-in fittings, 4 bedrooms, bathroom and two int. toilets. Rear unit comprises attractive living room with free-standing metal fireplace, small bedroom with int. toilet. Wall to wall carpet. Large carport area with broad drive. Vacant possession. Inspection welcome. $78,000.

After all the years, after all the laughs, the overcast mornings, sickbeds, Christmas tinsel, after the chirping cacophony of Susan and Jesse at the meal table excited about the new swing beyond the clothes-line, after the eyes of friends in our rooms, cradling drinks in our glasses. $78,000 for four lives sundered. It is the end of us in words in a newspaper.

When I slowly reel into the kitchen with the paper Patricia is sitting in the alcove in semi-darkness, a mug at her elbow, chin in palms, staring ahead.

'Did you see this?' I ask.

'Yes,' she says tonelessly. 'Jesse showed me. A desirable dwelling, eh?' She gives me a tired, phlegmatic smile and stares ahead again. Perhaps we're beyond feeling. Perhaps it's possible to sail beyond feeling and find that it has all been a mistaken dream.

The telephone cuts into my thought. Patricia starts too, then her eyes sweep the walls slowly, her mouth setting. She makes no move, so I pick up the receiver. It is the agent's voice – fruity, unctuous. Would it be at all possible to bring some prospective buyers through tomorrow morning? Yes, I say, of course. Yes.

It must be the last, saddest echo of a family.

—

It's when I'm a young man and I wear a sports coat. It's at the club in the rising street above the river in Kew. It's after I bump into Pat Friar again at the university. He's with me again. We've come in my little Consul. It's parked a few cars up the hill in the shadows of street trees in the cicada twilight.

Pat and I are here to hear Des play, to watch the girls who we fear and yearn for, perhaps to dance. I can see Pat likes it. It's the first time he's been here. There's been a bit of dancing and there might be dancing again later too, but at the club it's mainly listeners. It's when Des and Charlie, and Don on the bass, and ferrety, small Mark under his boater hat behind the spangled drums can let themselves out, slide in for proper breaks, then step out again, the clapping following them. They experiment, follow trails, have conversations with each other – sax and piano, sax and bass, Charlie's rolling voice and Des's piano.

But what am I seeing? It's Betty. She's left us to go back and sit at a table with a couple I don't know on the other side of the band. Now, she's on her feet, crossing the floor in front of the stage. She looks over at us, a grin on her face, and gives us a wave as she gets to the three short steps. Des is unaware. The band is deep into 'Bye Bye Blackbird'. He has finished his break and is leaning back at the piano listening to Charlie singing. The notes descend in their quickstep entreaty.

It's a cameo. I know already what Betty will do – and it fills my heart. She mounts the three steps, long and white in her sheath dress. Before he knows it she has Des by the shoulders, whispers to him, gives him a quick kiss, raises him from the stool, leads him to the steps, helps him feel his way down them, one foot, another, down to the open floor. She turns, holding Des's hand, then takes him in her arms and they dance. I hear voices as I watch them. I hear Auntie Jean saying: 'I hope Betty doesn't lead him on.' I can smell the beer on David's breath, hear him saying in his hammy voice: 'Go for it boy!' And I see Des shrunk into the stove corner, saying 'Don't worry about me . . . Don't worry about me.'

But Betty and Des are dancing close. Des is balanced, sweeping round, trusting Betty's guide. It says they've been practising on the quiet. Betty has coached Des to this moment. Now Charlie is on the sax. He's watching, half-smiling as he plays. He waits, playing, looking down on Betty and Des, waits the moment, then inserts a trill, just a touch of 'You Are My Sunshine' then flashes back to 'Lover Please Be Tender' on the sax. There's a rumble of glad laughter from the jazz crowd.

Des is complete, taller than I've ever seen him, controlled. His head nuzzles Betty. He speaks into her ear. Their bodies twine and turn together. They kiss. They dance. They kiss again. They are lovers, I know. I hear my mother's lament that Des might never marry. Might never marry. I hear my own voice countermanding, saying: 'No need for marrying.' My thoughts catch fire from the watchers' eyes among the jazz crowd and Pat's leaning face beaming at me and his mouth saying: 'They're an item, aren't they. They're an item.'

The band is winding up the song. Betty relinquishes Des's long, thin body, leads him to the steps again. She is beautiful in her white sheath dress. She is a woman direct and dignified. She no longer seems to belong to the little Austin that used to putter away from the Mont Albert house when Pearlie was alive.

I watch Des. Betty leaves him at the piano. He feels for its shoulders, its music rack, makes contact, sits down. Charlie comes to him to laugh and speak with a happy passion. He points a warning finger at Des, then laughs again, his head going back. Des reaches for a handkerchief, drags it out, mops his forehead, wipes his mouth and chin, then sits back trailing the white handkerchief in his fingers, happier than I've ever seen.

—

Is it that I catch a glimpse of the racquets, three of them, where Jesse has stacked them in the corner in the Hawthorn bedroom? Is it those oval reminders? I am proffered a deep, slightly scratchy voice – it is close by – and yet I don't know how I come by it. Then I hear the words and know it is Mr Tremearne, solicitor. It's as if he is in the room. I can hear pages being shuffled. 'From what I've been told,' he is saying, 'this is something that will be to your benefit and peace of mind . . . to your benefit and peace of mind . . . your peace of mind . . .' The voice fades and my eyes reel momentarily in the light from the window. The chill comes to my heart, and yet I seem to see a vista ahead. I see the outlines of the three racquets in the dim corner, their heads like interleaved oval reminders of something I should know.

—

Sydney has its Harbour

'Sydney has its harbour, which I love and which I know you love,' says my father Will, the glass of beer in his hand, the light coming in behind him to catch the spines of the books beside the fireplace. 'But Melbourne has its hills, which I have long ago also come to love.' He leans towards Bob Bristow confidentially, brow knitted exaggeratedly by the beer. 'In fact, to make the ideal city we'd need to string the Dandenongs across that stretch running out to Parramatta and south as far as Camden, say. Superimpose the Melbourne hills on Sydney! Then we'd have everything!' He laughs. Bob Bristow laughs.

Louise chuckles. 'There's an admission from a Sydneysider, Bob!' she says. 'There's a confession!' Bob Bristow is my father's Sydney friend from the rowing years, down for the holidays. He has a glass eye now where shrapnel spattering in the Western Desert took his sight during the War. He is a teacher of English. He sits in his slacks and open-necked shirt near the window at the Emerald shack. Our Emerald shack on its three acres comes after the Upwey shack, and the Upwey shack follows the Kallista block under its deep bracken. They are Will's shacks. They are his answer to the absence of Sydney and its bright water. Alistair and Greg are somewhere along the cloudy ridge picking blackberries for pocket money. I sit in the threadbare arm chair. I'm fond of Bob Bristow. I have fingered his Anzac Rising Sun badge during the War when he leaves his battle jacket over the chair at Cicero Street. Then he has two good eyes. I like to hear Louise and Will talking to Bob, see their eyes shining with pleasure at seeing him again. Bob is younger than either of them.

—

The secret of fire, I think, is surreptitious air, of interstices between sticks, between logs. I watch the flames at first lick the twigs, as if they might not go on. Then they feel the secret draft round the back. They firm their hold, they crackle. Then a short subsidence, then a building to a territorial yellowness and warmth, yellow and orange and rising, blanketing to themselves, certain, steady. So, lift a fire to revive it. So, if necessary kick it to command new surfaces to settle on each other.

133

I listen to the flames hushing to each other in the steady fireplace that doesn't move, but seems to waver in the light. I sit looking into the fire. How many fires have I watched?

What is the secret of music? Beautiful Ellen and music go together in my mind. What has Ellen in her bathers, dipping her toe in the water – I can see those beautiful long legs reflected at the edge of the pool – got to do with music? I weep inwardly for her when I think of it. Where is she now? Why do I hear music when I think of her plaits and her shoulders? What has music to do with writing? Why do I want Ellen to read what I've written, even if she doesn't know I know she's read it. Why do I want her eyes at least to have seen it? Will we ever meet and talk without anyone else near, while the light changes, while the trams keen up the hill? Where is Ellen now? We have never really met and talked, beyond lunch with all the others on the grass at school. We've never had hours together, although against hope I've dwelt on those dark, nervous eyes, that bubbling laugh.

—

I am thinking under my eyelids. I find I am thinking of my mother. Has she died? I am not sure, as I lie in this limbo of time in the hospital. My eyes will not open. But Louise must be dead. Slowly, it comes to me. Slowly I can see the detail of it.

Louise, my mother, is dead. Betty is dead long before her – so young. Des in his white shirt is dead. And Frank and Flute and Candles. So Louise has gone – and so has Will. I am parentless. My eyes are closed with sand. Parentless at forty-seven. I am sure now. It is the future.

I hear instruments clash in a stainless-steel dish. I can feel the morphine warm in my toes and washing like a tepid sea around the intricate workings of my gut. Blessed morphine. I now have no gall bladder. I see the warm sea washing its space. The sea I know is pink and smells like mouthwash. I can feel the fledgling birds moving around in my wound, hear the dripping of my blood in the loops of tubing. The white walls rear up before me like a screen where body parts writhe and change colour.

I am parentless, I think, but I don't care. My eyes are closed. Rosa will come. Is it Rosa? I will open my eyes to find her face leaning down to me. It is the future.

—

Will I become strange Uncle Tim who lives by himself? Is that what will happen?

All this time I spend thinking dismays me. Sometimes I can sense Rosa's orange circles there and it gives me hope. But other times I cannot reach her. I think in shadows. All this time devoted to thought that leads down, down. Susan and Patricia will be in Frankston in a kitchen where there is sun and voices when Jesse visits them. But there are no voices here – nor likely to be. I have been slumped here in the beanbag now for an hour trying to draw a plan that shows all of us, that sets us out as characters each with our own special sadness about the splitting up. I loll there, trying to accept that now I have lost the four people I hold dear. Will Rosa come with her warm circles? I can't reach her. I have let the shadows of the afternoon deepen through the house. I have not strained upright, groaning, from the beanbag to switch on the light. It is better without light. Here I am, pitying myself in the shadows, I tell myself. I could almost laugh.

I see Jesse's face, one weekend when he comes to visit me. He doesn't stay overnight. He seldom does – and it is nine months before Susan stays with me for a weekend. Jesse's face is scouting, urgent to assure itself that together we have covered the necessary ground. I can see from his slow blink that spells conclusion that he can't wait to go again, to return to his students' house shared with voices and laughter in Brunswick, in a narrow, tucked-away street lined with an assortment of cars and utes, their left tyres riding up on the hot bitumen footpath.

I do all this thinking back. I think in the shower, the creepers of water curling round my mouth. I sit and think at the desk. Going to do something else, I subside into the chair as I pass it and fall into thinking. It is not good. Will Rosa come? Sometimes I lose faith. Sometimes, sitting or slouching there, it seems that I exist only to be alone and to think, that that is why I get up and have breakfast, shave, shit, brush teeth – in order to prepare myself for a day finding a corner in shadow to think back, to see the faces, to hear the voices, to wonder how this has happened, to wonder who I am now, who I was then.

Am I becoming strange Uncle Tim whose marriage broke down and who lives by himself? I can hear my two nephews and three nieces thinking it to themselves and asking Alistair and Greg about me. I can hear Alistair saying to me in the car, the door ajar before I get out: 'Watch yourself, boyo. You have to move on, don't forget. Everything passes. You'll move on eventually. You will, don't worry. Pastures new!'

Yes, I hear myself saying, but currently I ain't got a dream that's workin'.

—

It's David's words I hear again.

I have lived now for forty-six years. I am here again, thinking back, finding the threads, following them where they turn, seeing the path they take all the way to my feet. I am fearful. I am marvelling. The days seem to go on deepening my wisdom, but I have never been wise enough, it seems. How can I not have reached behind the cruel, cutting truth of those words until now?

It's David's voice I hear. My heart beats chill again with the same dismay. David has never had goodwill in his words for me. But now it's my name and my mother's name on Uncle David's lips that I'm catching again. It's the flaking weatherboards of the old storeroom at Mont Albert that I see, and Joyce's hair spilling over her face, her shoulder backed against the wall, down, down on the ground. I can feel again the wire handle of the billy weighing in my hand, hear my own holding of breath.

It's David's words: '. . . dear little teacher Louise, eh? . . . what little secrets has she been hiding? Eh? . . . poor bloody Tim, eh, who can't even get out of his own way? What about little Tim?' It's David's words.

Ah, a tree to make one wise. A tree tall and unequivocal against the sky, against the slow energy of the days.

Flute is gone, the refrain in my head is saying. Flute is gone.

Frank, Flute's son, is driving us in the old Holden. It's the day of the funeral. We've been at the cemetery. Now, we have turned off the side road that runs to Swan Hill and onto the highway for a few yards before we will turn again and cross the railway near the silos and head to the new acres that Flute and Frank bought only last June on the other side of the town. Frank wants to show us. Jean is with us, sitting with feet either side of the differential's hump in the back. Des sits beside her in the driver's side corner. Behind me in the back is Louise.

There have been a few moments of silence, but they don't last. We are glad to be joined again after all this time. I'm trying to remember, in fact, whether this little congregation has ever occurred before. Have I been with Louise, Jean, Des and Frank together? These are my close people. I can feel an understanding that walks blithely through time and absence to bind us. Why have I been separated from them? I feel I have come home and have forgotten what home is like. In our thoughts runs a refrain. 'Flute is gone,' it says quietly. 'Now Flute is gone.' And yet we want to talk about other things, to test each other, to remind ourselves of our voices, of our Barnes body language.

It is crackling January. The day is bright, but not too hot. I look at the detritus under the mallee as we pass the roadside ridges running to the crop land and I hear Flute's voice again from a day far away: '. . . Won't do him any harm . . . won't do him any harm'.

'Oh, yes, Jean. Jean?' Frank says suddenly. 'Jean. That's the Fishers' place down that drive. Sugar gums. Remember?'

'Ollie Fisher, by cripes,' says Des's singing voice from the back. We hear him slap his knee.

'Yes,' says Jean. 'Young Ollie. Everything happened to him. Everything! He'd tell you, and you couldn't believe it. Is he up at Echuca now? He and Evie? Is that right? They're still together?'

'I think he's still up the river,' Frank says. 'And they're still together all right. They'll never be apart.' The Holden chugs on. The other four are dwelling in their thoughts of Ollie and Evie. I don't know them. I've merely heard people mention them.

'Yes, there's nothing that can't happen to Ollie,' Frank says suddenly – and he laughs. As he curls his arm round the steering wheel he turns to engage the eyes of the three in the back, looks as if he's about to say more. But then he just smiles, winking briefly at Jean, and turns back to his driving. His smile still hangs around his mouth. The big Holden chugs on. I can hear each piston-stroke tick home.

'I can't work it out. Ollie and Evie! How did they get into this?' Frank says suddenly. 'A funeral! And Ollie and Evie take it over! Funerals! Here we are, talking about those two. And Dad's gone.' He pauses, changes his grip on the wheel. 'It's strange, strange . . . I can't figure it. What're we doing laughing? But it takes us over all the old ground again, I suppose. And Dad's gone. Dad is gone.' We can hear in his voice's slight break the double edge of grief and then the need for new ways, the sadness and yet the cementing of the past to make sure that we know that it happened and was good. We're all feeling it. I can still see the tautening velveteen cords that lower Flute's coffin into the earth this morning, only this morning, and here we are. Five people in a car, laughing through our tears.

Frank slumps back as he drives, looks to the front. Then he rouses out of his grief, sits further forward, turns half on to the three in the back seat. 'You know how Ollie and Evie were always made for each other,' he says. 'No one else ever entered into it. Not even close. Well, Ollie told me one night, hot weather, they're fucking there on the bed and suddenly they hear a little voice. Yeah, come on Dad. You can beat her. You can beat her. It was Tommie – remember little Tommie – about three years old. Standing there in his pyjamas. Came out for a drink of water. Bloody 'ell!'

We hear Jean's hissing laugh and then throaty cough. Des gives two loud ha-ha's. Louise bubbles with a laugh and then hums.

Jean is not often trumped by a story, but she is by this one. 'Oh to be Ollie!' is all she says. She falls silent. I love them all. They are sitting around me, my close people.

I think of Jesse and Susan back at the house with Marie and Candles. I think of Patricia standing formal among them, not having the keys to reach them with her words. It's very hard for her.

—

Secrets? Truths?

The secret of the body is to risk it, I think, to challenge it again and again climbing the hill in the deep bush, on the tennis court when you don't think you can breathe again, in the sea, up the leaning volcano's rim, through the forest of beech, in the paddock, riding the edge of the ocean. Listen to the heartbeat, listen to the breathing. But my body's an old rind now. I look at the body's marks, guess how long it has to go. I finger the scar from the operation and remember that my body has been a servant invaded. My fingers encounter a fine valley under the skin all along the wound and into the little well in my side where the drain tube came out. I remember.

I must give my old rind some time. I must give it leeway. Sometimes my body speaks to me like a voice coming out of the ground. It often says, yes, I can go further with you. Sometimes it says no. Then I must wait for things to turn over, for my limbs to signal all right again. Look at my scars, my body says, here where the sharpened nail on the billycart went through this finger, here where the orange-peeling knife sliced, or this knot in the elbow where the arm was jammed between the bricks and the steel of the ladder as I plunged, this knot that was huge, blue, in the hospital, and then turned butter-yellow and purple with bruising. I look at this arm that was saved. Then there's this scar on the forehead running up to the head's crown where straightening up under the tree in the dark I ripped open the skin on the sawn branch and blood filled my glasses. Or here, where the T-tube went in to gather the bile, and this ghostly line a foot long where the scalpel ran, the blood following, where the stitches made a black-lipped purse. Please wait a while, my body says: please bear these assaults in mind. I can hear it.

The body's secrets. Give me a day, it says. Give me time to think about that pounding and leaning across the tennis court yesterday, the heat, the cicadas ringing along the river, the tree-shadow rubbing the baseline, the sun prying into my cheeks and the corner near the ears, searing my neck and the backs of my calves as I serve. Give me a day to think about it.

The secret of nature is trust. This grey thrush will come perching on my spade, I tell myself. And it does, regarding me with its eye. It is my doppelganger. The forest will open to me. It settles and settles contemptuously. The platypus will surface for me, and float as a stick, and disappear again in the river like a dark sleight of hand. The church trusts the valley and its trees, its ibis, its snakes, its water. It draws miracles to itself. I feel that God and past parishioners watch me from the wattles when I paint it. I can feel that they bless me, even though I blaspheme as I slip coming down the ladder.

The secret of the morning is to chant the day into being like the Navajo, even as the pale slice of the moon glides through thin cloud before the dawn, waiting for the light.

There are mysteries, too, in time and distance. I think the secret of time is what the future was and what the past will be. The trees I can see on the far slope of the hill speak of what has happened and what will happen. They perch on their shadows and wait in the hot stillness. Or sometimes the rank upon rank of lit cloud declining to the afternoon's horizon seem to contain aeons of time. Or I am watching the light slip around the rim of the dead volcanic cone where centuries have passed, will pass, over the scoria and the moss. When I am dead, the cloud shadows, the light, the faraway mythical trees will remain as on this listening spring day. The thought of that fills me with sorrow and yet a great content.

Sometimes I lie there on the bed and look down the long white deck of my body, over my skin and hair to my toes. It is close and hot in the room. The shadows themselves touch me, draping themselves from the dark spaces under the desk, from the square dark of the bookshelves and the liquid fall of the curtains. Shadows touching skin feel like warm smoke.

I haven't realised until now that it is to you I'm confiding, Rosa. I'm writing this to you, and yet you don't even know me yet. My word processor breathes and my fingers will tap it, making sounds like drops of water searching on slate. Those sounds and the words that come will find you.

—

I come upon my own letter. Can I believe now what I wrote then? How has it survived? Alistair must have kept it, tucked it away in the book. I wince at it now, when I read the words on the page. Who was I then? When Patricia and I were supposed to be rocks of certainty, the children circling us like trusting seals, seeking our eyes?

> Hazlitt St,
> Heathmont,
> Tues. 21 April, 1965

Dear Alistair and Deirdre,

Greetings, sun-tanned brother and sister-in-law! Make the most of Queensland while you may. Things are decidedly cooler inch by inch down here. The sun creeps just a bit further north along the Dandenongs each morning. One frost, more to follow soon?

Thanks for the birthday book. I've heard of John Gale, but haven't read anything of him, so *Clean Young Englishman* will be an interesting introduction. I say will be because I haven't had much spare reading time or energy. I've been 'volunteered' – I seem to remember that was the Army word – to edit most of the June and July issues of *River Country*. That, together with the normal inroads of student marking, has kept me busy every night. I'm afraid the creative energies that are siphoned off in editing tend to take some of the bloom from writing for the magazine for the time being. I will be pleased to see the end of it, although it's good experience.

Fancy being 29 yar-old! How many yars've I got left? Yars and yars, I hope. I only feel that age last thing at night, or for the first 5 minutes of wakefulness on some weekday mornings. Ho hum. Greg dropped in at about 9.45 pm on his way home from a guitar lesson the other night to find us in bed, me sitting up reading proof, Patricia already asleep. Greg was all aglow with 20 yar-old, child-less, art course sort of enthusiasm and oblivious of the hour. I don't know just how enthusiastically Patricia was welcoming his visit. He had some of his folio with him. We laid it out in the lounge – he's really got a talent with the brush, you know, our brother. At the moment it's going into brooding city landscapes.

Why were we so early abed when Greg arrived?

(a) because the night before I had taken some of the students to hear Yevtushenko read at Festival Hall. Patricia decided not to come although next door had offered to baby-sit. Yevtushenko is just a pretext for the Left to strut its stuff, according to Patricia. Boy, she missed something. A most moving experience that I can't detail here, with the place in darkness virtually and the red dots of thousands of cigarettes pulsing on and off among the sea of faces across Festival Hall – and then, there was Alan Edwards the Sydney actor, stepping to the table round the potted shrubs on the stage, then Dame Judith Anderson (also taking the long way round), then Frank Hardy (long way round), then a Jewish actress (long way), then a Russian interpreter (long way) and then Yevtushenko himself, who burst straight through the branches onto the stage. Theatrical? Typical? No one cared. Great readings – Hardy reading the English – Babiy Yar. Dame Judith with the City of Yes and No. Yevtushenko following with the Russian each time – the rumbling, rolling 'r' sounds. Some Nazis in the audience called out Heil Hitler at one stage. It stopped Yevtushenko for a moment – his concern was obvious – and it brought a comment from him later. Got home at about 2 am. Weary, but with a lasting impression of Yevtushenko and Russia – for good and bad, and despite the nationalist and propagandist element! End of first reason.

(b) because there's no longer any such thing as sleeping-in for this household. Susan and Jesse wake us up at first light every morning. The ritual runs thus: sun shows first misty-gold perimeter over Dandenongs (as I said each morning a bit further north along the ridge); Patricia and I sleep on. But little Jesse quits his virtuous three-and-a-half-year-old couch, and proceeds to let down side of Susan's cot and get her out of it, if she has not already performed this feat herself. It is done thus-wise. I know because I hid round the door one Saturday morning and watched the operation: Jesse, with considerable difficulty, brings chair to side of Susan's cot, and with suitable grunts and instructions pulls and half-lifts Susan onto chair. Susan has no difficulty in sliding to floor from chair. Both children, with expectant faces, patter through rooms to our bedroom, where Susan is cunningly placed to the fore. Parents in their half-conscious state hear 'Goodmorning' from Jesse, and detect Susan already trying to climb up bedclothes with wet nap smelling as sharp as ammonia. Parents reluctantly pull children into bed so that they won't catch cold, Susan chuckling with delight and settling her wet, stinking tail just short of father's face, while Jesse asks for a 'snuggle down'. This entails raising the bedclothes into a tent so that both children can enter it and investigate our lower limbs, ankles, toes, while allowing any remaining warmth to escape the bed. Father then realises that discretion – or surrender – is better part of valour and makes cup of tea, then carries Susan down dew-drenched front lawn to collect milk and paper. If milkman's horse not yet out of sight we watch that or else observe pigeons flying against the sunrise. End of second and I'm afraid chronic reason for early to bed.

Well – always say well at the ends of letters – it indicates sincerity and that there is more that one could say but can't at this juncture. Well, 'nuff of this. Thanks again for wishes and book. See you on your return. Have a swim for us in the meantime.

Love to you both,

Tim and Patricia (and Jesse and Susan)

It has become one of the echoes now. Do the echoes of a family ever cease? Will the sad joy ever be silenced?

—

It is the sea that has hold of me, Rosa. The sea that runs its horizon across my thoughts, that takes down the knot of my concern into its canyons and grottoes, takes it down and down in time until it is gone.

143

I have speared the one good fish in the sea's rooms – a sweep. Now I climb the cliff. For today the ocean has finished with me. The rope of the old Army bag, with the big fish in it, the fins, the mask, eats into my shoulder and the spear feels heavier. The sea sobs below me now into the sand, the sky runs its lips along the cliff scrub above. I reach the tussocks and I'm sweating, heart clamouring. I stop and slide the bag off my shoulder. I turn on the track to look back to the sea playing with the wave platform, to the swells coming in on the beach in that corner where the whiting gather and where further along on sunny mornings I look from the cliff and see rays moving like shadows just behind the break.

Now as I look out there's no ship on the horizon, no cray boat beating home to Port Chalice. The Twelve Apostles have glued themselves to the cliffs halfway to Moonlight Head. They might have been painted into the land by the sun's last light. I shoulder the bag again, take up the silver spear. There's no one, Rosa, as I mount and breathe up the steepening track. There's no one as I climb out of the cliff's curve and see the truck silhouetted against the sky, no one as I fish car keys from behind a tyre, load the things into the truck, no one as I climb out of togs and step into the dry warmth of shorts. Not a car on the grey-sand track, nor on the road astounded by the last light, the guide posts standing up white against the absorbent scrub. Only the twin figures of two big grey kangaroos looping away towards the she-oaks, ears and shoulders pink as they bound. There's no one on the road leading down into Port Chalice. As I descend towards the creek the little town is laid out in lights across the leeward slope of the cliffs, still, silent, as if uninhabited. Behind me the sea is pale blue under a brown-purple haze, and ahead, appearing like a new face above the run of trees is the yellow moon, Rosa, the change of guard. It follows me home, skipping the hills' flanks, beaming through the mesh of gum branches.

Hours later, after I've eaten, when the fire is a city of coals, Rosa, when the fish, washed at the tap, is freezing in the fridge, I come out with gloves, mask and fins to wash them at the tank. The moon is throwing itself in a white burning against the building, lighting the whole valley and its thin scarves of mist. There is absolute silence. Then I hear the waves sob from way down near the Gibson Steps. Not a dark leaf moves in the boobiallas.

That's what it is like, Rosa. The ocean does not care for me. It has finished with me. The sea and the land are bigger than all my thoughts, bigger than my significance, my very existence. It is humbling. But someone has given land and sea to me as gifts, and I have accepted them. That's how it feels.

—

I am not a good man. Like King John, I have my little ways.

I don't change both sheets on the double bed. I change one only and the pillow slips and that's it. Now that I'm alone I use both sides of the bed in turn. I even smell the pillow slips sometimes to see if in fact they need changing. I sometimes pick my nose when I'm tired and lonely and when no one is about.

I am not a good man. I eat the wrong things. I sometimes have ice cream, sometimes cheese. I eat chocolate when I come in cold and stiff from the garden in winter, or from hauling out grey firewood down the valley in the raking, frigid wind and humping it into the truck. My body seems to crave chocolate – it calls for fat around my bones to take away the brittleness and cold.

I am not a good man. I drive through a red light. I've reached the big intersection where the through road to the city hives off. I'm on the way home from the Institute and I've detoured to drop off the little heater to Susan at her flat. I stop at the red light. It is a week night – no one about, no headlights edging their way round the bend, no cars slipping from the folds of the hills towards the city. Just the concrete kerbs, the white lines, the acres of bitumen with its arrows, yellow light poles and the lit fronts of houses along the highway. All asleep. Why not slip through? I let in the clutch and drive soberly across. No one to watch.

I am not a good man. I let things go. I have let go my wife and my marriage. I have let go my children and they are somewhere off in the distance. I see them like two figures in the light out there, with what look like dark gowns swirling about them, moving off, always moving off. Sometimes they turn as though they are looking back to me, but they are so far away I can't be sure. It is in the nature of things that they should go, but not because of separation. For years I try to hold to Patricia and to them. But I have to give up in the end, have to watch the traces of love unravel.

I am not a good man. Sometimes I feel an isolate, a failure. Like King John, I imagine that no one has had a word for me for day upon day. It's not true, and yet if I wake in the night I feel alone. I find myself deep in some of the bitterness with Patricia. I find I'm reliving all of us sitting in the little room that the counsellor has at the Family Centre. Jesse's face is pursed with strain. He sits with his two hands gripped between his knees. Susan is dry-mouthed and gulping with the horror of separation and what it means – the sale of the house she calls home, the departure of Jesse for university. Who will she confide in then? She will live with her mother, although she says through her tears that she will never make a choice between her parents. In these half-waking dreams I see Patricia sitting well back in the chair, recoiling from the sneakers of the counsellor thrust towards her as she lolls, legs extended, papers in hand, and listens to each of us in turn. Patricia's face says that she is keeping her distance from these proceedings, from these elementary questions to which anyone would know the answers, and that she needs no opinion, just advice about the steps through which the marriage will totter to its end.

Rosa, it's you I can sense close to me again. I seem to have no doubt about confiding these things to you. It must be to you that I have been speaking. I am not a good man. I am an inveterate throat-clearer. I wonder sometimes whether it is physical or mental, my need to clear my throat, to keep my voice pure. I know that sometimes I use that throat-clearing to think, to prepare what I am thinking or going to say. Sometimes I do it as a nervous protection. But much of the time there is a quid of mucous waiting to be cleared, it seems, from the top of my voice box. I have to curl away at it, fish for it, loosen it. Then a slight cough and a swallow. Where does that come from?

I wonder. Am I a bad man condemned to be alone? And anyway, is being alone a condemnation? I have a strong urge to be alone to hear my voice, to write, to set things down. Solitude. There are times when I seem to have much wisdom to declare. Then I hasten to hear my voice. I seem to have so many questions to ask. Is it the Spiritus Mundi that wraps its arm about me, that stands in the shadows when I come home from the cliffs at 10pm and step from the truck into a moonlight so clear and still that from the steeped boobiallas near the gate I can already hear Alex Cumming's trophy clock ticking on the thin shelf inside the church?

—

I hear the voices. I'm aware of the heads near me in dim outline. I am somehow accompanying them as they travel. And yet it is not strange. I'm working after lunch lopping the wattles and boobiallas, then cutting up the larger branches with the axe, the afternoon waiting about me and up the valley to where it is closed off by the forest. The bull calves watch me from the far fence, slobbering and head-shaking and nudging each other with jet-black flanks and curly-haired foreheads, probing idly for weaknesses in each other with their shoulders, trying to knock each other off balance like teenage boys. As I work I slowly become more conscious of it against the beating of my blood, against the plunging of my breath. I seem suddenly to be hearing voices more sharply – or perhaps it's that they have been there for some time and I am now acknowledging them. Somewhere in my steady breathing rhythm I am encompassing four heads and voices coming across the country as they drive down its veins towards the sea. I know they are waiting to see the ocean's blue-green, slow beauty again under the sun, and perhaps the thin, black dash of a container ship slipping along the unimaginable distance of the horizon to the west. I seem to be conjuring it all. I sense four people. They are expectant.

The heads and voices stay with me as I chop and swing round, as I drag branches towards the pile near the truck. Am I following the pale blue car and its side mirrors as it slips past the trees at the creek crossings coming west from the city, as it slips past the cars of holiday families, past plunging tourist coaches and the baleful mammoths of transports, all riding west through the country on the large vein of the highway and then the smaller veins of the roads to the forest and then to the sea? The four are talking, flashing past the long perspectives of sugar gums down farm drives, boring on across the country towards the sun-stippled cones of volcanoes that are abraded by the clouds. Sometimes the four simply look out of the windows in silence as they speed inexorably south with the clouds and wind towards the sea. I cannot see faces. I know only the dim heads and the voices and their passage towards me. I know they are waiting for the first smell of Bass Strait on the wind.

Then I see two small-fingered hands lighting a cigarette. I see a driver's shoulder and ear and short dark hair. I see the scrub and grass flashing past the car's mirror outside. I watch one fine-fingered hand with pink-frosted nails reach around the headrest of the front seat, stroking the neck of a young man who is driving, fingers running up into his close-cropped hair, exploring around his ear. He inclines his head towards the caress like a cat. The fingers stroke lightly, reassuringly. Then the hand withdraws as though content. I still see the scrub and the blond grass sweeping past. It's just my mind picturing. It might be nothing.

Minutes later, I'm brought up short. I'm breathing, listening, waiting. And then I see the face of a girl stricken white, her fair hair slipping down the spars of a barrier, strands of hair catching here and there in the knots of the wood, falling free again, the face slipping down, down. I hear a crooning of grief. It is enough. It is enough for me to know. I hear grief's descant. This is something that will happen.

—

My mother is happy. She is talking about climate, the Koppen classification. She says she will have to simplify it, reduce it to essentials for her sixth grade, but it's vital that they get a feel for how climates mould themselves. It underlies all they might be thinking about in geography.

I look at her. She sits there in the lounge in Cicero Street, glasses shed for a moment while she's not reading, her favourite ballpoint pen near her hand on the low table, and the heavy dark bulk of *Finch and Trewartha*, the physical geography book, open beside it. This is my mother who goes one way on the tram to the school each morning, while Will catches the tram the other way to the college. I walk down through the blackbird singing gardens and catch the train to the university. This is Louise, her eyes baggy and tired from a long stint of correction at the higher table in the dining room. Teaching. Preparation and correction. Discipline. Union matters. Excursions. Sport. Staff meetings. Talk of colleagues. Talk of students with their buffed and yet hopeful lives. Lesson notes, the glasses going on and off at the table as she works. Teaching, she says. Paper and words. And the eyes. She tells me about the eyes. Even if you're dead tired, she says, the eyes are there. You can't resist them. You have to bring things to them, she says.

—

It is one leap and I'm there above the ocean. It must be that I write out of the future to make the past. Or is the past the future? I carry this heavy burden like a prophetic sack. I hear the crack of a big wave breaking. It is like a passage in a symphony, a passage that will come again. It may not have happened. It may simply be an idea. And yet I see, smell the wattle branches again, feel the beautiful pendulous weight of the axe in my hands.

It is one leap on time's circle. It is 1979. It's summer. The sea is like heavy, molten brass moving under the late sun. It has been hot. Port Chalice humps its houses on the headland. Their whitened corrugated-iron roofs and their orientation against the westerly gales make them look like animals in carapaces stolidly clinging in the slopes of scrub.

I have driven away from the town along the vein of the Great Ocean Road as it sweeps and curves, in dialogue with the cliffs. I have taken the load of branches to the tip along the creek road in the Nissan. Now, going the back way home, I am watching the sea through the gaps in the cliff line that give me a view every now and then of the waves' break along the shore. They give some idea of the size of the swell. I've decided to call in at the car park to see what the sea is doing. So here I am at Magnet Cove. I've come back to sit at my vantage-point, one knob of sandstone among a welter of wind-sculpted, spray-sculpted knobs of rock close to the cliff edge. From here, many times, I have watched the sea coming in towards the dark mouth of Cathedral Cave, estimating its swarming strength and looking at the water clarity in case it's worth trying a dive later in the day.

Then I see the two couples. They have come from the car park and are walking across the wasteland of salt-encrusted rock and clay towards the second level twenty metres lower. They are heading towards the National Parks barrier that seals off the old fishermen's steps. I see the dark bloke in the tee-shirt slip the hand of his girlfriend to pick up a couple of the small pieces of fossilised rock and punt them over the cliff into the wind with his boot. These people who I seem to know are suddenly only twenty metres away, the wind taking their voices.

I see them, register their presence, but I'm turning again to the sea. I look out over hill after hill of water. These are big swells that have come up from deep in the south, not answerable to local wind, not dragging up too much sand, keeping the sea's amazing green in its blue. I watch below me and slightly behind as a set mounts its power, thrusting into the corner, turning kelp-tressed water and the beautiful, pale whorls of bubbles that sketch depth in the blue into relentless white water that reaches up towards the wave platform, shudders with disappointment, its fingers sliding back reluctantly, retreating only to fumble and work itself up to power and try again. The wind carries its white roar and thudding blows.

But something calls me to look back along the cliffs. I see the two girls at the foot of the vertical planks of the National Parks barrier, looking up, entreating, and the tee-shirt bloke already over the top, dropping lithely down the cross-supports towards the eaten-out steps in the rock on the sea side. His mate in the denim jacket is nearing the top, his sneakers gripping the junction between wood and rock at the edge of the barrier, his fingers and arms straining. He makes it, swings a leg over

150

and is on the easier down-climb on the other side, aided by the cross beams put there by the National Parks during the winter lull. The two disappear down the steps. Fools! I'm left watching the girls who look at each other, exchange some words, and laugh. I see them slowly start the climb to the upper level to wait.

Fools! For a time I can't see anything further. The girls are reaching a point level with me and fifty metres away along the cliffs. Below them is a plunge to the wave platform, probably sixty feet. The platform runs round in the shadow of the cliffs to the blowhole entrance. Below the wave platform and its pools is another thirty foot drop to the shining kelp and the swarming waves. After the mounting of each wave the water plunges away again fifteen feet down the sea's sink, down the glistening leather of the kelp and the pale rock that is a honeycomb of razors.

Then I see the two of them, not far under me, moving across the broad road of the wave platform with its two huge blocks of rock the size of small houses that have rolled out of the cliff. I watch a shadow play. It is television with no sound but the sounds of the sea. Tee-shirt is skipping along, jumping between the shallow pools. Denim jacket is sauntering, looking for crabs. Strange how the roar of waves and wind blankets their thoughts, their breathing – how it cuts them off, puts their two figures in the eye of a lens, invests them with spectacle. I look over to the left and see that the girls are watching.

But I'm suddenly looking out to sea. There is a crack of water against rock on the promontory half a kilometre over, a big wave raking in, splitting itself on the point, ploughing on, others in the set developing green shoulders behind it. I have heard it before. It is the dire passage in the symphony that has come again. I look down. I can see both tee-shirt and denim jacket, but they seem to have no eyes or ears for the sea. There is a big set coming. Fools! I mutter a warning to the breeze. I look again. Tee-shirt is dancing, hands outstretched, out on the edge of the platform where it narrows close to the corner. First wave expends itself in white below him in the kelp, but reaching up. Second is larger, builds on the first, raises spray and runs white lips of water along the edge of the platform between the two figures. Denim jacket sees it, stalks quickly away from the edge and disappears from my view into the lee of the cliff. Tee-shirt dances on, looks back, pirouettes while the third wave musters power from a different angle and mounts behind him. He starts to sense it, makes to move back towards the watchers. The wave is huge, bounding over the lower rocks, engulfing the corner, mounting tonnes of white and green water high above the platform, swallowing the smaller of the fallen rocks, surrounding the other with white water, scouring the wave platform out with its huge tongue.

I'm standing now. I stand in dread, leaning forward. I see how cruel is the narrowing of the ledge between tee-shirt and his hidden mate. It has to be. It is something that will happen and the waves will still power in afterwards, the wind will still sound like a keening voice round the rocky corners. Yes, the third wave catches tee-shirt from behind as he runs and slides on the wet limestone, as he tries to come back across the narrow section before the corner. The green water sweeps in, rebounding from the cliff wall. It wipes his feet from under him, plunges waist-deep across him, converts him to a white fragile stick with dark hair. It hurries him to the lip of the drop, rolling him, his arms reaching for air, and washes him down. In the ocean's green and white sluice he is jack-knifed, straightens, and then is carried head first again into the froth and rich white that is boiling among the whips of kelp and the razors of protruding rock, while the fourth wave mounts its power and height, stands up and then runs roaring under its green shoulders at the rocks. It has to be. I see dark jeans and white tee-shirt regurgitated. It is something that rolls like a rejected doll with a terrible slowness in the water at first and then speeded up as if reluctantly, only to be sucked away. Next I see boots and shirt further down in the bowl of boiling pure white as the wave retreats and prepares for its successor.

Then I am seeing nothing. I catch just the edge of a rasping scream from one of the girls and the wind whips it away to the sea. Then I'm stumbling towards the girls across the rocky mesas. I know it must be. I know what it means. As the second girl runs, trips onto her knees, rises, runs again towards the barrier. I know. It means a pale-blue car up above that no one wants to drive. It means breath that tastes like blood in the mouth. It means a heart rollicking madly, catching breaths. It means the wet plastered face of denim jacket appearing at the other side of the barrier and sinking down, not climbing, and the girl with the fine fingers sinking face to face with him down the planks, her hair catching here and there on the wood as she declines, as she slumps at the bottom, knees splayed, crying.

Why do I know these things? Why do they seek me out in the world's long afternoon?

—

Sydney moves differently now in my mind. I have not known how important it is in what has already happened and even in what is happening as I sit here in Hawthorn. I have not guessed what a soft backdrop of greenery against water and sandstone it will make for what is still to happen, and how I will hear the murmuring of its traffic.

Now that I know, everything is more acute and meaningful. And yet it is more settled. Now that I know, there is no more guessing. Now that I know, in my forty-six-year wisdom, I can hear voices against the fussing turmoil of the ferries leaving, see faces I have never dreamt against the dark recesses of the Moreton Bay figs tucked into the North Shore bays. Now that I have been there again, armed with my knowledge, Sydney has become luminous with significance.

I can feel against my face the pure susurrus of wind off the Pacific. It is blowing through the thin curtains of Alex Cumming's unit in Sydney, bringing with it the sound of waves that lave the rocks with white below. This is his home, I have to tell myself. This is where he has lived all these years on the headland beyond the North Steyne pines of Manly. From this window he has watched the sun-filled, sun-dappled ocean. I have not known this, have not known that it should

153

matter to me, and so I have not been able to think about it – until now.

Then I hear my father's voice, Will's voice, as he leans towards his friend Bob Bristow all those years ago, with me and Louise there listening. 'Sydney has its Harbour,' he is saying. 'Sydney has its Harbour, which I love and which I know you love.'

Now it is as though Sydney and the ocean that is always stretching its pastures towards it have come to me with a towering, blue answer, generous but daunting. I can feel it swallowing the present and the future.

—

Susan is my little daughter. She falls asleep all over the house. She carries her little bit of rag with her – a bitty she calls it. She settles in the bean bag near my desk, as the jazz flows. It is Oscar Peterson, playing the Duke Ellington Songbook. From my desk I look over the white pages to see her eyes straining to focus, her head sliding into the vinyl. In two minutes, the sun highlighting her scuffed, tiny shoes that just touch the carpet, she is motionless, eyes closed, mouth slightly open. Her face is open, secure in itself like a pale buddha. The only movement is the steady rise and fall of precious breathing.

It is the past. Susan is a young lady now. She uses nail polish and then spreads her fingers to look at them. I have lost her.

—

I'm looking out the window, watching the figures going about their business through the trees of the campus, along the paths, up the steps, around the balconies. I should bring binoculars to the office, perhaps. But they are only figures. The more my eyes follow them, the less I see.

I swing around in the chair. The books on the shelves speak titles and spines to me. My gaze pauses at *The Prose Works of Henry Lawson* in two navy-black volumes. They are Will's old books. They have been in my eyes since as early as I can remember. I can see them at Cicero Street, low

154

down in the bookshelves. My eyes rove further down the shelves, but they don't see, don't read, because I'm seeing Patricia's cold blue eyes flattened with anger and ill will.

It is an echo. Sometimes I can't escape the echoes. They come unbidden and at the strangest moments.

—

How can I have lost my children?

I pine for them sometimes. I slip into the past and then I can hear their voices. I can see their eyes. Then I feel their knees settling, shifting with their words under the bedclothes beside me and I know where we are. We are alone. There is no sight or sound of Patricia. It is only an echo, but it is an echo of something we have had of goodness and purity.

'Once upon a time, there was a little girl called Susan and a little boy called Jesse. And one day their mummy said let's go to Howlong and Brocklesby.' ('Let's go to Brock-bee,' says Susan, her lips drawing back to expose her chipped tooth on the 'bee'.)

'Yes, so we got out the car and we put in the blankets and the sleeping bags and the bikkies and the pot and the little hockey ball and the little hockey stick and the milk and the tea and the sandwiches and Susan's case and Jesse's case and Mum's bag and Dad's bag and off we went to Brocklesby and Howlong.'

'Yes,' says Susan.

'And we drove and we drove and we drove and at last we came to Howlong. And when we got there, what did we see?'

'Barry and Libby and Katriona and Tommy and Socks,' says Jesse, breathless. ('Kautrina . . . Kautrina,' says Susan. 'And Socks!')

'Yes, and you had a ride on Socks in the house paddock and Barry said come in and have a cuff-os-tea. And we soon had our tea and we went to bed and next morning, what did we do?'

'Ah . . .' Susan says, and shifts her knees and looks to Jesse. 'Ah . . .'

'We went down to the dam and we saw the sheep,' spouts Jesse in a pre-packaged deal. ('. . . dam . . . aah . . . saw . . . sheep,' says Susan).

'Yes? . . .' Susan says.

'And we saw the cows too and we threw stones in the water and we went for a walk along the road, didn't we, and what did we find?'

'Some horns off a sheep,' says Jesse, making excited eyes, then letting the light go out of them.

'Horns,' says Susan.

'And then we had lunch and had a sleep and had tea and went to bed and NEXT morning, what did we do?'

No response. Mornings become confused.

'Don't you remember? We got up and we had a cuff-os-tea ('Yes . . . cuff-os-tea . . .' says Susan) and we drove out the road a little way and we didn't even have our breakfast because there was something going eeeeeeeaaaaaaarrrr-um across the paddocks . . .'

'It was a PLANE!' says Jesse.

'Yes and the plane went eeeeaaaarrrrum and it sprayed the crop and then it went eeeeaaaarrrrum up over the trees and the telephone lines . . .' Two right hands, and a left, are making sweeping plane movements over the undulations of the blankets. Knees shift against mine under the covers.

'And then we went back and had another cuff-os-tea and had our breakfast and we went to look at the calf in the shed and we went for lunch and we went for a walk and we had tea and went to bed and the NEXT morning . . .'

'What?' asks Jesse. A note of impatience at not knowing what.

'We went to the Brocklesby Show . . .'

'Yes, the Show,' says Jesse and his eyes light, ' and we sat on the grass . . . and . . . aah . . .'

'Yes, we sat on the grass and had lunch and we saw the trains go past, and then we saw something way up in the sky going (raise arm as far as it can reach, let wrist turn down, allow two fingers to sway and gradually descend like pendulous legs) and what was it?'

'A man in a parachute,' says Jesse.

'Choot . . .' says Susan and leans back, trying to pull sheet and blankets around herself again.

'And the man came down and down and down – boom!' Fingers descend to tickle Susan's stomach. 'And then we saw cows and horses and chooks and tractors and jam and fairy floss.'

'Yes . . . fairy floss,' says Jesse.

'And we went back to Barry and Libby's house and we had tea and we went to bed and the NEXT morning, we had to go home and we drove and we drove and we drove and at last we got back to 21 Hazlitt Street, Heathmont. And that's the end of the story . . .'

—

My brother Alistair is calm. He is like Candles and Flute. I watch him, think about him. He doesn't look at the future. He can't see it, or he doesn't want to. I'm never sure which. We are brothers, but we're very different. Alistair reminds me of Flute. Both of them, I see, are pushed forward by the past, pushed forward resisting, pushed forward still trying to hold onto the present, slow it down, make it stay. And they don't see evil.

I am like Louise. The future is a territory I go to without intent. I look up in my mind's tramping, and I'm there. I'm seeing where things will end, what will happen. Sometimes it's prophetic and frightening. Sometimes it's a matter of where evil will appear. But who is to say whether this is the future or the past on time's circle? All I know is that these things have not happened yet, as far as I can see. All I know is that they are things that will happen to people, the people who are my faith, some of them close, some more distant. I know Louise can feel it too, can see where the good and the evil will come in – and so can her sister Jean. And yet my father Will can't. It's strange.

For some people, I hear Louise saying, there's no rest, no break from considering things. I can't stop being curious. With me, she is saying, there's no holiday from reading, either. 'I'll second that,' Will says. Will is sitting near, fingering the tablecloth in the Mont Albert kitchen. He's watching Louise, but he's sceptical. He knows when it's not wise to speak too much. Louise is talking to Jean, and I know what she means. It's just after David is caught out, and everyone is wondering what to do about it. The thing is, my mother says to Jean, that I've known about it. That's the thing. I know it's been there. I might have known for years almost. It's as though the flavour is there, the likelihood. But you can't put it in words, can you. You can't say you know. Then it might turn untrue. Jean nods. Yes, she says. We always seem to have to wait for it to happen, to wait for it to be uncovered. Will shifts his legs under the table, lolls back in the kitchen chair, but doesn't say anything.

A holiday from curiosity and thinking? A respite from probing, trying to find out? I don't have them either. I don't want them. I look at my father, but he's far away.

—

Des is talking to me about playing jazz standards. They're the real test, he says. And now that I've come home I'm lying in the dark and I can see it. You can only truly tell when the sax or the piano or the cornet or the guitar show you how many stories they can make out of the dream of a melody and the words that lie back and look at you with their hands behind their heads. Even though the words may not be heard, even though you mightn't know them all, I tell myself, they run along the back of your mind as you listen. They slip themselves under the chords and the progressions. That must be one of Des's jazz truths.

—

I see that Alex Cumming will be waiting in the Kooyong darkness under the stands.

This moment swims up to me again, as it has done before. It is a distant day in the sun. In the way it unravels its significance in the light it ensures that I will never forget it. Every detail is there. It's as if it knows its own deep meaning. It's as though I already know its own particular luminosity for me.

I remember the shadows falling to the left. Always and ever to the left through that afternoon. The court shadows are etched there in my memory. Yes, I'm there again. I can hear voices and the low murmur of the crowd relaxing between games. The shadows creep, but it is still early in the afternoon.

I see Alex Cumming's face now. He has taken off his hat. He is fingering its band in the shade under the stands. He spreads his feet, looks over his shoulder up the steps to the sky that opens out into the rows of seats and the bowl of the courts. But he doesn't move. I can see that we are sitting above the bowl of white-marked grass under the dome of the Melbourne sky. My father Will is beside me on the right, and Louise sits on the other side, the canvas bag with the thermos and sandwiches near her feet. But it is earlier in the day. I can feel the sun probing my acne like hot fingers under my shirt.

I am there again. I know it all. The cicadas string the afternoon from tree to tree on the Toorak hill.

The shadows have barely started leaning from the umpire's chair, the net-posts, the flags around the heights of the stadium. It is a steady, reassuring 90 degrees. The pure sun reels overhead. I think how it will spin slowly to the west over Government House and the hidden river. We sit at the Scotch College end. A bastion of hats stipples the far stand.

But is it not that time? I am there and yet not there. I can see myself, but I am watching my mother, sensing her tremor of excitement. I am seeing her handkerchief dredged from the bag and returned to it. I am watching her eyes under her broad straw hat.

And then the crowd claps. We look to see Victor Seixas step onto the court in a creamy-yellow blazer and carrying racquets. We watch him walk to the chair, set down the racquets, choose one, swing it in an arc, let it drop to the others again. Now he takes off the blazer. He wears a white tee shirt. He was in the American navy. He holds his head erect and dark, like a bullet. He is neat in his crew cut. He is deep brown and fit. He is ready to play. Behind him is Ken Rosewall with his racquets. His hair shines. Rosewall's shoulders shuffle out of a green blazer and he stands looking up into the crowd for a second. Then he pulls on a white sweat-band, settles it on his wrist, bends to his racquets and selects one. He is ready. They stand near the net and watch the coin spin. They walk to their ends of the court, looking at the ball boys as they advance, taking the balls that float on the bounce towards them, setting themselves, then sweeping the balls into their first flights over the net again and again. I can see their white flights. Rosewall sinks along the baseline like a tango dancer, right foot forward, to sweep his racquet through, cutting under the ball on the backhand. The ball doesn't waver. Rosewall hits it joyously, a slight smile on his face. And the ball spins, undercut and joyous, down to the far grass in its green and sap. I watch, and wish for that grace. I can feel Will and Louise beside me, watching.

But even now I can see that Alex Cumming will be waiting in the soft, even light under the stands. He is in his pale-blue summer shirt. He wears a broad, brown grazier's hat. Now he takes it off and wipes a hand across his brow.

I'm seventeen. I play tennis. As I watch my hands ache for the touch of a racquet. I hear the players' racquets ring tightly. They're strung tighter than the Dunlop Maxply I use when I'm playing matches. In the bowl the balls go tuck, tuck, tuck as the players hit them. They know where each ball will come. Each ball flies like a fast white dove, making an arc that descends, touches the grass, and is arrested before it can rise. The dove buries itself in other strings, dies a death, and before you can see it, is flying again, rising, back down the court, descending so that it meets the grass two feet from that final white line. It is flight. And the players' ways of bending to the ball are distinct – like different signatures. Their muscles sing. The matches roll over one another, each one a separate drama, each one pregnant before it starts, before the first service streaks down and is arrested.

We watch Tony Trabert. He is from the other side of the world. He might have stepped out of *Life* magazine or the *Saturday Evening Post.* He is so tall that his back and his buttocks bend inward as he serves. He has light-coloured, candid eyes. Bovine. He is a long machine, all white. When he plays and comes into the net it is ballet. This is the Victorian Tennis Championships.

The sun rides above us. The match inches forward point by point. It is a tournament in air. The players are polite, but their legs are swift and forthright, knowing where to go. Sometimes I find I am watching only the players' shoulders, the way they dip and right themselves, reach down, stand up and punch.

The sun creeps golden and westward towards the river and the trees that usher Government House to the sky. But where is Alex Cumming? I look down on it all, the courts, the nets, the white figures. Will and Louise loll and shift position beside me. But where is Alex Cumming? Ah, he is still at a grey concrete entrance to the stands. Now the sound of the crowd's clapping swims down the stairs to him. He shifts the hat in his hand, runs his fingers vacantly round its band, then its brim. The stairs are still and empty above him. For the moment he is alone in the midst of all these people and their attention. He looks at his watch. He paces, thinking. Now he sets the hat on his grey hair, straightens it, walks towards the imminent line between shadow and brilliant full sunlight. Now he is back in the brilliance, the sunlight smiting his shoulders. He walks towards the white plateaux of the clubhouse.

Over against the Toorak hill the trains gurgle up the long slope, coming from Flinders Street and the city. I think of the mothers and clerks and nurses and accountants and office girls and schoolkids in the snailing train. They will feel the sudden quiet and hint of night in the veranda shade or tree shadow when they step down onto the platforms that run out through Tooronga, Gardner, Glen Iris towards Mount Waverley. They pass the tennis by. The white ballet of the tennis in this green bowl goes on without them in this valley that runs from the city and the river. This is Melbourne. This is how it works.

I look up from my dreaming. People, hats, shirts, flowered dresses move like swarming insects in the stands at the southern end. Louise stands to stretch her legs, to jiggle her feet at the end of the game. Will rests his arm along the seat's back and looks steadily at the people in the western stand as they swarm and twitter.

'Ha!' says Will suddenly, then drops his voice sotto voce. Now he's looking at the southern stand. 'Ha. There's the Prime Minister.' He leans towards me, points to the stand that bubbles with colour at the other end of the court. 'See in the front row. That's Robert Gordon Menzies.' I look where he points.

'No relative!' Louise says, and laughs. She shifts the thermos beside her, settling back more comfortably against the seat, giving a placatory smile to the lady on her left as she moves. 'He's always liked tennis and cricket.'

I'm looking, but I can't see him. Will leans to me. 'See, in the front row,' he says, pointing again. 'There he is – big man with the blue tie and white hat and no one sitting next to him on one side.'

Ah, yes. The Prime Minister has taken off his dark jacket. He wears a white Panama hat. He leans his jowls to his companion on his left and we can see him say something.

'He's hatching a plan,' breathes Louise. The people from Toorak are there around him in the southern stand, under their white, smart hats.

And then I'm floating in time again. I am in the past. I hear my father Will's voice. He is raising a glass of beer, looking at it, then looking at me. I can see it. 'To thy two bright eyes! May they never meet.' And he laughs. It is a nervous sound. It is a laugh that comes from another time. Someone else is there but I can't tell who. It is another place, and for the moment I don't know where and when. It fades. But I am disembodied. I float above the tennis in the bowl. I see the three of us sitting there in the northern stand, the sun on our shoulders. I am watching my mother. I am watching my father, Will. I am slowly studying the rows of watchers in the southern stand as though looking for something. I sense it and then I see it and I know I have to follow it. Two rows behind Robert Gordon Menzies, in the official seats, a man sits with his dark-tanned arm along the back of the seat. White slacks and pale-blue shirt open at the neck, and a broad grazier's hat that shades his face. He wears sunglasses. I can see he is relaxed, not formal. He seldom puts his hands together to clap a good shot or a close-fought rally. Below him now are Ashley Cooper and Mervyn Rose, busy with their walking between points, their nodding to the ball boys who hold balls up for them to see, their stepping preoccupied to the line, their deliberate setting of feet, their roll of body, flight of ball, their anguished eyes looking up as they serve, and the smite of the racket as they enter that passionate ballet. They are chasing the white dove to its death.

The man in the grazier's hat simply reclines there, watching, on the end of the row, the seat next to him vacant. He sits. The sound of the balls in the bowl drift over him, drift over us. I am looking down from above, hearing the pluck . . . pluck . . . pluck and the brief clapping of the crowd. The game ends. The man, I see, gets to his feet, stretches his back, points both his feet in turn and finally stretches his legs, leaning one way and then the other. Then he takes off his hat to smooth his hair, looks around, nods to a man and a woman two rows behind. That is what I see from above. That is what Louise, my mother, sees too, I know. I am beside her and yet not there. I seem to know what she will do and why. She looks down suddenly, and I can feel her face draining for a moment. Her eyes are suddenly pinpoints below her scalp as though she fears something about to fall on her. I watch her. I can feel her confusion. In some way I seem to be able to understand it. Louise is busying herself among the things in the lunch basket under the seat. Then she sits up again, face composing, and looks unswervingly for a moment direct at the front rows in the opposite stand. Will and I are standing, too, it seems, stretching, yawning. But Will's eyes, I see now, are all for the tiers of faces looking down on us from behind.

I watch my mother. I know what she will do. I know her thoughts. I know that she could tell us, over the sudden churning of her stomach, that the name of the man in the grazier's hat near Robert Gordon Menzies is Alex Cumming, and that he knows what he is seeing in the green bowl.

—

A Vase of Years

I think I must be far north. I can sense the grey walls of red gum along the river. It must be Mildura. It must be the future.

And yet here is the vision of the two tennis racquets again. Cressy Perfects, and the flounce of the feather logo below the lettering of the transfers. New racquets, but racquets from the past. Why am I being offered this? I am in a dim room, carrying a piece of paper to the light of a window. It will tell me something. It is something I will handle and read – or have I already handled and read it? I will read and re-read it at times down the years, and it will be important. It will be a touchstone. I know I will be in this room – is it years hence? – and I will hear a small clash of cups and the rake of a kettle on a stove. And when I take the paper to the window I will read the words on it and try to puzzle my way through them, try to find my way into the past. I can feel it will be urgent. I can feel that it will be another clue. It will sidle up to me, offer itself like another piece of the jigsaw. I know that.

1953
DAVIS CUP CHALLENGE ROUND

The President, Sir Norman Brookes and Council
of the Lawn Tennis Association of Australia
request the pleasure of the company of
Mr. Alexander Cumming
at a Dinner to mark the occasion of the Davis Cup Competition
at the Hotel Australia, Melbourne,
on Thursday 31st December 1953 at 7 pm for 7.30 pm

RSVP by 14th December to the Secretary L.T.A.A.
18 Queen Street, Melbourne

Dress: Dinner Jacket

—

It comes back to wash over me when I least expect it. Where is my mother? I'm small again. Where is she? I need her words, her eyes. I can even feel the rough edges of the canvas chair and the beauty of the sunlight again – and then my chill of fear in the midst of it. Why don't my brothers and my father know that I'm watching them? Why don't they feel my sudden drop into loneliness? I see their three sandy heads there, concentrating. Behind them is the darkness inside the shed door. They seem to have what they want.

Here is the apricot tree. There is the sandpit that spills up against the sleep-out wall. I can hear the cold of the wind shivering the lily-of-the-valley in the shadows. Where is my mother? I need her words, her eyes. I'm suddenly small again.

—

Sometimes I can cut everything else away from it and look at it. Then I can see the pattern, the stupidities, the cruelties, the wounding, the pettiness, the learning. How could I ever have allowed it to happen?

In the mid 1950s I am a university student in a sports coat, carrying a satchel. In the early 1960s I am an eager teacher in Gippsland's hills. I meet Patricia Williamson when she comes as legal officer to the building society in Traralgon. Patricia's father is a doctor in Brighton. Through a spring and summer, a winter and another spring we swim at the white, sculpted beaches of the Promontory, we go to Melbourne for concerts, we play tennis on the grass courts at places where the curious heads of cattle swing up from the pasture across the river, where the lips of the ranges run blue and thin along the summer horizon. We sweat and kiss in the closeness of the car, and in our entwinings along the river. I have never smelt a woman so closely. My erections are triggered by a brushed forearm and by Patricia's perfume that promises what I know. Within eighteen months we are married. I have known Sandra, Ellen, Valmai of the beautiful legs and eyes but I have never slept with a woman until that wedding night at Partington's International Hotel with the dying throb of the city traffic outside. My body is dry and taut with excitement by the time everyone else has gone. My penis throbs erect and painful all night against Patricia's thigh, against Patricia's bottom. We make love twice, inexpertly. I hold her warm, soft body into the dawn noises of the city. I am already discovering how little she talks.

How marriage goes on with its insistent echoes.

—

Sometimes – it seems like a dream – I lie alone and beside the water in the lee of the cliffs during the heat wave, waiting to have another drink from the thermos, waiting until the day calls me to go in again and dive. I think then that perhaps all of time comes to me. Everything that I can see then, or hear or smell or taste or touch, is elemental. Salt on my lips, sea-washed pebbles under my fingers, the sky deep blue, the rock of the small cliff running yellow brown against it, stained deep brown where the last heavy thunder rain has run red-brown soil from the scrub along the cliff top. I hear the water running fingers in among the rocks, then a pause, then the start of a tiny chattering again, mounting to a chuckle as the wave ambles in. The cloud nations advance across the blue, cirrostratus far up, baked against the dome, frozen permanent lace, although in half an hour it has moved imperceptibly from north west to south east. That's when Rosa seems to be so close to me that I could turn to speak to her.

That's when I know I am somewhere in the long afternoon of the world. It's then, when I come back to the church and make a meal and watch the dark come down and sit out late into the night under starlight, that I'm sure people come to talk to me from far off, from beyond the grave. When I sleep later in the dark church with my hands lapped over each other on my chest, when I dream, my close people come to me. And I imagine Rosa's exquisite weight next to mine as I lie there.

That's when I see the sister we never had standing beside

169

my mother and I catch the grip of their tears in my throat. That's when I see my brothers bending with my father over what he is making in the shed, and no longer feel a dread at those three fair heads concentrating and at one with each other. That's when I marvel at Alex Cumming putting down two sparkling tennis racquets and taking up a white towel. But I wonder no more about their portent or why these things should be. I see my close people clearly, listen to their messages and feel as old and assured as the cliffs and the implacable sea.

—

It's Charlie's voice I'm hearing. He cradles his sax in the crook of his arm. He's talking about Des to Pat Friar and me. It's a hot January night. Des is over at the piano, trying out a version of 'Sunny' with Don Wendover just shading in the bass behind him. The chords come across to us at the tables. The gig hasn't started. Charlie looks over at Des for some time, listening. Then he leans down to us, almost whispers. He's a great ear man, he says. He looks at us both. He gives a down-to-earth little laugh. He has to be, he says.

Now it's another time. It must be after Betty has gone. I can see the change in Des's face that never leaves him after the accident. But does Des play with the band after that? I'm not sure. I seem to be listening to Des and Charlie and the band playing at the club again and I can hear that it's the chords and runs that count, and all that pretence, that rejection and denial, as though the sax and then the piano might desert the song, just go off somewhere and never come back, but then there's the sheer risk of the chords climbing back to court the melody, to woo it. It's the piano's drops of water, it's the deep wood of Charlie's baritone sax spilling over into the dark corners and the field of dim faces.

But now there's no Betty – no Betty any more.

—

Louise brings me further vignettes of the children in her grade. She knows them all so closely. She'll put down her glasses and tell me about them, this cast of small characters, their eyes appealing, their faces declining with hurt, their voices chiming and struggling with words to tell their tales. She knows I'm interested in the misunderstandings, the secrets let out, the injustices, the shadows of parents that she sees hanging over their children, about George who soils and wets himself, his eyes doleful and deep with shame, about the girl twins, the one quiet and lacking self-esteem, the other a sharp-tongued bully who dominates her. Will the parents allow them to be separated at school? No, there's scornful laughter, negatives repeated out of the sides of their mouths in Louise's office. And there are updates on Big Ross and Little Ian. Big Ross, who struggles, almost drowning, in the classroom's books and paper, whose mind works in slow and wide ellipses of incomprehension. But from the window Louise sees Big Ross protecting Little Ian – another Little Ian, she says – from the nudging football and cricket players in the yard. Little Ian is the most scintillating mind in the school – small, adjectival, quick, questioning with a surgeon's skill to get to the point – but physically vulnerable and inept, a gift to the school's larrikins. They are a team, my mother says – brightest boy and the big boy slow to comprehend. They tuck into each other.

I look at my mother's face, at the crouching creases under her eyes. I try to imagine her at the school. I can hear the classroom pause around me as she speaks about it. I smell schoolbags, fruit peel, sweat, the dust in the lazily moving blinds. But for a time I can't see Louise against all this. How does she sit in the room? What is it that brings her to her feet and takes her to the door? I hear echoing voices in a stairwell. Now I think I can see her threading her way up the corridor to morning tea. But I wonder is she too old for this? Should she have to teach now? She doesn't have to financially. It's strain and slow work at home under the standard lamp at night. She needn't do it, I tell myself. But when she speaks I know it will only be rarely she complains about worry or work. She's always speaking out of fascination – and a constant thread of delight. She has to teach. She has to touch people. It's the appealing eyes.

—

There I am, sitting on the bed's corner, listening to the noises of the house, moving one image over another in the pile of photographs, searching, amazed, wondering . . .

It's a winter Sunday, cold overcast weighing down on the house outside. I'm tired and yawning, sneezing every now and then with the dust coming out of paper undisturbed for a long time. But I find the bundles. Greg and I are moving Will from the larger Cicero Street house to the smaller one in Overton Lane. I can hear them out in the kitchen, Greg asking where Will wants things to go. I can hear Will's mumbling replies now and then. But it's quiet here in the front bedroom. That's when I come on these other photographs, photographs I've never seen. It's quiet. They lie there on the candlewick bed cover in the silence. I'm clearing one drawer at a time. What if it had fallen to Greg and not to me to clear them? That's when the questions grow vaster and vaster. There they are above me, like straining, unreadable dirigibles against the blue.

—

It's someone else's dream, but it fascinates me.

Always shoot the bitch first, he tells me. It's the man who knows foxes speaking. I'm listening to him talk on. He is taking me into his dream of landscape and life and death. Here is the sound of his voice in his valley which is not my valley. Here is the way he looks over my shoulder as he speaks and up onto the big hill that looms over another creek just one valley away to the north where my church nestles beside its tank in wattles, gums, boobiallas.

I don't reckon any fox is born smart, he says, but they learn to be smart very quickly. Once they've seen the spotlight and heard the dogs and the shouts and the shots in the air the smart ones remember forever. You'll see them on the run, trailing round to get out of the light, to get

172

into the darkness behind the truck or the ute, or sloping off to the side and out of the paddock. The younger, inexperienced ones are still silly. They'll stand still, staring at the spot or trying to catch moths in the light. Then they're gone!

As he tells it to me I find myself going into his dream.

I've seen a lot of dawns, he tells me. I go to some of the volcanic craters further west, he says. I wait up there on the lip, he tells me. I wait for the first light and then the dawn. The foxes with burrows in the crater have been out across the rises hunting during the night and they come home. In winter they'll be looking forward to going down into the crater and camping from about 8.30 in the morning. They'll camp in the burrow all day – some of the burrows are twenty feet long. But if I'm ready there on the rim before dawn I'll see them coming up the side of the crater and shoot them as they come home. Not difficult, he says. Not too difficult.

The foxes start pairing up in July and August, he says. Later, you'll see them running together, the pairs. Always shoot the vixen first. Always. The vixen has no faithfulness to the dog fox if there's trouble. She just scarpers, disappears. You'll never get her. But if you shoot her first, the dog fox gets a bit of a shock. He runs on, looks for cover. Then he has second thoughts. Where's Mum? That's strange. Where's Mum? And he comes back to her – and you get him too.

Other times you'll see a pair teaching their litter, he says. Training 'em to hunt. A fox follows a ewe and its lamb, he says. She follows them to see if she can separate the lamb from its mother. The lamb always follows at the ewe's back leg. If the fox gets too close the ewe can turn and butt. If she's got twin lambs she's in trouble, though. One of 'em is quite likely to be left a bit behind – and then the fox is in. The fine wool sheep aren't much chop with their lambs. The merinos will put up a bit of a fight for a while against a stalking fox. But then they panic, give up, leave the lambs. Crossbreed ewes don't leave their lambs so easily – they stay and defend them. But the fox is always more patient. He'll wait. I saw a fox once with two lambs, he says. They'd been left by a fine wool ewe. So here's this fox, with a young litter, playing with the lambs like a cat plays with a mouse, a rat, a bird. Letting them run a bit, then catching up with them and slapping them down. He'd let them up again and they'd head for freedom, but he'd follow them again, slap them down, again and again, and they'd be losing strength. He was just playing. Just playing, showing the cubs how to do it.

He looks over my shoulder as he tells me. It is his dream, someone else's dream, but I can enter it, taste what it must be like in the dawn, what it must be like seeing the vixen go down. I can hear the crack of the rifle, see her topple and then try to rise, reel away sideways, trying to rise. Then she falls.

I didn't know these things. One day I'll tell Jesse about this. I'll watch his uncertain student eyes, their curiosity shaded, to see what he thinks of it. It is a grim, active part of the life tapestry that doesn't touch everyone, I'll tell him. That's how I see it, I'll say to my son. Yes, I didn't know these things. Now I do.

—

It's when Will and Louise are abroad in the 1970s. I try to see their faces while they are far away. I try to hear their voices. And after Will's first postcard and then first aerogramme I think I can. Just how I do not know, but sometimes, thinking about them, I seem to be aware as in an indefinite print, where they are standing, what they are thinking. It's as if I will not be surprised at what places their next airmails might describe. And yet I seem to know also that if anyone asks me for detail the vision will evaporate. Is it a membrane of knowledge that hangs there unseen until it is challenged, threatened?

I'm surprised at first, though, that Will and not Louise does most of the writing. Then I realise I can feel a withheld excitement and a slow regret coming through his words and I know why. They shouldn't have left it so late to go overseas, he says. They should have gone sooner after they finished teaching. But ah, Florence! he says. Never too late! I didn't know that life could be art, Will writes. I always knew that art could be life. But Italy! Everything concentrates and presents itself so beautifully, he writes, not only in Florence but in the fields, in the palazzos and the barns we see from the train, in a woman and a man at a table in the shade of walnut trees one warm evening, or a man walking home down a white road with a hoe over his shoulder. We have been to the Uffizi, Will writes, his ballpoint lines of words coming perilously close to the bottom of the page that has to be licked and sealed for *par avion*. We saw that Cranach of Adam and Eve. And the sarcophagi. But when we come outside there is the art continuing in the square. People are sculpted there as they eat and argue or bend to touch a dog or walk through the pigeons slowly. There are people meeting and talking everywhere, meeting and talking under the loggia of the post office, at the newspaper stall, under the loggia near the Sabine Women! You'll have to see it.

Louise doesn't write more than a scribbled afterthought to Will's air-letters until they are in Paris. They've met Rona, Louise's old friend from days at the teachers' college, as planned. Rona has changed, Louise writes. She's become Italianate, if that's the word, somehow swarthy and Italianate or Spanish. But she's still the same Rona beneath it. She's the most knowledgeable and witty person to walk Paris with. A lot of walking. Today across the river to the Sorbonne. It was either the Sorbonne or the Eiffel, and you can see the Eiffel down every second street in the distance. We have decided another day, maybe, for that. There were few classes going on apparently at the Sorbonne, but students were sitting in the huge interior courtyard swotting last minute for exams. A far cry, Louise writes, and I can hear her voice saying it and see Rona's face listening in – a far cry from the exams Rona and I swotted for at Melbourne Teachers' College. Imagine, she writes, Melbourne Teachers' College becomes the Sorbonne!

As I read the aerogramme and hear the words, hear 'the Sorbonne', I see grey stone and a river running darker below it. I see a bridge against the light further down. I see the spines of books in rows and the pages of newspapers stirring but entrapped in a light wind. I see an old clock high up in stone, and a forearm raising a coffee cup behind glass, but reflections smother the face of the drinker. How can this be?

—

I write in the church. The iron of the roof cracks once alarmingly in the morning's slow bursts of sunlight. The church settles again to quiet. I write. It seems as though I'm carefully stepping through the generations. It's like placing my feet between the scented rows of a herb garden so as not to tread on a single plant.

I suppose I have seen a lot of death. First Grandpa John, who dies at the front gate in Mont Albert, but I'm not there. I'm at school. I see his face in the coffin later, so pale. Where are his red veins? Then Pearlie in the bed in the front room. She dies late in the afternoon. I'm out the back in the chook pens at Mont Albert. Do you want to come and see her, Will asks when he comes to find me. I've never thought about it, never thought I'd be asked like an adult. Yes, I say. Then I wonder whether I can do it. It is Sunday.

Only this morning I came into the room and felt her hand on mine and watched her lips trying to rid themselves of the rime of white. It's Tim, Pearlie says then to the pillow. It's Tim. How are you? Now, three hours later, Will takes me in and I can smell the room is different with the window wide open and the curtain rubbing against it. My mother is there, crying, looking past me, then at me and smiling through tears. They have made a stream down past her mouth. They wait to drip from her chin. Pearlie is grey. Her eyes are closed, but for a moment I think they might open. I look at the fat of her arms, her hands one over the other on the bed sheet. I look again at her face. No movement, nothing. Nothing. What has gone? I decide to go to the front steps to sit, to think. Something I can't explain has gone. It's so quick. Her eyes are still, eyelashes still, hair resting on her brow like her sister Mollie's hair. Mollie is not here. Mollie is still alive. Pearlie is dead. She is still. Still. No one moves or says anything when I go out.

Death. Where is thy sting? Death. Days of the Dead. The dead speaking. To be alive. To be dead. What is it to be dead? I don't know. When Mrs Abbott dies next door and I go in for Louise with some more flowers, her son stands at the door and says, 'Would you like to see her?' Behind him I can just see the handles of the coffin glimmering in the dark room. No thankyou, I say. Afterwards I wonder if I should have said yes. What would I know now if I had said yes?

—

51st Street, NY, NY.

11 September '71

Dear Tim, Alistair, Greg and everyone at home,

Hard to believe I'm here, we're here. Louise's feet are sore. So are mine. We mid-sixties are not as spry as we used to be, although we can both feel the added strength in our legs. A lot of walking, in a lot of places I never dreamed I'd see. But ah, Manhattan! I don't mind going on and on about it to you all, if you can stand it. I'll write you all a letter a day to get it down! So this is a longer *par avion* for an envelope rather than an aerogramme. It's a way of keeping a record of impressions. Can you hold these for me? I've had to become something of a writer because it seems mandatory to catch the flavour of these places and what's happening. I'm writing a few notes, too.

Savannah and Charleston were fascinating. There's Fort Sumter – far offshore in a bit of sea mist. The first shells from out there! The start of the fight for the Union – the fight that made Americans what they are.

Interesting to see Savannah away from the city centre. We went out on the bus, looked down the long roads of the black districts – gunshot roads they call them. We met a black cab driver later who was very bitter, said he'd blow the whole country sky-high if he had the power. He hates Savannah and its black/white divisions. We spoke to another Savannahian, white, with an office down near the port sheds who told us that once there was snow in Savannah – a freak December cold snap. Panic! Nobody prepared for snow, no snow ploughs, no snow tyres, no procedures. But people turned out and became choristers from door to door!

There's much more to Charleston than we had time to see. We saw one of the old plantations. Miles of plantation dykes dug by the slaves, for rice growing. West African slaves were prized because they under-stood rice-growing. Many alligators through the swamps and canals.

177

Then Manhattan! We come from the South and I'm thinking of Whitman. I hear Whitman in a lot of what we're seeing. We came north from 'I Saw in Louisiana a Live-Oak Growing', so to speak, and 'Lilacs in the Dooryard' and I'm thinking of 'By the Bivouac's Fitful Flame' and that silent procession of soldiers' faces in the dark – that's what I imagine. And now New York: 'Walt Whitman, a kosmos, of Manhattan the son . . .' Here it is and I'm seeing it: 'My own Manhattan with spires, and the sparkling and hurrying tides and ships . . .'

We walked the base of Brooklyn Bridge, but not across it. We'd be quite a long way from the relative protection of either shore, we thought, out there in the middle, if someone wanted our wallets. Of course Whitman went by water. We stood there and I swear we could hear Whitman's '. . . Ferry': 'Ah, what can ever be more stately and admirable to me than mast-hemmed Manhattan . . .'

From here I could sense his sweep of time – the continuity he saw, or foresaw:

'Gorgeous clouds of the sunset! drench with your splendour me,
or the men and women generations after me!
Cross from shore to shore, countless crowds of passengers!
Stand up, tall masts of Mannahatta! stand up beautiful hills of
   Brooklyn
Throb, baffled and curious brain! throw out questions and
   answers . . .'

This is getting a bit messy, but far beyond Manhattan I wonder how Whitman got about so much all up and down this eastern side of the States. Must have been slow and arduous and uncomfortable – and dangerous a lot of the time.

North America – a remarkable continent physically. The New World, prairies and mountain spires. This place pushes it at you. You can hear that wonder in its writers. As you know I've often had occasion to think about it! And that's it. Whitman – but for that matter Thoreau and Melville, Frost, Lee Masters, cummings, Stevens, Williams, Eberhart, Steinbeck, McCullers, Marianne Moore, bullish Hemingway, McLeish –

the lot. You can feel it in varying ways in them all. They are all the time thinking what it is like. They are having to try always, having to try to say what it is like. Just being in New York brings a lot of that together. It's very strong – we've got the best and the worst right here in front of us.

Anyway, much more of this anon. I can see we'd better go out. The Metropolitan Museum of Art. Fifth Avenue – and a walk back along Central Park. I'll post when we're out and add more in a later letter. I'll keep writing so that you can preserve. Please pass around – but please keep them for me. Love to you all, Will and Louise.

—

Louise doesn't write us as much as Will, but she sends us word pictures. No day-to-day, hour-to-hour account – but pictures that start out of the page. She can write, my mother!

Americans touch beautifully, she says, in a way Australians don't.

In Central Park, she writes, the leaves are turning. As gentle as finger-tips, she writes, they fall past us onto the paths. Just over there there's a jogger stretching his legs, pushing against a pole. And ten feet from him, a down-and-out who'll probably be freezing in snow in three months time, is washing his face at a bubble tap. His bundles are beside him on the path. Neither takes any special account of the other.

Louise tells us about sitting in the little red booths of the coffee shop to have breakfast, watching and listening to New Yorkers on their way to work having their breakfast and talking about cash-flow and Thanksgiving that will come soon. Breakfast of French potatoes, scrambled eggs, toast and jam, perhaps some wheat cakes, and 'corfee', the ever-flowing good 'corfee'.

Louise writes about the Statue of Liberty reeling up like a dark figure far off down the bronze river, the pavement (sidewalk, she says, sorry) gratings that trail a steamy breath under people's feet in the wind.

The dark of the shoe-shine stands, Louise writes. The only thing luminous against the dull corners is the white man's face and perhaps his hat, while he looks down on the negro cap, the dark neck, and the fingers wielding the flashing, polishing rag. We've seen it in New York, she says, we've seen it in Charleston. But how impoverished American society would be, she writes on the thin, pale-blue paper of the air letter, without the black presence – their good humour, lack of inhibition, their wit, their rhythm, their flair against European dourness. Mercurial, volatile. But what suffering the blacks are capable of enduring, she writes. We can see it all around us.

She can write, my mother.

—

People die. Candles dies after all these years. Flute is dead five years ago. People have their life span and then it's over. Candles has had his years. Like Flute's heart, his heart has stopped and he with it. We sit in the church and listen and watch – Louise and Will and Greg and Alistair and Patricia beside me. Where is Greg's Carolyn? Where is Alistair's Deirdre? Further along the row Auntie Chris sinks back in her tears behind her veil. Rod, my cousin, her son, ranges beside her in his suited, broad shoulders. I look towards him. I haven't seen him for nearly four years. He is three inches taller than Candles, his father, but when I look at him there are Candles' hanging jowls, and when he turns and sees me there are Candles' eyes coming to mine now in a sad smile from beneath dark eyebrows. On Auntie Chris's other side, Frances, Rod's sister, has an arm linked through her mother's, her fingers patting her forearm gently, constantly.

I look at the blond wood of the pew in front of me, I look at the triglyph repeated in the carpet about me. I hear the organ gurgling towards the twenty-third psalm. I think about it all there in the pew and wonder why it has taken me so long, stumping towards the gathering at the graveside at so many funerals, smelling the milk and the woollen care of bunny-rugs nuzzling the cheeks of new babies, new cousins, to realise this about life's span and about death and the luck of the game that determines what happens to those allotted days and nights, all those summers, all those autumns when for Candles and Flute the Mallee must have seemed to wait without declaring itself – no utterance in the still, warm sun for the season of no growth, just waiting for the first frosts.

It's no use being sad about Candles. He has enjoyed what the after-noons give him when things are quiet in the newsagency up country. For so many years he drinks the sharp air of football training, the canny joy of moulding a team out of toughs and lairs and quiet family men who don't say much, the shouts way out in the ground, the sound of fast footfalls and then panting breath and grunts of effort in the dark. I can see him there, a football in the crook of his arm, the training lights bouncing off his bald head, his waist and legs in shadow. The players jog around him as he has asked and then dash off in a race to the fence, boots creaking, breaths fluttering in the cold. Or I see him straightening up from his bending in the long rows of the potato plants on his block in Ashburton after the War. He reels for a bit, calls something to his partner Freddie further up the slope, then steadies himself, leaning there on the tilling fork, one shoulder bunched under his old shirt, and he is looking about him with satisfaction. It is Melbourne Sunday morning, and he can hear a train far over in the dew and he and Freddie have turned over half the planting and he is happy. They'll get to the rest after work during the week. My uncle Candles is happy.

—

How does the truth get into photographs?

I'm thinking about this picture I've turned up. This one has Jean's husband Cec in it. He is in khaki shirt and shorts. No hat. Behind him are palm trees and shadows and some splintered timber rearing out of the earth. At his feet are two Japanese soldiers. One has his left leg bent cruelly under him and his shirt has been blasted and burnt into a six-inch diameter hole around the right pocket. The hole seems filled with blood or mud. Not all of the second Japanese is visible. His torso and his face lie against the thigh of the first one. He has no shirt. His body looks relaxed in its reclining, but his eyes are staring. His head is tilted uncomfortably against his comrade's leg, so that he seems to be scrutinising his own chest.

They are both dead. Cec's face is smiling straight at the camera. He stands straight, but not at attention.

The photo has no love in it – only unease. It is small and fading brown now with age.

This next photograph is the one I take of Greg with Barry McLellan in the creek. Greg's face shines in its complete cold rhapsody from the dark that hovers over the water. I take that when I'm twelve. Greg is only seven. When I take that shot Alistair is up at the shack with the chicken pox. I can remember the details. I look again at the image. I like looking at it. I think it has been taken with love. That shining face. And it has the truth in it about Greg.

Next is a photograph of Louise Barnes, my mother, reclining on a cane garden lounge, her dress arranged in a comely manner over her legs. In her hands she has a book of what I can guess is poetry – probably Robert Browning's, if Louise's stories to us as kids about her teacher training days are any guide. In the photograph she is a young woman looking down and beyond the book, rather than at the camera. She must know she is posing, and yet her face is unselfconsciously reflective, if not sad. A white picket fence runs in the background, with what look like jonquils growing at its foot. My mother's hair is parted down the middle and bobbed. The reverse of the photograph tells me that it was taken in 1929.

In this next one of mine, taken forty years later, I seem to be blessing the surfer from far above him on the cliff as he comes out of the water below, striding with his board through one throw of the sea's white lace, while further along the cove the fans of white spread themselves and then retreat in a series of scallops. I don't know who the surfer is, and that is as it should be. This is anyone. This is land and sea. I look through the tele-lens and see from the cliff top that it is going to come to this, that the sea will spill its perfection up the steep sand, that the surfer will stagger as he begins to stand in the shallow water and then will make his lone tracks across the beach from right to left, quitting his love, his neck nodding as he walks, his calves and shoulders silvered with weariness. It seems to me that it contains the truth.

There are two shots that have 'Adelaide trip 1932' on the back. Someone, probably my father Will – but could he have been in Victoria then? – has taken them both of Ken and Phyl, Louise's greatest friends when she is a trainee teacher and later when she teaches in the little single-teacher school at Gellibrand and later the one out of Edenhope. The three of them are posed above the Blue Lake at Mount Gambier. From the photo their laughter comes down to me even now, Ken on all fours, Phyl riding him with a superior grin and tweaking her beret with her other hand. Perhaps it's a parody of Adam Lindsay Gordon's leap? There is Louise, the woman who two years after this photograph is taken will become my mother. She's posing on the other side of the fence like a punter. She's waving a newspaper and smiling with an exaggerated wink. In the lower part of the photo is the shadow of a male body and shoulders and felt hat bunched round a camera. It crosses the grass from the corner foreground, almost reaching my mother's feet. It's clearly late in the day.

—

It is hard to visualise the principle of waves, because when you see water move to capture the sand of the shore or run in among the defiles of rock, the sight obscures the fact that out from the shore the same water holds its place, holds its place, while the wave moves its green, proud, stately swell through it and is gone, and is gone. I think of it like music moving through me.

That is one of the truths from the church where I write.

The window on the north side near the door, white painted inside, is my best thinking shape when I'm writing.

Looking at its proportioned rise to the Trinity, I sometimes think God has given that window to me. But I don't believe in God. I sit at the computer on the old dais that covers the baptistery and pour my thoughts into the swimming-green frame, draw them out again transmuted. The six-foot plunge of the window in the dark-panelled wall pictures the reaching branches and leaves of the blackwood wattle spreading outside near the door of the old vestry and behind that the more cavalier and blond limbs of the boobiallas close to the gate. There is little of sky, so the vision doesn't compete dazzlingly when I turn my eyes back to the words on the computer screen. I sometimes sit for a half hour musing again and again at the shadows and light, bark and leaves, all the time turning Alex and Will and Alistair and Greg in my mind, seeing the face in the photographs, hearing Alex's voice on the beach at Parkdale saying, 'I'm the king of the castle' – and smelling the blood of the sea up close. Parkdale is a magic word in my childhood, a word full of smells and sounds, where I find that as we come to it through the ti tree day after day, the sea always waits. I can feel again a stomach full of happiness as I squat to pat the wet sand of Port Phillip Bay.

If you pull the nail out of the lock on the big door of the church the catch will go home and you'll be locked in. That is a truth. If you leave scraps and crumbs on the sink and the kitchen benches at night the mice will come. That also is a truth. You can tell if you have the water turned on too far in the shower if the water whistles through the shower rose when the pressure unit comes on. Summer and autumn are the times for finding firewood, cutting it, stacking it to dry out for the next winter's fires. Eucalypt is good – some white gum or stringy bark. Boobialla is lighter and needs a long dry out. But wattle is the dense one – it lasts all night, hoards embers to start the morning. And remember dead boobialla branches have one aim when you are gathering them, chopping them, lopping them, splitting them, breaking them under your boot – and that aim is to gouge out your eye, to lance your hands, to trip you up, to deflect the axe into your boot, to kill you if possible.

These are all truths from the church where I write.

I want to be present at the ceremonies of the morning and the evening. It's half summer wasted if I don't see them, walk in them, listen to them. After the late evening meal I have during daylight saving, in the hot weather, the valley is rose and blond all the way down to the patch of forest in the west. It hoards the last light, stores it in the dry grass, lets it out long after the sun is gone, when the moon is rising. The far paddocks up to the horizon glow with so much wheaten light in the dark that you can pick out the fences. The willows and poplars along the creek are dark, but don't even whisper. The stars try themselves in the vault. These are further truths.

I move from bow saw and axe to computer and back again through the day when I'm down on the coast. Each day I get up with the sunrise if I am there by myself, with the Nissan tucked in under the boobiallas. Day is an elongated morning of wood and eucalypt smell, of sweat that smells like wine, and the computer screen to which I speak and spill the stories. It speaks back to me when I finish a section. Morning is the best writing time. That is a truth.

In the morning I can send my thoughts deep into the pining window that rises like worship, past the near wattle leaves, past the rounded boobialla limbs as thick as six arms, into the dome of the outer branches that make a veined globe against the light. I urge my thoughts, my problems, against those far branches.

—

There is a photograph of Alex Cumming. I hear his voice, strangely, as I look at it. It will later become more and more important to me, but I don't know that. What do I hear in Alex's voice as I write? Sometimes I can't hear it. But I can see Alex clearly again now. I hear him chanting: I'm the king of the castle. I'm the king of the castle. But his voice fades away. I'm not seeing him now on the beach at Parkdale. Here in the photograph he is young and hatless. His hair is near black, short-cropped like a small fright. I seem to be seeing him on the farm at Sea Lake. He is sitting half perched on a hewn rail fence near a post, one thigh thickening over it, his shoulders loose and muscled in the faded blue work singlet, hands crossed and loose in his lap. He seems to be talking to someone about wheat prices. The sun strikes down over his shoulder and catches his right pectoral and its nipple, then flashes to his thigh. Near him, leaning against the fence, is an axe. But there's no voice. In my picture of him the sun drills down from above, Alex's face speaks with an ironic smile, the light catches the cheek bones, leaving the eyes and mouth dark. But there's no voice. Then, when I least expect it, I hear Alex Cumming clear his throat – an insistent note curling round an obstruction, curling, pushing, loosening, and a slight cough and a swallow. That is all.

Louise and her friend Rona like going to galleries to look at paintings. We are all at the gallery. It is years before Louise's end. Will and I are watching Louise and Rona together, while we saunter separately. I think I can also sense Louise and Rona moving together behind the screen of their past.

The two were friends when Will came from Sydney to Melbourne, but not long after that Rona sailed for Europe to study fine arts. For twenty-five years and more Louise can only know what Rona is doing when she receives her letters. They miss each other. Louise tries to imagine Rona in Europe. She is trapped by the War in Paris. It's a story, an incredible story Louise tells me. Rona watches the Germans sweep in, works as a chef's assistant, marries a French artist, but it doesn't last. Rona's letters keep coming to Louise fitfully. The War ends, the years of letters pass. Then Louise and Will find Rona in Paris when they go abroad in the 1970s. It is the new and Italianate Rona they meet, Louise tells me. How can anyone have such a life, she asks. How pedestrian must life in Melbourne seem after all she's been through, after all she knows. Where life takes us! says Louise. Two years later Rona is back in Melbourne. She has sold her art shop in Paris, come back to be near her brother. She has never remarried. She sets up an antique shop in Caulfield. She is happy and knowledgeable, happy in her knowledge. But the first time they meet again in Melbourne, my mother tells me, she cannot believe she is watching Rona Ellis picking her way down the steps under the clocks at Flinders Street to give her a kiss and a hug.

So I watch Louise and Rona in the gallery. They are slowly side-stepping, close to each other and yet separate in their musing and assessing, as they look at the Arthur Boyds along the deep-white walls. Will is in the next gallery, looking at the sculptures, slowly coming back to us. Then he'll be away again after a couple of words, only to return by degrees, an eye kept out for us. I see Rona come back to Louise at Boyd's painting of the bride, the trees looking in on her, her lover cupping her pale face with his hands. Rona draws Louise close to the painting, points to its dark corners, says something brief in her ear, then steps back to take in the whole painting again. Louise's face remains considering, then she turns and smiles assent to Rona. They are two girls again, unselfconscious and in tune.

Later, sitting with our coffee before I drive them home, I try to find what lies behind Rona's steady gaze, sometimes lit by a half smile. She says little, her face teak and immobile beside my mother who is talking while Will listens, his coffee cup carried forward in his hands, elbows on table. Rona has been silent for a long time, watching Will and Louise. They are friends who have come together again after the years, after her absence from Melbourne. I catch a quick smile from Rona as her thinking gaze wanders. What does she know?

—

They never find the man who kills Betty.

His car sweeps her off the tram stop in Malvern. His bumper bar carries her along, throws her against the steel tram pole that holds the wires, and then he veers back onto the road. The girl who sees it says that his tail-light blooms up red when he's gone a hundred yards, as though he might stop and come back, but then she hears the accelerator go down again and he goes off speeding.

Betty is only thirty-seven. She dies so young. She is dead long before Flute, before Candles, before Frank, before Archie and Cec, before Jean and my mother, long before Joyce's David or my father Will or Alex Cumming. When she dies Des is left all alone. Their love is dashed away on a near-empty street at night in Melbourne.

Des, who never marries! Des and Betty. I can see their love, deep and candid, their bodies making vows again and again in song and dance. They touch and understand each other far from a church from when they first time meet. And that's what Will says at the funeral. That's what is so cruel. I don't like to look at the picture I carry of Des at the funeral. When Betty is killed Des's face changes and never comes back. From that time his face has a stare, no matter what is going on around him. He seems not to be listening. He no longer starts up and thrashes across the room, feeling his way to the piano. He hardly ever plays it from then on. The warmth and conviction is ripped out of him.

When the young policeman calls after the accident he stands there uncertainly near the kitchen table in his uniform. 'If the bastard'd hit the steel pole himself we might have tracked him down through the damage to the front, but he glanced off her and back onto the road.' That's what the policeman says, standing there, looking at us. He has already been to see Betty's parents. Now Des has to hear what he says. Des just grapples for the table's edge and grips it, then slowly lowers his head to his wrists. I can still hear his breathing, as though he doesn't care any more.

'That's the curse of the car,' Louise mutters. 'The cursed car and probably drink. I'm glad I'll never drive.' When she says that we all look at Will, who loves driving, who loves his car. He says nothing.

―

I remember Grandpa John takes my hand and draws it down towards Little Gwenda's tiny arms that flail and are still and then flail again. I smell the secure, moist answer-back of the wool in her jump-suit. She is my new cousin, five months old. She is Joyce's new baby, lying on the floor on a light-blue rug in the lounge at Mont Albert. I trust Grandpa John as he leads me. I kneel.

'Feel her little fingers,' he says. 'It's something absolutely beautiful and amazing – a baby's hand.'

That is a truth. I touch her fingers and feel them as unassertive and random and tender as gum-tips against my palm. That is a lasting truth that Grandpa John brought to me in the year that he died. And there's still the milky, secure smell of the wool around Gwenda.

―

All of time seems to come to me. The days run on in light. It is the future. I can feel myself wiser in my forty-six-year-old wisdom than I have ever been. I have read Louise's final letter to me. I have caught the curiosity mixed with concern in Mr Tremearne's eyes as he hands it to me. I have read the pages and reread them. They gather all else in. It's still difficult to know myself. I am no longer the person I have known. I am a different person, even though the days run on with the same steady thunder in my skull. I am made of days. But now I am made anew. If I be not I then who will be? I shine in a new joy sliding out of sadness. The words written by my mother's pen on those white sheets of paper gather all else in. And then there are the further days, the days running on in light.

—

Do you remember the day we swam in the thunderstorm when you were little? I am saying it to Jesse. It is you sitting there, isn't it? It must be two years after our divorce that I am saying this to him. I think I see his dark eyes burning in the corner of my small back room where we have not put on the light even though the sun has set. It is you sitting there, I say. Your name is Jesse Menzies. Mine is Tim Menzies. I am your father. Patricia is your mother. You are not me. I am not you. But we are each other's close people. Neither of us is Patricia. Neither of us is Susan. It's as though we can look down on it all and on ourselves.

Patricia and Susan are at Patricia's house now, where the highway swings up over the hill above the water and the lights just out of Frankston. They are not thinking about us or these things at this moment. But we are, Jesse. There is no one to parallel you, no one to parallel me, no one parallel on earth beside Patricia and Susan. You and I are both alive. I think I can remember my birth, like an opening into light. I remember your birth, your head misshapen when you emerged, Patricia's seizing of the gas before you came, her desperate eyes and the words of the nurses. I remember her grunts, her urging. We both were born. We both will die. So what is it all for? I have had longer on the earth than you, and my death is nearer. I know things that you cannot know now, but that you might one day know. But you have youth. You have much longer now than I have to experience how the world works.

Will you do it? Here we sit, each in our own singular envelope, each with our own moment of time. How far will you get in your discovering of what can be done with this time alive on earth? We look down on ourselves and we see that we have this time and this chance to find out its meaning. Billions of other people have had the same time and chance. They have all had different places in their hearts, different close people around them. What is there to know about people and life and death? What is there to find out about good and evil and death? What is there in us of good and evil and life and death? What will happen when we die? Who is it that we think we hear calling from somewhere else while we are alive? Does everyone hear those voices, feel that hand at their elbow?

I can see Jesse's young face with the down still on its cheeks and his dark eyes looking at what I'm saying. He is in a bean bag in the corner of the room in floral shirt and board shorts. We are talking now as we have never talked. I'm sure I can see his answering dark eyes.

—

Louise has told me about it. She and Rona have already paid it a visit over the weekend. It is Greg's exhibition in the city. Greg's oils and acrylics. My brother's work! My brother who used to do drawings of Flute's tractor on the back veranda table at Cicero Street.

I've come to have a look late in the day, the city bent on making home from work in the streets outside. It's a long, echoing gallery, white walls, the deep windows at the far end giving onto the dusty plumbing of a building on the other side of the lane. One dove and then another flaps down into the gloom of the lane out of an unseen sky as I watch. I hear their cooing. I swivel on my heel and look back down the gallery. The owner is busy in a side room. I have the long lines of paintings to myself as they run to the daylight.

There are some cityscapes. They are light and open, with a sense of the sky. I think of some of my brother's folios years back, full of watercolours with buildings and narrow streets treated in blues and greys, steeped in shadows. Greg has changed, has he? His view of the world is more celebratory now. Down the other wall I find I'm seeing suggestions of rooms and food, window-light, figures on couches. I've seen two or

190

three of them before – ones Greg has been working on in the old laundry building behind the shops close to where he and Carolyn live in Altona. They live near the sea – a calm sea that runs out in a blue sheen to creep into the sky, the pale ghosts of sails far over.

Now I find a still life four feet wide but only eighteen inches deep. I would like it for our kitchen. It is abstract and warm, the paint thick and enticing. It is bread and food, with just the suggestion of knife and table top and crumbs. Ah, my brother, your maturity and understanding! I stand and take it in, the balance in the light, the airy table top backed by a room's darker corners, the golden promise of the bread. I find I'm thinking of Greg at high school, when even then he knew what he had to do, when he struggled home up the hill with his big folio, talking to his mate Rod who carried a guitar in its case that flapped around his knees as he walked. Ah, my brother.

Voices. I look to the entrance and yes, my brother, yes, coming down the stairway hand in hand with a dark girl I don't know in cloche hat and warm blue coat. They don't see me. Greg draws the girl towards the door of the side room and waves to the gallery owner. Hi! I hear answering words from within that I can't make out. Then the two saunter past the catalogue table, looking about them, surmising, thinking about context, preparing for appraisal, like someone nosing a wine and thinking before they drink. Then Greg sees me, starts, looks again, and I see the Barnes creases in his face deepen as he grins at me. He starts towards me, pulling the girl forward as he comes. She looks distracted for a moment, then looks full at me and smiles.

'Greetings!' Greg says, his voice unnaturally high. 'I thought you'd be in some time. What d'ya think? We've come back for another dekko. This is Fran. We're fellow book illustrators, you might say.'

Fran smiles and says hello. 'Your brother?' she asks Greg.

'Yes, my brother, come to appraise the works,' Greg explains and shifts his feet. 'My brother Tim. '

Yes, we are brothers. My brother, Greg. My left-handed brother, now painter, illustrator, teacher. I see his arm curling round the top of the butcher's paper, see his mouth pursed, watch his vacant-eyed thinking again before he dips the brush in the water and hovers over the paints on the old table at Cicero Street.

And already I can see Greg and Fran have a non-dependent way of tucking into each other. They move as if one, in a way that I've never seen in Carolyn and Greg. But what of Carolyn? Where is Carolyn in all this?

—

Here it is again.

I seem often to be granted a special sense of where I am. There are places in the Otways and along the coast where I have never been, but I find I know them when I reach them. Am I like a child? When we dawn on the earth as a child do we come from a state of knowing to one of not knowing and then from our birth work towards a state of knowing again? I can feel places where I have never been, as long as I can make a mental swing about, so that the directions are right, so that the path skirts the broken fence to the left, so that the cathedral is away on the rise in the west and I can see the sun behind it and its trees. Then I can know places where I have never been. Then I know where I am.

I read Louise's words about Central Park and the streets of the Upper East and West sides. I read her descriptions of the black women who are child-minders. They come out into the leafy aisles with the white children of absent mothers when the sun has become warm enough. And I'm not surprised. It is not new to me, and yet I have never seen it. I can hear their voices. I can hear how rude and spoilt the white children are. I see them prop and refuse to move until there's an ice cream, until there are French fries. There's a mild, ongoing threat in strange figures who skirt rock outcrops further over under the trees. No, I don't want to walk. I want the bus. No, I'm not coming. See? Where are the black child-minders' own children? I see the desperation on their faces as they reach for the white children's hands and find them withheld. It is not new to me, and yet I've never thought about it before. But it is a place and a day I will come to.

I put the air letter aside and I am seeing a steep forested slope, fir trees, cedars, and other huge trees that rise through green, kissed by mist, to small snatches of sky. I see surprises of white snow filling the perfect pudenda made by the trees' roots. It must be America, but I can't think about it because I don't know. But I will come there. I am hearing a creek rustling deep in the woods. I can feel how the forest waits. I will come there, and there will be a voice by my side. It is the voice, the foot-fall, of someone who ushers my gut down to a far-reaching joy. I feel a sense of warm completion in my throat as though I am about to sing. It is someone who will accompany me in my wondering forever.

I wonder if it's normal to know places before I've been to them.

—

Wood Smoke Rising Around
Us in the Hills

That winter Sunday at Cicero Street. The voices from the kitchen, saucepans clashing. And the photographs on the bedspread in front of me. My back sore, my eyes tired, my throat dry with the dust of things forgotten until now. I've found the photographs. An overcast and cold winter Sunday. These are other photographs, photographs I've never seen. I look at some of them side-on, guiltily, as the lantana twigs rake at the side window in the wind. I come on one photograph after another and the questions bear down on me with an urgency that dispenses with my fatigue. There they are above me, like great unreadable dirigibles riding and creasing against the blue . . .

It's as though everything is happening at once around us. Louise stalked by cancer, Will's ill-timed move to Overton Lane, my fragmented days and weeks in separated loneliness, our children, our work, our hopes. Louise is still in hospital, not due home again for another three days. But she will come home to the new house. I am emptying the Cicero Street drawers, throwing out, saving, bundling, carrying out cartons to the front door ready for loading into the cars. Will and Greg are at the other end of the house, deciding the fate of things in kitchen and laundry.

That's when I find them. In the back of the drawer of the dressing table my fingers encounter two folders and an envelope with a metal clasp. I'll slip some twine round them to secure them for the last of the day's trips to the new house in the back of the station wagon. But a quick opening shows me that the folders contain photographs – small, almost square prints in black and white in the old way. Can I resist having a look at one or two of them? As I begin to pick some out I find I'm looking at shots I've never seen before. I look at a few, turn them over, and immediately I hear a voice of intuition insisting that this collection has not been made by Will, although it seems he has taken some of the photos. The further I pry the more I tell myself that these are pictures of the past that Louise has put away, looked at again, pondered, put back in the folders. This is my mother's selection, I'm sure.

I feel a sense of urgency, knowing that Greg and Will are working two rooms away. There's no time to look further now. What's in the envelope? I snap up the wings of the metal catch, draw out a tied bundle. It is a tight wad of letters secured with wine-coloured tape. The tape has etched into the paper of the outer letters. They are yellow with age, but the ones in the middle are white, pristine, where I can prise the sheets open with a finger to get a glimpse. I'd say the bundle hasn't been opened in years.

I sit there on the bed's corner. I listen to the noises of the house. For the moment there is silence almost complete, then the sound of a kitchen drawer being pushed home. I feel covert. I can't hear anything from the others in the kitchen. The photographs challenge me, look at me like small, hard nuggets of truth. I'm intrigued by them. I want to know if they represent my years at Cicero Street – but this is another version of the years. The further I go the more I sense a difference in these. I can see they must mean something deep to my mother. I decide I've got time to delve a bit further. I pick out others, my mind weaving, trying to see what they are telling me. I wonder again. The sun on people's faces and shoulders is soft with other days, other years. Will is there – and Louise. There's a shot of Candles and Alex Cumming on a beach. There are girls around them in heavy, dark costumes that hang over their thighs. Candles is kneeling on one knee in the sand like a muscled Samson. A frizzy-haired girl is balanced like a dancer on his braced leg, one hand on his head for support, the other making an exaggerated arabesque. Her face is intent with keeping balance before the camera. All the other girls are smiling or laughing. Alex Cumming kneels beside Candles, supporting two girls who lean towards him like shop dummies on rigid legs. Alex's face is earnest with effort.

I decide I'll take the photographs and letters home. I slip the pictures back in their place, then put the folders and envelope in my briefcase. No matter, I tell myself, if they reach their destination a few days late, perhaps next weekend. I feel strangely furtive about it all.

I take the last load to Overton Lane and head back against the headlights to Hawthorn.

In the good light of the front room I sit again with the photographs around me. They still seem to me to be mysterious objects of truth and time, but yellowing, fading. There are two other shots of Candles and Alex sitting on a beach – the same beach? And there's another shot of the · two of them in the scrub somewhere, Alex standing with his fingers curled loosely around the barrel of a grounded rifle. Alex and Candles in tennis gear, wide hats in their hands, a racquet under Candles' arm. A group of tennis players disposed on the steps of a clubhouse, some with racquets, some in blazers and turned-up white collars, some of the girls in comely white dresses to the knee, some smiling, some morose, others turning just as the camera clicks. 'Swan Hill tournament '33' it says on the back. I look again and pick out Louise and Alex, sitting close together, his hand on her knee, her hand resting in the crook of his arm, her hair gathered to the right side in a woven bun. I want to look at her face for a long time. I love her there, her eyes direct and happy, her shoulders and waist womanly and young. Next I pick up the shot I've seen before of Louise reclining on the chaise longue with her book. I turn over others, check dates. 1929, 1932, 1933, 1934. I sense even more strongly as I search that the tone of this collection is different from the shots that Will and Louise have shown me. These are taken earlier, running through years in the early 1930s that have always in my mind made a vague approach to the month of August in 1934 when I know Will and Louise marry.

And then, still looking at the backs of snaps and searching for dates, I read: 'Port Chalice Harbour Summer 1931.' I turn it over and there is the inlet I know so well, the inlet only five kilometres or so from the church where I write. In the photograph the waves are raking white onto the outer reef where these days the surfers appear like dark seals as soon as there's the hint of a northerly. There is the harbour clutching the jetty against its landward side. Louise stands at the picture's left, and where now the takeaway and tourist buses and the new surf shop cluster near the beach there are only paddocks running far behind her towards the old post office and the store. She is in a long, hip-tight dark skirt, a sweater and beret straight out of a touring car. She is beautiful, and I see the Barnes candour, insouciance, engagement in her eyes. 1931. 1931? Is that the year before she meets Will when he comes down from Sydney? Who are her eyes for then behind the camera? Alex Cumming? The writing on the photograph is not Louise's. I riffle back through the other shots, turn up the Swan Hill tennis photograph, look at the back. It's the same hand – an oval, looping handwriting. It must be Alex's hand.

There are others. I keep picking up and putting down. Alex standing against a wire fence, trees leaning down to it. He holds two racquets under his arm and raises a silver cup high with his other hand, his mouth admitting that he's exaggerating the pose for the camera. 'Geelong Singles Easter 1932', says the back. Alex and a white-trousered doubles partner I don't recognise, standing as if bored against the brick pillar of a veranda. 'Dubbo – Mens Doubles 1931'. Then a shot showing Louise standing with another young woman at the top of a rough track that drops away from their feet towards a river and its red gums. The faces are serious, waiting for the shutter's slur, as if the two do not know each other well. The back says in Alex's writing 'Louise and Else – Mildura Jan. 1932'. It is Alex's sister Elsie and my mother. It is Louise's past in the Mallee. It is almost as if I smell a whisper of eau de Cologne drifting to the massy tree trunks.

A jolt. I turn up a print that shows Louise and Will together, standing formally, faces strained through their smiles, Will's blue eyes exposed and vulnerable. It has the air of being taken by a professional, printed on backed paper. Will's dark suit with button-hole white flower, Louise's lipstick and hair veil, trimly cut suit and expensive handbag and shoes seem to say important occasion. Their wedding? I turn the picture seeking details. There is nothing on the back. I have seen only one other shot of their wedding at the registry office – a picture of them both with John and Pearlie on some steps. It sits for years on the picture rail above Pearlie's dressing table.

Then more. Here is Alex Cumming carrying his racquets, a white towel cascading over them from his shoulder. His arm is tightly around Louise, pulling her waist towards him. She is in a summer frock and carrying a broad hat. Both are backed against a balustrade overlooking

200

a vista of tennis courts. Who took the shot? I wonder. A friend? The photograph's reverse, in Alex's hand again, informs me: 'Louise at Vic. Championships – Kooyong '31'. The next shot I turn over is Louise again, in the suit and veil of her wedding day. She is imperfectly photographed, head and shoulders, from a few yards away. Someone has taken the shot on the run. There is a suggestion of Will's shoulder and arm and white shirt collar beside her. But the truth of the face is etched into my mind. Louise appears in that split second riven with sadness, half turned away and yet aware of the camera. Her cheeks are wet with tears. I turn to the back for information. Nothing.

—

'Anyway, you know that Grandpa John wrote some poetry,' Will says to me. 'He did, didn't he,' he says, turning the words out of the side of his mouth towards Louise, where she sits in the armchair on the other side of the fire at Cicero Street. 'He did, didn't he, your father?'

'Yes,' says Louise. 'He did some rhyming. That's what he'd call it. He had a sort of journal he kept it in, but it's gone.'

'And I'm guessing that at some stage he actually met John Shaw Neilson. I reckon he was the poet – remember that? – the poet that was there on one of the jobs your father did.' Will's eyes rest on mine pointedly and then turn to Louise's. 'Fancy that,' he says. 'Just fancy that – and he probably didn't know.'

'Quietly as rosebuds talk to the thin air . . .' My mother's voice is wandering. I have heard this before. I cannot place why I know it, but I know how her voice will sound, how it will try the words. Her voice seems to be considering, weighing the lines. 'The thin air?' she says, her voice rising, questioning, admiring.

'Quietly as lovers
Creep at the middle moon . . .' Will says, and falls silent.

'Quietly as lilies
Their faint vows declare . . .' Louise responds.

'Came the shy pilgrim:
I knew not he was there . . .' says Will, and his eyes take on a far look.

Then they just stay staring into the gas fire, its glowing mantles. Finally he says: 'Yes, I'll bet he met Neilson. Who else could it be? Out there? Doing that work?' All I can hear then is the gas and its steady seething and the sound of Louise's needles clicking and advancing as she knits.

—

It will come to us all. I have watched the dogs die, one minute aquiver with expectation on the concrete floor awaiting a game, the next pinioned by gowned elbows and a muzzle. I'm there doing the story, taking photographs for the magazine. Already the vet's green syringe approaches, while the words of endearment flow. Then the plunge to the syringe's haft, a final tremor, and the gloved hands are spinning haunch, head and ears, flanks on the stainless steel to look into the eye, the black bag waiting for the word. Later the fur of heads and ears shines like jet, the eyes stare far away, from two bags that have fallen open in the back of the truck. The indefinable has gone from the eyes. The faces are still with a huge, vague stillness. It is over.

Ben Lodz is gone. I miss him. I just hear that he's gone. I don't get to the hospital. I do manage to make the funeral. I miss Ben, even though I have lost him before he dies. After the funeral, I go down into the toilet in the main building of the crematorium, before I head to the car. As I stand at the urinal words and sounds start coming to me as if from silence, as if people have just entered an echoing room somewhere below me. Through the air vent in the wall I hear: 'Who's this one?' And then: 'Lodz. L-O-D-Z. Got him marked off?' And then the ringing blows of hammers on metal handles, and further indecipherable words from voices retreating. It is over. Ben has gone.

As my mother Louise is dying I can see death sitting behind her eyes, a second face looking out dispassionately.

When Taffie is killed by the car in Riversdale Road, Will finds his body later, discarded under a lilly pilly tree near the dentist's surgery. He brings him home. When he opens the car door and draws a wheat bag back, there is Taffie in the place where you put your feet in the back seat of the car. He looks asleep, but he's so still. When I reach and touch his chest he is hard and cold. He doesn't move.

When is it my turn?

When I go out with Flute in the 1940s drought he takes a knife and a stone into the paddock and pulls the long gate rattling up behind us. We walk towards the bundles of the sheep where they lie against the fence or far over under the trees. He gives me the heavy bullet of the whet stone to carry. He tests some of the sheep with his boot. They don't move. They are dead. But one lifts a head, feebly rakes a leg behind it and is still again. Flute leans down, grasps the wool of the crown of the sheep's head, pulls it back, baring the whiter folds of wool under the throat. His knife plunges in so easily, the blood following it, as he saws across the throat to make sure. The head slides away at a pitiful angle from the body. I watch the sheep's eyes flutter. I watch its last tremor. It lies as though it were pleased, relieved. Flute moves on, finds a movement in another, and again the knife leaps in and the throat gapes, the sheep's back legs lunging briefly, then lying still. I watch. I look at Flute's closed face. I listen to his breathing, his cursing. I hear his rough blessings. 'You poor bugger. You poor bloody bugger. Better fuckin' out of it, aren't you.' I watch and start to count. I count 18 sheep we've killed. We walk and kill and Flute asks for the whet stone. When we finish we have been doing it for more than an hour, going far up the paddock to the end where the line of sugar gums has always been a mystery to me. We are alive. All the sheep are dead. Flute has given up. 'Shit!' he says with a savage hiss. 'Shit it.' He hurls the whet stone against a fence post, his anger forcing his body round so far he nearly falls like a clown. The toes of his boots are red with blood. He stands for a moment as though his legs might crumple. His eyes are wild. They're not seeing anything. Then he kicks his way through the dust to the whetstone, picks it up, looks over at me as though he's emerging from a reverie. 'Ah, bugger it all to hell!' he says. 'I suppose it's home James.' He slips the whetstone into my hand again to carry.

—

I can feel what matters to Will even when I'm only twelve. Sometimes I can stand aside and watch him, listen to him. I can see him at the block at Upwey, with the evening coming down in grey and blue. He is still working in the bracken towards the creek, the fire sending up its thin smoke. He works in the old Army shirt, his shoulders seeming to heave of themselves in the disappearing light as he chips with the spade and then rakes. Sometimes he drops the rake and reaches for the slasher with the long handle, spreads his feet wide so as to cut low, and grunts as he sweeps down, severing the stringy stalks of the older bracken again and again in an arc round him. Louise is in the lighted kitchen on the other side of the shack making soup, setting the table. Greg is playing on the floor.

Alistair and I have been helping Will, doing the gathering and the raking, plying the fire with bracken and leaves until it stifles, rebuilds its heat and sends the dense smoke of green burning aloft again against the trees. We like that slow, thick cauliflower of smoke rising. Now Will comes up the slope, hat off. He stacks the rake and scythe against the fibro wall for the morning, slowly wipes his brow with his sleeve, then digs the spade into the ground, leans on it. He looks at us and raises his eyebrows quizzically. We know he includes us. We know he is tired but in a celebratory mood. We like the silence he leaves ringing. He looks down the darkening valley. We watch him. We feel time swarming, then stilled. We need no words, but we are waiting for words. We know that this might have happened before. We know in our fresh-air tiredness and languor in the dusk that this might happen again. I know in this silence that this will become a scene, a story that I will tell. Alistair is unaware. He is thinking about the distance he can shoot in this bush with his plane-tree bow and arrow brought from home. I know what he is thinking.

Our father watches the fitful fire he has created for a moment, and looks further down to the Billington's chimney in the valley bottom. He sighs, leans on the spade, taking it in. I can tell what he will say before he says it. 'Look at Billington's wood smoke climbing,' he says. 'Straight up to the stars. It's going to be a cold night. It'll be a sunny day tomorrow. Don't you like the way the wood smoke rises around us in the hills?'

—

'See that cow over there that is a bull? Well, look what very big shoulders that cow has – because it's a bull. I'm glad she's in the next paddock – given that she's a bull. I think she thinks we're intruders. What do you think? Do you think that fence is strong?' It's my mother talking, as if to herself. I wish Susan and Jesse could be here. Then they could hear this and see this. Then they could understand. But it's the past. It's too late for them. It's too early for them. It's far back when we're kids. We're here in the green paddock corner, the sun shining, the white clouds slowly mounting like optimistic faces over the gums along the creek. It is the Otways. We've brought a picnic – the old rug, the old bit of tarpaulin, the old basket with some sandwiches and fruit.

'Look at the line of the body, though,' Louise is saying. Now, she's talking only to me. Greg and Alistair are further over chopping at the grass with sticks. In any case it's just the four of us in the world, or five if you count my father Will, who we cannot see any longer in his walking further up the sweep of the valley. The valley is so generous in its green space and its chancels of deep shadow under the trees. We have never been here before, and yet I feel I know this place. I love it and its green peace.

I am looking where Louise points. The bull takes just a couple of rolling steps and its head goes down to feed again. It's a Hereford with a white neck and huge tan flanks and a blunt, wise box of a head. I like watching it. Its face is creased and hoary.

'Look at the stretch of its body,' my mother is saying. 'Look at the chest. Look at the frothy décolletage! Look at the curlicued brow and the horns. Look at the hindquarters narrowing in. Look at the sheer reach of it. It's magnificent, isn't it?' The bull, not thirty yards from us beyond the thin line of the fence, stops feeding, swings its head up to regard us, motionless. Then its tail switches at a fly. Then again it is motionless, its eyes on us. Is it thinking?

'What's it thinking?' Louise says, jumping into my thought.

'It's thinking that it would like to lie down in the sun, but it's still hungry, so it has to keep feeding,' I say. I'm sure I can sense the vague thoughts shifting in the fog of the bull's mind. 'It can feel the sun, and it knows about the line of trees along that top fence because that's where it goes sometimes, but it's forgotten how it's supposed to lie down.'

My mother's face seems to accept this. 'Yes,' she says. 'It knows the smell of each corner of the paddock and where the water is. And it knows where the cows are, but it can't remember why they're there. It'll remember that later in the day.' She looks at me, drags her mouth down with mock seriousness, then laughs. 'Look at its cock swinging there. Fancy dragging that round all the time. Willie's the wrong word for it. Tossil? That's better. Have tossil, will travel. He's a bit of a lair – that cow that is a bull!'

I look at the bull again, look at its cock thinking about coming out from the middle of its belly. I look at the distance between its cock and the heavy dark hanging of its balls so far to the rear. Perhaps I've never looked at a bull before. My mother is always looking and then thinking and imagining. When I am with her I see things and think things for the first time. Greg doesn't see that way. Alistair doesn't see that way. But I know that Louise and I see so directly sometimes that it hurts. It seems that is what we are meant to do.

'Anyway, whatever it's thinking, that cow that is a bull seems happy enough,' my mother says. 'It doesn't have to be borne down by the woe that is in marriage, does it.' And she looks away from me with her thought. The birds are busy along the creek. We can hear them chiming.

Would Susan and Jesse understand this? Would they fold into this hillside, hear these words with their hearts?

—

It is 1977. It has been all over with Patricia for four months now. She has filed for divorce. All the sorting and packing is over. All the stepping round each other in the house with dismaying concern, even with a sort of tenderness, is over. All the weeping inside is over. I am desperate and happy by turns. I go into the tunnel. It is a limbo. I wonder whether I will ever emerge. I have my new love of Adela. It will be the year's end in 1978. It will be 1979. It will eke into the hot days of 1980. I am lost. I am found.

I watch other people weep in the quiet rooms at the Centre while we sit on the cushions around the walls. I'm surprised how I open to the support group – all those hands that hold me, stroking me, lifting me. I stroke, lift, clasp others, feeling the concern and acceptance that floods out from my fingers and forearms. And my love for Adela is new and bright. I push through thickets of glad terror. I drink its bitterness, sadness, sudden light. I feel wounded. I feel more alive now than ever before. And more fragile.

Patricia has moved to Frankston now, and Susan with her. The small and modest house I buy in Hawthorn is sometimes so quiet and unnerving on a Sunday that I have to quit it. I don't like the mid-grey curtains, but they become familiar. I cook for myself and become three parts vegetarian. I sometimes weep with loneliness to the flowing jazz in the lounge room – deep, deep sobs from the gut. I am finding there are many forms of weeping. It is good to weep – it is somehow an affirmation of worth. It is cleansing. It says this is me and I will come through and be wiser.

I see my children's faces register separation and divorce, their faces pinched under the light in the counsellor's office. I sometimes hear Susan crying in her room, her throat musing with each sob, when she stays with me. Even so, I have to love Adela now. Adela is new. She has bowled me over with joy. It is part of the pattern. We must use each other. But Adela doesn't want to meet Jesse and Susan. And after Adela, who then?

—

It is 1980. I am desperate, alone. At other times I feel as tense as fine glass in a happiness I don't trust as the sun sets beyond the window. I am fine glass. I am lost and found, growing older. I love Adela – and she will hurt me. It is 1978 becoming 1979, just eking into 1980. And I have wounded her in my questing, in my weighing of her. Adela walks away from me into the forests of faces and voices. The days pass. I see Adela emerge and smile. But she walks away. Then I see her still. She is standing looking down at the meagre pool she has made with the ragged builder's plastic in her smitten backyard. I love her, the swimmer, the woman of pools, who sees with me, knows when things will happen, when things will end. For a time I think we will never end, but we do. Her husband returns. Does she know he will? She has been unhappy. She will be unhappy again. Our love ends and I am lost, and yet I will be found in another place.

I walk the long paths of the forest, listening for the rush of water through the trees. I watch the swifts arrow across the sunset as the tree-tops close around. Then I emerge. He that I was is lost. He that I am is found.

—

I come into the room from the hall, look to find Louise's face against the pillows. I register that her eyes look clearer, more enquiring than yesterday. She is recovering little by little from the operation. She's pleased to be home. From the bed she can see the big maple across the street riding there against the sky carrying its last few flags of golden and russet leaves. I drop the two library books at the foot of the bed. She smiles.

'Thanks for getting those,' she says. She sets hands and wrists beside her in the sheets and raises herself against the pillows. As she moves I pull the top one out, leaning over her, dig it down again vertically to support her back. She lies back, sighing. She looks at me, then looks away at the curtains and window for a moment.

'Do you want to see my operation?' she asks, and she's mumbling with uncertainty. 'Do you want to see my scar. It's expected that everyone exhibits their scars, isn't it?' She laughs dryly, looks at me.

'Yes, if you want to show me.'

She reaches across with her left hand and pulls down the right shoulder of her nightie. She exposes her breast. I see a sad, blank plain of white skin like a kettle drum, the wound crossing it like an unsure, clamped mouth. That essence is gone, that essence that says woman in its nippled globe, its beautiful falling, always beautiful in its falling and rounding – that is gone. My expectation makes me still see it there, but it's gone. The pricks of the departed stitches march like footsteps in a snowy waste. It's a sad taking away from her.

'It's neat, isn't it!' She almost questions me, but there's a bitterness in her reaching for my opinion. 'He's done a good job, hasn't he!' What is a good job, my head is saying, and I have a clutch of fear that she can hear my thoughts.

'Yes, very professional and tidy. But very sad.'

She appraises it herself, chin tucked into neck, for a moment. 'They're going to monitor the other one for now,' she says tonelessly. 'Monitoring,' she says. 'They love monitoring.' She draws the shoulder of her nightie back, pulls the light cardigan around her again.

'Are you going to make a cup of tea?' she asks. 'I'll have one if you are.' She lies back, mouth working, against the pillows. I shift the library books from the foot of the bed to a place within reach of her left hand. I nod twice solemnly, turn, leave the room for the kitchen.

Of what use am I? Even my widest embrace can encounter only a loss that is creeping on, a gradual concluding. I am turning the tap to fill the kettle. I look out through the window curtain. The grey stucco bungalow next door blots out all of the sky.

—

I am in Mildura to teach. I will do the classes arranged for me at the college in Redcliffs later in the day. But swarming beneath that purpose I can feel a secret, urgent current – a current of fascinated fear. Yes, the current runs with chill and fear and a sadness I'm unsure of. It's something more secret and important that carries me along in these sun-filled streets now like a steadily advancing moraine. I am seeking my mother Louise and Alex Cumming through the Mallee, even though I can see Louise's wan face against the pillows, and my heart and breathing fade. I am pursuing them up to the Murray. Packing before I leave

Melbourne, I think I can see both their young faces together against the river. I am seeking them and I'm fearful and yet fascinated at the thought of what I might find.

As I drive north I am trying to break through to them, but more and more I can hear the doctor's gravelly, practical voice saying only a week ago that Louise's mastectomy is in the nature of a holding operation, that it may be six months, or as much as eighteen, but probably not more, and I nod and find my throat clogged around my next question, so I study Will's face where he sits looking down at the carpet, his hands pressed between his knees. And yet still as I drive I can hear Louise and Alex, as though those photographs are invested with movement and presence. I see the two of them in Melbourne. I see them against the coast during the summer at Port Chalice. It is a cruel intrigue that has hold of me. I can see them walking above the river where it spreads resting and brown in the sun. Where else are they? I am trying to break through. I have to know this past, this past I have seen in the strange set of photographs, this past that unselfconsciously trails before me out of the cards and letters in the envelope.

I don't know why I want to know these things. I don't know from where the conviction comes that tells me not to mention my discovery of the photographs and the letters to Louise or Will. I can feel the strength of my intuition, but I seem also to have to excuse it, to tell myself it is not the best time – when Louise is recovering from the mastectomy and has been called to account again by the cancer in the next months, while Will sits tired and unseeing in strange new rooms.

I can feel something even deeper staying me. A cool hand stops me. The photographs and words are shaded with another view of the past that has its own right to the light. But it has not been granted it. Why? In all of our poring over family pictures I've never seen these. Will has never spread them out for Alistair and Greg and me to look at. Louise has never produced these folders. Why? Jean, my mother's sister, drops in at Overton Lane in the evening to see Louise, her face older than I remember, her voice rich, though, with its old jazz hoarseness. Just as she is going, no one else about, there on the back veranda I take a chance and ask her a tangential question. I tell her that in the move I have found a couple of interesting shots of Alex Cumming and Candles going back a long way, and another one of Alex and his sister Elsie.

'Ah, yes,' says Jean. 'Elsie Cumming is in Mildura as far as I know. Strange lady. Strange. Last I heard Alex and his family are still in Sydney somewhere. But Elsie's always stayed close to the home farm. She's a strange Mallee lady.'

It's not like Jean, this talk. Her mouth is pursed and ungenerous as she says it. She looks quinces and sideways at me. I search her eyes for more, but she stares me out, says nothing, then looks away to the dimming back yard. I should question her more, but my mind is trying to process what I'm learning – so I don't.

When Jean has gone I still see the photographs, hear their legends: 'Port Chalice Harbour Summer 1932' . . . 'Louise and Else Mildura Jan. 1932' . . . 'Swan Hill Tournament '33' . . . 'Louise at Vic. Championships Kooyong '31'. I am seeing Alex Cumming's loping handwriting.

So now I am walking towards the river in the first light. It is an atavistic thing. It comes from the journalism I used to do, from landing in towns with questions to ask. Spy out the land. Remind yourself of this place. Far over, the sun has come up rose, dusting the grey of the vines that are still in shadow. Like a darker frieze behind run the shocks and recesses of the long armies of river red gum. Behind me a single car door shuts tentatively down the far end of the motel, as if testing the dawn. There will be *longueurs* of heat later in the day, I think, and the tresses of the willows along the river will lean down to the water near the wharves' white stanchions. I can remember many days like this. I've forgotten the brown strength of the river, the echoing bends, the cloisters of red gum. For me there has been the sea for all these years.

But I know I am here to see Elsie Cumming. I know her house and its old palm in the quiet street in Redcliffs. I will visit her. I will have questions for her. Will she answer them?

I walk to think. But I am conjuring with Elsie Cumming's face – the one I have seen in the photographs, the other face with my mother's on the slope above the river bank all those years ago. At the same time I feel

211

as though I'm walking to find some pure solution to the slow sadness in me. But I know there is none. I'm thinking of my mother, and I know she is going to die. She knows she is going to die. How can my mother die? Why must she die? Why is she leaving us while the clock beside the bed trips on, raking time, raking time? I look at the Murray's morning business, the flash of white cockatoos in the red gums and I'm angry that she won't see it any more. Should I be grateful that she has known it? Twaddle! She deserves it forever. Curse cancer! Curse the steady stare of death!

—

I'm sitting watching Pat Friar's lips. I'm half smiling. There's a half-smile on his face, too. He's carrying on, and he knows it. He's declaiming.

'Fortunately, given the phenomenon of frequent and fortuitous er . . . fraternisation afforded farmers with their er . . . fiancées or feral female partners, itself facilitated by er . . . ferocious following of the, the er . . . fine-day passage of the sun from first light to final frisson, few farmers forgo a frangifying fuck in the forenoon followed by further er . . . femur-frying fornication far into the night . . . and so on,' says Pat, his eye holding mine much of the time as though he fears losing the forward movement of the phrases. Then he stops and sighs, relieved to have found the final words. 'And let that be a lesson to you,' he adds and smiles his self-deprecating smile. He's trying to brighten me.

'So, one thing's for sure,' Pat is saying, travelling to the real issue now. 'You're too young to live by yourself. You're too young and spritely, my boy, to spend the rest of your life alone! Too spritely, for want of a more salacious term. I don't agree with your psychiatrist friend that you should not seek another long-term relationship. Long-term relationship is the going thing – and it improves each time, you old bastard!'

I smile at Pat. I'd like to believe what he says, but I can't. I think my smile is wan.

—

I am thinking about it again, but I don't know where the truth lies. Nevertheless it persists there in my mind. And I hear a voice. I hear lines being spoken. I think it's the poet who worked with Grandpa John. And I think, as Will guessed, his name is John Shaw Neilson. The proposition sits there like a dense stone in my mind and I can feel the weight of the fact that it must have happened.

I hear a voice I don't know. I hear it saying, '. . . his case is grievous.' Then it repeats: '. . . his case is grievous, his strength doth fail . . .' The voice is wandering. It seems to be considering. It is trying the words. 'The dews have draped with Love's old lavishness,' it says, and I can hear it is in the open air. There is no echo, no resonance. But for the first time I catch a slight hiss in the voice, a slight slurring sound. It's not the poet's voice. It is my grandfather's. It's Grandpa John, sitting legs splayed wearily before him in the straw and red earth. His back is against a taut bag of wheat and other filled bags crowd around his shoulders, looming like rough escarpments above him while he is on the ground. He is a young man. His voice is a young voice. It has not developed the raspiness that I hear in the shed at Mont Albert when he is in his sixties. 'Through stilly hours . . . the dews have draped with Love's old lavishness . . . the drowsy flowers,' says the voice, separating and savouring the phrases. 'Love's old lavishness . . .' it says. 'Love's old lavishness.'

The poem is in a little notebook that Grandpa John is holding. The poet is near him, sitting astraddle two wheat bags, nursing a pale hat in one hand, the back of the other hand slowly and thoughtlessly spreading sweat and red dust across his forehead as he listens. It is his little note-book that Grandpa John holds. It must be morning lunch time in the wheat-bagging. Morning lunch the workers call it, and the shearers. Morning lunch when the farm wife and her daughter in their broad white hats come in the buggy from the house far over on the road with the scones and the tea-billy and cloths.

Grandpa John is still trying the words in the air. The poet is still camped silently behind him, leaning on one ramrod arm and shoulder on the stack of bags of wheat to stay balanced, looking out into the stubble. He is wordless, but these are his words being read by another man. The two other workers are lolling in the shade of a gum in the paddock corner where the tea-billy sits on a couple of planks, where the horse stamps in the shafts of the buggy.

'An evil time is done,' Grandpa John reads. 'An evil time is done.' He is not shy of saying the words into the air, leaving them there, saying them into the air again. Grandpa John has written rhymes. And the poet understands. He is happy to hear his words in the air, happy that someone likes them and sounds them there in the paddock. But he doesn't want the other two workers to be near. He doesn't want the farm wife to be near either. He can see her on the other side of the buggy, talking to her husband, her skirt billowing briefly. Words are not for any of them. He looks again to where the other two workers loll in the shade, their hats down over their eyes now.

'Again, as someone lost in a quaint parable,' Grandpa John recites. 'Again, as someone lost in a quaint parable, comes up the sun.' Now there is only the sound of the steady, dry wind in the trees in the paddock corner for long seconds. Then the slightly slurring, considering voice:

'An evil time is done.

Again, as someone lost in a quaint parable

Comes up the sun.'

The dry wind, the low, blond rise of the hill towards the town, the horse nodding in the shafts of the buggy, seemingly asleep under the dappled shade. Then Grandpa John says, 'It's beautiful. Your rhymes are right. Will someone print it?'

'Don't know,' says the poet. 'Perhaps if I write away they might. Who knows!' His voice is quite thin and breathless amongst the dry jute columns of the wheat bags.

—

It's mid morning. I am in the airy front room of Elsie's house. The bulbous old palm in the lawn looms over the front veranda. The traffic murmurs from Redcliffs into Mildura at the end of the street. I am poring over paper clippings, snapshots. I am reading Alex Cumming's name in the passenger list for SS *Sonoma*, sailing from Sydney to

San Francisco via Honolulu and Pago Pago. It is 1934. I am in the year 1934. I read: 'Mr. Cumming was born at Waitchie in the Victorian Mallee district in 1908, but grew up primarily near Sea Lake. As a boy he learned his tennis strokes hitting against the wall of the Sea Lake bakery. He played his first tennis on the ant bed court of neighbours near Chillingollah. Alex Cumming won his first local tournament at Berriwillock when he was thirteen years old . . .'

I read. I believe. Who is telling me? I turn over the clipping and find that it is the *Ouyen Standard.* I pick up a denser single sheet among the newspaper clippings. It is embossed paper. I read: 'We note with regret that you were unable to join us at our 75th Annual Dinner, and feel you may be interested in having one of the souvenir dinner menus . . .'

I'm aware of Elsie Cumming somewhere near, but I read on, shuffle the clippings towards their box. I'm finding other yellowed newspaper pages. I see in the prickling screens of the old press photographs Alex Cumming's high-browed face, a shock of dark hair on the right. I see the pinched patrician nose, the eyes in shadow, the face waiting for the camera to let time run again. I see Alex Cumming's bunched wrist tendons and the strength of the right arm and the shoulders. I read the caption: 'The concentration and style of tennis player Alex Cumming is captured in this action shot taken on the Australian team's New Zealand tour. The service is one of Cumming's strong points.' Who is telling me? The *Swan Hill Advocate,* March 13, 1934.

But I can sense Elsie Cumming hovering behind me as I turn paper, read, turn more paper. She wants to sit down.

'You're welcome,' she says, as she's said before. 'You're welcome.' Her white hair is in a bun. 'I'm nearly eighty, so I don't move about so much now. They're all a long time ago. But you're welcome to take them with you. I can't let you keep them. Alex might want them. But take them back to the motel if you like. You'll be staying a bit longer, won't you? Take them.'

'I'd like to, if you don't mind,' I say. 'I can sift through them. I can drop them back tomorrow. I'd like to have a look at some of the other clippings.' I'm still idly plucking a further wad of photographs from the blue, stippled cardboard hatbox as I speak. My fingers are surprised at their weight. Elsie shuffles around me to put the kettle on.

'It's all a long time ago. Some of them in there are from that Davis Cup tour in America and Canada,' she says, her back receding, her white apron lighting the way. 'It's all a long time ago now.' I look up at the room dim around me. For a moment I can't believe I'm here. How did this come about? Why is this imperative? Why do my fingers go on searching even while I stop to think? What is it that I sense bunched in Elsie Cumming's stooped shoulders?

I need more light. It will be better at the motel. I start to collect, dump the sheets into rough order, stow them in the hat box. There are a few photographs. I encounter a pin. It pricks my first finger. It is orange with rust where it spears two photographs together. I suck finger while I glance at the first of them. It shows my mother and Alex at a table, both looking up, eyes luminous, Alex's arm round Louise's shoulders, other couples behind them in dimness. 'Louise at Kooyong Farewell – May '34'.

'Kettle's on. I'll sit down a bit.' Elsie is back in her slippers.

I turn to her, the picture brimming in my mind. 'My mother's here,' I say. 'She and Alex knew each other for a long time, didn't they? Didn't they know each other up here and down in Melbourne too?'

'Yes, they got round a lot together,' Elsie says. 'They sometimes played as a mixed doubles team for fun. Alex played with her brother too – ah . . . ah . . . Murray.'

'Yes, I know Alex and Candles played together at Swan Hill a few times,' I say.

'Ah,' she says. 'Candles, yes. Everybody called him Candles. I'd forgotten. Candles.'

'What about in Melbourne?' An imperative burns now in me that I have never suspected is there. 'Louise and Alex must have known each other in Melbourne for three or four years after they were up here. Did they ever get engaged?'

Elsie makes as though she hears the kettle, as though she is going to get up from the chair, as though she might not answer. Then she sits back again, looks pointedly at the fireplace, her hand resting along the arm of the chair. 'They weren't properly engaged,' she says. 'They were going to get married. But they didn't in the end, and that's that.'

'What happened?' I ask.

'You'd have to ask Alex that,' Elsie says. 'All I know is that Louise didn't want to wait until he came back from America.' She flashes me a smile that is not vacant, but not genuine, that her searching eyes directed too long at me betray. 'It's a long time ago now. It all happened down in Melbourne. It's water under the bridge, as they say. Water under the bridge.' Elsie sighs. I can see that she is relieved to be able to give events that finality. She will go and get the kettle. She slowly hauls herself up from the chair.

'So, where is Alex now?'

'Ah.' Elsie swings round uneasily and leans heavily on the back of the chair for balance. 'Alex has been in Sydney for nearly thirty years now, I'd say. Meg died about eight years ago, I suppose. But there's still Lorraine. Their daughter. And Keith. But he's overseas. Alex moved again not too long ago. Lorraine tells me she's not far away from him in Sydney these days.'

'I don't suppose you'd have an address or telephone number for Alex, would you? I'd like to talk to him one of these days when I can get up there, ask him about the tennis and the Davis Cup trip.' I'm surprised at how easy it is. I've become cunning. And yet in some way I don't know what I'm asking, why I'm asking, why I can already picture myself in Sydney. But my heart is beating sharply.

'Yes, I've got it somewhere. I've never been to the flat he's in now, or even the one before,' says Elsie, rummaging a hand under her apron, making at a shuffle in her slippers for the kitchen. 'Remind me when you bring the cuttings back and I'll look it out for you. Lorraine's too, if I can look it out. Now, milk in coffee for you? I haven't got any cake, but there are some biscuits.'

Can this be happening? I have been down – groping my way for days in the dark of the tunnel – when Adela Priest rings. That's how it starts. Jock Newsome, a colleague of mine at the college who teaches evening classes with her in Kew gave her my number. She has heard from someone that Patricia and I have separated. Tough, isn't it, she says – and my dear husband Les thinks he's in love with a young woman, an audio-visual person in one of the universities. He's always been my mate. He's moved out, though. I don't know. So join the club, she says in her throaty voice. It's a voice I remember from a curriculum committee of five years ago when we talked a couple of times over a drink. She laughs. Ah yes, I remember her laughing, her deep lashes, her challenging eyes, her dark curls. That's how it starts.

Yeah – my mate, my mate! she says again. But enough of that. Would you have the time to look over an outline for a book I'm getting together on computers and English teaching? Very early days, she says, but could you? She could drop the pages over. She's only in Auburn.

That's how it starts. In another twenty minutes Adela is sitting on the stool in my kitchen, her legs crossed, swinging her foot in rhythm to 'Telegraph Road'. I look at her. She is drinking the coffee I've made, reaching for it on the bench, sipping, putting it down again. Have I ever really looked at her before, really seen her? She is my first importunate woman. Her cheekbones are beautiful, with the dark ringlets of hair framing her face. She is wearing a white sweater with a gold chain hanging between her breasts. Can this be happening? Already we are wondering if we will go to see the Fred Williams exhibition in the city next weekend. Can this be? What about dinner later in the week after I've read the outline? Thursday? Yes, we can get together then.

When Adela can get together she gets together. That's how it begins. And yet even as it starts, I can sense its ending.

—

Butter, the stomach settler. That's one of Pearlie's truths.

Boobialla and peppercorn trees round the house, I hear them say. Because they are more fire-resistant, slower to burn than eucalypts and wattles and mallee. That's a truth I hear from Jean and Joyce and Louise when they're reminiscing. I hear it from Flute. I hear it from John and Pearlie too, far up in the red Mallee, but they're thinking of the Wimmera.

Writing is discovery, giving my own twist to happenings and yet remaining honest. That is a truth.

There was a man up near Waitchie, still quite young, in his thirties, who slipped and had a sliding fall when he was carrying a bag of wheat on his shoulders. The fall twisted his spine. He was part paralysed in the legs. Even though he was big, had strong arms and shoulders, he had to spend a lot of time in bed in the side room of the old weatherboard house. But he was the best person on the place at killing chooks and roosters when only the women were home and the others were out in the paddocks. So his mother or his sisters used to hand the chooks through the window to him where he was sitting up in bed. One twist and their necks were wrung. He'd hand the chooks back to the girls to be plucked and dressed. That's not a truth. That's one of Candles' stories. He used to play football with the man before he had his accident. But it's a story that has the truth in it.

Good rain, an autumn break by Anzac Day, is generally a pointer to a good season for the crops. That's a truth. I hear it from Pearlie and John and Candles and Louise and Flute. But they're thinking of the Wimmera.

Des never marries. That's a truth that catches at my throat. Des, my uncle who is blind, never has a wife. He often holds his head on the side, listening, waiting to see if he should smile, as he gets older. That's after Betty is gone.

We are all very good actors. That's a truth designed for Jesse and Susan, but it will be too soon to be of use to them. They will have to be older, to have seen how cleverly people can pretend to be confident, happy, unperturbed until they encounter pressure or think they are unseen, when you can watch their faces suddenly fall away, drained of joie de vivre.

That's a truth to be learned from others but also to be found in one's self. No one is exempt.

Photography is about walking, moving, seeing perspectives change, climbing, looking for repetitions and distances. It is about walking, looking again and waiting, knowing something is about to happen that has not happened before. That is a truth. Afterwards I have forgotten what steps I take, how I kneel quickly to get the photograph. But I know it is about waiting.

Even while I'm thinking these things I'm waiting. Waiting for what?

—

Adela is reading. I love her. I hear my mind whispering it. She lies beside me in the bed, pillows plumped around her. I won't disturb her. Out of the corner of my eye I watch her.

Yes, I love her. We flow together – her bubbling laugh, her soft voice, her occasional cigarette, her need to tell me her stories, quietly slipping into them like a country person. But she has secrets somehow. I don't see her at the main shops in Hawthorn. Perhaps she shops in Kew? I'll have to ask her. Her answers are vague when I ask her about her years with IBM, before she returned to teaching. Yes, we get together, but we seldom go to her modest stucco flat. She says she doesn't socialise much. She's sometimes strangely quiet in company. Now and then, when I least expect it, she'll sweep her hair back and talk about her husband Les and their one daughter I've never seen. It sometimes sounds as though she's telling it to herself. Her face drops, the lines around her mouth more pronounced and sagging. I can feel the secrets, the yearnings there. She looks riven – then brightens and smiles. So for the moment she is my beautiful Adela, my importunate woman.

Now, she closes her book, looks at me, knowing I'm thinking about her. Enquiry in her eyes turns into a coy smile. 'What am I doing reading? Can't waste a good man!' She reaches over, switches off the light on her side, straightens, and drags her nightie over her head in one movement. She slips down beside me.

'Never ever waste a good man! Things my mother taught me!'

I work my left arm under her, hold her to me, murmuring into her hair, then feel for her bottom, fingers stroking round it and down her thigh.

People, I'm discovering, organise levels for their lives, and step from one to another carefully. That is enough for me for now. I know I'm putting questions on hold.

—

I'm sitting at the desk in the motel room late in the day after the classes at the college in Mildura. I'm riffling through Elsie Cumming's photographs and yellowing cuttings again. And there it is – a letter, written on quite stiff paper:

21 Halibut Drive,
Hartford, Connecticut, USA.   20 July, 1934

Dear Mr Cumming,

Please, please don't put this letter down just yet!

You might think me a scatterbrained American girl, and perhaps I am, but I wanted to write to you after watching your marvellous play at Newport. Yes, I was there with a girlfriend, in only about the third row back!

We have talked about nothing but you since we saw you play. You have such a beautiful smile when you are coming back to fetch the balls. I'm writing to you on a dare. Belle, my girlfriend, calculates I won't do it, but she is really just as fascinated with you and curious about you as I am. Please, please, don't stop reading!

I can't imagine how you can play such tennis. You must be very strong. How any of the other players return your serve I cannot think. I play tennis, too, but not tennis up to your standard. Much more hit and giggle and give in. I suppose you know a lot of Australian girls like that.

And speaking of girls, we want to know what sort you like. Blonde? Brunette? Tall? Short? We are two business girls who live together here in Hartford. I am brunette and 5 feet four, Belle is 5 feet two and blonde, but not extreme blonde. We like swimming, dancing, going to the theatre and the movies. We like reading. And of course we like watching tennis stars like you!

You should meet some American girls like us. Maybe you will. We'll both be at the tennis at Long Island Cricket Club next Monday and we'll both be in the main dining room wearing Stars and Stripes hats wound with white ribbons. You'll think we're forward, but if you meet us you'll find we're not like that.

Your most devoted admirer on a dare,

Stacey Bloom.

So – here are Stacey and Belle on an American dare. Then in my fingers I find a photograph of white-attired players practising on grass courts that sweep away to a large, steep-roofed clubhouse. The back carries the words 'Canadian National'. Then a picture of a man in a workshop with the ovals of tennis racquets like eyes on the wall behind him. There is nothing on the back. I turn over another shot of jacketed men and broad-hatted women on a sunny balcony among tables. The back of the photograph tells me it is Monticito Country Club. Another shot, inexpertly taken, is of players rounding a net on a grass court. I turn it over. The back says: 'Nassau (NY Cricket Club) – first hit on grass.' It is written in Alex Cumming's looped lettering.

Then two heavier professional prints in an envelope. I slip them out, and look at the larger of the prints. There is a girl's face, immediate, striking. She is beautiful, her blonde hair mid length, sweeping away from her forehead on one side to nestle her neck, just above the loose chemise she wears. The skin of her open throat looks tanned and smooth. She stands edged against a white-clothed table, looking candidly at the camera, her mouth and eyes just smiling. She is waiting, right hand holding a champagne glass. Beside her is Alex, unmistakeable in long white trousers and dark blazer with an indistinct pocket. His hand nearest the girl hangs uncertain. His other is loosely hooked in the side pocket of his blazer. He looks serious, head tilted slightly back, regarding the camera and its expectations rather than looking at it. Behind him there is a suggestion of a potted palm and a spacious reception room. It is clearly a professional print, probably bought from a newspaper.

I turn it over. Attached to the back by paste that has turned to concrete is a caption cut from a paper, a slim sliver of yellowed words: 'Miss Belle Ormiston, of Hartford, Conn., is pictured with Mr Alex Cumming, the Australian Davis Cup player, at the reception given yesterday at Long Island Cricket Club for visiting overseas players.'

Belle Ormiston. It takes me a moment to recall the letter. Yes – Stacey and Belle. The other smaller photograph is still against my palm. I take it to the window. It is turning sepia. Holding it to the light I see the same fine-featured face and blonde hair of Belle, turned upwards and smiling pure love from under a hair braid at Alex Cumming. The girl's arms reach to surround his neck in its white, turned-up collar, her breasts in a woollen jumper turning towards him. His arm is reaching down to clasp her waist, his face intent on hers. Neither seems aware of the camera. Taken by whom, I wonder aloud. Taken by whom?

—

I'm standing near the desk holding a sheaf of assignments, my hands not knowing where to put them down. For the moment I seem lost. Someone on the radio begins to play 'St. James Infirmary'. I hear the voice, the words. Is it Jimmy Rushing singing it? I feel the sadness of the notes climbing. It floors me – this sadness that has nothing to do with me. I hear the words persisting – '. . . so sweet, so cold, so fair . . .' it is saying. I hear a trumpet coming in from the side. And suddenly I find I'm weeping. Deep sobs start to come from somewhere that is nothing to do with the blues, something much further back than Patricia and our hopes, further back than Jesse and Susan. My sadness surges towards them like a steady wave and gently washes over them and then on towards me where I prop against the edge of the desk on this Sunday late afternoon, the weekend traffic murmuring home to the living places of people down Power Street. I weep, and 'Ridiculous' an inner voice says. 'Childish!' it says, 'Stop this self-pitying nonsense!'

But I go on sobbing. I feel the sense of it, the warmth of it, the dignity, integrity and responsibility of it. I weep through to a dignity in my tears, in my learning, in my sadness. Dignity – that's it. The inner voice fades like someone departing down an avenue. Dignity remains, slowly burning. I'm real. I'm true. I'll survive.

—

Jesse, I am writing to you. Have we lost each other? Jesse, you may not be listening, but you are my son. I want to tell you some of what I know. I am telling you about what happens as the world turns and the sun departs and the moon rises.

This is a gun, Jesse. This gun in the corner with its cold, grey barrel is made so that it can suggest a path through air for the bullet that will kill the rabbit, the fox, the feral cat. That is a truth.

It is a gun in a church, leaning against bookshelves.

It is no good being afraid of the rifle. With its receptive golden butt it is made to be controlled, to do bidding, to be fondled. I have slipped it inside a pair of pantyhose.

Jesse, there are things I want to tell you. I'm trying to reach you again. Our lives are governed differently, just as my life and my father's have had different refrains. But now that we are apart, now that you are older, I want you to see some of the things I see and have seen, hear some of the things I hear and have heard. It has become important to me to tell you. I suppose what I want to say is a sort of passing on to you – if you want it. It's one set of thoughts among many that I could share. Why at this moment it should be about foxes I don't know – but it is about those half-ghosts of threat that thread the landscape near Port Chalice. They slip through the grass and the timber, they slip through my thoughts with their ruthlessness and intent.

I go to the church to write, quite often with the company only of trees. Sometimes as I work I hear the fox's rising cry from the darkness up the valley on nights of frost and moonlight. Sometimes the shrieking cry goes up just near the church, so close I can hear the throat pulsating. The dogs at the two farms further up the road bark wildly, then questioningly. But the fox is gone.

Foxes are cunning, Jesse. I hope you can picture it. It is a truth worth knowing, something far distant from the streets of Hawthorn or

Frankston, far from all of the Melbourne that we both know. Yes, they kill, the foxes. They waste as they kill, because often they don't eat. Perhaps twenty lambs in a night, while the sheep murmur, starting in the dark, then run, sweeping away across the slope, the fox getting down to its business of claws and teeth behind them.

The farmers tell me about it, Jesse. I'm passing it on to you, as part of the picture of how life runs in my experience. It's something I've learned, something that comes back to me when I'm thinking. The farmers tell me about the killer fox who has survived to become successful, to thrill to the feeling of the lamb struggling under its paws, in its jaws. It rejoices in the smell and taste of the blood. Can't get him, the farmers say. He's gone off to the side at the first sweep of the spotlight across the paddock and the scrub. Less experienced foxes stay too long or skelter back through the bracken where the light has passed and will sweep a second time and the men get them on the return. But not the killer.

The foxes can wait, Jesse. They are like dogs. They are natural hunters. They think of prey, they detect when something acts as prey. They love it. They play games too. I have seen a young one play a game with an old ram, waiting to get to his water tin in the corner of the house paddock, luring the ram out to butt at him, but keeping out of range, retreating, returning from the downhill side, luring the ram out, retreating. And the foxes know when a cow is going to calve, when she is weaker than usual. They watch. They smell blood in anticipation on the hillside above her where she stands. They circle. She panics just a little more. They go away to watch. The cars go past on the road half a kilometre over. The foxes wait. When she gives birth they know. They watch to see if she can stand. But sometimes her legs are slow to come back. She goes down, licking the calf, mooning to it, finding her legs part paralysed, wishing for the warmth of the day. But it is nearly night. The foxes come, Jesse. They circle. They see where she has placed the calf to protect it. They see her try to rise. They circle. They lunge in at her udder. Their teeth tear it, the blood flows. They return, flash in again to bite and tear. The blood flows now like a stream. The foxes come in to kill the calf. The cow can only swing her head. The foxes come to tear at her udder. Multiple teeth. The cow will not last the night while her blood flows and she weakens. The foxes are cunning, Jesse, and they can wait and they know when to strike.

The farmers shoot and try poison. They electrify their fences but the killer stands off delicately from it all. One of my neighbours, Jesse, lives in a farm where the cypresses lean out over the sheep-yards at the head of the valley. He has lost all of his late-drop lambs to a couple of killers. He has organised shoots, with the men bagging ten or twelve foxes in a night, but still the killers come. He has electrified his fences at the low wires and along the top strand. But the killers jump the fence at the fence posts, spurning the wood of the top of the post with their paws as they go over, and still get to the throats of the lambs.

Over on the Lightning Point Road is a man who has been in the bush all his life and who knows foxes. He is steady, patient. He will try to poison these new killers with a paste made up of meat and vixen's urine. It may work for a time.

I sometimes look at the gun, Jesse. It is a single shot .22. I know I will have to be very close to the fox to shoot it with that. I will have to stalk, sit out in the twilight where I have seen the family of foxes playing along the creek in the summer evenings. I will have to go on learning, go on experiencing.

Shooting is not my way, Jesse. But I suspect that one day I might be called to plan it and do it. I can see the grassed banking where the mother fox will go down when I fire like a brown sack suddenly heavy. Second time I will get only one of the cubs. It will lie at my feet, twitching, a soft-haired puppy. It will snarl. I will have to find a bit of greyed wood and kill it. I think it will happen. I think it is one of the things I might have to do, even though I'm city-bred. It's part of tooth and claw. I suppose it's part of what happens when the natural world is kicked out of kilter by an introduced rogue. It's about acting against evil, perhaps, although the fox wouldn't say so. It's an act against cruelty, isn't it? Is it a male thing? I pass it on as something I wonder about, as part of what makes me, for good or ill. Does that make sense to you? Can you accept what I'm offering you?

—

Des will never marry, says the voice. I don't know where it comes from. I hear it again as I once heard it long ago. Des will never marry. The voice draws me by the hand into the past.

Ben Lodz and I are sitting together at the concert. It is the Melbourne Town Hall. It is the Melbourne Symphony Orchestra. Eric Lansell sits a few seats away, too. He has slipped in a bit late with his dark-browed father to hear the Hungarian pianist play. Behind the soloist, the organ pipes glissade upwards into gloom. We see his startling white collar. We see the light pouring into the absorbent dark sleeves of his coat as he plays. But suddenly, in the midst of a long andante passage, he lifts his fingers high from the keys as if they might burn him and looks up at the conductor. Then he sits back, his shoulders drooping, the orchestra's sounds trailing away around him.

Des will never marry, the words say. As I remember it, I hear again the voice I heard then. The words whisper to me. The conductor has announced that there will be a short delay. The orchestra members are melting away to the wings to wait for a new tuning for the piano. Ben and I speak briefly, then watch the drama under the stage lights. Around us people are standing, stretching between the rows of seats. The voice comes again. Des never gets married, it says. He never marries. I see in my mind's eye Des's tentative figure stepping along the street. The wait goes on, minute after minute. He never marries, the voice is whispering. We wait. We sit, taking in the people around us, the suits, the frocks, the sleek hair, the glasses. The minutes pass – and then I see him, unbeliev- able, led onto the stage of the Melbourne Town Hall, led with his bag of tools across the yawning space under the lights by a suited orchestra official to the piano – the lapsed piano. It is Des. It is my uncle. Some orchestra members still stand near the curtains, watching. From my seat in the middle of the hall I see the official and Des my uncle exchange some words, and the official departs. I watch Des unlock his bag, roll out a housewife of tools. People murmur around me. This is my uncle under the lights, seeing nothing. People in their concert-going suits and frocks mutter, make self-pitying faces to each other at the delay, at this piano that has lapsed in the middle of a concert, at this hunch-shouldered figure tightening, playing, tightening, listening, tightening, playing, head on one side to hear under the stage lights. This is my uncle. But no one cares. I am fifteen. Ben Lodz is in the seat beside me. I haven't told him yet. My eyes are full with the surprise. My heart is beating quickly.

It is far from me now, but it all comes back to me with the voice.

—

Suddenly, when I least expect it, it's the Army again. I can smell it – the dust, the heat in the leaves. I can feel it – the sun stinging my forearms below the shirt sleeves. I haven't known that it will swim into my mind. I've forgotten. The hot hills reeling into the distance from the Hume Highway remind me as I drive north to a couple of classes in Benalla. We tried to be soldiers in those hills, I'm saying to myself. I look at the proud, tough slopes and their few trees blue in the sun and I feel it again. I'd like to be saying this to Jesse or to Flute and watch their eyes – but I can't. This is when I was someone else, I'd say to them. That's what I'll say to Adela when I get home. And as I tell her, and it sounding so foreign to her, I'll think I'm reminding Pat Friar and Bobbie Chappell about it, putting it into their minds again, because we were there together when we were young men.

This is the Army and most of the time it's about the country, if you forget the way we practise at destruction and feinting at ways of killing in amongst the glaring rocks and the hot hills. That's where we go out in the trucks, where we fire the guns. After all the guns' thunder and the practice at killing, the country is still there, waiting. When I'm in the Army it lets me do the things that I have always done since Flute takes me out in his arms at Berriwillock when I'm no more than two and a half to feel the morning before a hot day, and says won't do him any harm, won't do him any harm, and the chickens run to the hen and I know then that this smell is important, that this smell and this last silky feeling in the air before the sun booms out are Victoria, are the Mallee, are Australian heat, are the baking Army camp and are somehow close to my close people and how they feel about things.

The Army lets me get up at first light and put on KDs and boots and leave the tent quietly without waking the others. I can walk without a shirt towards the creek, my boots pluffing in the dust of the Army track. No need for a hat or gaiters. The air is silk on my skin. The birds are already busy in the branches of the trees near the camp. But the camp is still asleep. Twelve hundred men asleep. Only the cooks stirring yet. I keep walking until I get near the river. Then I can lift up my eyes to the hills on the other side and think about the rocks that are always natural where they fall in the grass, about the big trees there, each one alone and still, just catching the sun.

Where we are in the hot hills seems a long way from Melbourne and its streets where we grew up. Now it's later in the day. There are no trees near us, only the grey rocks and the sun-pale green lichen on them. When we're unloading the shells from the shell-boxes we can glance at the boulders waiting around us as we work, but they don't care about us. They've seen too much. At the centre of what we have to do and all we have to think is the gun. We stand around it. We are young men. That's what the Army wants. We are here on the hillside. In the Army it's often hot. And on this hillside there are no trees. The sun is burning brass above the earth. The earth sings and writhes in its silken mirage. Lying here in faded working dress we feel we can swap places with the sun, look down on this stumped hillside strewn with men moving on it like blotchy weevils. We can look down and see ourselves. But we are standing around the gun. We know what the Army wants. It has to have yelling and the slamming shut of metal. It's about obeying orders. It's about being dour and enduring. The Army likes detail and ways of survival. It likes water, ablutions, food, equipment, transport, smoke-ohs, lectures, squad drill, communications, dummy runs, swim parades to the river, boredom, maintenance, sentry duty, stripping-down of weapons, leave passes, regulations, more boredom and waiting in the dirt, mopping up, greasing of parts, bodies lolling in the only shade, making camp and breaking camp, boredom again and the sudden, beautifully inclusive scent of cigarette smoke in the clear, dry air. We can hear the dry caa-ing of crows in the hills. We can hear the far, quiet thunder of other guns firing and the brassy crump of shells parting the earth. So we stand ready around the gun, waiting for the orders to come down. Our gun is like a mother. We cluster around it like chickens, doing its bidding. It's big, but not all that big as howitzers go. Its khaki sides and barrel are slim. Its breech is fat with steel and sweet and heavy like a woman's arse and hips. We have known it a long time, have seen it in all weathers and in many moods. When we first hear it speak, its huge word splits our perineums. We reel, our eyes for a moment seeing only a white wall of shock. Now, when it speaks we all feel a guttural urging like sex in the throat. The breech block flashes back in a blur as the gun utters its tearing consonant and falls back silent. The breech sinks away to its expectant position, like a lip closing over a statement. It sits there, awaiting the tickle of the next shell and the brutal, gasping thrust of Number Two's ramrod. There are just the five of us sweating on the gun, our mother, bringing up her food, making sure she eats it. It's the gun, our mother . . .

This is when we all are someone else. This is when I am another person, I'll say to Adela, and yet I suppose it's the making of the person I am now. Adela will stare and then laugh uncertainly when I tell her. It's when we are very young, I'll say to her, when we are learning how to feint at ways of killing and destruction, and how to defend until death.

—

I carry the story with me. I carry my close people in my head. They know when I write about them. I look back on them and I think I can see them all walking along a red track in mallee scrub. I think I can detect the gait and the pace of each one, although they are just outlines in the half light.

I carry the story with me wherever I go, trying to hear the voices. Sometimes the story covers its tracks and I can't find it. Sometimes I seek it all day and yet there are so few words to show for it. Sometimes it's like this beloved, secretive valley I write in when the last light of the day is falling. It holds itself aloof, waiting to declare itself ready to open to me.

Pearlie and John and Flute and Candles are gone from the earth. They are resting, but when they hear me seeking them they sometimes speak to me quietly. My mother is saying her goodbyes day by day to this world as the cancer advances. She sees redemption in small things – the silver-eyes tumbling from branch to branch in the tamarisks in the side garden at Overton Lane; her first cup of tea at first light, just as she has always woken with the sun, taken her first thoughts, assessed the morning, with tea's dour tannin. Ben Lodz is gone. Betty is gone so soon. I see in the story I carry with me that they will die, and I am dismayed. Ben, whose dark eyes are looking for answers. Betty who loves my uncle.

Oh, Jesse and Susan, I can sense you listening to me. I see your uncertain eyes that I love. Come into the light, I hear myself saying to you. Don't leave it too late. Come to the world with goodwill. Hazard yourselves to see how far your love and intuition can reach. Don't wait for dress rehearsals. This is where you step into time's circle to play.

Joyce's David is gone. I hear about it from Jean. It's twenty years after he leaves Joyce. He's dead, we hear, in a car crash coming home from the races at Hanging Rock, the car's bumper-bar riding up out of his speed on the bend and striking a red gum twelve feet from the ground. It rocks Jean. 'The bastard's been allowed two more years than Cec,' she says. She laughs ruefully 'There's no justice.' For a moment her eyes flare, and then it's as if her shoulders cave in. She stares at the sarsaparilla that cascades from the side fence outside the window. She stares a long time without moving. Then she looks at us with sad, softened eyes. 'I hate the thought,' she says. 'Car crashes! I never could like David, the bugger, but I wouldn't wish it on anyone, and not on his new lady either. I'll never forget the police turning up when Cec died. I saw them coming to the door through the garden. Even before they reached the porch my heart was sinking. Car crashes!'

Des will die, his sister Joyce nursing him to the end, watching his scrotum grow huge with a dropsy she can't manage and doesn't understand, washing him, describing to him the days outside that he can't see.

Des, my uncle. Des who plays jazz and loves Betty and never marries. How can I know when I've heard him speak and will never hear him speak again? How can I know when I am watching his tottering walk for the last time?

Jean's Cec is gone. And in a car accident too. You'd think his death would have been sealed by his time as a drenched fighter in the Islands, Louise says, that it would creep up on him, coming from a strained heart or return of malaria or complications. I picture Cec waking day after day wet to the skin and ill beside his Owen gun in the mud of dripping jungle tracks in New Guinea, while I am a swimming boy at the baths who lives in Cicero Street, Camberwell. Cec who loves Candles like a brother when Candles comes to Melbourne. Cec who could sing and dance and be a comedian and wag his moustache.

I carry the story with me. Flute lies beside his son Frank who is only thirty when the tractor crawls so slowly over him far up in the back paddock and kills him. They are buried beside each other in the Sea Lake cemetery. Their grave is not marked. That is a truth that appeared as if from nowhere. I didn't know that in the story I would go up the paddock with Flute carrying the whetstone when he went out to kill the sheep. It's another truth that appears from nowhere. It's inevitable, undoubted, and yet I don't know how I came by it.

There's a time when I hear a voice speaking in French far in the future in a huge hall with a tiled floor and views to a river. I hear the word 'blesses' – the wounded – and then I see it. There is a red cross and under it the words: *'Ici furent 2254 blesses pendant la guerre* 1914–1918'. There is somewhere where these words are true. I do not know where. And yet I sense that some day I will be there. I will discover how all those soldiers have changed the air and sounds of that place and kept them slightly rapt and cold even in summer with their suffering.

I can feel the story will become about happenings that have to do with love and a deep plunge that will desolate me and then galvanise me. I can feel love and gratitude somewhere further round the circle. I can feel a wisdom that I've been waiting for, that I want to put my arms around. I can see white sheets and window light.

When I think of Will at Overton Lane I see his books' spines lined behind him, hear him talking about the surrealists and wondering that Magritte's mother suicided when he was only thirteen. Look at the sadness of those shoulders and the face that you can't see under the bowler hat, he says. Then he falls into a quietness, listening for Louise. As she is dying, Will helps her, brings her tea out to her on the cane lounge on warm days, then retreats into himself, into a doggedness as though he is pacing himself.

I carry the story with me, and it lets out vignettes. One night as I write long into the darkness I find myself staring under the church's lights and I hear the pluck . . . pluck . . . pluck of tennis balls being hit. I'm standing beside a river. It is surely Mildura, I think, but then I see Louise and Alex Cumming in the photograph sitting together on the steps at Swan Hill, and I'm trying to remember Alex Cumming's address in Sydney. My head seems suddenly full of immoveable sand, endless tiredness.

—

Kodak

Susan Counts the Thunder

'Have you ever seen this?' Adela asks, and looks at me with such a direct gaze, drawing in her coquettish cheeks slightly, considering my face. She has beckoned me into her bedroom. She reaches up to the bookshelf near the bed, pulls out a book and offers it to me. Adela, who reads with her shoulders straight, her breathing even, her head tilted down a shade. Adela, who becomes a young girl again when she reads. I love her.

I glance at the dust jacket. It is a book of Japanese erotic prints. I look at Adela. She smiles, looks away out the window, looks back at me, purses her mouth, draws in her cheeks, makes eyes conspiratorially again. Not a word. She swings around and goes to the kitchen. I prop on the bed's edge to read. The sketches are skilful, beautiful, with grey swirls of garments, limbs, faces, swept up hair, buttocks, breasts, ample cocks approaching generous thighs and a string of text that I yearn to decipher in the top right hand of each. The book is in Japanese: there is no translation. I see the sword of a penis ranging near a cunt's dark secrecy and think of how many times I have run the pads of fingers along that moist surprise in the darkness. I move to stand near the window, still reading. Adela comes to me from behind, reaches over my shoulder to my top shirt button. She undoes it. I put the book down on the window ledge, reach over and draw the curtains. We undress each other slowly, my penis dropping out heavily. Her breasts emerge and sway as she throws blouse and bra aside.

We make love, each knowing where to go, I thinking it marvellous that I love this peremptory woman. In her body's sure clasping I can feel her thinking this is my lean boy-man who is steady and warm. I don't want to calculate this love's end. I stroke her bottom, her shoulders. I kiss her neck, hold her with delicious sadness. Now, after thirty years of love, bitterness, joy, perhaps I'm learning how to keep only this moment, knowing I am my own educator, my own pilot.

—

It is my mother's head I am seeing embedded in the pillows. It is wedged there, the thin wisps of hair framing it. Her eyes have nowhere to go. They are further embedded in the cancer's yellow puffiness and the shiny red or deeper, wine-coloured pustules reaching from near the crown of her head down her cheeks, around her mouth, beneath her chin, into the fold of bedclothes coming to meet her neck. The evil monkey sits there in her face even as she is dying.

There have been months of pain in every movement. Her back is locked with it. There have been months of retching. Her eyes have been intense with pain and misery. Now she has a skin made up of what look like faded red peppers, so ready to break into blood. I look at her, wonder how the blood can be contained. I reach for her hands, her swelling forearms above the sheets. They are hot. Her eyes are distant with the morphine. I let her hands drop. I look at Greg. My face is incapable of movement or expression. We are the only ones at the hospital.

As we leave I am watching Greg walking ahead of me towards the hospital entrance. For a moment it's almost as if I can feel his heart-beat. He and Carolyn have separated. He and Fran are living together. As we reach the end of the corridor he makes to kick the wall as we go. Then suddenly we are aware that our final footfalls to the heavy door are almost in step. Greg's face is set with anger. 'The bastard's just romping through her,' he hisses. 'It's just romping through her. I can't stand it.'

—

I am not a good man. I must be like King John. Although I often hide it well, I am sometimes filled with anger.

My anger frightens people even when it is not directed at them, when it is expressed against inanimate things – a folder that I dash to the floor, the pages of student assignments that lie there demanding things of me, words that will not be ordered, the gas pilot that will not light, the starling that falls, scratching and scuttering, in the flue of the fire at the church and brings my tapping of sentences to a stop, that loses me my place in the story. It is not often anger against people. But when it is, what am I capable of? Am I a bad man?

Patricia and Jesse and Susan have felt it. Adela now too. I know Rosa will feel it, hating to see my eyes blazing empty. I suppose she will be burned by my impatience. Then I will have to climb down from it and apologise, knowing that it will happen again. Is it my idealism? Is it because I am driven? It is my railing against the gods, I suppose.

—

I seem to be speaking to my children in a dream. You must have encountered evil, I am saying to them. Jesse? Susan? You must have smelt and heard evil. I fear for you. You must have felt it reaching for your ribs with its steel knuckles. You must have seen it. I am saying it, although you are not here. I say it and wait for your response, although I know it will not come. I hope you can detect evil and life's sudden ruthlessness far off: that might save you. If you can't, I fear for you.

The face of evil, I tell my children, is often calm, almost switched off, because it is so sure of its power, until things turn against it. Evil is the face of Little Caldwell at school as he bashes Ditsy Corrigan's head into the cricket pitch's concrete again and again in the yard, the sand battered into Corrigan's hair, the blood coming from the corner of his eye, the skin torn off his forehead, and sometimes we see his eyes glazed with pain and concussion, streaked with tears, and then we can't see it as his head goes down again on the concrete, crack . . . crack . . . while the cricketers stand around. No one goes against Little Caldwell, because just yards away in the big yard is Big Caldwell and no one knows when Little Caldwell might run to get him. I have seen it, Rosa. I have seen it, Jesse and Susan. It is power and the evil of power.

Evil is the twist of the nipple in the cookhouse in the Army. The Sergeant Cook who runs the open-air brothel out in the blond grass is waiting, watching for a pretext. Too slow with the potatoes? Too fucken' slow. I didn't say fucken' tomorrow! I said now! And his fingers grip and twist until I am forced cringing to the floor. Don't respond! I must carry the files of pain that run from my nipple and through my chest to my neck. His regular Army mates are just across the way in the OR's mess. They can be here so quick you wouldn't believe, and they'll hear the story and their eyes will narrow slightly with disbelief and joy, so that they can hardly save themselves from laughing. And there are stainless-steel shelves with sharp corners just behind me. I'll have an accident while on cookhouse duty. I'll have slipped and knocked my head, my eye, my elbow, my knees. I won't believe how comfortable, well-used, well-ironed their faded khaki shirts and regimental badges will look in the flashes I have of them as they bash me. I have come close to it, Rosa. I have seen it.

The sound of evil and danger is so often the sound of the crowd. I have forgotten what steps I take, how I climb a bench to get the photo. I hear the crowd, see their shoes and boots coming, shuffling in the dirt. I see the seconds escorting the two men, both in long-sleeve shirts, one with sneakers, one with boots, both dark-haired, dark-eyed. I know something is coming. I go back for the camera. Now it all comes back. I don't know any of them. There are men and boys in shoes and boots and hats. There are just a few girls in jeans and blouses and young women in skirts and tops. They walk in groups of three or four on the outer flanks of the crowd. They are linking arms, looking to each other's eyes, looking to the other groups sometimes with suspicion, sometimes with a secretive recognition. They have all come to see something settled. I can see it all, the red gums leaning down in their grey bark. But nothing can ever capture the sound of the crowd when the blows strike, when the thudding blows strike, rattle jaw and teeth, when they close averted eyes, when the shirts became dusty and spattered with blood, when we see the eyes and brows so keyed with effort, and the cut under the eye bleeding into his mouth and the rip behind his ear. It is a baying from two hundred throats, and then a sighing of evil, an expelling of hundreds of breaths as the head snaps back, as the smaller of the two falls on his shoulder into the red grit of the carpark. The fence of the cricket ground is strung white across the top of the picture, unbelieving, unbelievable. The smaller man hits his head sharply on the gravel when he falls. He lies still, one arm across him, his shirt half open. That's when the deep baying comes from the crowd, then a low thunder of approval, and then a guttural murmur full of deprivation and disappointment. Someone must have told the crowd that it is to be this afternoon at three on the dusty flat of the cricket ground carpark. They come there in the afternoon, some of them having waited for this all the week. They come into the photograph with their hopes of blood, of seeing a man beaten insensible, of feeling a full and evil satisfaction in their gut that they can take home to bed with their girls, their wives.

Evil is always there. It is so sure of its power, and by then often it is too late. That is what happens time and again, Jesse and Susan. That is why sometimes I fear for you, I pray for you, around time's circle.

—

There are strategies of love and waiting and joining and joy for the moment that I would never have dreamed. Adela brings them to me. She has taught them to me with her words, her changes of direction and mood, her eyes. Her words have fainted away telling me about her past. She has shown me how to return after bitterness, how to declare need. She has taught me about anger and forgiveness, about duplicity and smiles. She tells me about her life when she was a swimmer. She deliciously manipulates me. She is direct, though, in her loving. At other times she is overtaken by happenings. She looks lost. She talks sometimes about Lesley, who was the man of her life. She laughs a hollow laugh. Then she smiles again and looks down.

—

I can't get past my anger at the way death is stalking Louise. I find myself disbelieving, then angry wherever I turn. Even though no one has told me I can tell that there will be no more visits. If I come again tomorrow my mother will be gone, the bed will be empty. What if I come back and see this bed made up, empty, and try to call her to me? Could I reach her? I am ridiculous in my disbelief. I know this is the end and yet, standing here alone, I am not supposed to know it. She will have gone from this room, these streets, this city, from the gentle, greening rises, the stately platoons of Wimmera sugar gums, the low red sun that rakes the mallee at the end of day. She will be gone from among us.

I look down on her from the doorway. I carry her voice, soft and dry, barely audible. Not three minutes ago, leaning down to her, I see the lips I have watched so many times utter gentle words, lips sitting swollen now in her terrible face. 'Goodbye, my love . . .' Louise lies against the hospital pillows that hear her breath, her pain, the pillows that in a few hours will still cradle her head even though she is dead. My mind shrieks again in disbelief – and yet there is no sound.

Will, so much an old man, and stolid with tiredness and doom, has visited and gone home. He will be lighting the fire at Overton Lane, taking the chill off the air, stopping to stare into the flames. I will not call him back. In the morning the night nurse, who will not discover the stillness in the room until the grey light is widening again outside in the street of pin oaks, will ring the doctor and the doctor will ring Will at about breakfast time. That is how it will be done.

—

When it comes, even though I have expected it, even though I have rehearsed what will happen and how the eyes will close, even then it bears down on my shoulders with an unexpected bleak weight. I have not expected it to well up so quickly. Louise Menzies is no more. My mother is no more.

I cannot credit the effects of the grief that takes me over. I walk on sponge rubber, it seems, and find myself laughing and crying in the one sentence as I squat to talk to my aunts in their chairs among the cakes and sandwiches back at the house after the funeral.

There are only Jean and Joyce and Des left now. Susan and Jesse are with them. It's huge and warming to see their eyes for each other. My heart swells and then subsides, choking. It's the generations. Des has got to his feet. He's leaning against the kitchen door jamb, his eyes fixed, his head cocked to one side, so that he can separate voices. I see my daughter Susan pressing him with sandwiches. He nods, smiles at a point away to her side and down. She puts one in his hand. He looks beyond her, feels the bread with his fingers, conveys it to his mouth unselfconsciously.

Jean and Joyce huddle with Little Ian near the far window. He has come down from where he's doing wheat contract work near Walbundrie. It's strange to see chairs there, profiles of faces against the wall. Ian's hands look huge. His face is tanned and polished. There is none of the city drawing of the skin in his face. His face speaks the country north of the Divide, speaks the strong sun that edges into whatever he is doing. I look at him, marvelling. The little boy I was bidden to mind at Mont Albert and who I have not seen for more than twenty years. He sees my gaze and my reminiscing smile. He winks.

It's family. Suddenly, that is all there is. My close people in the sad-happy room.

—

Sometimes, even now, I'll be listening to jazz, hearing the songs, and I'll find myself thinking of Des and what he played and sang and what he told me. I'll be thinking of what he's laid before me. Des is dead a long time now. I'll hear him saying it again there at the piano at Jean and Cec's place at Mentone: 'I'd be black if I could. Them's the ones that have the words. Them's the ones that have the blues and the songs.'

And what is it, I'll be saying to myself. Is it knowing that the world makes its way in grief and loss and joy? Is that the blues? Is that under-standing? That the world will always make its way in sorrow and joy? And again I hear Des exploring a path into 'Danny Boy' on the piano in the church hall near Cicero Street. I can see his white shirt in the darkness. My father Will is looking over my shoulder too, I know. I hear him singing it with his sister Grace. Yes, 'Danny Boy' is a white-skinned, sandy-haired blues, I suppose. Blues is transcendence, is it? It seems to have the wistfulness and terseness of haiku. Blues seems to be honesty and coping. Jazz is a whistling of black grief and joy. How much did Des know? What about the black soldiers who sat in with Charlie's band during the War? He tells me about them. What did they say to Des? He was singing and playing their wistfulness and celebration, wasn't he? How much did Des know? Where is he now? How can I thank him for what he gave me. There doesn't seem to be anyone I can tell about this. I think these thoughts must be mine alone.

—

I sit at the table in Hawthorn. I'm going to read, turn pages, read again. I cannot relax. I keep seeing my mother's face. Day by day I see the world go on without her. Photographs of other faces demand attention from the scatter on the table. But instead I've picked up a letter. It is headed 12 Swift Street, Richmond. It is addressed to 'Dearest Lou'. It's one of the letters I've found with the photographs in Louise's dressing table. I've flexed its creases so that it will open itself to me, felt the resistance of its staunch paper folded for years. It is from Alex Cumming to my mother. It is dated 8 December 1931. I am familiar now with Alex's spidery hand and its flourishing loops. I try to see him writing it. I see the heel of his hand wafting over the paper, sculpting the lightest of impressions. I imagine he writes as I write. He does not bear down. Alex is writing from Melbourne to my mother in what he calls 'the western border districts' – it must be when Louise is teaching her last year in Edenhope.

'My lovely girl. Here's another brief missive from the big smoke! How are the crops in the western border districts? The weather up here has been good. We've had some late day practices on the grass at South Yarra and I played three sets with Harry Hassett last Friday at Kooyong. Won in three! Yippee! But god his backhand is good.

It looks as though I might have to go up to help York with the crop during the best practice time down here. Blast! I'm feeling fit and I know I'm knocking on the door – for some good wins, I mean. Anyway, we'll see. The harvest might be clear and give me the two weeks before the Australian. That'd be good.

There's a chance of a new job at Hartley's. You know – Flinders Street. I could do with that to keep me going, keep me close to tennis people and the tennis trail. We'll see. I'll write you about that and my new address as soon as I know it.

Any news from Candles? He must have finished the season well. You don't get best and fairest every day. I hope it's a bumper year for him and Flute. In her last letter Else is better than she was, but the doctor has told her to watch out for things like bacon. Fat's no good for the bile duct apparently and she loves bacon! Our mother had a gall bladder, too. But Else is pretty young to be having trouble. We'll see.

I wish you were here. I'm counting the days to the 17th. I want to hold you again. I want to just hide away with you. It's you I want. So, please close down the school early and come back to the Big Smoke! The kids'd love you for it. But remember I'm the one that loves you first. Perhaps I should come and stay with you down there at the Bowmans! That'd get them going at the church! You're lucky to have such good board, though.

Love and kisses and . . . and . . . and . . .

Write me something soon.   Alex.'

Next in the pile my fingers find a postcard. Behind the pale-gold word Pasadena it shows long rows of orange trees and workers on ladders far down its perspective. The back says: '16 May '34. My beautiful Lou, Are these better than Mildura navels, do you reckon? Played at Sacramento on Tuesday and here on Thursday – just exhibitions. Stanford and San Francisco next week and then to Albaquerque and Chicago.

My love and kisses . . . and . . . and . . . Alex.'

But then another letter, headed 'Winston House', 172 Toorak Rd, South Yarra SE2. It is dated 20 December, '33. It is Alex Cumming's words again, loping along: '. . . What am I doing down here while you are up there in Mallee dust. Seriously though, it must feel good to be really home. Remember me to everyone and don't get too hot during harvest.

You've fallen on your feet at Richmond – it's been a good year. A strong headmaster must make a big difference. But I can't stop thinking about your kids on Susso. Who decides who's lucky and whose unlucky in this world, that's what I wonder. You can only give the kids as much of a chance as possible, I suppose.

I might get home for Christmas, depending on when the harvest has to come in. It'll have to be soon, with the Australian coming up in January. The Australian is everything, and I'm going well. The practice is so good here at Kooyong, South Yarra. Had a long go with Hopman earlier in the week. He's fast, good reflexes. But over a long haul you can feel him go off a bit. He hasn't got the strength for really long matches. O'Hara Wood was like that. Good wind, but less strength in the legs and shoulders. I suppose I've always had the staying-power in the legs from walking behind the harrows and the plough, and what I get from lifting and lumping. But I don't get the running the others get down here. Hopman is always at it, skipping, running. Anyway, I've got my regular beat now through Hawthorn and South Yarra, or around the oval at Scotch College. They let me run there.

Remember the run I used to do out the Swan Hill road? God!

I'm going on a bit. But my match against Willard in the Victorian is still standing me in good stead. Norman B. dropped in for a look at us at South Yarra the other day. Enough of that, anyway.

The work at Hartley's is easy enough, but I don't like being inside all the time. I'm sick of looking at Flinders Street station! I'm sick of selling racquets! But I can't complain. They're pretty good to me in there. I'd feel a lot better with the 'Pitnacree' sun over my shoulder, though. I don't know just how good the season is up at Sea Lake, but expect a letter from brother York any day. If they're short of hands I'll take the train up and help him and the others bring it all in. I'll have to be careful – stay fit for the other tournaments. I can always run out to Old Friends' Lane, I suppose. But no draught horses stepping back on my toes this time! Bugger that! I can still feel those toenails!

What about our 1934 dream? It's good to think about it, I suppose. I can see us in Honolulu now! Question is whether the great Norman B. would let us do it if I get selected. We both know he wouldn't. But if I make it to America I'll be back by October and we could think about making it official then. What do you think? Am I proposing by long distance? Hell! I wish you were here to talk about it. I want to hear your voice. Not much other news. All I can think of is that 1934 has got to be the year. I'm going to keep plugging. I've got to do better than Willard and Sproule and Gar Moon too. They're on my tail. Crawfie and Harry H are in, I'd say, no matter what happens. But so far so good. I think I can do it. The Australian in January is the trick. I think I'm hitting better than this time last year, foot trouble or no foot trouble . . .'

I look at the words and I am there. I see Alex's face more closely than I've ever seen it in photographs. I see the shoulders, the farmer's wrist leaning down to scoop the ball up before it kisses the grass. I see the grace. I feel the passion in the eyes that are all for the crucial sphere of the ball. And I hear Alex's dream. I can see it in the air, Louise looking at it too. She sits reading and she's thinking about it. She feels her belly tighten at the thought of the future that Alex paints. It is suggestive. She reads on in her book, not seeing the words. I think she is beautiful and uncertain. She is the woman soon to become my mother. She is young and candid and her beauty is in that.

Louise's youth has hold of me. The past has hold of me. For a time I see this young and aspiring vision of her. Just for a while it rides across the dark place in my thinking where now there is a slow, womanly dying, death at my mother's shoulder and in her eyes, then death sitting in her wracked face.

Then the vision and the words can hold out no longer, furry darkness descends, chords tolling. Then all I know is that Louise Menzies is no more. And yet here in my hand are words that say that my mother has been young and I can remember. My mother has loved. But my mother is no more.

Louise has loved Alex Cumming, I have to tell myself, even though in the letters I can do no more than imagine her part of the conversation. It is somehow flattering that she has loved Alex, that I can think of her young and attractive and lively with a tennis player in his white shirt with his towel and racquets. I think of her in Hawthorn and South Yarra. I imagine her dancing with Alex – I can hear the thin, plaintive strings of the orchestra. For a moment again I see Alex a figure beneath the perfect, gloomy columns of the trees at Fern Tree Gully. I hear his voice call again from the sodden bridge with its fungi, I smell the leaf detritus and bark in the damp. I smell the slow-burning resignation of the billy on the fire in the rain and see my mother walking towards Alex in the glade. I am aware of Alistair there. Then the vision is gone.

—

Yes, here in my head are the images of faces, tennis skirts, my mother on the lonely coast. I want to know more, but at my shoulder at this moment is Adela, hovering. I'm distracted. Yes, I pore over the letters, but here's Adela, standing in the shadows.

Adela is gone. She hasn't finished telling me her stories – but she is gone. She has been talking about her days as a swimmer, how she coached children, how she trained along the sweeping eastern shore of Port Phillip Bay where the clear water takes on a sheen from the sky and runs out in fields of palest blue to the shipping channels. She has only just told me about her breakdown when she and Les moved to a new suburb where the trains sigh out from the city up the Fern Tree Gully line, and how she built a succession of pools with builder's plastic in the backyard dirt so that she could see the sky reflected and pretend that she heard the sea. She has only just told me these things, as though we might go on together, and yet on her last visit to Hawthorn she is somehow distracted. And now she rings to say that she must come over. She laughs a nervous laugh. There's something I have to impart, she says, and this time there's no laugh. Soon she is with me, her eyes somehow clouded with pain – is it fear or impatience? Les has talked to her again, she says. Yes, she says – and he wants another meeting, wants to try things together again. At first her eyes are confused as they look at me – and then they look for a moment almost eager to hear my response. Les has overtaken her again, I can see, for good or ill.

I carry those eyes with me. I've never seen them rapt with that expression before. And so I surprise myself. OK, I find myself saying. OK, it's sad. It's sad. I suppose that's the end of us. We've shared a lot. But I've watched you wilt sometimes, I say, heard you wondering. I've heard you being torn. So I suppose it's as far as it can go. Can we cope with it? I find myself laughing sadly, just as she often laughs. I'll just have to cope with it. It's the end. It's where you'll have to count me out.

I'm amazed at how adamantine and certain I am. For moments she is silent. Then we talk again. Our words sound final as we look into the fire. The lounge darkens around us. I know she is gone.

I walk with her out to her car. She slips into the driver's seat quickly.

I feel dead inside. I can't smile at her. I watch her face as she starts the car and slowly backs out. She doesn't look up. She doesn't wave or bip the horn.

So she is gone. The interlude has ended. I suppose I knew it would. I think of her and Lesley sometimes. I see her in my imagination in another territory, carrying her books to a class down the school corridor in Caulfield. I can see her switching woman's walk, and the way she sweeps to a halt. I miss her laugh. But we have parted. Over the days I come eventually to the reality – her car will not come slipping into my drive at Hawthorn any more. We have parted.

Time passes. Then Adela, I hear, is overseas. She and Lesley are no longer together. I think that one day I might see her again, but I don't. The next thing I hear is that she is dead. She has died in Spain of complications that follow pneumonia. Even though by then I am a different person, for a day after I hear the news, I barely see other things, thinking of those eyes. There's a chill desolation in my heart.

—

I'm at the table in Hawthorn again. The photographs are around me in an arc. I've been searching. The letters are to one side in pink-taped bundles. I've tried to be systematic in looking at them, returning them to their bundles, to their places in time. But who is Alex Cumming? He has loved my mother. The letters have told me. My mother has loved him. Although there are no letters carrying her words I can hear it behind her silence. But who is Alex Cumming? What about Belle in Connecticut? What about the beautiful Belle of the photographs? And where is Will, my father? Are there no letters from Will?

Different handwriting? Is there? I pry into the bundles I haven't read, turning down pages without undoing the tapes, to look at the handwriting. Yes, as I pick up a bundle, pry into it, I discover a smaller, flatter hand. I untie the wad, careful to preserve the letters' intactness in their folds, not attempting to read at first, merely to scan. Aha! I turn up three or four tight-folded ones on a pale grey paper – the same smaller, disciplined hand. I unfold a thin one of them. It's two pages. I turn it over, find the final lines. Yes – 'Your loving and rowing (never skiing!) admirer, Will'. I go to the other sheet, find the first page. It's from the Mount Buffalo Chalet, on Victorian Railways paper. It's Will writing to Louise in June 1932. It's Will describing Lake Catani fringed with snow-filled scrub. It's Will lamenting his legs' disobedience on the skis. It's Will saying that postcards don't allow him to say enough, hence this short note. It's my father writing to my mother. He is occupied, but not happy, he says. He has been horse-riding on one finer day after overnight snow. It is a new experience, he says, the snow so delicate against his ears, collecting in his collar. At night, he says, there's the fire in a fireplace 'big enough for a herd of cattle'. But all the others, he writes, want only to play cards or charades. He sits and reads in the corner where it's warm, then heads for bed. He wants to see Louise again as soon as he's back in Melbourne. Au revoir! Au revoir until I can see your face again. Your loving and rowing (never skiing!) admirer, Will.

This is my father writing to my mother. They know each other well. They know each other, they miss each other. Ah, my father, Will. He is here.

I see a tinted photograph, a frayed edge, and there's a postcard. A photograph of Mosman Bay in a frame festooned with leaves. '19 Jan, '32' it says, hard up against the stamp, and the message in Will's fast, small hand. 'Dear Louise,' he writes, 'no turning back now. I'll be on my way to the sunny south day after tomorrow (Thurs) and wanted to let you know. The Williamstown board with the Carruthers is set up, I think. The other board in Canterbury was beyond me. I hope you don't mind if I drop in on you when I'm established. Yours, Will Menzies.'

This is my father writing to my mother when she is still only a vision to him. They don't know each other yet. She must be a dream, a voice, a vision to him not fully known. They have spoken to each other, perhaps. Perhaps they have never touched? They must be six months from knowing each other. But it is my father writing to my mother nevertheless. I can hear Louise thinking about Will's words, trying to conjure his face and his voice and hold onto them.

My fingers rove on, not directed, but under some compulsion I don't understand. There is a torn page folded. It drops from my hand to the table when I pick it up. I reach for it again, unfold the page, the pages. There are two, but no conclusion, it seems. Just an opening, dated 28 June '34 – Colac. Colac? The second sheet is a dense page of Will's fast, low hand, running on, running on, reeling to an end in mid-sentence.

'Beautiful Woman,' the letter opens, 'I'm still remembering the Rowing Club dance floor and afterwards. I'm remembering you. And now I'm writing rather than telephoning to say everything is OK for the weekend. I'll pick you up in the chariot first thing on Saturday. It's no use trying to do it on Friday night, more's the pity, by the time I get back from here. Thank heavens the chore down here is finished. The classes I've done have been OK, and the staff, but four weeks is enough. And why did they choose me? After Sydney and Melbourne I run out of Colac very quickly, if you get my meaning.

Anyway, we can be up to Fern Tree Gully and beyond in an hour and a half on Saturday, judging by what I remember last time, as long as there's not too much road ripped up. Then it was blowing dust. Now it'll be mud!

You've already met three of the crowd. Convivial, passionate, they are. Enquiring, of course! Lance and Margaret Cressy you know, and Bob Mercer, you remember, with his stentorian voice and his Whitman. You haven't met Merle Cassidy. You'll like Merle. She and Bob get round a bit. Six of us? The place is rambly, so there's plenty of room. Beautiful places to walk. It's actually closer to Upwey than to Fern Tree Gully. We might tramp over to the Glenfern track and look down on that beautiful valley. Or sometimes we go up Mast Gully Road a bit. You've been there. Remember those massy trees reeling up?

And at night there's a big fire. I'll remind you to bring warm sweaters and a rug.

Lance has sounded me out about doing some reviews for the Artists Society mag. That would be good. A start in Melbourne for a Sydney-sider, you might say. It'll be interesting. You'll hear the crowd – we call ourselves 'the crowd' – talking about Vance Palmer and Nettie and people like Frank Wilmot that they know. They're keen on some of the

American writers too, and of course Neilson and Furphy and Lawson and others like Palmer and Prichard from our own people. I've been trying to get hold of some more of Carl Sandburg, but without the library where would we be? Nothing in the shops. So little American stuff comes over, doesn't it. Bob Mercer sounds Sandburg's praises. It's people, people, people he says. People in all their pain and joy and strife. He's an interesting chap – goes to the Fitzroy stadium every now and then to the boxing, he tells me. He likes it for its basic sort of animality and blarney. Crude and sad, he says.

This is getting a bit disjointed, but I love writing to you. It's better than the telephone because I can declare myself, take more trouble in what I say, talk about the deep things. I love you. And you're not sure, I know. I just feel that I can talk to you, that we understand each other from the outset. We're easy with each other, aren't we? We sit easy with one another. We dance easy with one another. We read to each other. It seems to me we compare notes a lot. And we laugh at the same things, don't we?

I love you, but I can understand that you are unsure even now about your tennis-player friend. I know only what you've told me about him, and it's good that you have told me honestly. I suppose his image will settle down in your mind in the next few months, and then you'll know. In the meantime, we can be a duo, can't we? I'm looking forward to being with you and having the smell of the gums and bark and wood-smoke around us in the hills.

I want you to write to me too. It would be terrible not to have some letters from you to savour, even though there's the telephone, even though we meet. You can write to me when you go up to Berriwillock and the river in the holidays. You just have to think of me in Williamstown and write to me about what you're doing, what you're thinking, what you're reading.

I've been putting down a bit about the sort of things I've come from in New South and what I'm discovering here. Not a diary, really: a very sporadic journal I suppose I'd have to call it. I'm making up for lost time in Melbourne, I think. I was on the Harbour and up the river so much in Sydney with the rowing that I didn't get to feel the literary or painting scene at close hand at all. I heard about it. I knew some of the names. But that's it. Lindsay – and you might have heard of Slessor, Hugh McCrae and so on. I've no doubt it's there and it's vital, but I never managed to touch it. Now I'm more mature – ha, ha – and I've fallen into the Melbourne scene very happily. And it's lively. It has been the luck of running into Lance and Margaret. They seem to know everyone, know what's what. I'm hoping I'll get up to Kalorama with Lance one weekend to meet the Palmers! Let's both of us go? What do you say?

There's so much good writing and painting that has come from this landscape, from the antipodes, from Melbourne and Sydney, when you look at it, even though as a nation we're young and small. I'm doing a lot more reading since I came to Melbourne – the air sharpens the mind? And I'm concluding that we have a lot in common with the Americans. America is such a rich story, as I know from the history. So there's a lot to learn from them for me, at any rate, although I'm not a writer as such. Emerson, Herman Melville, Whitman, Hawthorne, Clemens. There's a woman called Willa Cather, there's Sherwood Anderson, Marianne Moore, Sandburg, William Faulkner. I don't know some of them except as names. I hear about Sinclair Lewis and Scott Fitzgerald and Robert Frost. Frost will even write using the sole of his shoe as a desk!

Anyway, 'nuff of this. Glad you're reading the Henry Handel Richardson. You know what we'll . . .'

The words stop at the page's bottom as though they have been severed. I check again. A further sheet? No further sheet. I sit as graven as a sculpture. I feel my body, my mind portentous in a way I haven't felt it before. I am seeing my father Will before me as I've never seen him before. I can hear his voice young and earnest beside me. He is writing to my mother. He is speaking to her. And behind them I'm sure now there is something bigger, something that they don't know about yet. I think Louise might sense it but not be able to reach through to it, like *deja vu*. I sit and I feel the filmy, fine envelope of *deja vu* surrounding me. It is palpable and puzzling – and I know that soon I won't be able to escape pricking it, letting in the cool air of more knowing. I've got to talk to Will. But not yet, not yet. I feel my heart speed up. But I can't talk to Will yet. Not for a while yet, at least.

—

I am in the tunnel again. That's what I call it. It has been more than a year and a half since I was there. I talk about it with Axel, the psychiatrist. I have three sessions with him in his old terrace house.

My mind, I know, is sometimes raw, like where a sandal strap chafes against a cut. That's what separation and divorce is like. Although I seem to be coping, seem to be efficient and balanced at work, in keeping my little lone household intact, in shopping, in cooking, in planning to see Susan and Jesse, when I look back I see that I've been erratic. Even as I do things I realise I can't completely trust myself or my judgement. I've lost Adela. Regrets, guilts, sadnesses stop me in the middle of a sentence, or halfway across the yard. Sometimes I find myself in the corridor at the college, intending to go somewhere, but standing as if poleaxed, deep in a bitter reverie. I am hearing all the voices, seeing each face. I see Adela. I see Patricia behind her sometimes. What have I done to them? Where have they left me?

But Axel, the psychiatrist, and I – we seem to know. We seem between us – on the three or four times I see him – to be able to see what will come. We loll on bean bags in the semi-dark.

Axel knows the questions to ask me. 'Are you writing something at the moment?' he says, and falls to rubbing his chin.

—

My mother's voice has trailed away. My mother is gone. And yet she is still there. I hear words from Will's letter. Phrases return to me. I sense Louise receiving the words. Your tennis-player friend, he writes. Who can tell me? I'm gathering books after a tutorial and the voices are repeating themselves to me. Will and Alex. They transport me from the room. I am not seeing the corridor, I realise, even as I walk and reach the office. I am aware of walls that run on down the building, leading to questions, leading to light. Will is writing to my mother. Alex Cumming's handwriting loops before me. Am I proposing? He writes. Am I proposing? My beautiful woman. My beautiful woman. Watch over them – Will and Alex. Watch over Will and Alex. Who will tell me? My father is so old and lonely, thin in his clothes. I must know the past. I must speak to my father. But not yet. I must make an appointment with Mr Tremearne about Louise's will. But not yet. It's too early yet. The words in the letters wash into my mind, then out again.

—

Sometimes I'm seeing the essence of Rosa, and wonder if she still exists? And yet I am sure. I can see her even now where one day I will photograph her, here where I prop on this steep track coming up from the waves at Campfire Bay. I have been thinking love is gone, now that my marriage to Patricia is ashes, now that Adela has departed – but no. I am discovering how it will shyly appear again, how it gives its permissions, declares its needs. Yes, I have been treading the tunnel. It has been loveless, close, fungoid. I have been halted by loss, my heart like leather cracked in the heat. For weeks I have been faltering. I scarcely remember the sun. Sometimes I deny to others that I have ever felt its warmth. I have doubted whether I am a citizen.

But now I catch snatches of that contralto voice again when I'm alone. Now my mind registers again that suggestion of Rosa's warm orange presence. It gives me hope. Sometimes I imagine I am close to seeing her face. Now I am certain of her, although we have never met. She will come to me. So now as I study them people's faces change. I falter no longer. Although I know my joy lies ahead of me in the sun, I see that the eyes of others now engage mine. They tell me I am a citizen again. Eyes and mouths shatter before me into plainsong smiles that flow around joy and the daylight's long lasting into twilight. And I know Rosa will come through them all to me.

So now I move again. So now I love people. I think they are leading me to Rosa. I stand under a new sky. I walk in a forest of broad leaves. It seems I carry the sun like a warm orange that touches the inside of my elbow. I will kiss. I will be privileged. My lips will trace brow and eyes, rediscover the tongue in the mouth. I will lave shoulders. It will be final. Somehow I know that Rosa is my finality. I think she knows in her deepest well of knowledge that I am on my way to her. I have learned. I have stroked shoulders. I have failed – and yet I have succeeded. I have watched my fingers make a soft shearer's blow along thighs as white as shell. So love has come and gone. So love walks away and I am wiser. Love brings its risks, its hurts. Love flicks out its reminders of death, places the soft of its fingers in my navel, does strange things to the clock, rushing the sun down before it has had time to pick up its towel.

Sometimes I have wakened to find myself standing on the wave platform. I watch the sea as I have never seen it before. I sense Rosa there and on the track up the cliff, looking back at me. Here there is acceptance and love, laid down on the wave platform's pure level of glass. I stand between the miracle of pools and the desperate patience of the scrub. I stand before life's biggest pool. This rock will always be here, rinsed by the sea's pourings, hearing all night the om of the surf.

—

Susan is counting the lightning. She is counting to the thunder. I can hear her. It is years ago.

She is small and deep-backed in her jeans and yellow tee shirt. She plants her feet when she stands, thrusting her knees back, just as I do. The thunder showers come down in the evening through the last hot sun. On the veranda she looks up away from the light into the sky over the church yard and the smaller wattle and the new blue gum sapling. There's a tongue of rain hanging from a grey cloud. The lower, broiling clouds are dragging their inky feet across the country. Behind them, far up in the light, there is a rearing of huge dobs of flowering yellow cumulus. They expand, expand into the blue. Susan knows it is magic. I feel her touching the magic with her eyes. Now she is standing with the same stillness as Patricia, leaning forward, all eyes, three fingers in a front pocket for security. I feel a sad pang. And then the rain falls against the sun in millions of sequins, coming out of the sky's vault, turning, fading, then catching silver again as it comes down to us, down to us in the green valley. The lightning staggers in white brilliance down the grey walls of cloud towards the sea, then glimmers to itself again deeper inside the eastern clouds.

Susan starts counting the lightning to the thunder. One two three four . . . one mile; five six seven eight . . . two miles; nine ten elev . . . and the thunder thuds against the grey sky's dome, then grumbles to itself up through the day's eastern curtains. Nearly three miles, Susan says, and swings her hips and eyes to me with excitement. It is magic. I love her voice trying to space out the figures in seconds. She is counting the lightning. She tells me. From where I am standing, book in hand, I love her.

It is the past. It is the fifteen-year past. I have lost that Susan. She was only loaned to me. That Susan no longer exists.

—

I think it is Rosa I meet when I'm starting to climb the landslip on the way back from Campfire Bay. She is kneeling before a woman friend with her hair in a red kerchief who has sat down on a rock, heart palpitating, for a rest and a drink from her bottle after their descent, just where the sand hill gives way to the rising scrub near the bottom, where the track is worn into a small gulch by the water coming down in the winter rainstorms. When Rosa looks at me, and half laughs in greeting, when I see her hair against her forehead and her neck, when the smile crosses her face, I feel certain I know her. I'm sure it's Rosa. My heart is suddenly beating, but then I think stupid, stupid. How can I be sure? I climb on.

—

I am searching. Is this real? I could be flying, looking down, my questions beetling to the ground. My mother seems dry miles to the north still. Alex as a young man, I suppose, is out there to the east. I'm convinced I will touch Berriwillock by lunch time, sun time, this time round, this side of time's circle. But my mother who lived there must be dead now some time. I sense her like a deep red dahlia that is gone. Against her presence I hear the words again – the words in Will's letters.

It's a dream, surely. Where am I? Who am I?

—

I'm facing the mirror again. It's the Hawthorn house. I'm looking at my face. As I study myself I can see that some of the people I once was are now gone. They have learned their lessons and are gone. So who am I now? Dark, tired eyes; dark hair with a tinge of grey. I look at the shine of my forehead. Greying hair, receding hair. Not long and I'll be fifty. My eyes look away, but cannot resist. They come back to regard themselves. So much is registered in them that I have to know. I watch my eyes watching my eyes. Who am I now? Why am I still here?

I can see a deeper drinking of experience in my face now. I can see a sadness that will always be there. Adela is gone, my face says. I realise now how much she has given me. I can see her propping on the stool in the kitchen. I can smell her perfume. I can see her eyes provoking me, and then the false batting of her eyelids. It's a game we play, but it's over. And now you realise don't you, my face is saying to me. You know now how important to you it was to hear the purr of her car coming into the drive, to think she still comes to you, she still comes here to this house in Hawthorn. You're lonely again, my eyes say.

Yes, the slight sadness is there in my eyes, but I can catch another flicker of thought. It's as if my mind, my eyes, see an avenue of trees lit by the sun, running away, away into the distance into a welter of rich leaves. It is promise in the light. It is prediction. Something, someone is waiting for me there. I can't see detail, but soon I will know, my eyes are telling me. I'm surprised. I study myself in the mirror. My eyes are shining.

—

Sometimes I sit on the primary dune above Campfire Bay, not far from The Well, not far from the reef off Tortoise Rock in the other direction. I climb up there for the swatches of light-reflecting warm sand when the wind is from the east or south off the water. If I step down from the dune's lip, away from the sea just ten yards through the scrub, towards the wetland held in the dune's clasp, I can hunker down in complete warm shelter. Inland the broken rises and cliffs start from the other side of the small lake, running up through clumps of she-oaks with their secret grey rooms inside. The wind pumps inland over my head, the sea's gathering and roaring off the sweep gutter is reduced to a steady surge at the back of my hearing. The birds in the scrub stab tiny points into the air with their delicate notes.

It is primal. I think about it and I know that Rosa one day will feel it too. Could I become an Aborigine, sitting there on my old diving towel? Sometimes I think I know this place better than the surfers, perhaps better than the Aborigines. What is knowing? I certainly know the secret geography of the sea bottom off the wave platform at my back. Many times I have waited there twenty feet down in the gloom of the overhang for the big fish to emerge. One wave, then another, and yet another on a breath. But then I realise I don't know anything. How can I know anything to match a million days and nights of knowledge on this gentle slope of quivering scrub raked over by clouds? I sit looking down at my calves, at my toes insinuating themselves into the fine sand. I can imagine myself as an Aborigine, as I lean forward to pick up shells from the midden that runs under me in the sand. It is a midden made from all those thousands of years of dawns, all those ticking hot mid-days, and then the long afternoon of the world and then all those gilt evenings when the sea hoards its blues and runs them through with black and gold. All those fires, the shells clinking down, the fingers starting forward to them. All the high singing that covers country in the warm nights, the eyes watching the coals, watching the smoke waver up until the stars take it. I know nothing. I know I am nothing. I might drown one day off this wave platform and no one will know. That is as it should be in the scheme of things. That is the risk.

—

Rosa, I still can only dream about you, but I have always known you will come. I have had this hope – that somehow you will see Louise before she dies. But it is too late.

I think it is the second time that I find you on the way to Campfire

Bay. I seem to know in advance. As I overtake you at the flat rock in the scrub I know what you will do. I know how you will look up at me. I'll stand there in my old canvas hat, the long diving fins rising high behind me in the haversack. This time, as I say hello and stand back to let you onto the better footing in the scoured track, I know that you will stop, turn to me, say something.

—

'You call him Dig?' says Alex in my dream. And his hands are huge as he tries to pull Will down from the high, rusty bonnet of the tractor. At first I fear that they are angry with each other. But Will is smiling as his feet touch the ground again and Alex stands back with a wave of goodwill and satisfaction. 'Yes,' my father says. 'He's always Dig to me when no one else can hear. Aren't you, Dig?'

I see we are at Kooyong again. The tractor has begun sidling through the mud of its own accord and into the grey overhang of the Kooyong stands. I look at Will and my face is suffused with a warm rush of love for him. Behind him, beyond the tennis courts, there is a house burning, but it is all right. It is expected. I can see that Alistair is asleep in a cot under some trees. 'Yes,' I say. 'I am always Dig until someone comes.' And it seems a very happy answer.

'In that case I need a spanner,' says Alex, and laughs. He walks away towards the darkness under the stadium. Eventually I can see only his fawn hat bobbing in the dimness and then it too disappears.

—

One day soon I will tell Rosa about the day when I spear the big sweep. I will tell her how the swells hold up so long in the northerly, how they break with such crisp drama, such detailed white offertories. I will tell her that when I am offered the sweep and its afternoon and evening, I know I am privileged. I am vouchsafed two hours of time so pure that I might be the only person on earth. So in that bright month I swim with the big sweep. I woo it, I lure it, I stalk it. I spear it as it moves through the water's rooms. I bless it. Later, in the cool of the church, I write about it, I hope without cleverness, because it is my duty, my joy, to say what happens, to say who I am, to say what it is like. Rosa will come to know me.

—

I watch Will. I watch his old neck straining below the grey-sandy hair. I watch the shoulders retreating bowed into his coat. It is not the time to talk to him. I can't talk to him yet. But I hear phrases and it's as though my gut is punched by doubt, by disbelief and uncertainty and a sort of loneliness. I hear phrases from the letters. My lovely girl, they say. And I hear Alex's question: Am I proposing by long distance. I hear Will chiming in. Your loving and rowing (never skiing) admirer, he writes. Beautiful woman, he writes to Louise. Now, I tell myself, I have heard my father speaking from the past in his letters to my mother. I hear the phrases again. I have questions I want to ask. But I cannot ask them yet. Will is so old, so alone, his thin neck so vulnerable. I know that the questions will come if I speak to him. I hear the phrases. But I put them aside. I stop thinking about them.

—

Now I have had a meeting with Mr Tremearne, the solicitor for Louise and Will. He has shown me my mother's will. There it is. He reads to me about a letter from her that awaits me a year hence, or earlier if my father concurs. He looks down as he tells me, then his eyes come up to study my face. I catch his brief look of curiosity to see my reaction and then his face becomes one of professional dispassion. I am not surprised. It is as though I have known that there was always to be a further message for me from Louise.

—

It is the mirror again. It starts at me from the wall – disconcerting, clear. Nothing escapes it. Here is my face polished by the years. Wrinkles at the corners of my eyes, the crouching sacks underneath them that sometimes I see are grey-black with fatigue. And the upper lids rest sometimes along the eyelashes like crinkly awnings. It is not a pretty picture, and yet if I step back and allow my candid whole face into view – what then? I look at my plain face, neither sad nor happy, the eyes merely curious. There is determination and hope there, I think. The brow becomes important. It will face the world and discountenance it. The mouth is square, the teeth behind white and even. It is a dour face, but not weak. It seems to spell experience and yet it seems always to be coming forward quizzically, coming forward with enquiry. I hear words as I look candidly at my appraising eyes. '. . . A tree to be desired,' I hear a voice saying. 'A tree to be desired to make one wise.'

Ah – to make one wise, to make one wise.

—

For the first time, I know I am speaking to Rosa. It is late autumn.

And yet I have been wrong. Rosa is not her name. Her name is Greta, but on the track I have yet to discover that. Many times since I have listened to myself, watched myself, marvelled at myself, as I learn her real name later in the day. After the funeral, after my slow grief over months, there, on the track to Campfire Bay, is the woman I have thought of as Rosa. This time, when I hear her contralto voice asking me about the rock pool, I am quite certain. It is like being rediscovered.

In my visions I have been mistaken again. This beautiful woman now will never know my mother as I had hoped. Our meeting is too late. The fact that they can never know each other is a steady sadness.

On a warm weekend I am at the church. I mow, dig away at edges, chip the spent iris beds in the secret corner. I clear, rake, burn the summer's sheddings in the green valley. I have been away from the block too long. Now the northerly is blowing off the land. When I go in to Port Chalice I see the wind stroking the sea, the water smarting and moving under it offshore. I decide to go to Campfire Bay to check the swell, perhaps to dive in the sweep gutter.

On the way down I round the steep corner of the track in the scrub and there she is, sitting on the flat rock. She is watching the sea running its lips along the wave platform far below. Elbow on knee, chin in hand, she sits with the small, faded pack beside her. Her thoughts are lost somewhere in the blue-green water behind the waves' break. Then she hears my steps. When she sees me she starts, looks at me again, rights herself. Hello, I say. Hi, she says, and swings round to get to her feet. She picks up her pack.

I gesture towards the narrow, scoured defile of the track plunging down through the scrub. There's no room for two of us.

'No, you first,' she says, reaching to straighten a shoulder strap. She turns back to me where I stand. Her eyes look into mine for the first time. 'I think you'll know,' she says. 'People tell me there's a nice rock pool somewhere along Campfire Bay. But I haven't found it. Do you know it?'

'Oh, yes,' I say. 'Probably the one people call the Blue Pool. Easy enough to get to. It's off to the left when you get to the bottom.'

'Ah, the left. I've been going to the right.' She laughs, flexes one foot and then the other in her sneakers. 'Well, you first.'

We start down. I marvel that it is we two now in all the world who are treading the track that I have trodden so often. I can hear her feet padding behind me, her breathing as she lets herself down the steep pinches, using her hands on the rock. Down, down to the levelling out in the stiff grass. I turn to check. She stops, looking at the little catchment that holds the trigger plants near the bottom.

'Where will you swim?' she asks.

'Oh, I'm going to have a look in a sweep gutter further along the wave platform. There's an overhang there. I might get some photographs in the sea gardens. If the water's clear.'

I look at her. Her skin is darker than mine, her eyes brown, her hair dark too, swept up above her head. She is beautiful. Can she know that I have been writing to her these months, these years?

'Well, I'll be happy if you can point me towards the rock pool,' she says. 'I haven't brought my flippers. Only a mask.'

'OK,' I say. I step on down, haversack's weight half relieved by a hand to the strap and a braced elbow, until we come to where the track lets out of the scrub and onto the sand of the dunes. I stop, wait for her, point to the small grotto catching the sun just this side of the rock pool. 'It's just in the lee of that little cave affair that comes out onto the wave platform. See? There? If you stay up top till you get past that, you'll find a way down to the pool. Go carefully though: if you fall the rock's pretty sharp.'

I look at her. I want to take my vision of her away with me down the wave platform. Everything is possible. This all has its own pace. I cannot lose her. I can't believe she brings such beauty to me. I know we'll meet again soon. I touch my feelings about it and find that I'm not even impatient. Everything is possible. I know we are found. I have her voice, her eyes, to keep for this bright morning.

'Well, get some good shots – and thanks. See you soon.' She smiles, turns in her blue shorts and green denim shirt, starts plodding through the sand into the sun's alley of white. The scrub sings in the warmth up the track that runs behind us to the sky.

—

In my grief I hear voices. How long does grief last? I hear the steady stepping rhythm of Longfellow. It is my mother's voice reading to us in the back bedroom at Cicero Street. It is a story about America, a place I want to go to if the War stops. It is a patient, steady story about Hiawatha, with the fir trees and lakes and the mountains behind and braves in canoes paddling up the rivers. Alistair flops over towards the wall. He can't stay awake. I'm swooning too. I hear the book close and the light click off. I feel lips gently touching my brow and then nothing but the warm dark of the bed.

Louise knows her poetry. She recites it because she loves it. It is what makes sense of the world for her.

'I will arise and go now, and go to Innisfree, And a small cabin build there, of clay and wattle made . . .'

I can hear her voice. I can see her mouth pursing as she utters the words. I can see her eyes even now, saying that this is worth remembering, this is worth committing to my sense of what life is and what might happen. Sometimes she is so tired that her mouth sags and her throat dries and she yawns so long that she struggles for breath as she closes the book.

There are worlds in the poems. There is Australia, even Victoria in the poems. 'The Morning Star paled slowly,' my mother is saying at the door of the little holiday house at Somers when I can't sleep any more and she is making a cup of tea in the grey light. '. . . the Cross hung low to the sea . . . and there's the Southern Cross. See? There!' Or sometimes she'll say, 'Oh to be in England now that April's there.' And she'll swallow and look around at the japonica blossom and the swooning pale purple of the tamarisk near the front door at Cicero Street. Her eyes seem to be thinking far away as she listens to the birds in the garden. 'That's the wise thrush,' she says to herself and then looks at us. 'He sings each song twice over, Lest you should think he never could recapture the first fine careless rapture!'

I hear voices. It is holidays. Will and Bob Bristow are talking each other down, quoting each other down, as they walk the path to the lake at Emerald, Bob's glass eye sadly roving the near side of the scrub, his feet sometimes tangling in the grass-knobbed centre of the track. 'I have seen old ships sail like swans asleep . . .' he says. Will, my father, walks like a squire with his hands behind his back. '. . . See the mast burst open with a rose . . . and the whole deck put on its leaves again . . .' Will volunteers. Louise has picked a bouquet of wattle and veronica as she walks. She chips in, looking pointedly at the lone derelict house swathed in its wild garden on the upper side of the track:

'They left the vine-wreathed cottage and the mansion on the hill,
The houses in the busy streets where life is never still . . . and . . .
   er . . .
The pleasures of the city . . . and . . . er . . . ah . . .'

'Very polemical!' says Bob Bristow. 'And a long way west!' They all laugh. The sombre wattles are silent around us in their grey, turning dark. It is the past.

I hear voices. I hear someone say, 'A chiel's among us taking notes' and they all laugh again and trip their lips and look at me. I hear the voices. How have I lost them? It is the past, I suppose. But what is the past? And are the voices lost if I can hear them?

—

What will my father say? How will he answer me? I can see him backing away from my words, busying himself with his meagre washing for the line, sorting, lifting the old cane clothes basket that Louise lumped outside on so many days. The questions must be asked. They hang there in what my mind repeats, in the words I hear. '. . . your tennis-player friend' – I can see it on the page. And then: 'Beautiful woman, I'm still remembering the Rowing Club dance floor and afterwards. I'm remembering you . . .' My father wrote this. What will he say when I ask him about it?

—

I've barely stepped in beyond the plastic ribbons at the door of the restaurant when I see her sitting there over a cup of coffee. At first she is looking out the window. But then she turns. She has noticed me. A slow smile takes over her face when she looks at me. She swivels towards me on the rough bench, smiling.

'Hello. Any pictures from the sea gardens?'

'One or two,' I say. 'Hold on. Let me get a coffee and I'll come over.'

I have a momentous calm. Can she hear me thinking while I stand there? The Port Chalice tourists step between us as I wait. Ben, the proprietor, eventually can lift his head from the wrapping counter, gives me a wink, calls out the numbers of a couple of orders, then asks: 'Latte?' I nod.

So we sit. How young a face, her eyelashes so soft and dark. Her cheeks have the faintest dimples. Can she sense me looking at her? She is happy, smiling, as she tells me about the Blue Pool, that now she'll know where to swim, that it was cold but bracing. Revivifying, she says. I love her. But does she know how much I have told her through the weeks, the months, how much I have confided to her?

She sips her coffee, asks me if I'm a local. No? A writing place. Ah, a writer. Of what? So where do I write. A church? A church! And where am I in Melbourne? Hawthorn – heavens, she's only down the road in Malvern. She was helping with an anthropologist's study of Aboriginal history and stories further along the coast a year ago, and stayed at Port Chalice. She liked the coast then. She hadn't really known it before that. Now she is back sometimes at weekends and free days, on off weekends, through the summer and autumn. She stays at the motel, usually with a girlfriend, sometimes with her son, but not this time. She is Greta, by the way. Her name is Greta as in Garbo, she says, and laughs. Greta Pirrone. Her father is Italian, her mother French, both living now in Adelaide. They came out from Europe in 1952, so she grew up in Melbourne from the age of three. With each thing she tells me it is as though I already know it or should know it. And yet I have to learn it again, treasure the knowledge like a fresh apple. It is proffered to me. It is a gift to me of part of her life.

I feel calm and yet I cannot believe. I look at her face, and I feel the hardness of the bench beneath my thighs, and I look away at a wave feeling its way up the sloping beach like a secretive pale hand and retreating again beyond the tourist cars and I still cannot quite believe.

She has to get back to Melbourne this afternoon, she tells me. It is her son's eleventh birthday tomorrow. He will be coming back to her place in Malvern from his access with his father. Joel's birthday, she says in her deep, soft voice. He is a long-legged schoolboy. She wants to see him. His father is living in Berwick now with his new girlfriend, so he has some driving to do on access weekends. Yes, Joel has been with Gavin. Gavin is the father in Berwick.

Gavin and Greta divorced three years ago, when Joel was eight years old. She uses her unmarried name again now.

She wipes back some strands of hair from her forehead. She asks what sort of camera I use underwater, about the distance of the church from the sea. No telephone at the church? No television?

She thinks about that. I watch her eyelashes, her cheek, from the side as she ponders. Beyond the road the waves still push their hands up the sand of the beach.

She shakes herself out of her reverie, looks at me, smiling. But you've got to have music, she remonstrates. Her lips almost pout. I'm smiling at her. Yes, I'm saying. Jazz. Depending on the sort of thinking and writing I'm doing. But sometimes I find I'm chasing the deepest silence. She nods. She works to music too, writing reports and papers. She's an anthropologist. She can work to Copland, Sibelius; sometimes to Faure, Delius, perhaps Elgar. Where you can feel the land, trees, weather, the season, she says. And – yes – quite often jazz. Brubeck, Mulligan, Thelonius Monk, Ella, Wynton Marsalis. What about them? And Miles Davis and Billie Holliday, especially Miles Davis and Lady Day. And what about Dire Straits, what about Sting, what about Peter Gabriel! Her eyes shine at me and then she draws them back as if she has come too far into the light.

She tidies a strand of hair with the back of her hand, finds it again, begins to curl it absently against her forehead. I love her. I love her!

There is a silence, both of us looking at the waves raking in beyond the dark skirts of the pines and the inert cars, the sky waiting for a look-in above as the sunlight changes. I can feel the sea uniting us – its indifference, its beauty, its unfailing presence, the light on its shoulders. I can feel it helping our thinking towards each other. Always the sea. Always as if for the first time.

'How about the Marsalis concert in the Concert Hall?'

I'm asking without even pondering it. I see a golden evening. I hear the hush of people finding seats, see the lights on polished wood, the sound baffles hanging there above the stage, waiting above the music stands, the drums. 'He's here this week. You know? I can probably grab another ticket?'

'Mmm . . . Marsalis. Yes, I know.' She looks direct at me. She raises her eyes towards the dark rafters, thinking. 'Yes, Marsalis.' She laughs, her face breaking into something pleased. 'Yes,' she says. 'Marsalis! Why not!' She thinks again into the rafters, looks back at me. 'When is it?' she says. 'Any day after Tuesday I could. When is it?' She looks deep into me again. I see hope unfeigned in her eyes.

'Thursday.'

'Then, yes, I'd love to come if we can work it.' She's reaching for paper in her pack. 'Marsalis in Melbourne. Great! I'll give you a phone number.'

There is a golden evening somewhere ahead of us. There are lights on polished wood, the first light stirrings of a drum, the figures coming on-stage. I hear it through a momentous calm. Greta has waited for me.

—

There is a letter from Louise. Mr Tremearne holds it in his safe. It is designed for me to read in a year's time, unless my father agrees to release it to me before then. A letter for me alone? There's no letter for Alistair or Greg. Even though they're not here, my brothers swim in my mind now. I'm seeing their blond heads shining in the shaft of sun that throws itself in among the scattered pieces of wood in Will's shed. It's what is called the past again. It's a scene I know. I see my father's fair head behind my brothers as he works with an awl. He probes and probes again at a hole in a length of wood. I think of Mr Tremearne and the letter again, but I see my father's head starting to look up at what Alistair is doing. A momentary panic nudges the backs of my knees. My mind swoons as though it might shut down to sleep.

The past has come back. In my darkness I am still alone – and now my mother, who might have been on the veranda, is dead. I needed her words. I need her words. Am I alone in my dark difference?

The voices are still there, too. What about our 1934 dream? We could think about making it official. I hear the words of the letters. My father Will loved my mother. Alex Cumming has loved my mother.

At the end I see Mr Tremearne's face again, looking up from the papers on his desk. I catch the brief shaft of curiosity as he glances at me, then looks away at the pink-taped files on a corner desk. The curiosity is gone. A dispassionate, professional calm has taken its place. I must talk to Will. It will soon be time. It will soon be kinder to him, when his thin neck in the collar can stand it. I find my knees are shaking.

—

Greta will know me as no one else does, although we have been in each other's lives for only three weeks. We have met for the first time on a track five months back when I am so stupid with sadness that I don't know then that we are meant to join, although she does. I catch her looking at me and her gaze doesn't stir. We go to a jazz concert and I am aware of her beside me all night, generous, warm and knowing me already. I realise she wants to be with me alone. She moves past me and stirs me. She is woman through and through, the other presence, the other sex, the wise round circle that goes with my hard line. Against all the meretricious coyness and false smiles around us in the city world, in televised Australia, I can see our love will speak itself truly all the time. Sometimes it seems that Greta and I will tell each other every day, every hour, how much we love. We make love and we are close and pure – a pavan of tongue and hair and thigh and buttocks and breasts and shoulders and cock, moving. Her body is beautiful, full of soft circles and eyes and deep contralto sighs. My throat thrums as I spear to reach her.

—

I speak to Will at last. It is Saturday morning. I have called in, knowing I've given him time to get up and have breakfast. Down the yard the silver-eyes are tipping about like urgent drunks in the recesses of the fig tree. They seem to be trailing yellow-tinted coats.

My heartbeat says that I do not look forward to this, and yet I am driven. This is something I want to punch home, even though it means punching my father. My fist is clenched as I think about it. But I must be deliberate, and I must hold out hope, something to progress to. In the afternoon I will meet Greta in Collins Street. I see her face. It is what I yearn for. It is hope. It is where life goes on.

But now I am studying Will's face across the table. He's in dressing gown, his pyjama collar appearing at his neck like a faded, unkempt flower. The face with its surprisingly blue eyes below the grey hair. The face that I have sat with over so many mornings, over so many plates and

270

crumbs and desultory knives and spoons at this very table in another house.

'Will? Dad? I think you have something to tell me, haven't you. Something pretty important?'

There is an instant flash of naked fear in his face, but it is quickly gone. His eyes rove to the window. 'Something important? What sort of thing, Dig?' he asks. I have expected this parrying question. I could have scripted all of this. I slug on.

'Well, something to do with Louise. Something to do with you and Louise and Alex Cumming?' I leave it on an upward questioning inflection. I can feel my own deep and vague cunning. I'm like a cat crouching.

'Oh, yes, Mr Tremearne told you about a letter that's coming to you, didn't he, when Louise died? That's what you mean?'

But he is not looking at me. He is putting his knife through a half piece of toast and jam.

'You tell me, Dad. I don't know what the letter says, and it doesn't come to me for another year unless you say so.'

I see the flash of fear again in his eyes. I catch the beginning curl in his mouth that is his way to tears. He has put down his knife. He has forgotten his toast and the half-drunk cup of tea. He pushes the plate away from him so that he can rest his forearms on the table's edge. He might take his head in his hands. I feel pity. He might weep. He doesn't. He lifts his forearms gingerly from the table, settles back in the chair looking for ease but not finding it. He sits there uncomfortably. He expels a breath, looking at the wall. Then he brings a hand to his chin, starts running his thumb just under his mouth. His eyes rove from one end of the small wall shelf opposite him, from cookbook to cookbook. He is studying the spines as though his life depended on missing nothing. I pity him. I pity the thin neck and the grey swatch of uncombed hair. But I could punch him. My teeth grit. I do punch him.

'Dad? Are you my father?' He sits still. I punch again. 'For God's sake, Will, I've got to ask you. You don't have to say yes. Are you my real father?'

He doesn't look at me. He takes the punch and his body remains still. I watch his breathing as it raises and lowers the collar-button of his pyjamas. I swear that for a full ten seconds his eyes look straight ahead at the chair opposite where its shadow reaches to brush the wall lightly. I could hit him. I could hit him again. He doesn't have to say yes.

'No, I'm your stepfather.' He stops to clear his throat, to swallow. 'I'm your stepfather, Tim. Alex Cumming is your father. He's your real father, as you have concluded.'

As I have concluded! All at once I could punch him and yet kiss him. Faces resolve and then dissolve before my eyes. I see the figures in the photographs. I hear the words of the letters.

'It's all gone on much longer than it should,' he says, and his body looks so fined and weary in the dressing gown. He's rocking with relief in the humble chair. 'You should have been allowed to know. Long ago. Long ago!' His voice rises with surprising vehemence, then breaks.

'So why didn't you tell me? Why didn't Louise tell me?' Now I find a deep anger reeling up and locking to my heart with the shock of a train coupling. 'You take my breath away. I'm forty-six years old! For God's sake!'

'I did want you to know,' he says. He lets his eyes rest on mine now for the first time. They are the leaping, thinking, blue eyes I have always known. They soften me. 'I always felt it was better you should know. But your mother didn't. And then it got later and later.' He swallows and waits as his Adam's apple moves against his pyjama collar. 'There was one time we were going to tell you. You came in feeling very mixed up. You'd remember? You told Louise you felt different from the rest of us. You asked her why you felt so different from us all. You asked her why you weren't like Greg and Alistair. Do you remember? You were nine or ten.' Again Will pauses. But this time his eyes stay with mine. 'So we were going to tell you, but Louise got cold feet and we didn't – and then the moment was past. From then it got harder and harder.'

'Did you think I was made of delicate china, for God's sake?!'

'Huh! It was Louise who was the delicate china. And yet she suffered for it all these years. It wasn't that she wasn't strong. She put a brave face on it.' My father casts about him on the table cloth with extended fingers as if searching for crumbs. 'It was the one thing she felt she had to hold to herself through thick and thin. And I thought I should abide with that if she wanted it, but maybe I shouldn't have.'

'Well, you better tell me the story now.' My anger simmers with sadness. I want to escape. But I want to know. For a second Greta's face swims up to me promising the world as I have imagined it to be. I picture her waiting in Collins Street, looking in a plunging shop window. But the vision fades.

I have to know. My anger simmers. I say again with a bitter edge to my voice that immediately I want to retract: 'Spill the beans. Go on, Dad. Spill the beans!'

Will looks levelly at me, the dark eyes with their creases, the jaw set out slightly. He starts to respond, stops, chooses his words deliberately. 'I can understand what you feel. It can only be a feeling of betrayal. I can understand that you want chapter, line and verse. I won't deny you anything I know. But I think you should have the letter first. I think you should have Louise's account first and then we'll talk.' His eyes seek my permission. And I'm nodding acquiescence.

'OK,' I say. 'Can I ring Tremearne? That's all right with you?' I'm suddenly weary. 'Can I tell him you'll write him a letter?'

'Yes, if you would, Dig. If you would.' He sits still for a moment looking from the window down the yard. Then he stacks the two plates, brings the coffee mug over to them. 'Secrets and lies,' he says, and leans back from the table. He looks at me. He even smiles. 'You know, down the track you'll probably be able to look at it all as a piece of human drama, part of what people do, what they carry about with them. But certainly not now, I suppose. Not yet.' He groans and pushes himself to his feet, starts reaching for the plates. But he decides better. He extends a hand towards my shoulder, feels for the bone. I can't respond. So he draws away, picks up the plates, thinking of the sink.

I sit on, looking down the yard. I can see only two silver-eyes now in the fig tree. They are still propping, glissading, prospecting among the leaves in the morning sun.

Ten Thousand Thousand
Fruit to Touch . . .

Don't move, my voice says – it might break the spell. If I don't move I can hold the story, although I don't know yet where it has to go next. I can see my close people. I hear their voices, feel their rhythms. I have caught them on the screen in a net of words. There are snatches of phrases I don't want to lose. I hear some voices I cannot place. Near me on the desk are other parts of the story in the camera lying on its side across white printouts and proof sheets. If I get up, the image, the order, the urging momentum might vanish from me. If I sit and dream, on the other hand, the image might consolidate like a sculpture until I can hold it. I need the net of words, the peremptory slap of the SLR to help make up the world.

Will's face is here, drained by sudden fear. Greta's face waits for me where she sits chin on hands at the table. It seems I am thinking how to live next. I think by writing words, by stopping the bewitching light and rhythms that come through a lens.

Ah! My camera! It's a beautiful mechanism – the angel of time and light. Here is a shark boat that I see, just come in from Bass Strait, and in its resting against the wharf, in the pile of shark on the rough planks, in the swearing men in their oilskins, there are many things I must not know. How else can the mystery hold? The lens consumes the pale boat's side beautifully, the men's faces working lower than the wharf's decking. I can almost touch the light sculpting the boat's bow, I can feel the shadow drawing in the wheel-house. Writing and taking photographs is a constant asking – again and again, what else is there to learn? What will I never know? My photographs are mine alone, taken to see what I can discover. I press the shutter, feel the delicious slap of the mechanism, of the mirror going home. It captures time in glass so that it can be laid out on paper to be thought about.

In the steady beat of the night truth stands against the dark. It is my origins I search for. I know that something is incomplete and I see that there will be a revelation. Will, my father, is still my father and will be revealed. Alex Cumming, my father, will come into the light and I will know him. Greta who I love will be revealed to me. I will be revealed to her. I think I will unearth again a credo I thought was lost and find new leaves springing from it.

'Yes,' says Mr Tremearne. His voice is metallic on the line. I can hear paper shuffled. He speaks as if he's in the midst of reading something at the same time. 'It poses no difficulty. Get your father to write me a note . . . ah . . . stating that your mother's letter should be released to you. Make sure he states his permission and . . . ah . . . identifies the letter as the one by Louise Menzies, dated . . . er . . . what is it . . . 12 October 1980 . . . that I hold pursuant to her will and . . . ah . . . ah . . . over which she has given him discretion. It might be best that you word it for him. Can you do that?'

I say that I can. I hear him pause at the other end of the line. Then he clears his throat and continues in a lower, engaged tone. 'From what I have been told, this is something that will be to your benefit and peace of mind. Help him with it and get it off to me. OK?'

—

I miss my father's voice. Rhythm, he says, that's what it's all about. I remember far back round time's circle hearing Will saying something about rhythm in photography. Then he talked about the rhythm in a book's structure, too, in how the pages fall, in the balance of line and drawing and text. It's all rhythm, he's saying. I did not understand then. I can hear his voice again now. I can see his words on the thin letter paper. New York's rhythm, he writes. New York's rhythms – plural – he says, in his air letter from abroad. The camera moves with me, he says, in these places where I have never been before. It seems to unearth the rhythms. And I'm bracketing, he writes. I'm taking multiple shots of the one thing. That seems to be the way to see through to the best rhythms. Rockefeller Center – its base of different levels, different horizontals and people moving, and then its white rhythms reaching to the sky, the lower levels falling away. How do you capture it? There has to be a better way to express it. Move, look again, he writes to me: move, compose another shot, shoot again. It mightn't be there in the light tomorrow. Move again – change the mood with another rhythm. Bracket it with three or four shots, make sure you've given it a chance to speak. Rockefeller Center bracketed. The Louvre bracketed. The Museum of Modern Art set down in the well of New York's buildings – bracketed. The Guggenheim's stack of saucers, too.

I look down at my black Pentax with its lens as pure as a calf's eye. I hear Will's words, see his fingers wrapping round his cameras, then sneaking towards the shutter when he's found what he wants. I look out at the world and it flows. And I sense Greta beside me. It is the future. We are watching the world repeat itself, the steady rhythm of the expected. We watch the planes lifting from the runway, one every minute, while we wait beside our bags in the airport. I think we're watching to see the order of things, of human movement – the order in which things happen, and how they'll happen again. I am coming towards Greta slowly, touch by touch, kiss by kiss, over the months, perhaps over years. In the end I will look into the eyes of this woman I seek and I see that I have known her all along. It's like the city's beat from shadows left to shadows right – and then the fading light. It's like the sharp, hopeful risings of one silver plane after another above the buildings of the airport. We will know each other's rhythms.

—

I have only to look at her and I can feel the circle there, firm and calm. It is as if the circle is her friend and companion, her essence – just as it was Louise's. It is in her voice, her movement. It is in the air about her. She knows much more about it than I do. My line persists against her circle. Greta is circle after circle, circle within circle.

She tells me. She is thirty-nine years old now. She is only thirty-six when she divorces, when Joel is only eight. Her husband is a metallurgist. Gavin. She is just twenty-two when she marries him. She is still a student, but he is already working. Gavin proves to be very ambitious, driven, self-absorbed. How has she not seen this in him before she marries him, she asks me, she asks the air. Then after she finishes her Masters, after she starts working, but more particularly after she stops to have Joel, Gavin begins blaming. She and Joel are weights around his neck. There are chances going begging. Then he sometimes becomes violent. She leans away from me, baring her neck. She touches a finger to a white wisp of a scar below her ear, feels for another beside her eye. Not often, she says, but sometimes. So, fourteen years of time wasted, she says, before she calls it quits. Fourteen years.

But not absolutely wasted, she says. She has her work again for the last few years of her marriage – some teaching at the university, some consultancy. She has Joel to watch as he grows up. Gavin is doing a lot of work in Western Australia for three years or so of that time. Then they separate for two years and the divorce rolls up at the end of it and they know. Nowhere further to go.

I watch her swallow those years away in silence for a moment. Then I see the circle close around her again – and she smiles. You see, her eyes say. You see. Later I will tell you more, say her eyes.

—

There are other things that happen that I cannot explain.

I'm driving south from Mildura – coming home from a lecturing trip. It's before Louise's letter, before Sydney, before the susurrus of wind through the curtains in Alex Cumming's unit above the ocean. It's the Mallee, still hot, late in the day. I'm not attempting to reach Hawthorn tonight. I'll probably stay in a motel in St Arnaud. I've come down past Hattah, Ouyen with its cattle yards still wreathed in the final dusty throes of a sale, down past Lake Tyrrell on the long sweeps of highway, the sun smiting me from the right window. I've cleared Sea Lake. I'm in the country of my close people now, but I've got to keep going, think about distances, hours, fatigue. I'm running down the road through Boigbeat, the aisles of mallee running the low hills to the east. I should stop and take a photograph of the house at Berriwillock. It's unoccupied now for seven years, gradually mouldering into the ground, assisted by young bloods' drinking parties now and then. I've monitored the house's fall on other trips – the smashed windows, the veranda posts pulled away, the stubbies and cans on the floor in the old kitchen and under the mallee within a throw of the gaping back door.

I'm thinking about it as I drive. It must be twenty-five years since Flute died, and Frank six years after and then Marie selling out before she died. Who farms it now I don't know, but they don't use the house, although there's sometimes an old truck parked in the long shed.

Here's Berriwillock ahead, the silos rising like rose bolts into the paling sky, there's Flute's old house and its mallee to the east and the old sheep yards that Grandpa John first built close to the highway, where Frank and Flute often work down the hot days, grunting at each other, at the dogs, at the press of dust-rouged sheep's backs. As I approach I can see the spars of the yards, the leaning posts in the long blond grass. I'm sweeping on towards the offshoot to the hotel over the railway line. But as I pass the old yards I see movement, two figures bending and straightening in hats and shirts against the yard rails, the low sun lighting them. No car or ute. It could almost be Frank and Flute working there. I'm past them. I'm nearly abreast of the town's first pepper trees when I decide on a whim to turn and go back. While I'm here I'll find out who runs the farm, other news, ask them about the house and what state it's in. I swing round on the empty highway and I'm back at the yards in a minute. I pull off, reach for the door handle, look over to the yards. No one there. I get out, stump the few yards towards the split rails of the yards. Perhaps the two men are hidden by long grass. No one. I look around me, turning slowly on my heel. Three hundred and sixty degrees. No one, nothing, not a movement in the sunset. And yet I saw the sun lighting their shirts, their red-stained hats.

—

It's something I never expect. Des and Joyce in my valley, at the church that fate gave to me as my place, the place above all where I'm meant to be.

They've gone out down the lower road to explore a bit. From the kitchen I can see them mooching slowly in the late light, the long green hill looming treeless over them. Joyce is looking back to Des, telling him what she's seeing, telling him when there's a big drift of road gravel. He's guided by her voice – and he's got his white stick. She doesn't want to lead him by hand, but sometimes she comes back a few steps to guide him to the best path in dips where the milk-tankers have exploded out potholes, thumping into the surface day after day in the wet. I look at the two figures against the hill and I can't believe it. It fills my heart. Des and Joyce at the church where I write. Des and Joyce in my valley. These close people, brother and sister, hearing my birds, smelling the grass in the dairy paddock next up the road, feeling my valley's wind on their faces.

It's eight months since Louise has gone. It's only three months since Jean has died. It's more than four years that I've been in my own limbo. It's so long now since David walked out on Joyce and went to live with Nancy. And then when Louise is in hospital we hear that David's dead in the car up near Romsey. It's probably twenty-five years now since Joyce takes Des in, to look after him – her brother, her blind brother. What has happened to us all? I feel the present romping over the past, and even though I'm alone and lonely, it seems inevitable. It even seems right. It's sad, and yet somehow I don't mind. I test what I think and it seems like an unravelling that has to come. Most of the time I can see it as a peneplain in high country where the trail leads to further mountains, further valleys, further long, tramping stages.

Tonight we sit by the fire and talk. Des is telling me things I don't know, about how he and Charlie started in jazz. Joyce sits to one side, looking into the fire, listening. Yeah, Charlie's still going strong, from what I hear, Des says. Still going strong. I hear he still plays a few gigs here and there. Joyce cocks her head on the side and says you and Charlie and Mark Shrumm go back a long way. Yes, Des says and hesitates. He swallows. He goes on quietly, as though against some inner resistance. Yeah – you know how we got together? Mark and I are in the street in North Melbourne one night, and we hear a sax being played somewhere. We find a bit of a jazz club above a shop. We go up. I can still smell that place and feel the stair-rails – cold iron. We sit in and listen. It's Charlie playing, but we don't know him then. Anyway, in a break Mark gets talking to Charlie and he's interested in our piano and drums. We're away. They sit me down and I play a couple of things. They already had Don Wendover playing bass, but the others with Charlie are blow-ins. Anyway, over the next few weeks we start to practise and we team up as something permanent. Des's face falls with memory – then he rallies. Charlie's bloody Vanguard, he says, looking past us both at the fire he can feel – I can still smell that car. It had a petrol leak somewhere. Charlie . . . Charlie. He took me all over the place. Mark took me about a lot too. They'd tell you where. And then . . . Betty came in one night . . . when we were playing in St Kilda. Des swallows again, can't go on for a moment – and Joyce and I know why. Then he says with sudden clarity: that's where we met. But his voice trails away, the emotion taking his breath. I haven't heard from Charlie in a long time. He's been in Adelaide now for years.

Now I can see Des's white shirt again on the stage. I can hear the piano. I'm hearing 'The Londonderry Air'. I'm hearing 'How Long Has This Been Going On?' I'm hearing 'Lover Please Be Tender' and a little smattering of 'You Are My Sunshine' coming into it. I can see Charlie's face smiling as he plays. I can see the veins in his neck standing out. I can hear clapping and then the piano coming through in front of the floating circles of faces that have disappeared into darkness like moons into cloud – because it is the past.

Des's voice seems to lose intensity and die. We hear the wind outside in the dark wrapping its webs round the church and its trees. The fire seethes quietly. Then Joyce says it was good Will and Louise got overseas when they did. It's a change in subject. Joyce says it quietly in her small, piping voice. So we talk about Louise. We talk about Jean and how quickly the cancer took her after Louise. Two sisters in the blink of an eye, Joyce says, and she spreads hands, then open her legs in her skirt like a man does to trap the fire's warmth. So common now, she says, her voice going high with disbelief. It's bloody cruel! And I hear Flute's phrasing in the way she says it. We'll talk about her kids – Little Gwenda and Little Ian. I haven't seen them for a long time. Gwenda's in Perth. Ian is in Griffith. Des will be silent, listening. I saw Ian when he came down for David's funeral, Joyce says, surprising us with the mention of it. He went. I didn't. So that was a chapter, wasn't it, she says. She thinks a bit, and sighs and looks into the fire. Chapter ended, she says. Huh,

David didn't stand a chance from the beginning. Pushed by his parents, his brothers. Always defensive, always flighty.

I'm thinking to myself about the joy of having them here. I'm thinking I know how this will go. I'll put some more wood on the fire and go to get us all a cup of coffee. This is how it will be. We'll still be talking. Then we'll settle again in the warmth and cradle the coffee in our hands and talk about Flute and Candles and Archie. But there'll be no further mention of Betty. And yet while Des sits there staring past us, and feels for the shelf near him and puts down his coffee and places his hands between his knees like he sometimes does, I'll know that he's thinking about her among all these others who are now away from us round the arc of time, who were once with us. And I'll see Betty's face, so young and frank with love for Des before she died. I'll see her leading him as they dance at the club. I'll see their bodies entwined. I'll see Betty's white sheath dress. I'll see Des kissing her before she hands him back up the steps to the stage and the piano.

The fire will shift against itself behind our words. The metal surrounds will crack a few times in the stirred warmth when I put another piece of wood on. Then they'll go silent again.

—

I hear the echoes now and I think: what did you expect? Did you expect her to be another person entirely? Did you expect her to be other than she is? Expect her to change? I think: surely all the signs were there, but you didn't heed them. I think: were you too young to know? Too inexperienced? I think, sitting inside the hunk of myself, where I am unassailable. I think: how did you yourself come across to others? How easy are you to live with – always seeking, always pushing, always lured? Not relaxed, even when you think you're relaxed? I see Patricia's face, and I'm sorry. I see her as I saw her in the supermarket unbeknown to her – a face without youth, a stolid face pushing into the wind of what has happened, what will continue to happen. No frisson. No frisson of new fields ever again?

I listen to the echoes now and I apologise to Patricia. I look back now and I forgive – but my forgiveness vanishes like smoke into the air. It leaves an empty pit at my centre.

—

I remember. Yes, I'm at the door of the church, leaning against the jamb like Will often does back at Cicero Street. I'm watching Joyce in the yard outside. Des is asleep on one of the camp beds inside. Joyce is wandering, looking, taking in this valley that's strange to her, a church set in dairy hills. She's seen the half sheep-shear from the Berriwillock farm. I've shown it to her on its nail just inside the door of the church. She knows it's just a talisman, that it serves no useful purpose except to remind. To remind. To put me in mind of Berriwillock and Flute and Pearlie and Grandpa John. To put me in mind of Joyce herself and Bing and of that other dog called Bull sitting beside me in the old car in the shed years ago when I was three. I can still smell him, still know when he'll suddenly fall to scratching himself there on the front seat.

The old heavy spade and old garden fork, stuck upright in the ground, are marking the ends of the small vegetable patch. I see Joyce's eyes go to the spade. Perched on the wooden handle is a grey thrush. It has come down from the sugar gum. It has sung its three notes and awaits a reply. It cocks one eye at Joyce thirty feet away near the wattle. I watch. Joyce seems to go into herself. It's as if she has known this valley all her life. She's standing quite still, a bit of kindling she has picked up hanging in her hand. She raises her head slightly and delivers an answering three notes, whistling. The thrush cocks its head again and answers. Joyce whistles the three notes again, the last rising like a question. It's a good imitation. The thrush warms to this, sends its rich three messages, then loops down towards Joyce, perches on the fork. Joyce has moved a couple of steps closer. Now only ten feet separate them. Joyce speaks again. The thrush is alert, as though it might come to sit on her shoulder, look quizzically at her neck and hair. It waits. Joyce moves another step. She whistles again. The thrush waits. Now it responds, cocks its head, then seems to look away down the valley. Joyce whistles, three clear words. The thrush waits, does not reply. Joyce takes another tentative step. The thrush crouches, cocks an eye at her again, then flits off to the sugar gum and then in a grey loop in air to the older wattle. Then it responds – the three notes ending in its question from the shadows.

It's as though Joyce is coming out of a trance, starting to move again a step at a time. I'm watching, trying to reach my feelings, this mix of rightness and sadness against the trees. I look at the dark run of forest that marks the valley's end. I come back to my sadness. It's for Joyce and for Des. It's even for absent David, I realise. And yet there's joy and busy-ness. Now Joyce has stalked further up the block to the little nook where the lilies grow towards spring and flowering. The thrush has dropped down to the trunk of the wattle. It is quick, silent – a grey curator intent on picking insects from the stretchmarks in the bark.

—

Sometimes after making love to Greta my words sing. That's a truth. I come from her so beautiful in her circles of haunch and breast and bottom, from her voice in the clinging, warm dark. Ah, she says – a marvellous cock – and my mind swoons with power as I plunge, joining with her. She is answering. We breathe and join with generosity. Just clear of my skin, just clear of her silken skin against mine I can feel an electricity of possibility, of insight. And now, sitting up in the sheets to put her hair up, she is watching me, her eyes lying back in themselves in dream and languor, her breasts globes as she turns. She watches me swing out of the bed, go to the desk, scrabble there and make notes, write phrases in the light from the window, then come back to her arms in bed, kissing shoulders, neck, breasts, drawing in warm cunt smells, the eager butter of semen. Later, before I have a shower, I sit at the notebook in boxer shorts and old jumper and make the poem from the start that I hear in my head, from my notes and phrases and insight until it sings for the first time on earth. Then I leave it, knowing it will survive and grow and change and sing again. That is a truth.

—

Des and Joyce at the church in the valley. I never expected it to happen.

I will tell Des and Joyce about the penguins, how they will come out of the frigid water down near the Bay of Islands in the almost dark, how they will walk like little dark personages up the sand, how if you lie prostrate across their path to the cave and the burrows they will strut up and over your chest and down your body, pausing to savour its warmth, before they go on. I promise myself, after they've gone, that I will remember to tell Des and Joyce about it. I thought of it when they were here, but then forgot to tell them.

—

So this is it. Here it is, delivered at last into my hand by Mr Tremearne not an hour ago – my mother's letter.

It's not a particularly long one. Quite a short one, in fact. Five pages. Now that I've read it, its words surround me. I read it again, trying to discern things that are not said. It washes around me a third time. At first I resent seeing my life's origins set down like this. And yet I marvel. Because it is as before – what I'm reading I seem to have known all along. I hear Louise's ironic, typical voice here and there, and it softens me. But I hold my head aloof, wait and listen. 'I suppose I have led you a merry dance,' Louise writes, ' and I am sorry that my courage became less and less as the years passed. But you deserve to know, and you deserve to know from me. I'm sorry that it has taken so long, and that it has cost Will some anguish too. He would have told you years ago. The fact is that you are not Will's son, as I think you have dimly guessed in some ways perhaps as you grew up and yet not been quite able to confirm. Your father is Alex Cumming, who grew up close to us at Sea Lake and who now lives in Sydney. How can I explain it to you . . .?'

The words are there. I go back to them, back to that sentence, that bald turning around. I look at the ink, not quite black. I know that Louise has written these words with her favourite gold-capped ball-point. The school presented it to her. Where did she sit to write it? When? The letter is dated October 1980. So she knew. She knew that the cancer would take her over, that there was not much time. So she wrote

287

it probably sitting at the low table in the lounge at Overton Lane. That fact nudges me uncomfortably, then stabs me with disappointment. Is it possible that Louise looked out from the front window at Cicero Street and debated whether to tell me? The unburdening should have come from Cicero Street, rather than from the bland rooms at Overton Lane, rooms I don't know and can't feel behind the words. I can't picture Louise writing it there. It's a touch of cold air, a reminder of transitoriness. For a moment I see death's face again looking out of my mother's gaze. It sits there in her eyes, insisting that she is to die. She has little choice where or when. Oh, I wish the letter had been written at Cicero Street, so that I can see Louise leaning over the paper – but how could it have been?

And then I find I have read myself into a state of calm, into a state of curiosity, even prurience, as though these things are outside me, as though I have dispassionate enquiries to make about what lies behind the photographs I have looked at of my young mother, of gatherings and couples in the 1920s, those letters, postcards, snapshots of the 1930s. All bewitching light on another time. But how much do I know? Louise is telling me that Alex was three years older, that he grew up at Sea Lake, that he was a cricket and tennis friend of her brothers', that she and he were at school together at the Sea Lake school, but that Alex then went to Geelong College for four years – 'where tennis was king' – while she boarded with the Bethunes and studied at Stawell High School. 'Alex was often at our place during the holidays,' she writes. 'So you see, we were a bit like brother and sister, and then we took up again when I was in teaching in Melbourne and Alex was chasing after tennis fame.'

The paragraph ends. It seems to me as I read that the break in the letter rings like a canyon. I can hear my mother drawing breath. Then, beyond the stressed white space, I hear her voice again and feel the anguish of her life in it. 'I suspect from what the doctors tell me that I haven't much more time to go. It seems that this is when things must be reckoned up. So how can I give you a balanced picture of it all?' she writes. 'The first thing to say is that it is possible to love two people at the same time. I loved Alex. A man of action. A man of good fun.

288

A generous-spirited person. And I'm sure he loved me. But I didn't know my mind, as so many don't. I had met Will in 1932 when he came to Melbourne. He and I had grown very close, too. He had even suggested that we live together. I refused. But there was something very strong under the surface with Will. He began to be in the ascendant – I was just beginning to see how rich a person he was – when Alex's love seemed to wane, seemed to be taken over by his dedication to the 1934 tour overseas.

I always loved Will. How could I not? We used to haunt the gallery. We'd go out to Footscray sometimes, sometimes to the university, to hear poets read. Not the man of action, Will, not at first glance a person of good fun. But much deeper than Alex. My darling, never underestimate Will. He is someone of great consistency, great moral strength, great love. But you know that, having grown up with him. We are both lucky to have had him.'

Again the paragraph ends. Again there is the stress seething in the white space. I find I am marvelling in tears at this woman. I crave to see her settling in the window at Cicero Street to write to me, but I can't.

'I'd rather do anything than rake over the details of all this again in this way – but I'm trusting you as a person who has seen life. You deserve to know all about this, and I beg you to bring all your experience to bear to understand what I'm telling you. I had great love for Will. And yet at the same time my love for Alex went back so far and had been so slow and relaxed that I felt it was almost pre-ordained. I seemed to have very few people in Melbourne with whom I could talk about it. You remember Bet, my friend from teachers' college. She was one of the few. And she saw things pretty clearly. And Rona Ellis. She came to a tennis-club ball with Alex and me one year. She watched proceedings. Afterwards she said: "Vanity, thy name is Alex." And then she'd say, "But where there's a Will, there's a way." And she'd wink. She knew them both. That was a just assessment of Will, but probably a harsh one of Alex. Rona thinks that all sport is vanity. I could pretend to laugh at it, but I was still divided in my mind. Many times I was sleepless over it. Sometimes I couldn't eat. Alex was preoccupied with the overseas trip to America, the Davis Cup team –

all that. I was fearful about it. Our relationship was not purely platonic, you must understand, and hadn't been for some time. Alex was not one to deny his appetites, and I was an accomplice anyway. But we were very careful. And we'd even got to the stage of talking sometimes about becoming engaged. We thought we might when he got back. Even then I had doubts, but I put them away. I postponed them. I was still drawn to Will and his books and his quiet reason. I could talk with him about things literary and cerebral that I couldn't ever discuss with Alex. Will knew about Alex, but Alex didn't know about Will. I should have told him. It was terrible. And yet, when I think about it now I'm certain that marriage with Alex would have failed. His single-mindedness was there for me to see, wasn't it! I chose not to. Pursuit of tennis at all costs. And what a player he was – a joy to watch. But how wise and knowledgeable was I when I was in my mid-twenties, in love with love, in love with life, and torn two ways! So Alex went away overseas. Five weeks after he'd gone I knew that I was pregnant and that he was the father – the only person I'd ever made love with. You came from an act of love, be assured. My first wire to Alex missed him. When my second reached him he wrote saying that he couldn't come home in the middle of the tour. I could tell that the news had panicked him, and I thought I could also hear that he was still more concerned for himself than for me. He thought we could wait until he got back in October. I was distraught.'

Again the paragraph break. Again the tension like a steel band across the white space. Did my mother write this in one sitting? How did she wring out the words? Where did her eyes rove as she composed, the pen limp in her fingers, and then bend to the paper again? I'm sure I hear her breathing.

'The long and short of it is that Will had asked me to marry him a month before Alex sailed for overseas. I asked him to wait. And then when I was distracted over the pregnancy he tumbled to it, wheedled it out of me. He said we could cope with it, that it made no difference. I think he knew more about me than I did myself. He could think for both of us. He is a rare person. The longer I've loved him the more I've marvelled at what you could say was his wide view. And it revealed to me so convincingly what he felt and what he'd been going through watching me and hearing about 'my tennis friend'. He used to refer to Alex as 'your tennis friend'. We decided to get married quickly and claim you as our own. It was in a registry office in Bourke Street. Then later his name went down as your father on the birth certificate. Some raised eyebrows about your birth in January when we had married in June, but we managed. You were a beautiful baby – a slightly lop-sided, dark-haired baby after the forceps!'

This time the white pause on the page simply rests under my eyes, tension released. The near-black words flow on. Suddenly I see Louise's view, a woman's view. Her words reveal her unthinking dedication to – what is it? Creating and nurturing life? It's something that isn't to the fore in my male thinking.

'The rest you know – or rather, the rest you have some inkling of. Alistair born two years after you, Greg another one. Pearlie and George have never known any different. In fact my whole family – all but one – saw you, still see you, as Will's eldest son, and I've always been proud of you as my eldest son. For a time Jean was the only one who knew. She had suspicions and dragged it out of me. She says nothing but still blames Alex for 'abandoning' me. Later she told Joyce about it. None of Will's family knows any different. Alex's sister Elsie thinks that I wouldn't wait for Alex to come back from overseas in 1934 and that I rejected Alex for Will – which is true in a way. That's all she knows. But now you know you have a half-sister and a half-brother in Sydney. I think you should talk to Will about all this – make your peace with him, now that you know. You should talk to Alex too. He has always known of course. He came to see me years ago, during his leaves in the War, so that he could see you, too. But since then – nothing. Meeting him won't be so easy for you, I suspect. But it will help you both.'

I hear Louise pause. I scan the paper. I feel a flood in my head, held back.

'My son, I'm sorry I have presented you with this situation. I think I've come to terms with my part in it as far as I can. I've been watching you and Will over the years in ways that you'll never have guessed – and

I think your life has been rich enough. That's not luck. It's due to your make-up and outlook as much as anything. You will be reading this after I've gone, and that's sad – and that has been part of my weakness, I suppose. But keep with you the thought that there is only human fallibility and I suppose courage. Keep with you the thought that it has all been for the best, that it has been rich despite the sadness. That's what I take with me, my love – Louise.

—

I am alone, standing close to the fence up hill from the church, the tree shadow around me. Alex's face is with me. I turn and scan the paddock, but the face is still there. I look back towards the building. Now I sense more than a face remembered. It's as if my mind is reaching out towards a nature, a character, a being with the name Alex. Who is he, my father? Yes, my father.

Now I am walking back to the door. The thought of Alex still walks with me. I am seeing the ovals of two tennis racquets and a plunge of white towel. And yet I am watching a blue wren darting across the succulent grass below the church's step. Now I am inside, catching the hints of jute and dust in the air and the deeper, ascetic smell of drying mud that comes from around the church's stumps. I can hear a blowfly meandering in a minor key in the cupboard corner of the church beyond the bedroom screens. But Alex is still present, his tincture there in the air. I imagine I see him with flashes of Sydney light and water behind him. Through the window, as if in another world, I catch sight of the white flotation of a Scotch thistle seed ball moving in the breeze across the green promontories of the boobiallas like a slow hot air balloon against deep green clouds. Where am I? Why is everything in suspension? Where do my feet want to go? I see Greta's face, smiling, the sun picking out her red lips. But Alex's face swims between us, tanned and lined as I remember it at Fern Tree Gully, the khaki drill collar of his battle-jacket below it with the Rising Sun badges speaking against it. Where must my feet go?

The thoughts come, one after another, prompted by the letter. What the letter's pages tell me is paramount. Perhaps I have just been born. I am Alex's and my mother's son. I try to look back down the past. I have lived longer than forty-six years now. Can it be that in all that time my heart has never stopped its treading of the boards of the minutes, hours, days, seasons? Can it be that in all that time I have not known who I am? Just when I seem to have reached an accommodation with the light, the wind, with people's angers, with loss and hope. It seems now there is so much more to know. But the proposition of that unerring heartbeat seems unbelievable. I multiply it out. Forty-six years – close to seventeen thousand days through which I have assumed that my place on earth has been within one niche of family and faces and voices in the broad tapestry, while all the time there has been not only the circle of my close people but another one I have scented, another circle of faces that will come to touch me! Even without any other faces and voices and bodies in their familiar ballets there is the fact of all those days, my days alone. I cannot credit that around my breath and walking and hot, thinking nights and rhapsodies in water and my busy-ness and grief; those thousands of days have circled and completed themselves. It seems too much.

—

About loving, for instance. The thought echoes. The notion of marriage echoes. How exclusive is love for woman and man? Is marriage a pretence that it is exclusive and that people can be owned, as the words of songs say so often? I think of Patricia and Adela and Greta and I hear Maya in Vizinczy's novel saying to untutored Andras that the idea that you can love only one person is the reason why most people live in confusion. I hear Louise saying it. I can look at her words saying it on the page from beyond the grave: 'The first thing to say is that it is possible to love two people at the same time.'

—

Greta, you are not here, but there are things I want to tell you. I miss you. I can't wait until I can hold you again. I can see your face and hear your voice around me. I yearn to touch you. I want to tell you how much I love you. I want to assure you that I am whistling.

If I'm whistling it means I can see forward. If I'm whistling things are all right. If I'm whistling I can feel where the story leads. Sometimes when I'm whistling I can see the future. I know you are learning these things about me. And at the back of the songs I sing and the things I whistle are the songs' words with their wisdom. Some of them are so wise about love and its sweet sadness. I think they know so much about individual loves and past loves and improvident loves and practised and experienced loving and doomed loves and never-to-be-expected love like ours. This is what I want to tell you. It is my funny valentine to you.

I whistle. There always must be music. It's a sort of salvation. The slaves sing and the prisoners sing. They say to the new inmate: 'Learn to sing. Learn to hum. Learn to whistle. It will save your identity.' They know they must do it to preserve themselves against the mean men, against cruelty, degradation and desolate time. They must sing their beliefs so that they can hear them and others can hear them, so that when they join with each other's voices they know they are one. There is rhythm that echoes the sea, or people striding or working or dancing or making love. There is rhythm that is a steady stroking. There is rhythm that is urgent and searching. I hear the brush and the drum slurring beautifully just behind the beat. I hear the trumpet like a plaintive voice. It sings about the dearness of a person. Its message is pure. How dear she is, this funny valentine! It is Chet Baker's trumpet, recorded in Los Angeles all that time ago in 1953, when I am a student and know little about jazz. Then I hear the slow thinking of the saxophone. It is speaking hardly above a whisper. Yes, it says to the trumpet, you are right, and I will tell you more. The sax is baritone. It thinks in its deep throaty way, its eyes directed away. It speaks, it sings about sadness and yet it wouldn't be without love's grieving and reverses. It is Gerry Mulligan. You know him, Greta. When the saxophone finishes I can sense that the recording people know they have plucked some magic about being human from the air in the close studio. I can see their nods, their eyes full of gladness before they speak.

—

I am amazed at the male triggers, how quicker than any computer screen they zero in and capture me in sadness and joy.

At this distance it must be the way of walking, the hips, the neat peach of the round arse rising and falling that says female, female. But it can be hand brushing back hair. It can be abandoned shake of head. It is often leaning to a stocking, or a red mouth pouting, or eyes rolling towards the ceiling in disbelief. It is often hair falling, falling in golden plunge over the shoulders, down the back. It is thighs so far away, the beautiful switching of a walk like Adela's.

The cues can come from such a distance – a glimpse of legs or shoulders through trees, breasts turning away far over in a crowd, the upright carriage and sweeping feet coming down the platform. And each time there's the thrill that feels like hope. That's what it is – hope renewed, a fullness in the eyes and gut, and a lemon touch of sadness. Just a hint of shoulders and hair sometimes, or a dress sweeping along far over on a balcony – that's all it takes.

But this is Greta, these are her breasts rolling towards me in the bed, her belly understudying them, concave and deep. I want to kiss it. But her body says no. I can feel her thighs warm with mine. We have been talking about experience as we undress. But listening to her flippant mood I am wondering how many photographs of her I can take to catch her changes. Now she is confessional and mad in the bed.

'Experience?' she says, rising on an elbow. 'Virginity?' She rises higher, tantalisingly over me. 'Ah! experience! What an experience! Did I tell you I lost my virginity under palm trees in Micronesia? Did I tell you that? To a young anthropologist from Utah – you've guessed it. I was lucky. It was a serene introduction to sexual experience. He was kind. We had a month or so of loving. Do you want me to tell you this? Of course you do. But I soon found out he was fussy. I found out that he was always going to have to please his mother. We ended fussily.'

She sighs. 'We ended fussily, fussily, fussily . . .' She leans down and kisses me. 'No fussiness with us,' she says. She kisses me again on the lips, then burrows down against me, mouthing my chest.

—

There are things between us that will never be explained properly, never be understood, never resolved – between Susan and me. Many of them would not lie between us were it not for the marriage break-up. I think Susan blames me. I'm not sure about Jesse.

I think Susan believes I bring about the breakdown of our marriage and the beginning of her hurt.

I think back over the long camping afternoons near the Point, languor and happiness and the salt of swims. I think of bedding down children at night by torch and moonlight – then turning to find the sudden dropped faces of exhausted sleep. I hear the echoes of voice and footfall in the ballet school, then search to see her pointing in the far corner of the group and think – are those dark eyes, is this rapt, dewy, bending innocence mine? I remember birthday parties bubbling with faces. I remember Susan's eyes wide watching the procession in Swanston Street or the thrill in her that lasts overnight and all of a day near Gembrook, her concerned fingers round the jar with the frog in it concealed amongst the green tendrils of vine she has put there to make him feel happy. I think about it and I'm asking what she expects of childhood and love. What will she go on expecting of me that I think I have already offered?

I think back over my surly mornings, my impatience, my anger at being disturbed. I think back to how I must appear when my mind, my eyes, are raw with fatigue, when my study smells only of me and dissatisfaction.

And then suddenly somewhere ahead there will be a book I'm reading further round time's long avenue. And there I am. The book lies beside my wrist on the desk in the church. It is closed. This is what I treasure, this immediate book among many books past and many to come, with a slip-of-paper bookmark in it. The thin, throw-away paper shows just enough above the page's top – it tells me where I'm up to. The book tells me that I exist, that I think and will think and puzzle again and again. It tells me that I learn and still am learning. It tells me that the point of it all is chasing the mystery. It says that I am right in feeling a redeeming faith in people and nature, in seeking out people's lives and descrying what they will do with them.

And then I look up from the desk and the book. Beyond the window, out there, the near grass is bending in the wind and the far grass is streaming, streaming across the paddock and over the hill to the horizon. I see the clutch of cattle near the corner. I see a Jersey calf wandering lost. I watch it and with a stab I'm thinking of Susan. Susan is lost, partly to herself, and lost to me, isn't she? In spite of the wind I can hear the calf entreating. I can see it stepping far down in the green void of the dam paddock. Then, as if they haven't existed until I look up to impress them there, I see Perce and Barb, my neighbours, hands behind backs, walking far up in the big paddock checking the store cattle cluster by cluster. Two figures, slow against the land, small in the streaming grass.

Susan is lost to me, isn't she? How do I reach her again?

—

I will go to Sydney. There I will listen again to the harbour water wash shores made dark by the shade of Moreton Bay figs and see the sea pastures extending far out beyond the Heads into the Pacific and realise what I have forgotten and yet will never forget, what I will always regain. That is the way it will be.

Suddenly I can see Will and his fair-freckled brother Jack and his sisters as kids at Bexley in the sun-steeped wattle and scrub with Botany's beaches like a comforting rim of gold in the corner of their eyes as they play. Their dreams must be of sand and water. I imagine Will's father, Jim, coming home hot and sweating in his dark banker's suit to the house on the top of the hill and shedding coat and tie and shirt in the March humidity – but this is what Will has told me. I have no memories of his father, who fell dead coming up the Bexley hill. It was soon after

I was born. He had an aneurism of the aorta. Many times since I was a child I have pored over photographs of him. James Menzies' face with its sprouting, salty eyebrows and the steady blue-grey eyes and the surprise of pale neck remind me of Will. In one of the photographs he sits sidled on a rough saw-horse under a tree, his shirt-sleeves falling limpid over his shoulders and down his arms, rolled loose below the elbow, just as I see Will's forearms bared when he leans on the spade for a breather in the vegetable garden at Cicero Street.

—

Just beyond everything I do, just beyond what my mind is registering, as if hidden by a thin veil of glycerine at the edges of a lens, there is Greta. She is present. It's not her full face. It's not all of her body. It's more a suggestion of both. It's a warm closeness that I see in orange and brown tones. Sometimes, while I'm sitting in a meeting, fingering papers and looking down the reflecting plane of the table at others' faces, I'm sure she is by the window somehow or over near the door, beyond my wheeling vision. I find I am already thinking about her before I feel her there.

There are other times when I'm walking in the city crowds or shopping in Hawthorn or sitting entering expenses when I come to realise that I've been talking to her behind my eyes and yet I don't know what I've been saying. Sometimes she seems to have told me things and yet I cannot say what. Sometimes when I realise that I have been talking to Greta I realise that I've also been talking to Louise, whose face I can see dimly as I've seen it when she sits in the cane chair on the front veranda at Cicero Street before the move to Overton Lane. A lot of the time I'm saying the same things to both of them, it seems. I know they will both be receptive. I have no doubt about that. I know they both love me. And both of them have been telling me things that I take in but cannot name.

When I come out of it, finish the work, hear someone addressing me, come home from shopping, I'm thinking of where Greta most likely is at this moment and I can picture her there. My thought takes me to Louise and I can see her, know she is there – and there seems nothing final or dire about that, as though we are bound to speak to each other again. It's strange – and yet not to be wondered at. I know these things and yet I don't know how I have come by them.

—

I'm sitting at the computer screen, but I see nothing. I am in a waking dream. I hear music and voices. I realise my eyes are closed. They're tired, stinging after a day of assessing assignments. Eyes closed, I dream as I sit.

But now Alex Cumming's face is here with me. It's his face as I have seen it in one of the photographs taken of him at a tournament in the 1930s. It's a young face, dark and chiselled. He's there, but my eyes are closed. I feel my heart pause, stammer with dread, then beat on. I am uncertain. And yet there's something in Alex's face that I cherish now. It comforts me – a comfort like being warm in the church while the rain beats on the iron roof and the clouds roll inland like huge grey continents, while from the window I see the sad glimmer of runnels of water heading through the grass to the cold road.

—

Taken with love? Yes, I have been captured on film with love. There is just this one photograph of me, stopped short with the axe on my shoulder in the thicket near the dam. My eyes are querulous in the dimness. Greta has taken it, catching me off guard. We exchange no words, despite my surprise, despite my reservations about pictures of myself. It is a good photograph. I can look at it again and again, feel a wafer of satisfaction with it that settles on my tongue. It is a photograph taken with love. Taken with calm, certain, wordless love.

—

The thought of it jumps on me out of the blue. I can't even look at the image that comes to me when I think of Betty dying.

When I think of it I see Des walking in shining black shoes, his steps straying a bit towards the pews' ends as he goes up the carpet. I see

Des walking on Will's arm, like a confused bride. I hear people murmuring. But what I see is Des and Will walking down, down the aisle until they reach the front row where Betty's mother is sitting and Des half turns by mistake towards the people in the pews, his eyes searching the sounds of the air, before Will can redirect him, spin him, take his hand and bring it to the edge of the seat so that he knows and can sit down. That's the picture I carry and I can't bear to look at it.

—

Elsie Cumming's voice on the phone is edged with caution.

'All of that is a long time ago,' she is saying. 'Water under the bridge. I can't remember it all now. But I'm sure Alex won't mind you contacting him. If you want to. Good idea to write first. Yes, that's probably the best way. As I say, he hasn't been well. There's apparently a bit of a heart problem that they don't seem to be able to get at. And he's getting a bit vague sometimes, Lorraine tells me. He doesn't move about like he used to. Since Meg died he's been coping by himself in Queenscliff. Lorraine checks on him pretty often apparently.'

I am not telling her my real reason for seeking addresses from her. I'm sure Elsie has no idea that she is my aunt. Alex and his children will have to break that news to her if they choose. So I say coyly that it's just that I've been thinking that for old time's sake I'd like to drop in on her brother when I'm in Sydney in July. It'd be good, I say, to hear about his days playing football and tennis with Candles and his long connections with Louise and the family. And of course, I say to Elsie, I'm interested in the background to the photographs she showed me. I'd like to hear about Alex's tennis trips around the country. I'd like to hear about his trip to the USA and Canada.

'Do you think I should write to Lorraine first?' I ask.

'Yes, I suppose it might smooth things a bit. Yes, that might be best. I'll give you her address and telephone too. She's Lorraine Herbert now. She's in Chatswood. Do you know Chatswood?'

'Yes,' I say. 'My father's family used to be in Artarmon – not far away. 'As I say it I feel as though I'm trying to reach out, trying to picture those steep Chatswood streets that plunge away from the Pacific Highway, where my half-sister Lorraine must walk and drive. My half-sister, who doesn't know it.

'Have you got a pencil then?' And Elsie recites Alex's address and telephone number in Queenscliff for me in a sing-song voice, her inflection rising at the end of each dictation, then comes to Lorraine's too. Lorraine and Ralph Herbert, she says. I've forgotten that there will be a husband. I've forgotten that there will probably be children who must be half nephews and nieces to me.

'Lorraine's an intensive-care nurse at the hospital,' Elsie sings, as though divining my thoughts. 'Ralph's a marine biologist, I think you'd say: and there's Tommy and Melissa. Perhaps talk to them first and find out the latest on Alex. I haven't heard for a while. They don't get in touch very often, I'm afraid. That's families, isn't it.' There's a pause, as though she is counting out what should be told. When she speaks again I sense a thawing and a sense of relief. 'Well, goodbye now, Tim. I'll be running up your phone bill. So, goodbye for now.'

—

I wish Louise and Jean could have seen the church, but I first hear about it nestling among the farms in the valley too late. I hear about it waiting lonely there, I drive down to look at it and I buy it with its rusted roof – too late for both of them. I wish Greta and Louise could have met, but again it was too late. I meet Greta too late.

—

It is another night. It seems so long in the past now, and yet it is sharp, as though it might just have happened. I see Louise spreading her hands resignedly along the table edge at Cicero Street in her grief, looking at us through her tears the day after Pearlie has died in Mont Albert. Alistair gets up to put an arm round her shoulders and dries her eyes with his school handkerchief. 'Is that clean?' she asks him, looking at it in mock concern as it goes back into his pocket. She laughs and cries. Alistair reads her eyes, finds them recovering now. Louise laughs. Alistair gives a cackle. Will neighs uncertainly, and then we all laugh. We end up talking, even laughing, about the irony of life that hustles death away. Because in the same week in Oakleigh Joyce has given birth to Little Ian, her second child, but Pearlie is gone before she can see her new grandson. 'I suppose the world can't stop for poor old worn-out ladies,' Louise says. Will takes her hand in both of his, and warms it. We talk on, Louise telling us stories about her mother. The light has gone from the houses and their gables and walls outside. Our faces are sanded with dark around the table. I hear Alistair saying, 'And what about God? What about God?'

Sometimes we argue at the table. Then we come back to each other, reconsidering. Then we apologise, sometimes through tears. Sometimes we don't. We go to bed seething, hating each others' voices. But in the morning we say sorry somehow, whether it's in words or doing some little normal kindness, bringing the toast for someone from the kitchen, reminding them about their lunch that's waiting. Sometimes we tell stories about what has happened to us, to see how they sound in the light. It reaffirms us if we don't exaggerate too much, if the others listen, say something about it.

Now I'm thinking suddenly of Patricia. Patricia has never known any of this. This sort of storytelling and passionate argument was never part of her family. Patricia and I could never talk.

But Greta and I both come wanting it, looking forward to the way the orange words will arrange themselves against the dark, looking forward to what we'll discover. We put out the light, make our places in the bed and we talk.

—

You can only truly tell how good the jazz players are, I'm thinking in the dark, when they show you how many stories they can make out of the emotional dream of a melody and the words that lie back and look at you with their hands behind their heads. Even though the words may not be heard, they run along the back of your mind as you listen. They slip themselves under the chords and progressions. That is a jazz truth.

It is the rich slap of the camera shutter and then later the tone of darker trees standing beyond the sun-filled grass that makes your heart swell in a photograph, that means you have seen truly, that makes you treasure the final print. It is the flood of colour and vision and texture and the piquancy of the world's lines that rush on you when you step out of a gallery. It is the second stanza of a poem, the words dripping from the lines with their unique logic as you place them and wait for them to tease out echoes.

—

Greta and I sit and talk. Greta and I talk into the small hours when we lie together.

I have missed this since I was growing up at Cicero Street. Then at that table in the veranda room at the back of the house we thrash away at each other, the five of us, with talk and argument. I can see Greg's face swimming there across the table in the gentle dimness on summer nights when we avoid turning on the light in the heat but stay talking, fingering saucers, plates, fruit bowl as we speak, addressing our words to them as we think aloud, placing spoons out on the tablecloth to represent things or people. I can hear Greg talking about the best cars he's seen and how he's going to subscribe to a motor magazine and know all about them. 'And I mean everything about them,' he says, and looks round at us all to see if he's challenged.

I can still hear Will's voice deep with conviction, talking about fascism, how fascists don't like writers and thinkers, how they distrust artists. And thinkers and writers can't help it, he says. There's no rest or suspension for thinkers, because they're concerned. Writers and painters and ballet dancers, he says – it's the talent that is death to hide. We puzzle over those words. A talent that is death to hide. He looks at our faces. They couldn't stop creating, thinking, wondering, trying, even if they wanted to, he says in explanation.

Will talks to us about an Italian writer called Ignazio Silone who we've never heard of. He tells us about George Orwell and Erich Maria Remarque, who is German. He talks about an American poet called

Richard Eberhart who writes a poem that he calls 'The Fury of Aerial Bombardment'. Will starts to roll with words in the chair, his hands clasped in front of him on the table. He looks at them as though he is arguing with them:

'You would think the fury of aerial bombardment
Would rouse God to relent: the infinite spaces
Are still silent. He looks on shock-pried faces.
History, even, does not know what is meant . . .'

Will stops, raises his eyes, unlocks his hands, looks at us. 'See, Eberhart had to write that. He was right in the middle of it. He taught gunnery to American airmen going out in the bombers. And then he sees their names in the death lists. Killed in action. Because the Americans did a lot of daylight bombing over Germany. The British bombed at night. But in the daylight many more Americans were shot down. And Eberhart wrote the poem – or the first version of it. But it didn't move enough.' Will, our father, stops and looks out from the table on the veranda at the dry yard beyond the window. 'He looked at it and he looked at it. And then a couple of weeks later he looked at it again and he wrote just another four lines. He said they made all the difference, because they said what it all really meant to him, I suppose:

. . . Of Van Wettering I speak, and Averill,
Names on a list, whose faces I do not recall
But they are gone to early death, who late in school
Distinguished the belt feed lever from the belt holding pawl . . .

Will looks at us. Now we are thinking about the War and what Uncle Cec did in it and the man who used to bring the bread and the son of the lady in Della's fruit shop and Tommy O'Brien's father. They were all in it. The son of the lady at Della's was killed on a troopship. Tommy O'Brien's father didn't come back. He was blown up by a shell. Will speaks again, quietly: 'You see. He can't help writing it, if he's thinking it.'

Sometimes I think I'd like to be taught by my father, but then I think I'd rather not be in his class. I'd be embarrassed. He might look at me when he was teaching. I'd be embarrassed. Alistair and I talk about it. All the others would look at us then and they'd know. We'd have to look somewhere else. And what if he asked one of us a question? No, it's better just to be talking at the table on the veranda at Cicero Street.

—

I have written to Lorraine Cumming who is now Lorraine Herbert. I see her as a figure in a starched nurse's uniform. I have written to Alex too, suggesting that I might come to see him in the semester lecture break. I am waiting for a response. What will they think? Will they welcome a meeting? I am now thinking that I should have written only to Lorraine at first, as I planned, and allow her to broach the idea with her father. My waiting lies at the pit of my stomach like a leaden fear. Should I simply have telephoned, heard their voices, judged their feelings from that? It's ten days now. I have not sent them Louise's letter. I have simply paraphrased its sudden news. I have told them that it leaves no doubt. It leaves no doubt, but Sydney is a bustle in the smog far away. Alex's face, Lorraine's face are mysteries. Sometimes I wonder whether they exist. They hover against my fear like ghosts. I think of the photographs I have seen of Alex, but they are far around the bracelet of time. They are of another person. What I thought I knew through pondering and imagining is gone. It is all a starting anew. It is like a huge shifting of matted roots. I have to start it. I'm ready to start it, but it needs their blessing. I wait to hear their voices.

—

Once the light is out I can start to see Greta, this new woman who loves me, who was Rosa, whose past is strange to me. She tells me about her family, about Joel and what he has in him of her and what he has of his father. She tells me about her father Ugo, the stonemason, and her mother Therese, the dress-maker and cellist. She tells me about her sister Angelique – Angie – who is four years younger.

As she lies against me and tells it, Greta's life seems like a dream that I should know. Our faces are close. I can see the outline of her lips and her brow. I brush back the hair from her forehead, usher it down behind her ear to curl it against her neck. I kiss her brow, kiss her neck. Her words come to me close and moist. I can hear her tongue thinking, remembering. When she describes it I can see the street in Box Hill where she grew up after her mother and father had lived for eighteen months in the tin igloos of the migrant hostel down in the cold valley of Holmesglen. When she mentions the seminary at the end of the Box Hill street I see its pale brick girt by dark cypresses and then the paddocks taking over to the east and the Dandenongs running like hazed promontories far behind in the summer.

Greta is speaking of her father and I see him trudging through a threatening mist that is Europe in the 1930s when he is an apprentice in stonemasonry and comes to Paris, not knowing what the world is going to do. He comes there to work on three churches and to help at the Cimitiere de Montmartre where the wild cats materialise from the vaults like ghosts and melt away again among the aisles of reeling headstones. Greta is telling me what she has been told by Ugo but it is as if it is mine as soon as she tells it. Sometimes I find myself bending, straining like a navvy, to bring myself back to this room where we lie, bring myself back to this light, back to this murmur of Melbourne traffic we can hear from the distant freeway near Kooyong. I suppose it's because I'm bringing myself back from another vivid past, from another life, from the verticals of the Paris buildings stepping down towards the Gare St Lazare and the Tuileries and the Seine.

Her mother Therese is only fifteen when the War begins, Greta says. She is a music student at the lycee in Paris. She plays the violin first and then settles on the cello. Her mother in turn is a seamstress and has been a singer. When the Germans come marching through the Paris streets, when the sentries stamp in the cold in their dread helmets and demand passes, Therese tells Greta, the family survives by bartering their vegetables and patching up old clothing. Both the French and the Germans pay Therese's father, who is a printer, for small printing jobs. Therese stops playing the cello in public at the small concerts in Paris while the Occupation lasts. Her mother forbids it. They are long

War years, she tells Greta, and playing at the concerts might put her too much under the arrogant gaze of the German officers in their peaked hats and epaulettes. Only the inner room of their apartment hears the sound of Therese's voice singing sometimes and the deep tone of the cello as she practises. Therese meets Ugo Piccone one afternoon just before the end of the Occupation in the shaded aisles of the Cimitiere de Montmartre. They both have come to look again at the grave of Emile Zola.

Greta speaks and then pauses, thinking. I can hear her breath against the pillow. She sighs and yawns. I kiss her cheek again, then her mouth. With my fingers I retrace the fall of her hair over her ear and down, down against her neck. She breathes beside me, turns further towards me. Our lips explore. We part and lie back. We explore again and part.

Greta often falls towards sleep in a slow wandering of places she knows in the city. 'Now I'm in Spring Street,' she says, her voice soft and vague. She nestles closer against my chest. 'The trees in the Treasury Gardens are singing in the heat.' She'll hum against the doona. 'Now I'm in Collins Street near the Independent Church. It's all downhill from here.' She hums and sighs, disengages from me, lies on her back, stretches an arm across the pillow the other side of her. Her breathing matches mine. I am falling too, falling into nonsense and green-yellow pastures. We breathe. We slowly give up charge of our bodies. As we sink bit by bit, side by side, our dreams come into our heads like smoke.

—

It is Melbourne sitting in my mind, just as I imagine it is Melbourne I can hear growling behind the hill from the gutter in Cicero Street when I sit squatting there, watching the ants busy on their trails on the concrete, waiting for Sandra to appear at the top of the street on her way home from school. Then I am four years old. That is more than eighteen thousand afternoons ago now.

I hear the suburbs speaking from their hills and flats and house-filled valleys on the map. This is my city. This is Greta's city. This is Louise's city

307

when she is a mother and a teacher. It has been Will's and Flute's and Archie's city, even for a time Pearlie's and John's city although it often appears to them a mysterious, noisy humped back. It's the city where Des's white stick has guided him to street corners, to tram stops, to quiet halls with pianos in them away from the traffic's murmuring. It is the city of my children, Susan now with Patricia out at Doncaster and then at Frankston, Jesse in his rented house with the others at Heidelberg, close enough to walk with his canvas bag off-balance with books and folders to La Trobe University. It is Melbourne. It is the city of my other brief love with Adela. It is the city where Alex Cumming played his tennis, where he walked the blackout in his Army boots and uniform, where he and Louise arranged their faces for photographs, where Louise married Will tearfully. It is the city whose east I know better than its north or west. It is the city of Greta's sister Angelique, who is born there in Epworth Hospital, and of her father Ugo and her mother Therese who adopt its streets and summers and trams and its bay's waters running out in their delicate blue winter sheen to the marker buoys off Rosebud. Even now it is the city of Greta's dreams and our slide towards sleep together.

—

I know we are very wet, both of us. I can feel a warm, wet wind. Our clothes cling to us and warm us like a moist skin. That much I know – and I can see our bicycles, our *velos*. I see a sheet giving details of *velo* hire. I'm sure it is Greta and me. I am happy as I look down a dim track through green-lit trees. Now I know what the birds say in a French wood, I tell someone. I am no longer aware of being wet. It is another day. I hear someone say: *Monsieur. Monsieur! Il faut payer maintenant – s'il vous plaît.* It is a woman. Then I hear a male voice say: *Deux cent seize. Oui. Deux cent seize.*

Now I see a painting of three women in the nude, their pale legs and bellies lighting a dark background. And somewhere ahead of me I know there is a long, windowed gallery and through the windows the river can be seen passing underneath. But it is moonlight. I've never been there in the moonlight. The moonlight lays itself down through the windows, reaching across the floor. The drapes are white. There are rows of beds, white-covered, and white figures moving. I hear an intermittent groaning and the sudden ring of metal in a dish. It must be the past. I am alone, listening, reaching a toe towards the nearest moonlight flooding the floor. I want to go and stand in it, but I can't. But outside through the window I can see the moonlight spearing down to the head and shoulders of a gargoyle of stone. The rough, implacable face of the gargoyle is leaning out, leaning towards the night, the river water passing below.

Now I hear the voice I cannot mistake. It is Greta. I'm sure it's Greta. She's reading: '*Ici furent blesses . . . pendant la guerre.*' Ah. So this is where these words are true. It seems to be the future. I've heard the words before, but I didn't know where they were true.

—

He is pruning the Jonathon apple at Overton Lane when I get there. The year is just past its ebb. Houses on the ridges further east are taking on a terracotta magic in the winter haze, rising out of trees. Before I reach him, before he is aware of me, I stand and watch. I see my father standing further down the yard, musing at the spars of the apple, secateurs in hand, hat pushed back on his head. I can see his ladder angled into the tree where it rises against the grey Melbourne sky. This man I know so well, I think to myself, is standing there, one hand on hip, considering where he should cut next to promote balance, new growth, good fruit. How many times have I seen that stance at Cicero Street. This man I know so well, preoccupied, ageing, private in his thoughts.

Now he glimpses me out of the corner of his eye and turns. He laughs in my direction, takes off the hat, comes slowly up the yard, relieved to be required to stop.

'Ha!' he says. 'Half done at least.' He puts the secateurs down on the planks of the old garden seat. 'Half done,' he says, and he begins to address the unkempt privet hedge slowly. His voice croons.

'. . . For I have had too much
Of apple-picking: I am over-tired
Of the great harvest I myself desired . . .'

He sighs. 'Not quite apt,' he says. 'Not quite the right season. Five
months down the track, perhaps.' And he turns his eyes to me. We are
heading for the steps at the back of the house. He's happy.

'For there were ten thousand thousand fruit to touch,
Cherish in hand, lift down, and not let fall . . .'

He looks as though he will continue, one foot on the bottom step.
But he turns away. His voice trails off and he bends to take off a boot. He
suddenly looks tired and small. But I know he's happy.

So when we sit inside at the kitchen table I can already tell that he
knows he's given it enough thinking at last, and this is a day when he can
talk about it all. I too can sense it's at last one of those days and that he
knows he doesn't have to tell me that. We sit for longer in silence than
I've ever known. He's looking past me and down the yard, but his face is
relaxed. His eyes are ruminating, flitting with his thoughts from privet
hedge to shed and back again. I can see them come then to a conclusion.

'What do you remember out of the War years, Dig?' Will is asking
me. He is still looking past me to the darkening yard.

Ha! My mind leaps. I remember planes, warships. I remember you,
my father Will, doing Air Raid Precaution drills with incendiaries in the
street. You remember? With Mr Collins, Mr Davidson from round the
corner, with Mr Cashell? You all had helmets and navy overalls and
buckets of sand. I remember blackout curtains, the Kennedys' car on
chocks in their garage, sandbags under the house. Games of cricket
out under the streetlight, too. And the McLellans coming down the
street in their billy-carts. You remember the fruit cases on a plank chassis
they used to make with the metal wheels? You remember the races they
used to have, coming down the hill from Grantham Street?

Will's head is moving rhythmically, nodding, even though I haven't
spoken.

'You'd remember Mr McLellan marching up the street in his

310

Lieutenant Colonel's rig sometimes?' he says. 'But, more important – do you remember Alex Cumming calling in at Cicero Street? What do you remember of Uncle Alex?' His smile seems to be steering past me as he speaks. Then he looks at me.

My mind says, yes, I can see Alex in uniform. I can remember that. I can see him at Fern Tree Gully. I remember him having a swim with us at Parkdale one day when Alistair and Greg were still small. I look at Will. He seems to hear me, although I have not spoken. I'm waiting. There's an expectation and a flush of warmth and gratitude seething through me, and yet bound in with it is a slow, rolling anger.

'Do you know that Alex used to appear every now and then to check on you?' Will says. 'That was during the War. Amazing, isn't it? Louise all those years couldn't say the truth to you, couldn't bare herself and utter it. But truth won't lie down. She had to let Alex drop in to say hello.'

I'm watching Will's hands, the ginger hairs, the sun blotches on the fair skin. He has laid them palms down in disbelief on the table. 'It was as though she knew she had to reassure him. He needed reassurance and expiation.'

'Expiation?' my mind asks silently.

'Yes, expiation, I think,' my father is saying.

Alex had to atone, perhaps, before it was too late, before he might die. That's what Will says. Will had heard Louise talk about her and Alex together. Will had met Alex himself. Will had thought about Alex and Louise being together all that way back in the Mallee when they were kids. He came to the conclusion that Alex hadn't ever had a full commitment to anyone at that stage of his life. Will had to think about Alex a lot over the years. He could see that Alex and Louise had been companions, mates, close mates for so long that it was comfortable and predictable. It sounded comfortable, he says – but not deep. And then, he says, as Alex's tennis became more important, Louise's need for something deeper became magnified.

'I can't remember whether you know,' he is saying to me, although I haven't spoken: 'I can't remember whether you know that they were talking about getting married when Alex came back from the overseas tour in '34 or '35. So they had a parting fling – a fling that neither of them was sure about. That's more or less how Louise describes it.'

Why is Louise weeping? She seems to be retreating, sheltering against Will's chest and shoulder. He wears a tuxedo. I think it is their marriage. She is looking away. The tears run down her cheeks, but she brings no hand to them. She weeps pure, unregretted tears. I see figures who come close to her and say something soft and then pass on, fading into the background of a long sunlit wall and then darker trees. Alex comes and she watches him. He is not smiling. He says something to her. Louise makes no move towards him. She is weeping. She watches his head and shoulders as he retreats. Then comes my birth sister who I have never met. Her name is Lorraine. I can see her face clearly. I can see that Louise wants to go to her, but she cannot move. The dark brow, the heavy dark eyes pass. Someone else is coming, a woman in a broad hat. I look and see that it is Greta's face. She comes on and my heart soars. Louise's face lights with love. The two are close. They look at each other a moment, then they kiss. Now Greta is going. She is going. She is gone along the wall and into the trees' shade. Louise and Will stand together. Louise is smiling now. It is a pondering smile of someone unexpectedly reaffirmed.

'And Alex's expiation?' my mind is saying. I am groping, but I am prompting Will as though prompting a child, willing him to say something he doesn't want to put into words. I can feel the ruthless bit of anger between my teeth now. Anger at the three of them. Even now there's this analysis and explanation and yet lies. Analysis and explanation and yet subterfuge.

But what I see then in Will's eyes pours calm and sadness on my wrath. What I see is not stubbornness or denial or anger in return. It's a long concern that he knows he can never make me feel adequately, can

312

never make real in words. It's the years. He's leaning forward on his fore-arms, looking at me. And for a moment my anger is cheap. And yet I know what I know, I insist to myself. In some ways I know more than Will knows. What happened at Parkdale on that beach that I remember, with the waves slowly folding and refolding under a hot sky? What happened at Fern Tree Gully where I smelled wood smoke and damp, where the boles of the trees reeled in on us from around the clearing and locked us into that one day? I can't remember clearly and yet I seem to know.

'When Louise knew she was pregnant,' I hear Will saying, 'she was alone, except for me.' Now I can see his face again. I am with him. He is telling me that he was on the scene, as they say, by that time, that he had known from the first that he loved Louise, that it was almost as if he'd dreamed her existence into fact when he came down from Sydney and he met her. His eyes are searching mine now. He wants me to understand this. He has forsaken the darkening yard outside. We still sit without the light on, dim face to dim face. The light is soft as pastel on the walls. I'm not aware of my body – just our faces and voices.

Will tells me how he could feel Louise's panic. He could carry it somehow. He was waiting in the wings, he tells me, when she wired Alex. Alex's response was distant and non-committal. He certainly wasn't coming home. So that was it. He and Louise became closer, became inseparable, Will says, in the next months. We felt like whales swimming together, he says. Have you seen whales together? he asks me.

Yes, Louise and I were a lucky meeting, Will says, and his voice quavers. He is silent for a moment, his mouth working, tears coming to his eyes. Then he goes on, huskily, but determined to come to an end. Yes, he says, he and Louise decided to own me as theirs, to get married in August, to outstare the scandalmongers. And the rest you know, he tells me.

For a moment I accept that. Then my inner voice protests no, no, I don't know anything – but I stay silent because now is not the time.

'When Alex did come home from the overseas tour we didn't see him until the War,' Will says. 'He kept in the background. But the War rode over us all. War on that scale is such a huge lottery when it gets going. By 1941 there were a lot of men not coming back. There they are, we run into them in the street, home on leave. And then they're back to the Islands, or back to the Navy, or back to the Kittyhawks – and for a while no news. But later it filters through. They're gone. We aren't going to see them again. They've been killed.'

Will's voice halts. He looks round as if to find something at the far end of the table, but cannot.

'The Army wouldn't have me, as you know, because of my twist in the left leg and foot.' My father's words resume hoarsely. 'But while I was writing for Labour and Industry and later in the Education Unit, Alex was fighting with the Independent Companies in New Guinea – harassment behind the Jap lines, intelligence stuff. Not a pre-condition for a long life! So to know about you was important to him.'

His voice trails away. He is short of breath. Again his thoughts have brought him to a halt. He looks at his hat on the table. He looks at me, and I can see his mouth twisting.

'To get to see you, and his sister Elsie, and his father – his father was still alive then – that's what he did on his leaves. As though there mightn't be a next time.' Will's voice is low, but almost shrill with emotion. 'Expiation. Atonement. Making peace. Alex brought presents for you to play with. Since we all three knew you were his son, Louise and I decided he could come – no names, no background for anyone else, just a visit. No pack-drill. Elsie turned up her nose at it. Louise hadn't been prepared to wait for Alex to come back from America, she said! And Jean instantly disapproved. She couldn't understand. She was suspicious. She thought Alex had abandoned Louise at the very least. So I think it was harder for Louise than for any of us. She had the courage for that, but it turned out she couldn't face you.'

Why is Louise weeping? But I can see now she is smiling through her tears. What does it mean? She seems to be with us, listening in as of old, but not eavesdropping. I hear her voice, very low: 'Goodbye, my love' and I see the hospital

314

pillows empty, still carrying the indentation left by her head,
after she has died, after she has been taken away. Now in
the dimness, where she makes no shadow against the pastelled
light reaching to the wall, I feel her standing behind me.
I look at Will, my father. Can he feel her there? His face is
expressionless and tired. No, he cannot feel her now. We sit.
I realise that I am not allowed my anger with Will. I am
not allowed it with Louise. So what will I discover is my
anger against Alex Cumming, who I still cannot bring myself
to call my father?

—

Susan needs stories about my close people and about me. But she is not hearing them, because she is now distant from me.

'When did you start smoking a pipe, Dad?' she might ask me. 'When did you give it away?' I see her as a four-year-old watching me draw in on the pipe with the graceful, shallow bowl, watching my cheeks suck in to make the draft, draw up a first draught of rich smoke.

'Who was the uncle you call Candles again?' she might ask. 'I forget. What was his real name again? Did I ever see him when I was little?' If she asked I would be eager to tell her. 'He was younger than your mother, wasn't he? Wasn't he Louise's little brother? I saw a picture of him once in his football shorts, holding a football. Where did he play footie? When did he play footie?' I want her to ask me the questions. I want to tell her, but she isn't here. She never will be here now, I suppose, after the separation and divorce. I want to tell her about watching Candles sitting on the bench in the change rooms at Camberwell with one leg up, lacing his football boot, running the long white laces twice round the top and tying them tight. I want her to know the way my heart draws in to see Candles, my uncle, run up the race and onto the field at the head of the team, his legs kicking high at the back to stretch them, his team-mates running circles around him, then falling in beside him to advance like a wide header of red, white and blue across grass, the visiting team coming to meet them, small and blue and yellow from the visitors' change rooms at the ground's other end, also running, also circling, also kicking high behind. I'd like her to see the play begin, the rush of men following the ball to the distant dip near the other goals, and then the indecipherable dash and crossing and leaps and running, the players' feet and calves hidden by the bow of the ground beyond the centre – and then the sudden blare of car horns and cheering. I'd like to take Susan and Jesse there, but I can't.

'Dad – what's a pun? And what's a cliche?'

'Dad – how old were you when you got married? How old were you when you had your first drink and smoke?'

Susan, you need to ask me. I would love you all over again if you asked me. You need to know, but I fear that you will never know. Because this is not real. This conversation has never happened, never will happen. The thread of my close people is broken.

—

I pick up the brass sculpture, run the pads of my fingers over the Three Wise Monkeys. They always sit on the television set, propping up post-cards from friends overseas, their faces catching the light. I stand there feeling the sun sinking warm into the carpet around my feet. My fingers explore the tiny brass hands over eyes, over mouth, over ears. I close my eyes, feel the squat bodies huddled against each other. I turn the sculpture, run fingers across its smooth base and find that it is not part of the dream. Somehow, since Greta, I am relearning touch.

Jesse is home briefly. He lolls on the couch. Even now he is still like an uncouth tree, half asleep, and yet bursting bit by bit out of its bark. He bursts from clothes. He bursts through face stubble. I have told him about the existence of Alex and Lorraine in Sydney. He is cool, cool at first. Then he throws out questions as if not to throw them out, and comments that he won't own but which hang in the air. It is his way, and I can feel Patricia's lack of disclosure, her eschewing of ownership of dec-laration, in his words. So he has an unsuspected new grandfather. Hmm. And Lorraine – is there such a thing as a half-aunt? He laughs. Not the full aunt! And a semi-uncle! There is a long pause for consideration. He leafs through a gallery magazine, stopping here and there to stare disbelievingly at the pictures. Then – how much of this has Grandpa Will known? His snorts of gradual perception, gradual realisation are full of incredulity. How long has he known this? Why didn't Grandma tell you this? Did you ever suspect? It must be strange. Have you told Susan she's got these new relatives? God, it must be weird.

Further to the back on top of the television set is the African head, standing four times the size of the Three Wise Monkeys, as big as a grapefruit, but not as squat. I pick it up, look at the dark wood with its striations of blond. I look at the eyes first, as always. It is almost a fetish, this looking into the eyes that are strangely blank and yet sad at the same time. I sometimes look at them from across the room. But now my touch runs down the woman's hair feeling the cuts that have made the dread-locks in the wood, my fingers imagining the way the hair follows the receding line of her neck to the sculpture's base. I trace then the cheeks, the jaw, the delicacy of the neck. Touch takes me there, touch leads me to the pouting lips, the nose, the cheekbones. Touch. Another person. Greta and I in the dark are the mistress and master of touch. Touch informs, extends. Time and again we extend and inform each other.

—

It's Jesse who knows things, not Susan as I have thought. Again, I've been mistaken. It's Jesse who sees and hears what time is doing, what time will do.

On that day in 1980 when I'm called from the hospital and sit when the phone has gone dead and see that street of pin oaks – on that day I ring Jesse at Patricia's to tell him that Louise has died that morning. He comes breathless to the phone, and I tell him that his grandmother is gone.

'I know,' he says, his voice teetering. 'I know, Dad. I heard it when it happened. I've been thinking about her all day. I heard her calling goodbye. It was this morning when I was in the first lecture. I could see her face as though she didn't have cancer. I could hear her say it.'

I shudder. Tears well in my eyes. He doesn't say it's crazy or unbelievable. He just tells me, his voice teetering with emotion. I don't say it to him, but I know that one day he'll recognise that it's what we are meant to do – Louise and he and I. It's Jesse who will be the storyteller. It will be Jesse, not Susan.

—

Susan will know soon about the Sydneysiders. Susan and Jesse and Will and Greta and I will come together and we will think and talk about Alex and Lorraine above the glasses on the table. When I think about these distant people that I don't know, I hear at first the solemn wash of the Harbour waters in the darkness under the Sydney ferry wharves. But eventually I think I see sun dancing on the open sea and a horizon resting far off in unreachable purple fields of water.

—

The year when Pearlie and John come down the long miles from the Mallee and settle in the house at Mont Albert, is the year when some people know that the War is coming and what it will mean – and others don't. It is the year when Ugo Piccone escapes from Italy and comes to Paris. I see Pearlie rigging up a rough gate of wire netting to keep the chooks in their long, dark shed at the back of the Mont Albert block. She stops and stands, tired behind her eyes, tired under her wide maroon skirt, to listen to a train clacking down the valley towards Surrey Hills and Chatham and Canterbury and on to the city on its river. She has never heard trains so close before.

But now I'm seeing Ugo stepping into the huge courtyard of the Sorbonne and looking up at the walls. It comes from something Greta has told me in our depth-of-night talking. It is a place where he will never study, but he likes the sounds of echoing voices against the stone and the way the light falls on the girls' hair where they sit in the sun. He is sorry that his French is not better.

It is the same year for Pearlie and Ugo. They have no idea that one day they will be connected in a distant way by blood. Why are some years luminous when others are not?

—

It seems a long time since I wrote to Lorraine Herbert.

Now, suddenly, here is her voice on the phone. A woman's voice, suddenly, with a huskiness like Jean's in the words as they come down to me. We have all been bits of cowards, she says. Your news hit us like a bombshell. We had no idea that Dad had another child. He's an old reprobate, isn't he? He's told us more about it now, but it takes a bit of adjusting to. For a while it seems to change everything. You hear about these things when they apply to other people, but you don't expect they're going to hit you in your own family. We've all been a bit cowardly in a way, taking so long to think about it.

Yes, we've talked about it, she says, and we've talked to Dad. He hasn't been so well in the last month or so. He seems to have these periods of confusion that we can't pin down – and then he'll come out of it and be OK again. He's all right in himself. No trouble eating and getting about and so on. He's by himself in the unit, of course. You probably know from Elsie that Meg died some years ago. I've rung my brother in the States to tell him he's got a half-brother he didn't suspect! He's over there in Boston for the duration, I think. He's an American now, you might say. He's an architect. Anyway, the husky voice says, we don't mind if you come up and say hello in your lecture break if you want to. Best in the first week, perhaps. Ralph and I might be away in the second week of the school holidays. Perhaps you could give us a ring closer to the time. Yes, there's a motel not far from Dad's unit in Queenscliff. The Hacienda it's called. It seems to be all right. So we might see you then.

I sit looking at the phone when her voice is gone, as if expecting it to give answers. A wave of unwillingness sweeps me. Why am I doing this? There's no great welcome or excitement in Lorraine's voice or her choice of phrase. Just obligation. And embarrassed uncertainty and even fear. Why am I doing this? I hear the lugubrious wash of the Harbour waters in the darkness under the ferry wharves.

—

It's an 'off' weekend, a weekend when Joel is with Gavin, when Greta looks at me in the expectant way that the working week and 'on' weekends don't allow. Now she isn't so stressed. Now she laughs and clowns.

But I am thinking of Greta in the sea where she dives now confidently, riding the will of the water. I like what you call your sea room, she says, but I like the Blue Pool better. I see her on the protected side of the pool, where the water sluices in from the deeper water outside with each swell, bringing with it twenty feet down the enquiring wedges of the sweep and the long tresses of weed. In the green-blue of pure water, in the sheets of bubbles of the last swell along the rock walls, I can see her like a dim mermaid, willowing along the wall of the sea garden, fins treading and switching slowly, pale thighs and calves working with no hurry. The blue depths of the pool rake away below her, rock cod going about their messages in the weed, the swirling, dying gusts of bubbles from the last wave spiralling like a gyre from the darker blue of the fissure that is the pool's entrance. I like the Blue Pool, I can imagine her saying, because it is a circle sewn with waving weed against the light, because I can glide down its sides and look back up at the waves' tent straining against the sky.

Then suddenly I want her to quit these blue sluices of cold. I want her to rise. I want to see her out of the water. I want to feel her safe. I want to caress her body's circles in the warmth of the sun.

—

At last I have them all together and my cup is full. Jesse, who is cool, cool; Susan in her bewildered beauty breaking into smiles; Will bright-eyed in his lined face at the table's head in the bistro; Greta beside him, reading out the specials to him from the board behind his back, her eyes darting now and then to mine, then back to him, discovering nothing of me in his sandy-grey hair, his sandy-pallid skin. But she is drinking in his stories about me.

Will is addressing Jesse and Susan rather than Greta, but his picture is intended for Greta. It is the second time they have met. 'Have you swung any birches lately, you two?' he asks. 'One could do worse than be a swinger of birches.' And he is telling them about the silver birch at Cicero Street where as a child I used to climb with Alistair and swing like a monkey on the pliant dark branches, skirt and climb the white-silver trunk. 'Black branches up a snow-white trunk,' Will is saying. Jesse leans forward and is drawing a birch with his pen on the white paper table cloth. Susan watches, bemused. There is something coming together out of disparate elements. We all feel it. My cup is full.

'I'd like to get away from earth awhile
And then come back to it and begin over . . .'

Will looks at Greta.
'No, don't do that for a while yet,' Greta says, and laughs.

'I'd like to go by climbing a birch tree
And climb black branches up a snow-white trunk
Toward heaven, till the tree could bear no more . . .'

'No, promise me you'll put that idea on hold,' says Greta, and plants her elbow on the table between them, offering him her elevated, open hand. To my surprise, Will grips it like a teenager, smiles, pretends an arm wrestle and then gives her hand a squeeze. Will's eyes meet mine and I feel a lump in my throat. My cup is running over. Jesse and Susan watch, Jesse's eyes lighting with approval for a second.

But Susan's face is clouded by this scene. I suppose she sees it as a supplanting of her mother so publicly, so effortlessly. I can sense it, feel her confusion and sadness. She looks down. Then she reaches for a menu and begins studying it. I want to go to her, but she is a young woman. I can't move.

—

Yes, I'd like to have sat down with Robert Frost, Will is saying, but his voice echoes. I don't know when he is saying it. I'd like to have met Joseph Furphy, he says, up near the Willandra Billabong. I'd like to have met Melville and Whitman. I'd like to have seen New England with Thoreau. I used to think once upon a time, he says, that I might get to Europe, that I might meet James Joyce or walk the beach with Virginia Woolf. Will is speaking. I don't know when it is. I suppose I can dream at least, he says, and hear their words echoing.

It must be me remembering Will speaking. It must be me hearing my mother's voice, too, when she reads us to sleep. 'Oh, Ratty!' I hear her say with desperation and sadness that things are not otherwise. And I smell the river, see the winter woods, hear Mole talking, hear Toady brushing them aside. I can hear her voice telling me about Shere Khan and Mowgli and I see the Council Rock. She is telling me about Hiawatha, his world full of waterfalls and canoes, and the great lakes of America, and then I'm reading the words, seeing how they have invaded the soft, thick paper, and I'm gliding like Deerfoot through the forest, listening for footfalls, looking for the wink of fires in the dimness, hearing the gentle dip of paddles on the river.

Suddenly, I sense Louise and Will beside me. Here they are, giving out to me their rhythms, their experience, their geography, their words. I see Grandpa John here, too, his big dry hands roving the spines of books. There is his Wordsworth, his red-backed copy of Burns, the back binding cracking. There is *The World's Greatest Paintings*. I hear the filling of lamps, the breathless feeding of horses. I hear of a drowning near the Blowhole, a dust storm that shuts the farm in night. Will is showing me the long white wound where the nail on the old diving board tore his leg open, turning his foot in. I feel the pain extending behind my eyes and fingers. Louise's eyes dwell like coals as she thinks about the burning of the hayshed and the horse that died. I hear Flute's fingers playing notes that fall like pearls out at the woodheap in the sunset. I hear a requiem.

I smell the bookshelves and their mustiness. I don't know when it is. I don't know why I find myself in the midst of it.

—

There is a photograph I want to get. It is one that I see in my mind's eye. It will be of Greta coming from the shower. It will be a photograph that will keep her young. But I shudder to think that the time for it might never come, that I might never take it. I still see it there, ahead and above me.

—

I haven't seen Patricia for months, perhaps not for a year, and then only at the front door one day when I call to Frankston to pick up Susan.

But now, while I wait in the checkout queue at the supermarket near the railway in Auburn, I see her. What's she doing here? It is her, isn't it? I look again and assure myself. The eyes and nose I can't mistake. She must be visiting her mother. I watch her progress, a bit dismayed, a bit bemused, wanting to hide, not to be seen.

She looks tired. There's a weary desperation in her movements. She seems so small, smaller than I have known her – and there are touches of grey. She has a list in her hand. She looks at it, then seems to come to herself and realise that first she needs a trolley. She goes to the rank of them not far from the door. She pulls at the end trolley. No movement. She pulls again. I watch, hoping she doesn't look towards the queue at the checkout. She pulls a third time with anger and greater force. The trolley moves but angles sideways. Her hand loses its grip and she threatens to fall back. I cringe as she staggers, regains her balance, then stands defeated for a moment, her hands on her hips, her mouth a thin, exasperated line. Her hair is falling into her eyes. She raises a hand to tidy it back, and the note drops from her fingers to the floor. As she stoops to pick it up a young boy in supermarket garb and gob cap comes to her side to offer her help with the trolley. His voice, which I can't hear, apparently startles her. Her looking round to him is that of someone who is near tears and expects the world to fall.

In a quick, sure action, the assistant braces against the bank of mesh and wheels with one hand and one foot and pulls a trolley out for her with the other. I see her thank him, her eyes full of real gratitude and embarrassment. She seems so small now, in her dark pants and loose yellow top. She first pushes the trolley to an aisle where she is away from the gaze of the people milling closer to the doors. And then, with an uncertain glance at the list, she acts like someone about to dive into cold water, and rushes, half falls down the aisle and disappears behind its shelves.

I forgive her. She is mother of my children, someone it seems who belongs to a time years ago now, but who has always been present like a ghost nevertheless. But she is so small, so defeated. I forgive her, but it is too late. I feel for her, see that she can only be who she is and has always been when we lived together. She is frightened, defensive. My former wife. I did not expect to see her. I feel a shameful sadness. My heart beats fast.

—

I think the snow has risen overnight and gently erased the edges of these streets of the dead. I can see it. I can feel the cold. There is stone and bare trees and the reeling verticals of the graves. He is standing still, his breath feathering round the collar of his coat in the cold air. I know where it is. And I know it is Ugo Piccone I am seeing. At the lower end of the path, fifty metres away, the same two German officers he has been watching bend over a gravestone, reading the inscription. Then they straighten, the light catching their backs and then the peaks of their caps. He can feel his slow but constant hate of them warming his arms and upper chest. Nothing else moves. There is no one about.

How do I know it? Is it from Greta's quiet talking about her father? Behind it I can feel what Therese has told Greta and Greta has told me. I see him there quite clearly. It is Ugo standing in the aisles of Cimitiere de Montmartre watching the sun laying down long tresses of light through the trees. It is winter and wartime. It is still the Occupation. I know Ugo comes here to walk for sanctuary when the War seems too long, when he despairs of seeing his adopted city free again. He knows every narrow alley under the sky. He is still only twenty-one years old. He is pigeon-toed and quiet. His fingers know stone so well that they seem to converse with the past. He will not meet Therese for another three years and yet this is where it is to happen.

I have never imagined that Ugo will become one of my close people and yet he is. I think about his flight from Fascism in Italy. He flees, only to find that its grey face seeks him out again in the cold of Paris. I still have not met him, but I know I will on a day of heat and wind-blown grit in Adelaide, the sea at Glenelg like a face smirking under the blasts of the northerly. I know Therese will make me strong coffee and bring it to me with small biscotti. I will sit and watch and find Greta's face hovering there in Therese's eyes. They will be my close people.

—

I am cutting his hair and shaving him. We seem to be in his room at the nursing home, the window full of the blue and white globes of dahlias beyond the sill. My father is standing very still, like a child.

I can feel that these are last days. I can tell that the tea-bell will ring soon and he will pull to get away and I'll reassure him. I can sense a closing, and yet things are not sad. These are last days for Will, and yet it is still to happen. I can't tell when it will happen.

His face leans with satisfaction as I run the new red shaver down his cheek slowly, taking the grey sward, then down, down to his neck. His eyes squint away towards the window. He is cooperative like a child. He is pleased to be coming clean of stubble, to feel smooth again after his lost days in bed, after the delirium, and I am thinking that this is a simple thing I can do. His head is so old and gaunt now, the hair so fine. His swallowing under the neck as he stands there is gaunt and hollow.

It is a simple thing I will do. It has not happened yet.

—

Greta spills pictures when she tells me about her work in the Micronesian islands. She doesn't know she is doing it. They are human pictures. They are about belief and celebration. They are about how children and their mothers and fathers and grandmothers and grandfathers find explanations for life. They are about uniqueness and commonality. Greta's stories are strange, but they warm me.

She talks about storyboards and I can see them. I can hear a man crooning to himself as he makes the stories with his hands. I hear the chisel and the knife carving them into the honey-brown wood. Behind the small factory the trade winds are asking the palms about the sunset and the quick coming of darkness. The sobbing of the big waves far out on the coral at the edge of the lagoon is always there, Greta says.

She works with an American team there on the islands of the big lagoon when she's studying for her Masters. Only two and a half months, she says. Too short. She meets one of the women from the team at a conference who has heard her ask a question in a session and approaches her out of the blue. Would she like to do some preliminary enquiring to start a new data base for them in the long vacation and maybe even some interviewing?

Greta is a good storyteller. She knows how many ways stories will be told, how the same stories might play out in different ways in different centuries. There is always a concern behind the stories. She tells me about people of the sea who have been for thousands of years on the lagoon and how they have been used – by the French, and before them by the Spanish, by the missionaries, by the Germans later, then by the Japanese before and during the War, now by the Americans and the Japanese again. And still, she says, they try to believe, to the sound of the big waves on the outer edge, while the cargo ships bring in *Coca-Cola* and the television speaks with American voices and the Japanese developers strut at the hotel in its compound away from the thin roads and their corrugated-iron shanties and rusted cars. I listen. This is a Greta I have not watched before, have not heard before. She is telling me about the young men who suicide, how they strangle themselves with a cord that lets them loll away from a palm tree into asphyxiation and an oblivion that doesn't hear the waves' tolling or their sisters' cries of discovery.

Still she spills pictures as she talks. She has taken me out of the bedroom at Hawthorn and into the stories. She speaks close to my ear as we lie there. Sometimes she gets up on an elbow to tell me and seek my

326

eyes, my understanding. Then she lies down again. I love her. Sometimes for an instant I think I am hearing Louise in her words. Perhaps Louise might be an anthropologist or a sociologist if she were young now. Perhaps she was two generations too early for it. It crosses my mind like a breeze and then I don't think more about it.

In Greta's pictures there are Japanese caves and the big guns they sink into the hillsides during the War. There are bayonettings and forced labour. Old people have told her about them. There is the strong dream she has before she flies to Micronesia. It's a dream of a beach, she says, where there are gun emplacements and a funny concrete pillbox within reach of the waves. The dream is very clear, she says. She takes it with her when she goes to the lagoon. And one day after work when she drives along the shore for a swim with a young anthropologist from Utah, she finds the beach in all its detail. She walks her dream from the rusting gun to the pillbox. It is a beach where thousands of men died in a four-day battle towards the end of the War. She tells me. Then she is silent for a long time beside me on the pillow.

—

I'm playing a match. I'm searching for rhythm in my strokes, in my footwork. It is Melbourne spring. The photinias in a garden opposite the courts will soon declare themselves with a new density of soft red leaves. Some wattles have been and gone. Others are challenging the sun at midday. Sometimes at the college the scent of boronia along the paths near the lecture halls catches me like an arresting memory.

I am finding a rhythm. I am playing tennis. It is good how the plunging into rhythm begins again with every point. There are rhythms within rhythms. This is what Alex Cumming, my father, knew. He is my father. I can say it now, even though I have no clear picture of his face. But I have two fathers. Will is my father too.

In tennis, Alex Cumming must have known that there is the matter of pacing one's self – for this point, for this particular service game of all the service games in an afternoon. There is always the hopeful falling into the court ready to bound towards the first volley. There's a strategy for this game, the stubborn estimate of how to place slow, spinning serves that will arc in from the backhand, that will curve into the body of the opponent. There is the insistence of performing it again and again. The lines are white opportunities. Further off, and full of strategies and attrition, there is the prospect of the set, and the dour chances of the rubber beyond it, the wearing down, the joy of heartbeat and breath – all under the sky.

And there is the ballet of the others who are playing, and their voices. By their strokes I know them all, even far away, even in silence, even in the dusk – angle of knee, arch of back, dip of shoulder, height of toss, whip of wrist. We each leave our body's emblem in the air. Houses darken behind us as we play, drawing closer on the hill.

I suppose it is a dream. I've been in the midst of it many times, each time, each match a little different. And yet it is new – it has never happened before.

—

Sometimes there is just one thing, love, and the fingering and mouthing and probing of sex, and her body before me, as though I've swallowed her whole with all her allure.

I feel so alive, coming from the sea, coming from the underwater cave over the other side of the inlet, where the weed streams with each swell and I dive down to twelve feet to watch the sunlight through the water, to watch the wave surround the big rock like a spirit, stroking its hair, washing it with the brown weed, then leaving it and spiriting on into the sunlight, and then into the gloom of the cave.

When I reach the beach again, after a steady swim of two hundred yards under the brilliant yellow and brown cliffs, and stand in the shallows with my fins and mask, love is waiting. I can feel its urging in the pit of my stomach, in my tightened balls. It is waiting out there for me in the next hour, or in the night.

I am thinking of her. She is present in the sea, in the towel brushing my face, drying my shoulders. She is in the sunlight's leaning down. I know I can never stop, that my shaft will harden every day for her, that my dry mouth will yearn for her. We will lie together, the bed dipping deliciously as she turns, my shaft saying you are generous, you are open, you are opening to me alone. We will feel again our offering, our new searching which is such old searching. We have something sure. She lasts. I last.

—

I am parentless, I remind myself. I see the hospital in the street of pin oaks where Louise said goodbye. And I can feel that Will is dead and I seem to know so much that my heart is bursting.

But this is still to happen.

In between I see Alex standing wordless and confused in his unit in Sydney. I see his face there, standing at the wrong door, waiting for a sign to lead him. I see how noble his nose is, and his brow. I sometimes look in the mirror and think that I see him. I look across the room at his daughter and I see myself there somehow too – in her eyes, her cheek bones.

And yet it is still to happen.

I detect the sadness in his daughter's eyes that Alex doesn't see. I catch her watching his lost figure, knowing something is eating his awareness. But I know she is strong. That must be it. People are incredibly strong. I've never dreamed how strong.

How wounded people are! I've never dreamed how wounded, and carrying their wounds through every day, through every Christmas, every winter. Now I have heard Louise's wounds. I have heard what Alex says sadly about the past, felt his regret intractable as steel. With Will it has not been so much a wounding as a steady strain and endurance and wisdom. I have listened to him and learned how he has clutched his knowledge to him in silence. And now – has he gone?

No – Will's death is yet to come. I have learned about his resignation and then his love and hope and wisdom. I am lucky I have been able to make peace with his knowledge. It seems I have wept with him over his strength and patience and what it has cost. And yet it is still to happen. It seems that I have drunk his hope and strength now in order to be complete. I have been wounded, too, and come whole again. Greta and her presence in my life, Greta and the steady weight of what I know have done it. I feel complete. It has taken a long time.

—

And then it leaps on me almost before I can draw breath. The call comes.

In the dark of my study, sorting papers, half surrounded by a field of toneless music running in my head, working on bumbling automatic pilot, I'm thinking of Fern Tree Gully, and I'm seeing Alex Cumming's battle-dress collar and his slouch hat and smelling the mossed rocks under the trees and the damp around the rough timber picnic table. I can't see Alex's face. That's when the call comes.

How can this be? It is Lorraine. I recognise the voice at once, the huskiness again, even the way of using words. But this time there is urgency in her tone. Alex is worse since she spoke to me. She wants me to know that I might regret it if I don't come within a week or so. There have been scans done, she says, and her voice falters. There's a brain tumour. She pauses and I wait in the silence. Then I can hear her ready to proceed. It explains the confusion he's been having, she says: trouble with simple things – direction; the right way to drive through a round-about. She knows I'd want to see him while – again the faltering – while he's still at home and talking to people. We want you to be here, she says. We've been thinking about you and how it must feel for you. You are one of the family, she says, even though we don't know you – and her voice fades for a moment with emotion. I can hear her breathing. I'm sorry, she says when she continues, I'm sorry that I could only be pretty formal about it when I talked to you on the phone before. I didn't know what to feel. But now you've got to come over, and come soon. I've seen some of these tumours before. Don't worry about the motel. You can stay with us if you want. Her voice stops, waits for me to speak. I find I'm choking, suddenly close to a deep sob. I hear – unbelievable, my mind is saying – a sisterly concern in her voice.

—

It is all re-running through my head. It is like a tape. The voices are coming back to me. I even get that sense again of the Sydney summer that is almost upon the Harbour in early September.

'This is the Dire Straits room!' Lorraine is pleased, I can tell, to be able to speak of matters domestic. 'Tommy spread himself out here for a while last year. You can see he had a crush on Mark Knofler. He's doing music at Sydney now. You mightn't see him till tomorrow.'

I look again at her face, now that she's standing fingering the edge of the desk, looking about, thinking what I'll need for comfort. My sister! As soon as she steps up to me at the airport I see those eyes, dark and steady, heavy with – is it sadness? I don't know yet, because I haven't seen the obverse, haven't seen her smile very often. I seem to be more in control of the situation than she is. I am standing here in the room with its posters, awaiting what is new, ready to discover, and yet strangely untouched emotionally. I am so cool. And yet something deep in my core is saying be prepared, be prepared. Be prepared for what?

It is uncanny. Their house – the house of Lorraine and Ralph – is in those steep streets running west from the Pacific Highway, plunging down from the ridge in Chatswood. It is almost as I pictured it to be. It is Sydney. I am in shirt-sleeves. I can hear currawongs calling from tree recess to tree recess. There's a stillness and warmth in the air. Where is the fretting of the southerly and westerly stream that governs our moods in Melbourne, stirs the street trees, sways the powerlines, streams in cold through the main streets of the city against the bleak light of afternoons?

'I'm on at four,' Lorraine is saying. 'How about we go over to Dad now – you've had lunch on the plane? – and see him for a while. Then I can bring you back here. An hour or so might be enough for him at first. I've told him you've come up here. I'll ring him and say we're coming. Do you think? We'll have more time tomorrow?'

So it is his eyes that reach out to me, dark and with a touch of dolour in them, when he comes to the door, when I take in a gust of sea-smell and sea-wind and sunlight coming from the other side of his unit as he opens to us.

'Tim?' He peers a bit in the light. This is his daughter standing very still beside me, I remind myself. He peers again, but doesn't offer his hand.

'Yes, Alex,' I hear myself saying. 'It's me. How are you?'

Now I'm not cool. I'm gasping for breath suddenly, looking for words. And yet I go on speaking before I know. 'At last I've come . . .' I'm saying, and my voice is wrung out. It falters and breaks for a moment. 'At last I'm here . . . to see you at home. How are you?'

I'm not cool. I'm preternaturally aware of Lorraine beside me. I hear a little groan of anguish escape her as she sees us meet, as she listens to our mundane, ridiculous words circling each other in the doorway. But I don't look at her. I'm not sure what Alex notices. He waits. His expression doesn't change. It's just an enquiring, welcoming smile.

Then he starts as if he has been prompted and speaks. 'Me? Oh, I'm fit as a fiddle.' For a moment his face takes on a sheepish falsity. 'My only problem at the moment is to know which side to get into a car – things like that. I used to know, but I seem to have lost it . . .' He laughs a short laugh. He laughs again and it trails away.

'How about a drink, Dad?' Lorraine is taking over. 'Let's sit down and have a drink.'

There's a crush in the doorway. Lorraine edges past Alex and leads down the short corridor into light. Yes, says Alex, following. We can have a drink. Yes. I follow them both into the large room, into light. There, in the wide window at the end of the room, is the sea making its leisurely, green-blue advances in the sun. The sight of it, the far white offerings of the waves on the shore further north, begins to calm me. I think in a flash of Greta. I see her – and then she is gone.

I watch Alex. He moves uncertainly towards the drink cabinet against the far wall, but Lorraine anticipates him, says she'll get the drinks, asks me how a brandy will suit. So Alex swings about, walks to his deep chair, tells me to have a seat in the chair beside him, settles into his own with a relieved sigh. Then he looks to the window as if for rescue. Finding none, he turns and asks me where I'm living now. His dark eyes appraise me candidly. I'm aware I'm looking long at him, too, for the first time.

332

Oh, yes, he remembers Hawthorn he says. Not all that far from Toorak and the Kooyong courts. I watch him. He's waiting for Lorraine. He knows she is supposed to come. Like a child he's waiting for a glass in his hand. But then he's looking at me again, intrigued, then looking away to the windows. Those dark eyes, with their touch of languor, of dolour. Those loose, dark limbs made for sweeping down on a tennis ball. I remember photographs. I look back at him. I'm seeing my own eyes.

Then Alex has his drink, then Lorraine is sitting with us, then our gazes are roving, meeting. It makes my stomach creep. There is significance in this moment, in this room, in these chairs and voices and eyes. We are three. Father, daughter, son. Unimaginable! We are three. Father, half-brother, half-sister.

'We're awkward, aren't we,' I say. I didn't know I had it to say. 'But here's to meeting – after all.' We sight across our glasses at each other. Alex's face is neutral, as much as to say, yes, this had to happen, and here we are. Lorraine's brow is still knitted, caught by surprise. But yes, yes, she says. And we drink.

Suddenly Alex punches the soft arm of the chair. His eyes blaze for a second, his mouth turns to a grin. He looks away at the long window, shakes his head in disbelief. He punches the chair again. 'It's Lockie!' he says. 'That's who it is. I've been searching for it. It's Lockie, isn't it, Raine. That's who it is! Isn't he like Uncle Lockie? It's in the eyes, the jaw maybe – even the voice.' Now I realise he is seeing someone else in me. Someone called Lockie.

'It could be,' says Lorraine. She smiles towards him bemusedly. Then her expression, as she looks at him, takes on a certain sadness I can't place, even a certain dismay. 'You'd know, Dad,' she says. 'You knew him. You'd see it. I wouldn't. I only ever saw Lachlan once, I think, when I was very small. And a few photographs.' She turns to me. 'Uncle Lachlan Wishart was Dad's mother's brother – a great storyteller apparently. An editor at one stage in Adelaide, wasn't he?'

'Yes, Adelaide – and somewhere else,' says Alex. He half turns, looking at the carpet. Now it's as if we're losing him. He has to depart from us, searching the trail of his thought again.

Lorraine interposes. 'You're booked to go back on Wednesday, are you?' she asks me. 'Dad will be in with us by then.'

But Alex's face and voice have come back to us. 'That's what it must have been,' he says. 'I think I used to see him sometimes in Melbourne when I was working down there. I think he was in Melbourne when I was playing the championships . . .' Alex's words come to a stop.

Then he fixes me with a vague smile. 'Bookish,' he says. 'Are you bookish? It doesn't matter that I'm asking, does it? Lockie was bookish.'

As he pauses again I catch Lorraine looking at me to see if I understand his vagueness, to see if I'm coping.

'It's not in me, for God's sake!' Alex is coming again. 'That sort of thinking blows me out.' He laughs uncertainly, even bitterly. He falls to studying his glass.

Lorraine is watching us both. All at once she looks tired, a bit dazed. Could it be that suddenly she sees all these links she didn't suspect, of which she can't be a part, these connections that her father sees, but is losing? Perhaps she knows there are things coming that belong to Alex and me and from which she is excluded, from which her mother is excluded? That's how it runs through my mind, and yet my mind is racing elsewhere.

'Do you remember playing in the championships at Dubbo in 1933?' I ask Alex. 'Do you remember winning a travelling clock?'

He looks at me. His face blenches, thinking. He doesn't remember. I hear Elsie's words, his sister's words. Water under the bridge. All a long way back now. Water under the bridge.

'Anyway,' I say, boring on, feeling bright. 'Down at the church where I write – near Port Chalice – there's a travelling clock. I inherited it from Louise, I suppose. I can't remember. But it's yours. You won it in Dubbo for the singles in 1933. It says so on the case. I wind it up every time I arrive there.' I find my voice is choking. I've hit a shoal I didn't know was there. 'I wind it up every time . . .'

I see deep into Alex's eyes as I try to finish what I'm saying. At first I see him merely looking at me, trying to make sense of where I'm heading. This is my father's face, I'm saying to myself. It comes somehow as a new realisation. Then I see memory and feeling opening up his face, see his brow considering, remembering. Then his face drains somehow, the set of his mouth becomes uncertain again. But I'm boring on, the sweet wood of brandy in my mouth. 'I've never known why I do it,' I'm saying. 'I wind the clock and leave it going when I'm packing up too, when I leave. I do it every time. I seem to have to do it.' I'm appealing with my eyes to Lorraine.

Alex sits silent for a moment. He looks at his drink, brings it to his lips, swallows. He looks suddenly older. I get the feeling that if he weren't in the chair, if he were without the drink, he would be teetering, lost. I can sense Lorraine monitoring him. I can feel him trying to measure himself out, slow himself down to cope with all this beneath his grey, steely hair. He purses his lips intently, then passes a hand across his forehead and runs it back over the crown of his head.

Then he says: 'What's it got? Has it got little leather doors on it, has it?'

'Yes,' I say. 'You can close it up with a sort of keeper.'

'Ah, yes – Dubbo,' his voice rolls. 'Yes, Dubbo. God! I've forgotten that. That's the clock I left with Louie. That's going a long way back. It's all part and parcel. Louie was supposed to mark off the days with that when I was away on the Davis Cup tour. I'll be blowed! It was supposed to be a reminder . . .' His voice catches. 'So she's had it ever since? Or you have? I'll be blowed!'

He stops. He looks down at his feet. Then he brings his glass to his lips thirstily, as though he might not get enough from it. 'What do people do to each other?' he says.

Alex looks at Lorraine's strained face. She is following, as though along a strange path.

But Lorraine is setting down her glass. 'Dad, we've got to go. I'm rostered on soon. I'll hear more about it tomorrow. There'll be more time. I'll come over with a bag tonight and get you ready. Doctor's orders. Mrs Traill's got your tea for tonight. I'll ring you around seven to check. Mrs Traill, remember, if you're worried about anything. Don't forget – the next landing. OK?'

'Aah. Going, are you?' Alex's voice is thin, shorn of confidence now.

Lorraine steps forward to help him as he braces himself to get out of the chair, but he plants an elbow, writhes to one side, rises slowly without her. He stands as though to clear a reeling head, then walks vacantly towards the door facing the sea balcony, turns, waits for orders.

'No, Dad,' Lorraine says softly. 'Front door again. Front door.'

'Oh, yes – front door. Where am I going?' Alex laughs at himself, sneaks a look at me. 'Front door.'

So when I'm in the car and reaching for the seatbelt I can still feel in my fingers the warmth of his distracted handshake at the door, hear the curiosity in his voice: 'Come over again, Tim'. I can see him waiting behind the screen for us to pull away. Lorraine is silent as she slips out from the kerb with a final check over her shoulder. We're gone. The unit on the headland is gone into the blue afternoon. Somewhere behind us Alex, my father, shuffles back down the corridor to his sea-room of light and his modest table and his thinking about me.

But who am I? I keep asking myself. Who am I, being whisked about in someone else's car? Who am I in all this? And another voice comes in from the side. 'Too late,' it is saying. 'Too late.'

—

This is Will's Sydney, this morning Harbour and the beaches running north. This is his brother Jack's Sydney, where the wide pastures of the Pacific open up beyond the Heads. I feel the ferry plough on. I watch the shores reel around under their scrub. I think of Uncle Jack and his bananas and beer. I imagine the sun striking through his shirt, the gentle slap of the waves against his boat in the stillness, through the long day of stillness. I smell fish-bait and the baking of paint in the heat. I think towards Alex's Sydney, just round the corner of North Head, up past Fairy Bower, up past the glinting white combers at Manly, there on the Queenscliff headland.

I like thinking of places. They bring me voices. I hear Will telling me about the rowing up the Parramatta River, or sometimes at Mosman, sometimes at North Shore. I see words on a silver match-box cover, the impressions worn thin by handling. I've forgotten how many times I have seen it come up to Will's pipe, to cap it, to shepherd it, to get it to draw. Then when he throws the pipe out the matchbox holder lies unused at the back of the Cicero Street mantelpiece for years, until Will gives it to me when we move him to Overton Lane. 'Will Menzies', says the lettering. 'Gladstone Skiffs – 7. 3. 1925'.

But now is not the time. Alex will be installed at Chatswood when I get back there. Again as I talk to him I will be deciphering without a word what he can bring to mind and what he can't. I'll follow him with my eyes when he comes into the room with his rolling walk and stands abashed until Lorraine tells him what he is there for, what is going to happen next. Some times are better than others.

For a moment I think of Fiona and Kevin who will be talking to my tutorial groups, one almost at this moment, the other later this afternoon.

—

I've observed it so many times. My mother – looking first, and then thinking and imagining. She has taught me how to see, to feel. When I am with her I see things and think things for the first time. It's not the way Greg or Alistair or Will sees. Will, my father, sees when the best thinkers wrap their words around him. He's swept away by what he reads. And I think he sees through rhythm and through melody and music too. But he doesn't see directly like Louise or I do. He doesn't reach through to the secret spirit of what can happen. I think I know now. I seem to have no doubts. Has Louise taught me how to see, or did I know it anyway? I'm not certain – but I know that she and I see so directly sometimes that it hurts. It seems that is what we are meant to do. Now, who is going to carry it on? Who will take up the seeing? I look at my children's faces. Who?

—

She is standing at my knee, looking straight into my eyes, waiting. I don't know her name. It must be the future. Her eyes are dark like mine and Jesse's. She is looking up at me in unfeigned attention and intrigue. She has a glove puppet with a fox's nose and two beady eyes under her arm. She likes to keep it with her all the time, I know.

'Well,' I am saying to her in mock Socratic tone, 'you talk to yourself, don't you?'

'Only sometimes,' she says.' When I'm playing down near the swing I do.'

'I thought so,' I say, smiling conspiratorially at her, and she blushes and smiles back and I see Jesse there. It must be the future. Then I find myself thinking of my mother. Her page of life has turned and she has been gone now for some time, I find myself thinking, and she has never known these eyes that should be hers. It is the future, the next page and then another and then another.

'Do you talk to yourself?' she asks me. She looks as though she is considering drawing with her finger on the leg of my jeans as I sit there, then leans against my knee absently, looking up again.

'I do quite a lot, especially when I am at the church writing. You know my church, don't you. Well, when I'm down there, there's always this other person called Timmie there getting round cutting wood and working at the computer and stopping to make cups of coffee – so I talk to him. He's quite nice most of the time.'

'Don't be silly,' she says. 'That's you. Timmie. You're Grandpa Timmie. That's *you*. That's who you *are*. You're Grandpa Timmie.'

'Oh,' I say. 'Yes. I forgot.'

She looks at me with love and pity, pleased that we have cleared that matter up. And for a moment, bypassing Jesse her father, she could be Patricia when I first met her, when we walked and kissed along the river, and the Gippsland mountains were always in our view and in the back of our consciousness, when we both had hope.

—

Suddenly I can see Lorraine. Now I seem to see through and beyond my first impression of her face at the airport and in Alex's unit. Now I can sense something in her face and her bearing that is familiar, that is known in a deep recess in me. It seems that now I see her truly, despite the puzzlement, the dread in her eyes at yesterday's meeting with Alex, despite my dream about her tears. It's twice now I have had the dream, once back in Melbourne, and again last night.

Now I hear that her husky, spade-is-a-spade voice and declaration strikes a Sydney note and not a Melbourne one. It is not chic. Now I see how her eyes are Alex's and mine. Now I see that the stern, pinched nose comes from Alex. It is not my nose: mine is broader and deeper like Louise's. When I first saw Lorraine at Kingsford Smith that stern, narrow nose falsely led me to fear pronouncements. Now I know that they will never come. But it seems there is a membrane of awareness that hovers between me and realisation, a membrane I can't quite pierce and discard. It hides little indications that I sense are there when I watch Lorraine bending over vegetables in the kitchen as we talk – things I cannot yet discern, but that I think I should know. I felt them yesterday, too – the small clue that I sense in Alex's hand when he brings it to his face to help his thinking, fingers across mouth, thumb depressing the middle of his cheek. But I have salted that one home. I know all about that hand-to-face, that sort of considering. That is my way in the office, in meetings, or when Greta and I are talking about Joel and where he is going and how he regards my newness in his life.

It all seems so vital to me now, and yet it all wants to pass me by. Or is it that I am content to find the detail and yet let it pass me by. I am here, eager. This is Sydney. These are my people, I suppose. But a voice tells me that they are not my close people. I am here with a purpose: and yet I want to be home. At some moments it seems like no more than a job I have to do. I can smell the boronia in the small gardens on the way to my office at the college. I can imagine the yellow honey-sweat of the dandelions running down the hill to the lecture theatre. I can hear the trams grinding round the curve of the Power Street corner in Hawthorn. I see Greta's eyes, so dear to me, and the hair brushed back from her forehead – and then they are gone.

—

Things have come together. We have brought Alex to Chatswood. His modest suitcase and travel bag are in the corner of the back room. They make a pathetic, transient statement. For more than an hour he has been in the bed, asleep. It could be a short step to hospital, as Lorraine says, and her eyes study the carpet grimly for a second. We have been talking a lot.

Things have come together. We have been walking down the well of the Chatswood streets and up towards the sky again – just Lorraine and Ralph and I. Now we sit having a drink in the sunroom at the back. Melissa is home. She is studying in her room, with her music turned down. She is wearing patched jeans and a tee shirt. She has the dark Cumming eyes, the loose limbs.

Things have come together. Now I have met Ralph and had the chance to talk and walk with him. Now I am coming to terms with his bemused smile at the idea of Lorraine finding a half-brother after all this time, at Alex finding a son 'after, what, forty-seven, forty-eight years?' as he says with amazement. It seems that his are the first blue eyes I've studied for a long time. They look at me dispassionately quite often, but they are not unfriendly. They say I am Lorraine's concern and fascination, not his.

—

Greta – in half an hour I will be on the plane. It is almost over. I must be a different person. We have crossed boundaries, Greta, we have crossed one boundary after another. My heart stumbles over meanings, comes back to them. Sydney hovers at the moment like a different place in my mind.

This morning we sit at the table talking. They ask about you, Greta, and I begin to tell them. Melissa and Lorraine and Ralph. Alex is still asleep. I start to tell them, but Melissa laughs suddenly and slaps the table with her hand. 'He's a throat-clearer, just like Grandpa.' She looks at Lorraine and Ralph, blushes at the thought of cutting across my words. But she sees my wry, interested smile. I haven't been aware that I've strained to clear my throat as I start to tell them about Port Chalice and the Blue Pool and you coming up the track up from Campfire Bay in your sarong. Lorraine is laughing with her, concurring.

'Yes,' Lorraine says, 'and I noticed yesterday he sometimes has the Davis Cup stance, knees braced back, just like Dad. It's a bit uncanny, isn't it?' Ralph snorts and raises his eyes to Heaven. I catch his disparaging blue eyes. Lorraine turns to me.

'You look like Dad,' she says. 'You laugh like us. You cough and clear your throat like Dad, without realising you're doing it.' She breaks off and almost giggles at me. 'I hope you don't mind this body-language analysis. I've had long enough now to see it all. There'll be other things too. But the really fascinating one is how you touch things to see how they feel while you're thinking – that's Grandpa Cumming. That's Alex's father. Long fingers reaching out and stroking things without knowing they're doing it. And there's a bit of it in the way you hold the *Sydney Morning Herald*, too. Grandpa Cumming used to pummel it so that it'd fold, just like you do. It's partly the way you hold your mouth while you're doing it. Then in goes the nose to read! I've seen him do it a lot when I was a kid. He came up and stayed with us often before he died.'

What does it all mean, Greta? What am I supposed to feel? How can I ever make the right responses? How can I ever know enough to make them?

But Greta – I think it's all too late. Alex is confused for much of the time. I can't take his mind back very readily, although he's better with the distant past than with the here-and-now. But there are questions I want to ask him. There are times I want him to talk about. It's not going to happen. He'll be sleeping again now. A sleep and a forgetting.

We've exchanged a lot. I can call Lorraine sister. She tells me about Alex and his adjustment to Sydney. She tells me about his discovery of the sea. He used to fish off the rocks just under his unit until a few weeks ago. She remembers coming from Melbourne to the North Shore when she was nine or so. The light, she says, and water. The light and the Harbour. Alex liked it. The War took away his tennis career. But he used to say that Sydney wasn't going to keep reminding him of that. Melbourne did. So he liked warm Sydney. He did some coaching in Mosman and worked in the sports store in George Street. I need to know the detail of these things, and now he can't tell me. It's too late, Greta.

This morning I manage to get Alex to think about Will. Every word counts. He says that Will has always been a remarkable person, a person of uncommon understanding. Will is generous, he says, willing to give people the benefit of the doubt. He says – in fact Will is a saviour. A saviour! Such an unusual word from Alex. I can see him now as a saviour, he says. Every word counts. Alex wants to know where Will lives. He wants to know again how long it is since Louise died. Every word, every wound, every opening up to the truth counts.

I am not sure what it means, but Lorraine and I hug today. She says that when Alex takes a turn for the worse it might be very quick. She cries. I take her in my arms and hug her. We hug. We sway. You are a bonus, she says. She says she has been thinking about what it must be like for me to feel different and to know it, but not to know why. She asks me about Louise. I try to give her a picture of Louise and Alex when they were young – but I've only got the clues in the letters and photographs and what Will has told me. I find it hard to do. I find I'm talking about Victoria and the Mallee and feeling my close people about me with their stories. It is strange to Lorraine, although Alex has told her about the Mallee and some things about his tennis in Melbourne. I can understand her interest in this woman who loved her father. It is almost as if I can feel Louise listening to what I say.

Late in the day, when I'm leaving, I give Alex the clock. Lorraine is there. Tommy has been and gone like a gust of wind. He comes home to get a couple of books and is off again. I hardly have an impression of his face. Melissa is there. She will look after Alex when Lorraine takes me to the plane. She will help him until Ralph comes back from his conference in the evening. I notice how Melissa puts her arm round Alex as he looks at what is in my hand.

The travelling clock has little leather doors with a hook to close them. Alex looks at it and his face is a study. Then I can see he remembers. He reaches out a hand for it. 'Well ... I'll be blowed!' he says. 'I didn't think I'd see this again.' He opens the small doors, reads the

342

inscription on the metal below the face. 'Dubbo,' he says. 'Dubbo,' he croons to himself. Lorraine's face is riven with sadness, watching him. Melissa's eyes are wide with a huge compassion when she looks at me. But Alex doesn't notice. 'This takes me back a bit,' he says. 'Are you saying I can have it?'

'Yes, keep it,' I say.

'You know,' he says, looking at the face of the clock as though it might suddenly speak, 'this was a reminder of me to Louise when I was away. Did I tell you? This and some French perfume.' He weighs it in his hand for a moment, then lets his arm drop.

My stomach is sinking as I watch him. 'Yes', I say to him. 'It's told the time a lot for me too.'

'You know,' Alex says, as though he hasn't heard me. 'You know, for such a long time Louise was never out of my life.'

That's all he says. When I leave I put an arm around his shoulders. He looks surprised. The collar of my jacket has rubbed his fine hair into a small cocky's comb.

'Will you be coming to Sydney again?' he asks.

'Pretty likely,' I say. 'Pretty likely.'

That's all there is, Greta. And Melissa and Lorraine watching. Every word counts, every gesture. But now I just want to get on the plane and close my eyes. It will bring me down into Melbourne in the dark. If I'm asleep they'll wake me. I'll know where I am.

—

Finale:

A Carpenter's Level

I am looking at the jumble of the old tools in the porch of the church and I hear his voice. That's how I know it will come. It is the future. His voice comes again. It thumps me in the heart. 'Ah, that brings back some memories ...' I've dearly wanted to hear him say that one last time.

The eyes have been burning at me, not seeing me. He's in the chair, head sunk on his chest, his hands fidgeting. He's muttering. He can't hear me. He's away. He writhes, mutters, hisses. I lean down close to him, his face grey with stubble, the veins in his neck pulsing like mice under the loose skin. Such power throbbing under parchment!

'Hey, Will! Hey, Dad!'

The eyes burn in my direction. The urgent movements, the desperate words, the hissing go on. I look down at the ballooning feet showing under the blanket where his legs are supported by the chair. They are full of fluid – blue, potato-like. I reach for them and rub them. They are cold. Still the low, word-spattering voice and hissing go on.

'Hey! Hey! Will!'

The eyes burn at me now, but don't see me for a moment. The pupils are white light, like stars, so small. Then the eyes close again.

'Hey! This is Sydney, Dad. Will! This is Sydney.'

This time the eyes surface fully. I hold up the colour picture of the Harbour with South Head there, and North Head and North Harbour tucked in behind it, and further round Middle Harbour and Bradley's Head and Mosman and Cremorne. He can see it. The eyes strain, the brain dragging behind them, catching up. Suddenly the eyes soften, although the pupils go on burning unnaturally. The words come in the high-pitched whisper Greg and I have become used to these last weeks.

'That brings back some memories ... that brings back some

347

memories ... *but I can't remember much these days ...' His*
voice trails away.

The nurses are suddenly at my elbow. They have come to
put him back in the bed, to re-insert the catheter. It is
the future.

—

Why does this part of the story push itself forward, offering to tell itself?
Or do I merely imagine that?

—

What is a snake's joy? He lies in the sun near the front path to the
church. Or she wants the warmth of that grassy corner. I have no idea
whether it is she or he. She is a black, about four feet long. If I come up
quietly, don't rush, don't bend, I can study those scales, that small head
and light-green eye, that amazing sexy flattening just behind the head
like a cobra, the luxurious, ample coils of the body and the thin, black
trailing away of the tail. If she becomes aware of me because my movement is too sharp, because of my shadow falling across her, or my cough,
or my thud of boot, she withdraws under the concrete slab of the path
only six inches from where she has lain coiled near a single dandelion in
the grass just beyond where the lavender leans down from the weatherboards. Never a flurry, just a slow, inexorable black glide, thinning,
thinning to the end of the tail as it disappears, leaving nothing, like a
soft visual kiss.

I need grass, sun in corners, the smell of wood in the wind. I need
the water off the wave platform. I need to stand naked in the warm wind,
feeling the salt drying on my legs, stomach, on the middle of my back,
on my buttocks. I need to touch leaves, finger wet earth, watch the
grass stroked again and again towards the horizon by the wind on
the hill beyond the gate. It helps me separate the faces, the voices. It
helps me lean back from the vision of Alex, my father, standing abashed
as if awaiting orders at the door facing the sea balcony. It helps me to
think, yes, Sydney, far distant, and Lorraine my sister and the huge,

understanding dishes of Melissa's eyes registering my confusion and joyful sadness when I look at Alex with the travelling clock restored to his hands.

I can feel the physical, the primal, start the thoughts chiming quietly in my body again, just as the flow of realisation begins when I come with the spade and kneel to pull the first weeds in the bricky corners of beds in Hawthorn, my fingers encountering the forgotten, rough giving of the earth after days of paper and fluorescent light and carpet and inert white desktop in the office. Sometimes the brittleness takes days to come out of me.

The paddocks' bulking green shoulders loom over me and then run out of sight at the church. Greta will be down tomorrow when Joel has gone to camp. I stand a moment to think on the path. I need grass and damp earth and the cold fingers of the rock pools reaching round my shoulders. I need the sight of my black snake when I go to check the corner and find her there again.

I am stacking wood now, in the rough shed under the boobiallas. It carries the rhythm of strained wrists and the satisfying clap of the split blocks thudding into the corners under the shed's roof. Sometimes, preparing for unimaginable winter, for two days' daylight I have wood in my eyes, under my hands, raised by my muscles. In the provenance of stacking I start to dream. In forethought, hip swivel, wheelbarrow slew and fall, clatter of wood against metal and other wood, in the filling, emptying, filling again, I start to dream and the dream of Lorraine and Alex returns. Her face is wet with tears. Alex's face, the dark pouches dire under his eyes, is below hers, only half-inclined and half turned away. The eyes seem to be closed. Are they closed? It is important. I strain to see, but cannot. Lorraine's cheekbones shine with wiped tears.

I free myself from wood, from the dream. I step out towards the fence flexing my arms, squaring my shoulders. A Black Poll calf and a fairy-faced young Jersey wander almost together feeding at their own pace fifteen yards away in the paddock's grass. They wander, feeding and thinking. Suddenly the Jersey stops, raises her head, stands in a trance. The afternoon swarms down on her.

349

The dream of Lorraine and Alex returns to me at night in the warm dark of the church. No matter how I try I can't see Alex's eyes.

—

I feel it cut through to me. It is Lorraine's husky voice there all of a sudden on the line. After three days with them at Chatswood Alex begins just to sit in the chair, she says. He does not read or watch television, then next morning cannot dress himself or come to breakfast. He is in hospital now in a coma. Yes, she says, he sometimes drifts up to the surface like a fish and manages a few words but knows no one. Now it is just holding his hands, kneading his fingers, letting him register the warmth.

The darkness of coma. I try to imagine it. I see Lorraine and Melissa leaning to his face over the bedspread, whispering his name, faces pointed with urgency. It is not yet the semester break. I cannot be there. I can't go again. I hear his breathing, imagine the pouches dark under his eyes. But his eyes, I can clearly see, are shut. I watch Lorraine's face come up, turn away with a low sigh.

—

I know it will come. But I can see I am not prepared for it to well up so soon, there, in its place, just there, on time's circle. I will not be prepared for it to finish so quickly.

It has not happened yet, but it will. I will say to myself that this cannot be. But it will be, it will happen before me, and it will be natural. It will be the order of things.

Now it is after it has happened. I hear voices. I hear Alistair saying with a sad clucking: 'Now, what about the eulogy we never had for Mum, eh? We should have made sure of that, shouldn't we! Where was the eulogy for Louise?' I feel my cravenness and inexperience again. I feel again the lava of my emotions too thick, too slow to flow, when I think of her face. I see the hospital in the street of pin oaks, the late winter sun making espaliers of their branches against the walls.

But now, the blood, the ward Sister is saying, is not getting round. Will's heart is too weak to clear the fluid from the body. The catheter has to do that. The catheter has to empty the bladder. The blood is not getting round. I can hear her voice. I can see her hands holding the white file, pages spilling out of the folder at one corner. I will not believe it can come so soon, that it will finish so quickly. I am aware that she is poised in her chair to leave me, to go to another bed. I hear a falling metal tray chime in the corridor.

It is the future that I know and yet don't know. It is death calling. It is another death.

—

I am looking at the photographs again. Will has them out. He has brought the folders from his wardrobe when I ask – with relief, I think, with even a tinge of curiosity now that I know, now that I have visited Alex and Lorraine.

Will has never met Lorraine. What is she like? Is she a tennis player? How many children? Whereabouts in Chatswood do they live? Oh, that's not too far away to get over to Queenscliff.

On the table between us I'm turning the photographs I've seen before. And suddenly, among other faces, I see myself. It is me. It can't be me. It could be me – dark splash of hair, the eyes, the angle of face held on one side, as though listening, not concerned with the camera. Cheekbones of my middle age, the nose, the pouches under the eyes. It is Alex with a tournament group in Adelaide.

I push it over to Will, finger on the image of Alex until he can take the photograph from me.

'It could be me. It *is* me, isn't it?'

Will takes it, holds it up, finds Alex in the group, assesses it, looks away, assesses it again. 'Quite a likeness there, but I wouldn't overstate it,' he says and smiles with his blue eyes to convince me. 'You should keep these now, anyway. They're family significance now.'

'You know, according to Lorraine, Alex was fishing off the rocks below the unit at Queenscliff until he was diagnosed. Shades of Uncle Jack, eh? A true Sydney-sider.'

'Ha,' Will says. 'There you are. Alex ends up content in his adopted Sydney, while I finish my days happily acculturated by Melbourne. *C'est juste. C'est juste.*'

—

I'm glad I have done it, Greta. For the first time I have shed that feeling of incompleteness. I have been able to watch the Harbour waters and think about it. I feel somehow cleansed. I have a sister's eyes to return to. I have a father to remember. Under it all is a sense of waste, a feeling of loss that comes close to loneliness – a sort of retrospective loneliness. I have not had these people all these years. Have I been most alone of all of them? Possibilities have been lost. I can feel the edges of a richness that has been lost. And yet?

And yet, what would I have done if I had known my origins when I was a high school student? How would we have met then – Alex, my father, my half-brother, my half-sister? Could I have coped with it? I see the faces of Alistair and Greg, the brothers of my childhood, of the sandpit, of the street cricket games, of swims at the baths. Who are they now? Suddenly they have become half-brothers. There is the dismay I feel about such a confusion of new relatives, all these new references and cross-references I have to hear. It dismays me. It tires me. Sometimes it shuts my brain down to a doze.

When it bundles into my mind at odd moments, unexpectedly, I find that it comes down to eyes. Alex's eyes and their dark pouches, Lorraine's eyes with the same sense of dark sadness. It comes down to kindness – Lorraine's sisterly concern, Melissa's uncalculating compassion. As for Keith, my new half-brother, I have a photograph, that's all, until he comes home from the States. All I can see there is something familiar in the cheekbones and the ridge of the nose as he stands against a wall with some cracks in the masonry – a candid, dark face, a thirty-four-year-old man who is my brother. Am I as complete as I am ever going to be? I nurse a cautious joy.

—

Now it is over. Even as I'm deciding to ring Sydney, Lorraine calls. Alex has gone. About four this afternoon. Quietly, once they withdrew the support. About fourteen hours after. She and Melissa and Ralph were there. All they could do was sit and take his hands every now and then. I hear her voice break.

The funeral will have to be on Thursday. It will probably be in Mosman where Alex used to coach. They'll understand if I can't come, having been over so recently, Lorraine says. I've said my goodbye, in a sense, even though it was a hello. Of course, come if you can, she says. Come if you want to do that. It's cruel the way timing works out – you no sooner know the full story than things shut down. Alex mentioned you quite a lot, she says, after you left. The clock seemed to be something that kept the connections alive in his mind even when he was failing. He even had it there with him when he first went into hospital. He often just held it, opened the doors, looked at the face for a while, closed them again. Then he went into coma. We're not sure yet whether Keith will get back. He's way up north in Canada at the moment. Lorraine's voice falters and trails away again.

I discover that I have the same qualms in my throat as I speak. No, I say, it's unlikely I can get up to the funeral. I can't take more time very easily from the college, especially at this time of the year. In any case I think in a way that the contacts we three can make from now on are more important in a way – she and Keith and I. That's what I say. I'm still fascinated to know more about Alex. He clearly was a genuine person, a straight person. I hear Lorraine's short squeak of grief on the line when I say that. Yes, he was, she says. He was a good father, open, prepared to give things a go, to believe the best of people he dealt with. He was a kind father, she says, her voice wavering on, then stopping so that I wonder if she's still on the line.

Are you there? I say, and she is. I say that I'll ring her on the day of the funeral, or the night before, perhaps. Bear up, I say. And thank you for helping me sit down with Alex at least a couple of times. I've got no hesitation in calling you sister, I say. I mean it warmly. I can feel it. I can tell. Even on such short acquaintance. There's something there. We think alike, don't we? Thank Melissa for her understanding too, I say. Her understanding is amazing for someone of yet another generation back. So goodbye, sister, I say – goodbye for now. Goodbye, Lorraine, kind sister.

—

Who can foretell? We will watch someone who has been there all our lives just suddenly drop away. Who can believe that they will drop away so quickly leaving us only a shell that speaks no words, breathes no air, needs no warmth? I see Greg's face thin as I've never seen it with concern. Alistair has not come yet. We are waiting for him.

From the room of the meeting I catch the sound of the phone in my office down the corridor. I cast my eyes meaningfully round the others at the table. No time to wait. I get up, go to the phone. Yes, it's Eve from Brooklea Hostel, I hear the voice say. Your father's been taken to hospital with heart failure ... yes ... this morning ... not half an hour ago ...

Who can foretell? Perhaps this needn't happen? But I know it will come. I know it will come.

—

I send a card with a big bunch of roses through Interflora. I imagine, as I stand in the florist's in Glenferrie, that people I will never know are reading the card in the splash of sun against a church wall in Mosman, the gasp of the traffic on Military Road coming to them down the slope through the trees.

So I write something oblique for their eyes. 'Farewell with my love,

Alex – father and tennis player with the strength of the farmer's wrist – Tim Menzies'. Lorraine will explain to those she wants to know.

—

Yes, she will say. We've managed to retrieve him. I think he'll be OK. I think we'll get him back to 'Brooklea'. But we'll need him a week or so to stabilise things, bring the fluid down, adjust his medication. He's pretty confused, you know. We sometimes have to sit him out of bed in a chair with a bar for a while – just to keep him home. The ward Sister will smile, let her mouth decline to let me know the pity of her declaration, that I, just come in from the sunlit trees outside, should have to hear this.

—

When I think of Alex there is loss, loss behind the image of his vacant face there, waiting, at the door to the sea balcony. Too late, my voice says again in a whisper. Too much has gone with him that I've never seen, too much I've never heard him say.

—

I hear my father Will intoning: '. . . something to be desired . . . a tree to make one wise'. Am I wiser, here in these thin days of my forty-sixth year? I know now what I have needed to know through all my time on earth. Now I have the key. But even now, knowing it all, am I finally wise?

—

Just as I know that somehow I must pick up the travelling clock from its place on the rough shelf at the church and pack it in my bag for Sydney, so I know that this is crucial too. I pick up the old carpenter's level, feel the dust in its wood against my fingers. It has to go with me back to Melbourne. It will have to be washed and dried with gentleness, to come with me in the pocket of my jacket to the hospital. It has

355

lain to all intents forgotten now for two years or more with one of Will's old set squares, the inlaid patterning in the wood. They are both in the clutch of tools I inherited when we moved Will from Cicero Street to Overton Lane. They belonged to Will's father in Sydney before him.

I balance it in my hand, look at the pale wood. It is light, shaped for purpose but also for touch and finish and craftsmanship. It is less than an octave span long. I have looked at it many times and wondered, turned it in my hand. I know Will loves it, that it has always been somewhere near him.

—

I have just left Will. I have been looking at his thinking blue eyes, watching his fingers stray on the table as he talks. He has been asking about Alex. He knows too how much is lost. The stories now rest with another generation, other generations, he says. Keep contact with Lorraine and Keith, he advises.

I walk the Overton Lane driveway, past the maple, past the small roses before which Louise used to stand and ponder before she died, the sky over the houses pressing down on her tiny figure. I reach the Nissan, unlock it, get in, set a foot against the swelling of the gearbox, and sit.

I think of possibility, of time's circle, of what is called the past, of leaves putting hands in my pockets and starting my heart. I think of brother Greg mounting the steps of the pool towards me, his older brother, with his sandy curls. His face is beaming after he has won the breaststroke. I think of Greta's soft shoulder beside mine on the pillow, of our breathing, of the light going out, of our dreams coming into our heads like smoke. I think of Will's shed at Cicero Street, the rows of tins up the walls, the baleful eyes of the Chrysler's headlights behind him as he works at the bench, boot-mending. I see a cloud of bees pulsing against autumn sun along the side of the church. I hear Louise saying, '... Will and Alex ... take care of Will and Alex ...' There's a slow flurry of images and words, things that I've been thinking as I read,

356

television images – slave bones turning up in the soil beside a southern road; a woman expressing milk. Why now? And lending, my heart is saying: lending – the secret of family is lending. We are only lent to each other. Love is lending just this once on time's bright circle.

Then I am there, somehow, I am there, and I'm carefully, tenderly, trimming Will's hair. He is sitting completely still, intent on keeping the grey box of his head level, looking beyond me at his head and shoulders in the mirror, the thin towel swung round his neck and tucked in roughly.

—

When my father died, Will is telling us, Alistair and me, there in the slash of sun at the door of the shed in Cicero Street – when my father died I got most of his carpentry tools. See, these two planes, the little tack hammer, set square, spirit level – look at that, isn't it beautiful. There are the files, too, rat-tailed and otherwise, and the saws. There's this little mini-vice here, see, and the chisels, the beauty of chisels. You can make anything with chisels if you've got the idea in your head. If you've got the idea in your soul.

We look. We don't say anything for a long time. Two of the chisels lie there beside the spirit level on yellowing, paint-spattered newspaper. We watch Will's hands planing the board in the big vice, his shoulders leaning, his eye lining up each of his steady, forward blows. Then he stops, hits the vice's handle with the heel of his hand, releases the board, holds it in front of him, sights along it, leaning back.

Behind Will in the upper darkness on the wall, hanging like long, dim tongues, are the saws. And then the strange eyes of empty tins to the roof.

—

I put it in his hand. God, he says, the old carpenter's level. What do you know! Where did you get it? I thought it was gone.

357

Then the eyes strain back for a moment. It's the thought of the catheter.

Then he can look at me again, look down at the spirit level in his hand, resting across the cheek of his palm, lolling there with its inches spelt out in elegant figures. Inches, half inches, quarter inches. Eight inches marked, a bit less than an octave span in the hand, in Will's hand, where it belongs, on the hospital sheet. I want to hold the level myself. My fingers have been asking for it since the time I first wash it and smooth it dry and look at it closely.

I'm watching Will. He is more lucid than last night. And yet it is the future. His head seems tiny, fragile against the pillows.

I look at the blond wood in his hand, the metal corners let in, the metal let into the top too to house the horizontal bubble, the small hole on the right end housing the other bubble vertically. I know it now as well as Will does. The inches are marked on each face. 'Warranted Correct', it says in curved lettering on the right end. 'Patent No. 2207', says the wood on the other end. 'J. Rabone and Sons – Makers – Birmingham', say the curved letters near the centre.

'Well, Dig, I'm not much use now, am I? I'm not much more than a Whitman iota now, am I?' His voice surprises me. It comes from nowhere. "I do not doubt but the majesty and beauty of the world are latent in any iota of the world ..." Huh! I'm too tired for it all now. I can't remember much these days.'

He hasn't called me Dig for quite a time. It's a sign of acceptance, resignation. It sends a pang of panic through me.

'You still remember your Whitman,' I say. 'You're not doing badly.'

He uses his fingers to turn the carpenter's level slowly, face up, face down, face up, in his left hand. His right is inert on the hospital cover. He looks at the level, sinks back

358

deeper into the pillows as though they are now his home. He muses, working his mouth, his voice that low, dry whisper we have heard now for a week – '. . . trivialities, insects, vulgar persons, slaves, dwarfs, rejected refuse . . .' His voice fades to an indecipherable hiss.

His eyes close. His hand still holds the level. Against the intense white of the sheet the work-etched wood looks like a still life.

—

Alex has taken so much with him. Louise has taken so much with her. The Mallee stretches. I feel the itch of hay. The Suttons' youngest son, I hear someone say, is dead in the trenches at Neuve Chapelle. For two years after, Pearlie sometimes thinks she hears her brother's voice out among the sheep, with his cry of 'Come back, ya lag. Come back!' to the kelpies. But it's only the crows railing in the sugar gums. I see Candles' face, and then I see mine. Our brows, our foreheads are almost the same. I hear that John Barnes is good with the bat and the ball. I hear that he likes playing tennis on the new ant-bed court at old Rogers' homestead. And here is the wall of the Sea Lake bakery throwing back the summer morning sun. Here is the pluck of the net of strings, the smarting thud of the ball against the bricks, again and again. It is Alex practising. Flute is watching him from the shade at the angle of the wall, lolling there. There's a roll-your-own hanging from his lip. His left hand is swathed in a white bandage, like a signal.

Sounds. The chink of the side gate at Berriwillock, the neigh of the front fly-wire door. The slow sigh of the trains up the slope to Toorak station above the Kooyong courts, behind the gums.

Flute's ute is coming home. A mile over, on the highway, the yellow lights of Berriwillock sprinkle the mallee. The car sidles up the road, its headlights standing the taller gums up briefly as it passes and then washing them away to darkness. Flute knows the drill. Madge and her friend are talking in the front seat of the other car in the yard. He drives the ute past them, twenty yards off the tyre tracks as a concession to their presence, runs the Holden straight into the car shed. He appears under his rakish hat, walks inside on the concrete of the back path. He doesn't go for this nattering in the car.

And yet I've never known anything of this.

—

My father's face strives against the air. Yes, they say on the phone, he's sinking. There's been a reverse. He can't be roused.

Greta and Susan and Jesse are watching me. I take Will's hands from under the cover and stroke them, balancing his fingers on my palm, stroke again, listen to his breathing. It slows, becomes fainter, the pulse still working. No muttering now, no shuddering. Just the mouth open, breathing hectically, veins pulsing under the parchment skin. The breathing slows, slows. It stops. Two, three, four seconds. Then it starts again, climbing on one breath, then another, in rising intensity. The expended breath is dropped by the mouth so carelessly, the new breath taken in so eagerly. Then it levels, starts to slow, slows further.

I am still watching the throbbing of the veins. His face is thin, thin, as though the air of the room presses his skin against the bones.

I look up. Susan's face is a full peach, Greta's eyes are moist and full, her hair silken, her skin smooth, unwrinkled, resolute in the light. I see Jesse's forearm tanned and muscled under his tee-shirt. I love them. I will wait for them. They stream on after me, after Will.

—

Greta is sleeping again. We have talked to the murmur of the Hawthorn traffic. We have decided against marrying. We have both been bitten by marriage, by vows we could not keep. Anyway, Greta says, leaning on an elbow to look at me on the other side of the bed, I think we've made our own illicit marriage vows in action, you and I. Haven't we? That's how we see things, don't we?

I am picturing Patricia. I meant what I promised her, I hear my voice saying. I meant it sincerely without knowing how cold anger can be, how frozen love can become. It is marriage. It failed. We never hated each other. We failed.

Now Greta is asleep. I look down on her face. I look at the fall of her hair across her forehead. If I reach to pull it back I will wake her.

—

The Rev. Holly's voice intones. I sit beside Greta, Greg the other side of her. I am angled with a desperate sadness and excitement into the corner of the chapel's front pew. But I am hearing Will's sister at the piano back in Artarmon. It is Auntie Con saying yes ... yes ... I think I can do this. Far round time's circle she is pausing to let her fingers skitter amongst the sheets of music, demeaning herself, her head down, then coming up to say yes ... yes ... I can ... as she cons the key and the setting and then leans back to bring out the first notes and Will beside her clears his throat to sing. It must mean that Greg and I have forgotten – in what we have said, in what we have told Rev. Holly – to say how important singing is to Will. Grace's gentle contralto beside Will is reminding us. Will's pure tenor makes the words toll with sincerity.

He is gone. We have forgotten some of him already. I can see out through the door of the chapel to a photinia hedge glistening in the sun. He is gone. The day will bore on to evening, the shadows coming round to clasp the leaves.

—

Still I sit in the parked Nissan in Overton Lane's street of receding paperbarks. The sun is lowering across tiled ridges, across stark, rearing bathroom vents and the arrows of cypresses. I am seeing across

361

Melbourne's veins, the dip of the next valley, the dark windowless bulk of the old state school on the next ridge. And there is Grandpa John, muttering in his old garage at Mont Albert, hunched over the bench, making a cricket ball for Alistair and me with a golf ball core bound over and over with twine, his old mind grunting. He sews the twine under and over, ties the final knots, goes to the rough scissors to cut the ends, smooths it with his hands, tosses it a couple of times from hand to hand, looks at us standing there in our shorts and sandshoes. We are close people.

I dream, mind roving. And now I'm seeing Susan. Susan is there. It is the Otways. She is looking up. Her happiness pierces me. With the old tin she is dipping up more tadpoles from the runnel of cold water in the grass. She is blissful. Her face is a moon satiated with wonder. She is four.

—

I will know always that there is a photograph I should have taken in this hospital room with its blind drawn, with the light coming down evenly, softly on the patrician nose and the brow above the closed eyes. Nose and brow dominate from the bed. But already I know that I will never take it, that Alistair will blanch at the idea, that it is something for the heart to surrender, although it would be a photograph taken with love.

The Sister has left me. Now I simply stand there on the shining floor. It is the future. The room is the same as when Alistair and I left it last night. Bed 22 One South. Except that a blind on the east side is drawn down now. The bed seems higher than I remember. My father's bulk fills it, all under the sheet. I can know only his face. And it is still. It is the room's centre. Everything else loses focus around it. The nose is rising, commanding. His eyes are closed, his brow is pearly white. He is so still. I look for a long time at him, expecting to see a breath, a movement. Nothing. I look at the lines coming from beside the nose and down either side of

362

the mouth. And then the lines that fall from the mouth's corners down, glumly down. The face I have known to move for all my life is still – white and still like naphthalene, like white soap. I can't believe it. It is Will, but so still that it might not be, not a breath needed for that cold mouth, no lungs moving to greet the air. All cold. Alistair has not come up yet. Greg is an hour away. I look about. I am at a loss. I did not expect this. The stillness, the beauty, the dignity, the symmetry bowl me over. I keep looking, search the face. I wait for the mouth to twitch, the eyelids to flicker. Nothing. Nothing.

—

THANKS

I'm constantly thankful for my good fortune – for my warm, patient and supportive partner Judith, who is the guide to the voracious, wide-ranging and intelligent general reader that a writer needs; for my children and grandchildren, my brothers, my extended family. I'm glad to have been able to write in a multitude of coffee shops and libraries in Australia and overseas, a church sitting among dairy paddocks, a study with leaves eavesdropping, and a kitchen table looking out over Melbourne. I also write and teach at Deakin University in Geelong with sometimes the green plunges of the Barrabool Hills in sight, or sometimes the foggy pastel of Corio Bay, and surrounded by people who speak my language.

A number of people have helped to preserve in me enough equanimity and hope to see this story finished. Jenny Lee, quintessential editor, was first to discern that the tale had some distance in it and has, over several drafts, had to reassure me that it would be worth it in the end to endure my characters chipping away at me and me at them. Then there was a celebrated Australian novelist who heard me give a reading and asked a simple question – 'Have you written a novel?' There have been others who, like him, probably haven't guessed how much their interest and supportive asides have helped over the lonely midnight sessions on this and related work: and they range from dairy farmer to academic, fellow writer to pizza restaurateur, dwellers along the coast and on the volcanic plain, to naturalist and painter and gallery owner – Alex Skovron, Ron and Pam Simpson, Anthony Lynch, my remarkable aunt Bet Wilson, Manfred Jurgensen, Ron Smith, Michael Meehan, Les Murray, Noel McKinnon, Russell Grigg, Frank Moorhouse, Justin Clemens, Kingsley Tregea, Geoff Page, Gail Jones, Andrew Taylor and Beate Josephi, Dennis Haskell, Delys Bird, Bernard Corser, Paul Kane, Eric Rolls and Elaine van Kempen, Kevin Hart, Nicolas Birns, Laurie and Gunn Carlson, David Malouf, Tim Bass, Ian Williams, Ivor Indyk, Pete and Bett Killingsworth, Margaret Wagenhofer, Annie and Penno, Russell Davis, Josie and Niel Black, Les Smith, Russell Irwin, Ron and Helen Land, and Tom Griffiths among many other writers, readers, listeners and friends.

I am grateful, in a reaching across cultures, to Dikkon Eberhart in Phippsburg, Maine, and the Eberhart family, for permission to quote from Richard Eberhart's poem, 'The Fury of Aerial Bombardment'.

I thank the staff of the Adoptive Families Association in Canterbury, Melbourne, and the Austin Hospital's Psychology Department for their help in endorsing the verisimilitude of some sections of the story.

Finally, my gratitude to everyone in and around Wakefield Press for their professional thoroughness, faith and empathy – Michael Bollen, Stephanie Johnston, Jon Jureidini, Liz Nicholson, Clinton Ellicott, Julia Beaven, Kathy Sharrad, and Angela Tolley.

Inventing Beatrice

Jill Golden

When Beatrice Collins dies, her daughters discover the secret diaries she had kept as a student at Melbourne University in the late 1920s and early 1930s. The diaries reveal her passionate relationships with other young women in a group calling itself 'Mob'. They are defiant, unconventional women – *a slightly chosen race of free and original spirits,* Beatrice writes. Their closeness is challenged by the arrival of the charismatic Tom.

The second part of the book, written in Beatrice's own voice, takes up her story in Sydney immediately after the Second World War. While Beatrice struggles to live out her ideals about freedom, love and equality, she makes choices that will impact on her children for the rest of their lives.

Now her daughter must come to terms with the paradoxes of both her mother's past and her own.

ISBN 978 1 86254 704 9

For more information visit www.wakefieldpress.com.au

Paper Nautilus

Nicholas Jose

'They wanted a love they could take into eternity.'

In a small town on the Australian coast Penny grows up to marry the boy who has waited for her. Few know the truth about her birth. Her uncle Jack is one, for he shared with her father not only his childhood but also the horror of their wartime experience. Jack and Penny's special bond is as rare and precious as the beautiful nautilus shell they find washed up on the beach – entwined with its history are the secrets of their past and the tenacious passions of the other people who have had a stake in their lives.

ISBN 978 1 86254 733 9

For more information visit www.wakefieldpress.com.au

Cleanskin

Gay Lynch

'Isn't this how it should be?' Jerome murmured at her shoulder.

'Yes,' Madelaine lied, thinking of soft cheeks and the faint ammonia morning smell overriding the scent of the sea. A part of her hardened against him: a kernel of despair.

Five women share their lives at a playgroup, desperate for the company of adults.

Madelaine looks forward to the meetings, but they put her on edge. Amaretto biscuits, designer clothes, unwelcome advice – nothing seems to fit. Her relationships are forcing her out of control.

When one of the group begins an illicit affair, everyone gets caught in the deadly crossfire.

ISBN 978 1 86254 703 2

For more information visit www.wakefieldpress.com.au

Many Years a Thief

David Hutchison

'Why did God spare me? Did he spare me? He didn't. He did. He didn't . . .' She sighed, remembering those deaths: Jane, George, her baby Charlie, and her first husband John, and poor John Schoales. They were all too young to die.

John Gavin, a 15-year-old boy, became the first European to be executed in the colony of Western Australia. He had arrived in Fremantle just months earlier, one of a group of juvenile convicts taking part in an attempted rehabilitation scheme. John Schoales, the government guardian of the new arrivals, put Gavin to work on an isolated farm south of Perth. Soon after, he was brought back to Fremantle in shackles, charged with murder.

ISBN 978 1 86254 746 9

For more information visit www.wakefieldpress.com.au

Dodging the Bull

Paul Mitchell

Paul Mitchell throws a spanner into daily lives and watches his characters pick up the pieces. From the Bali bombings to the difficulties of unorthodox sexuality in a closed-minded community, back to the ripple effect of Australians returned from war, Mitchell's stories are socially aware and compassionate, but also confronting and progressive. Shifting with ease between the vernacular and lyricism, *Dodging the Bull* chronicles the lives of honest Australians confronted by the rift between ignorance and compassion that threatens to divide today's multi-layered society.

ISBN 978 1 86254 749 0

For more information visit www.wakefieldpress.com.au

Poinciana

Jane Turner Goldsmith

'Café au lait' *she calls him, the young nurse who finds him in the wet mud on the riverbank, hours after his birth. He is too shocked to wail, would have died in the tunnel of bamboo leaves feathering gently above him.*

Catherine Piron is in Nouméa, searching for traces of the father she barely remembers. She meets journalist Henri Boulez, her only lead in a foreign country. Their journey into the remote regions of New Caledonia uncovers an extraordinary story that, like the island itself, *brille à la fois claire et noire au soleil* – shimmers light and dark in the sun.

ISBN 978 1 86254 699 8

For more information visit www.wakefieldpress.com.au

The House at Number 10

Dorothy Johnston

Sophie Harper is abandoned by her husband, not for another woman, but 'a raft of girls – a floating, open-ended freedom'. Left with a four-year-old daughter to support, Sophie finds work in an old house in Canberra that is being used as a brothel. While the laws governing prostitution are being re-written, and prosecutions temporarily in abeyance, Sophie combines caring for her daughter with working in the house. She waits – for the sanction of legality, for the renovations designed by her architect friend, Ann, to be approved, and for her suspicious ex-husband to find out how she is making her living. She falls under the house's eerie, yet strangely comforting spell, and discovers within herself not only the ability to perform well, and delight in the freedom bought by an independent income, but the capacity to learn from, and be changed by, the men and women she encounters there. One of these men, Jack, teaches her more about revenge than she ever wished to know.

The House at Number 10 is a novel about the complex relationships people develop with the buildings they live and work in, about betrayal and the will to vengeance, but most of all it is about the resilience of friendship, and the transformative power of the imagination.

ISBN 978 1 86254 683 7

For more information visit www.wakefieldpress.com.au

Hill of Grace

Stephen Orr

1951. Among the coppiced carob trees and arum lilies of the Barossa Valley, old-school Lutheran William Miller lives a quiet life with his wife, Bluma, and son, Nathan, making wine and baking bread. But William has a secret. He's been studying the Bible and he's found what a thousand others couldn't: the date of the Apocalypse.

William sets out to convince his neighbours that they need to join him in preparation for the End. Arthur Blessitt, a Valley pioneer in floriculture, helps William deliver pamphlets and organise rallies. Others join the group but as the day approaches their faith is tested. The locals of Tanunda become divided. Did William really hear God's voice on the Hill of Grace? Did God tell him to preach the End of Days? Or is William really deluded?

The greatest test of all for William is whether Bluma and Nathan will support him. As the seasons pass in the Valley, as the vines flower and fruit and lose their leaves, William himself is forced to question his own beliefs and the price he's willing to pay for them.

ISBN 978 1 86254 648 6

For more information visit www.wakefieldpress.com.au

Wakefield Press is an independent publishing and
distribution company based in Adelaide, South Australia.
We love good stories and publish beautiful books.
To see our full range of titles, please visit our website at
www.wakefieldpress.com.au.